AGAINST A BRIGHTENING SKY

ALSO BY JAIME LEE MOYER

Delia's Shadow
A Barricade in Hell

Against a Brightening Sky

Jaime Lee Moyer

This is a work of fiction. All of the characters, organizations, and events portrayed in this novel are either products of the author's imagination or are used fictitiously.

AGAINST A BRIGHTENING SKY

A Tor Book
Published by Tom Doherty Associates, LLC
175 Fifth Avenue
New York, NY 10010

www.tor-forge.com

The Library of Congress Cataloging-in-Publication Data is available upon request.

ISBN 978-0-7653-3184-7 (hardcover)
ISBN 978-1-4299-4982-8 (e-book)

Our books may be purchased for promotional, educational, or business use. Please contact your local bookseller or the Macmillan Corporate and Premium Sales Department at (800) 221-7945, extension 5442, or by e-mail at MacmillanSpecialMarkets@macmillan.com.

First Edition: October 2015

Printed in the United States of America

0 9 8 7 6 5 4 3 2 1

For my activist son, Chris, who lives his principles and follows his dreams. Love you, boychild. And for the entire crew of Store 2251, all of whom work far too long and hard, for far too little. You are all my heroes.

ACKNOWLEDGMENTS

Writing novels is hard. You spend months locked in your own head, doing all you can to make the story on the page match the one you literally dream about. Writing can be a lonely way to spend your time. I can't imagine doing this without friends, most of them writers in their own right, as a support system. They make my stories better just by being part of my life.

I need to thank my long-term friends, the ones there in good times and bad: Rae Carson, Elizabeth Bear, Amanda Downum, Kat Allen, Jodi Meadows, Celia Marsh, Liz Bourke, Charlie Finlay, Lisa Clarity, Pam Thompson, the Infamous E, and Mark Alger. Newer friends Fran Wilde and Oz Drummond do more than their part in keeping me sane, A.C. Wise deserves thanks for never missing an opportunity to offer support, and I want to thank Lynne and Michael Thomas for just being generally awesome. I need to thank editor/writer Brian White for making me laugh, a lot, when I need laughter most; Heather R. for inspiring me with her courage; and author Stephen Blackmoore for going out of his way to tell the world about my books.

Thank you to all the book bloggers who go out of their way to spread the word about my novels, with special thanks to Angie and Stacee. My coworkers at Store 2251 come in for special thanks as well. I couldn't have a better cheerleading squad.

I'm sure all authors are convinced they have the best editor in existence, but I really do. All my thanks and gratitude go to Claire Eddy for making me a better writer, and a better storyteller. You are the best. Don't let anyone tell you differently.

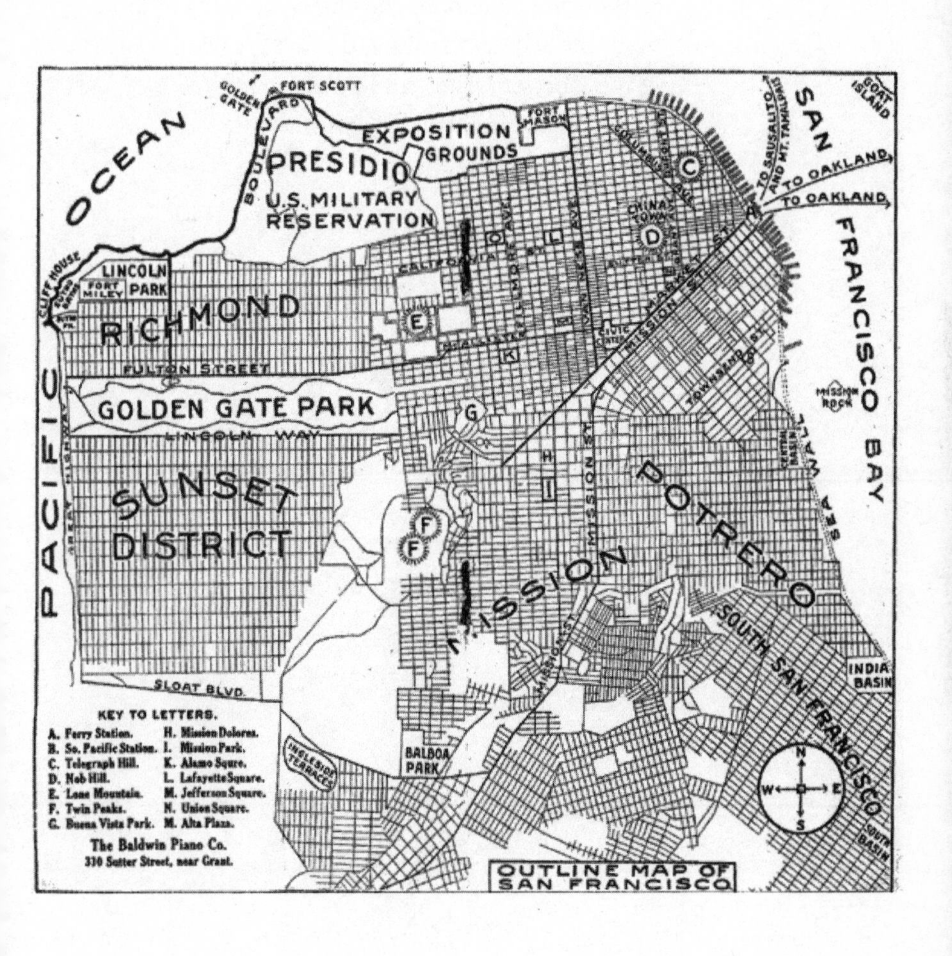
OCEAN
PACIFIC
GOLDEN GATE
FORT SCOTT
BOULEVARD
FORT MASON
EXPOSITION GROUNDS
PRESIDIO
U.S. MILITARY RESERVATION
CLIFF HOUSE
LINCOLN PARK
FORT MILEY
RICHMOND
FULTON STREET
GOLDEN GATE PARK
LINCOLN WAY
SUNSET DISTRICT
SLOAT BLVD.
MISSION
MISSION ST
POTRERO
SOUTH SAN FRANCISCO
CHINA TOWN
MARKET ST.
TOWNSEND ST.
FILLMORE AVE.
VAN NESS AVE.
CALIFORNIA ST.
SUTTER ST.
TO SAUSALITO AND MT. TAMALPAIS
TO OAKLAND
TO OAKLAND
GOAT ISLAND
SAN FRANCISCO BAY
MISSION ROCK
CENTRAL BASIN
SEA WALL
INDIA BASIN
SOUTH BASIN
BALBOA PARK
INGLESIDE TERRACES
N
S
E
W
KEY TO LETTERS.
A. Ferry Station.
B. So. Pacific Station.
C. Telegraph Hill.
D. Nob Hill.
E. Lone Mountain.
F. Twin Peaks.
G. Buena Vista Park.
H. Mission Dolores.
I. Mission Park.
K. Alamo Squre.
L. Lafayette Square.
M. Jefferson Square.
N. Union Square.
M. Alta Plaza.
The Baldwin Piano Co.
330 Sutter Street, near Grant.
OUTLINE MAP OF SAN FRANCISCO

AGAINST A BRIGHTENING SKY

CHAPTER 1

Delia

In an age of empires, princes were raised to rule, and often, to fight and die. That time of soldier kings was over by Armistice Day. Far too many kingdoms had shattered in the Great War, the power of their rulers broken forever.

Some kings and princes had gone into exile, saving themselves and their families. Others had simply vanished. The papers were full of their pictures and speculation about whether they were alive or dead. Fortunes hung in the balance in some cases, the peace of knowing what had happened to a loved one in others.

Far too often I saw faded and smudged images standing behind the somber-faced royalty posing for the camera. I knew those hazy figures for what they really were—ghosts. The men and women and children in those pictures would never be found.

Knowing their fate, being certain while the rest of the world wondered and waited, gave me nightmares. Each dream held the feeling of truth, not imagination, a glimpse into secrets and things I couldn't possibly know. That the details of what I'd dreamed didn't carry over into my waking hours was both a blessing and a curse. Not remembering let me hope the dreams would stop.

The ghost gazing at me from my dressing table mirror was real enough. She looked to have been no more than twenty or twenty-two, chestnut haired with dark-blue eyes and delicate features. Her skin was fair, making the roses in her cheeks all the brighter. I thought her pretty, but not a great beauty. She clutched a folded fan in one gloved hand and stared at me intently, as aware of me as I was of her. Judging solely by her beaded white silk dress, the tiara in her hair, and the strand of pearls at her throat, I guessed she'd been a member of royalty in life. I didn't remember her photograph from the papers, but that didn't mean she hadn't been amongst the missing.

I slipped a last hairpin into the twisted knot of hair at the nape of my neck, never taking my eyes from the ghost. She still appeared solid and lifelike, no doubt recently dead, mourned and missed by someone who'd loved her. This ghost had died on the other side of the world, yet she'd sought me out and managed to cross my boundaries.

That said a great deal about her determination. I feared it might say even more about the circumstances of her death. Those who'd died a horrible death made the most stubborn ghosts.

She'd haunt me if given half an opportunity, but I didn't intend to give her one. I pulled my wards tighter, doing all I could to shut her out of my house. My life. "You can't linger here, spirit, and I can't help you. Whatever you're looking for is far away. Leave this place and seek your rest."

The ghost stood fast, her gaze never wavering from my reflection in the mirror. I'd expected the anger common in strong spirits to fill her eyes, or a demand for me to bow to her will. What I saw instead was patience and a willingness to wait. I'd no idea what she waited for.

"Delia?" Gabe's image appeared in the mirror near the ghost, startling me. My husband couldn't see her, that was plain, but I'd no doubt from the way the ghost moved to one side that she was aware of him. "Are you ready to leave? We're supposed to pick up Jack and Sadie and the children in half an hour."

"I'm ready." The ghost was gone between one instant and the next, leaving me with a racing heart and a catch in my throat. I tucked a stray strand of hair behind my ear, staring at the emptiness where she'd stood. She'd gone because she chose to leave, not because I'd sent her away. "I just need to get my hat."

Gabe put his hands on my shoulders, worry in his eyes. "You're very pale, Dee. Are you all right?"

"I'm fine. A ghost took me by surprise, but she's gone now."

His frown deepened. He'd watched me deal with ghosts of all kinds for more than four years, becoming more sure of my abilities as I gained experience and knowledge. Isadora Bobet, a master practitioner of spiritual arts, was my teacher, mentor, and a good friend to both me and Gabe. Before she took me on as a student, I was awash in a world I didn't understand. Without Dora's guidance, I might have gone mad.

Spirits and haunts seldom surprised me now, a fact Gabe was quite aware of. I covered his hand with mine and smiled. "Truly, I'm fine. We should get going. Sadie's more excited about going to the parade than Stella. She'll be very cross if we keep her waiting."

"As long as you're sure everything's all right." Gabe kissed me on the cheek. "I'll pull the car out. Meet you at the end of the drive."

I hadn't lied; everything was fine. Still, I avoided looking at the mirror. If she'd come back, I didn't want to know.

There'd be time enough to deal with stubborn ghosts later.

San Francisco was always full of travelers come to see the sights or passing through to other parts of the country. Spring of 1919 brought an influx of well-to-do refugees from Europe into the city:

skilled craftsmen and prosperous merchants, minor nobility and retainers who'd served royalty for generations. All sought a safe haven or to flee memories of the horrors they'd witnessed before the final battles on the Continent stopped. Diplomats came as well, new faces to man the embassies abandoned at the beginning of the Great War or to carry news about the current state of the Paris peace treaty.

Diplomat or refugee, they'd all brought their ghosts with them. The haunts attached to most of the refugees were family or friends, people who they'd recently lost, missed, and mourned. Watching a dead soldier trail behind a weary woman clutching a child's hand struck me as very sad, but nothing about these ghosts appeared out of the ordinary. But not all the newly arrived spirits I saw were quite so mundane. Rulers haunted their subjects as well.

Phantom European kings and queens, princes, duchesses, and nobility of lesser stations roamed the busy downtown streets in large numbers. Some were dressed in ermine-trimmed capes, coronation robes heavy with gold braid and golden crowns, while other dead royals wore simple linen shirts and trousers, or plain summer cotton dresses. The richness of their clothes and their confident, often haughty bearing left no doubt about their station in life.

Many of these noble ghosts looked lost, bewildered at how they'd come to be in this strange city and unsure of where to go. Others followed closely on the heels of the person they haunted, holding tight to someone familiar or who'd known them in life. Perhaps the ghost in my mirror had come to San Francisco the same way, riding on the memories of someone who'd loved her.

Strolling down Market Street with Gabe, Jack and Sadie, and their two children, I found myself face-to-face with the spirits of European nobility at every turn. I might have said no to Sadie's invitation to watch the Saint Patrick's Day parade if I'd known how many new ghosts inhabited the city. The only saving grace was that few showed evidence of how they'd died, sparing me a small amount of distress. All I could do was make the best of things.

The majority of the ghosts I saw ignored the world of the living, too busy reenacting some part of their past to take notice. A few appeared keenly aware they'd traveled far from home, going so far as to stare in bewilderment at storefronts or reach out to touch people passing on the street. Those spirits turned to watch Sadie's children intently or moved closer.

That made me uneasy. I whispered charms, telling them to move on and forbidding them to haunt me or mine. All but two of the ghosts did as I'd ordered. A middle-aged man dressed in a formal coat and a slim young woman in a crimson gown resisted, but I won in the end.

I relaxed once they'd gone, determined to enjoy our outing. We hadn't had a free day to spend with Sadie and Jack Fitzgerald in far too long. Sadie and I had been best friends since childhood, and ours was a friendship that had endured through both the best and worst of times. Jack and Gabe had been partners since they joined the police force nearly fifteen years before. They'd grown close as brothers. Time with Sadie and Jack was always well spent.

March weather was often unpredictable, but we'd gotten lucky. A cool breeze blew off the ocean, carrying the scent of salt and seaweed, but the sun was warm and bright in a cerulean sky. Thick gray fog sealed the mouth of the Bay but showed no sign of moving inland. Flocks of ducks formed giant vees and raced toward the wetlands lining the Bay shore, while gulls and terns wheeled in thick, dark spirals, their keening cries echoing so that I heard them from blocks away.

"Isn't this a glorious day, Dee? I knew the fog would stay away until dark." Sadie set two-year-old Connor atop Jack's shoulders, her face flushed and blue eyes bright with excitement. Blond curls bubbled out from beneath her stylish cloche hat and framed her face, accenting her already considerable charm. Her shawl-collared dress was the latest fashion, made in chocolate silk and broken at the waist with tiny pleats. Bell-shaped skirts ended at her ankles. The day was warm, but she'd tossed a honey-colored mink shawl over her shoulders.

Half the fun of going anywhere with Sadie was watching heads turn as she passed by, a game her husband enjoyed as much as the rest of us. Most of our amusement stemmed from knowing those who judged Sadie solely on her looks vastly underestimated her. Given the opportunity, she never hesitated to set them straight.

"It's an absolutely perfect day." I sidestepped the ghost of a prince kneeling in the middle of the sidewalk, head bowed to receive a crown. "Not a trace of fog anywhere. I'm so glad we could watch the parade together."

"Oh, so am I, Dee." Sadie brushed a hand over her son's cheek, and her bright smile dimmed a little. "I just hope the crowd and the parade noise don't frighten Connor. He cries so easily when we're downtown."

Sadie didn't see the world as I did, but I suspected that her son did. Connor was wild eyed and flushed, trying to look everywhere at once. Not telling my dearest friend that her baby boy watched ghosts was a guilty secret that weighed on me; one I couldn't keep much longer. Since early infancy, he'd had that telltale stare Gabe said I adopted when ghosts were present. I couldn't deny that Connor watched unseen things in the corner of the room rather than the people around him. Not when I saw spirits in those same corners.

Dora and I had half hoped Connor might grow out of it, but as time went on, I became convinced that wasn't the case. The question had become when to tell Sadie, not if we'd be forced to.

At least I'd be there to help Connor and teach him how to protect himself. Slim consolation for his mother, but that was all I had to offer.

I reached up and brushed the hair back from little Connor's face. His hair was red and curly like his father's, but the curls were fine and soft like Sadie's, his eyes the same shade of blue as his mother's. Stella was the miniature of her mother through and through, including the ability to charm the moon from the sky. I could never firmly decide who Connor resembled most, but many days I thought it was his grandmother Esther. "I'll take him for a walk if he starts to cry. That way Stella can enjoy the parade and you needn't worry. Where are we meeting Sam?"

"Near Lotta's fountain and the Palace Hotel." Gabe picked Stella up, making it easier for us to move along the increasingly crowded sidewalk. She looped an arm around his neck and rested her cheek against his. "Sam said he'd be at the corner on the Palace side of the street. We won't be able to miss him that way. The parade turns right there, so it's the perfect place to watch. Sam and Miss Mills are going to save a spot on the curb for us."

Sadie's eyes lit up at the mention of Sam Butler in connection with a woman's name. Time and motherhood hadn't dulled her matchmaker instincts. If anything, fewer opportunities made her more eager. "Miss Mills? I didn't know Sam was courting anyone. Why didn't you tell me, Jack? We could have had them come to supper."

"Sam's not courting her, sweetheart." Jack and Gabe traded looks, but Gabe's amused expression made it clear Jack was on his own. "They're friends. Colleagues, I guess you could say. She's new in town and Sam's making an effort to introduce her to people."

"Colleagues?" Sadie appeared thoroughly unconvinced. Now that she had the scent of a possible romance in her nose, she'd not let go. She'd pointed out more than once that her matchmaking had worked with me and Gabe. Sadie lived in hope of another success. "Is Miss Mills a reporter as well? I've read that some of the more progressive papers do have women on their staffs."

I felt sorry for Sam. Samuel Clemens Butler was young, a successful reporter for *The Call,* and romantically unattached, and thus the perfect candidate for Sadie's efforts. We'd all been friends since he came to San Francisco a little over two years ago and helped Gabe with a case, but poor Sam had no idea what was in store for him.

Attempts to sidetrack Sadie usually failed, but I felt honor bound to try. "Libby Mills is a social worker. The *Examiner* has run several articles about her. Miss Mills negotiates with local businesses to provide respectable employment for soldier's widows at decent wages. It's quite noble work from what I've read, and she's gotten good results. I'm looking forward to meeting her."

The words "social worker" must have summoned visions of an older woman with ample bosoms and frumpy clothes. Sadie's smile dimmed ever so slightly, but she put a good face on things. "Perhaps I can persuade a few friends to host a luncheon or an afternoon reception for Miss Mills. Introducing her to San Francisco society is bound to do her cause a world of good. I could even ask Katherine to include Miss Mills in the garden party she's hosting next week. She's always looking for a new charity to support."

The corners of Jack's mouth twitched, but he kept a straight face. "That's a marvelous idea, sweetheart. My dear stepmother loves to throw money around in public. She has an image to maintain, after all."

Sadie laughed and slipped an arm around his waist. "What you really mean is giving money to charity eases her guilt. Katherine would never admit to that, but we both know it's true. If Miss Mills's people benefit, well, that's all to the good, as far as I'm concerned. I'll ring Katherine this evening."

Lotta's fountain came into view. All the people of San Francisco knew the fountain built by Lotta Crabtree, her gift to the city. Most had a story to tell. The brass fountain with its tall, ornate central column, lion's-head spouts, and griffin-guarded basins survived both the 1906 quake and the fire that swept away all the surrounding buildings. People used the fountain as a rallying point in the aftermath, a place to leave messages and post lists of who'd survived and who had died. Esther had brought Sadie and me to the fountain to hear opera soprano Luisa Tetrazzini sing on Christmas Eve of 1910.

Survivors of the quake still gathered around Lotta's fountain each April 18 to sing hymns and remember. Not that anyone would ever forget.

Sam was easy to spot. I'd always thought of him as tall and lanky, but today he stood inches above the people around him. His straw boater hat and the thin pinstripes in his ash-gray suit made him appear taller still, especially in comparison to the tiny woman holding his arm.

Libby Mills was much younger than I'd imagined, and her clothes far from frumpy, edging dangerously close to being fashionable. Her green dress had a square neckline, a large lace collar that covered her shoulders, and a pleated skirt that ended scandalously far above her ankles. She wore her hair loose, and soft black waves rippled over her shoulders and down her back.

My father always referred to small, pretty women as doll-like, but I'd never pin that label on Miss Mills. I could see strength and determination in her stance, even from a distance, and she watched everything with a keen eye. If she missed much, I'd be greatly surprised. She laughed easily at Sam's remarks, revealing dimples in an open, friendly face.

I glanced at Sadie, wondering if she'd seen them too. Her utterly blissful smile told the story. I'd no hope of saving Sam from her meddling. He'd have to save himself.

Sam saw us and waved. "Gabe, Jack, over here."

Police officers had already halted traffic for the parade. We crossed the street quickly and filled the space Sam had saved on the curb. Cheery music carried from around the corner, a sign the first band would be here before long.

Sam made the introductions. "Libby, you already know Gabe and Jack. These are their wives, Delia Ryan and Sadie Fitzgerald. It's a mystery to me why such smart women put up with these two scoundrels. Delia and Sadie, this is Miss Libby Mills. Go easy on her, Sadie."

Gabe winked and I hid a smile. He'd warned Sam.

"Why, Sam, I don't know what you mean." Sadie was positively beaming as she shook Libby's hand. "Pay no attention to him. I'm very pleased to meet you, Miss Mills. And please, call me Sadie."

"Only if you and Mrs. Ryan call me Libby. Sam's told me a lot about both of you." Libby gave Sam a sideways glance. "All good things, I promise."

I stuck my hand out in turn. "And please, Libby, call me Delia. Sam's a good man. I'd listen to him if I were you."

The music grew louder as the parade came around the corner, cutting off further conversation. Gabe set Stella on the curb at his feet, giving her a clear view as well as room to dance and bounce to the music. The first band was followed by another, cars full of pretty girls tossing paper flowers to the crowd, and solemn-faced men carrying banners for aid societies and fellowship halls. Policemen marched in full dress uniforms, while men from local firehouses drove old horse-drawn fire wagons and tossed candy to children. People clapped and cheered when a group of dancers stopped at our corner. They gave a grand performance before moving on.

I kept an eye on Connor, looking for signs that the crowd and the ever-present ghosts had gotten to be too much for him. Jack bounced his son up and down in time to the music while Sadie rested a hand on Connor's back. So far, he seemed to be faring well, watching everything with excitement and not fear. I stayed close, just in case.

A new group of men came around the corner, carrying flags and a different kind of banner. Some of the men had hand-lettered cards stuck into their hatbands that read *BREAD OR REVOLUTION.* The cheering stopped, the crowd growing quiet and subdued. Sam scowled and wiped a hand over his mouth. "I didn't think he'd go through with it. Dominic Mullaney should have more sense."

People booed loudly and a few shouted insults. I touched Gabe's arm. "What's wrong?"

He gestured toward the men marching past. "Mullaney and his crew are trying to organize labor unions on the docks. They've already started organizing waiters in the big hotels too. The business owners involved have done their best to turn people against the idea. Father Colm over at Saint Mary Magdalene was afraid there'd be trouble and tried to talk Mullaney out of marching in the parade. Father Colm was right. I just hope things don't get too far out of hand."

The shouting grew louder, people in the crowd and the men who'd been marching taunting each other. Ghosts appeared amongst the marchers: men dressed in miners' gear with coal dust smeared across their faces, blacksmiths in leather aprons and longshoremen in sweat-soaked shirts, phantom boxes balanced on a shoulder. There were child ghosts as well, barefoot waifs holding spindles from textile mills or battered lunch buckets. The spirits' anger rolled through the crowd, feeding the growing rage of union organizers and spectators both.

Spirits of dead royalty shimmered into view, clustered near a group of the spectators along the curb. These ghosts were nervous, afraid. I tried to discover who in the crowd they haunted, but there were far too many people.

"I don't think it's safe for the children to stay here." Gabe picked up Stella and handed her back to Sadie. He took his badge out of an inside pocket and pinned it to his coat. "Take them down the block and into the Palace, Dee, and stay as far from the front windows as you can. All the way to the back of the lobby would be best. Libby, I think you should go as well."

"There used to be seating areas at the back. We'll go there." I took Connor from Jack. He was shaking and crying, staring at the ghosts, and I'd no doubt their anger washed over him as it did me. I pulled Connor's head down to rest on my shoulder, doing what I could to wrap wards and protections around him. They must have done some good. I felt Connor sigh and relax against me. "Be careful, Gabe."

He smiled and turned away, wading into the thick of the angry mob. Jack and Sam went with him. I met Sadie's eyes, knowing what I'd see. Fear for Jack struggled with the need to get her children far from danger. She couldn't protect all of them at once. Neither could I.

Libby was small but adept at making her way through crowds. She went ahead of Sadie and me, forcing openings to let us through, and going so far as to shove a large man who tried to block our way deliberately. I couldn't shake the sick feeling that something was very wrong here. Few people made an attempt to leave. Instead, men and women both pushed forward, faces eager, and scrabbled to get closer to the heart of the disturbance. I didn't understand why.

We broke through to a clear patch of sidewalk. A large plate glass window on the front of a jeweler's shop loomed in front of us. Black moiré taffeta lined the window display and showed off rhinestone bracelets, necklaces, and earrings to their best advantage. The crystals glinted rainbows, mimicking the pattern in the fabric.

The window glass was flawed, full of ripples that distorted the reflection of the milling crowd behind us and the buildings across Market Street, buildings that overlooked the parade route. Images wavered, appeared to move as I stared.

All but one. The princess ghost I'd seen in the dressing table mirror stood in the center of the glass, still and calm. She'd known I'd be here, in this place at this exact moment, and waited for me. I couldn't say how I knew that was true, only that I did.

The ghost raised an arm and pointed, the fan in her hand touching the reflection of a building directly across the street. I turned and saw tiny figures moving on the roof, men who appeared no bigger than children from a distance. One carried a bundle to the iron railing that edged the roof and stood there, waiting on his partner. The other man got down on one knee, arms held at a strange angle. He shifted position, and sunlight shimmered dully on the long barrel of a rifle. "Oh, God . . . Sadie! Sadie get down!"

Libby looked up immediately, instinct or divine intervention drawing her eye to the same rooftop. Shock froze her in place for an instant, but no more. She grabbed Sadie's arm, dragging her into the shelter of the jewelry store doorway. I crowded in as well, heart hammering, and jammed Libby, Sadie, and Stella up against the shop door, little Connor wedged between us.

The door must have been unlatched. We tumbled inside, landing in a heap of tangled skirts and frightened, crying children.

Explosions sounded from outside, followed quickly by panicked screams, frantic shouts, and breaking glass. A clerk came around the front counter, an older woman in a prim gray dress, who stood and stared at us, mouth agape. "What . . . what are you doing on the floor?"

Libby lifted her head and glared at the woman. "Trying not to get shot. Get down, you ninny."

The front window shattered, spraying glass into the shop. Shards skittered across spotless marble floors to land at the clerk's feet. She squeaked in fright and scurried into the back room, yelling for Mr. Perkins to call the police. I curled over Connor as he sobbed, and made shooshing noises in his ear, trying not to think of Sam and Jack out there.

Most of all, I was trying not to imagine Gabe lying in the street, cold and still.

CHAPTER 2

Gabe

Gabe and Jack were fighting a losing battle against madness, but they fought anyway. They didn't have any other choice.

Five streets met at the intersection surrounding Lotta's fountain, forming a large, open square. People continued to crowd into the square, ignoring all Gabe and Jack's shouted orders to disperse, ignoring everything but their eagerness to enter the fray. Pushcarts selling ice cream, roasted peanuts, and sausage on a roll were abandoned by the vendors and overturned. Fistfights broke out in pockets on every side of the fountain, onlookers cheering on the men flailing at each other.

Women were just as crazed, using anything at hand to pry out cobblestones to throw at the union organizers. Children huddled against walls or cried in prams, apparently forgotten by their parents. Gabe prayed none of the children would move. They'd be trampled and he didn't think anyone would notice.

The crowd's fury was unprovoked. Unnatural. Gabe was rarely frightened after nearly fifteen years on the force, but this mob scared him. He saw the same fear in Jack's eyes.

Word of the riot near Lotta's fountain spread quickly among

the cops stationed up and down the parade route. It took only a few minutes before they all converged on the area, their ranks swelled still more by the officers who'd been a part of the parade. The one bright spot Gabe found was that whatever mania had taken hold of the crowd left him and Jack, and the patrolman coming to their aid, untouched. Reinforcements helped, but the police officers were still outnumbered three to one.

Dominic Mullaney wasn't faring any better in his attempts to restore reason. Again and again he tried to separate men shouting at each other, stop fights, or convince his supporters to walk away and go home. They argued right back, and more than a few took a swing at him. Mullaney had a darkening bruise on one side of his jaw and a split lip, but he didn't back down. Gabe gave him credit for that. Whatever was going on, Mullaney wasn't a part of it.

The first gunshot caught Gabe by surprise. He saw a man crumple off to the left, blood blooming in crimson petals on his chest. The ringing echo of gunfire was swallowed by the roar of voices and shouts, and he couldn't tell which direction the shot came from. A second man standing a good twenty yards away fell and didn't move. No more than ten feet from where Jack stood, a third man went down, clutching his leg and screaming. The victims were spread across the square, the shots fired with too little time between to have come from close range.

Someone was shooting into the crowd from above. Gabe spun in circles, desperately searching the rooftops for the gunman.

He saw the gun barrel and a second man toss something off the roof an instant before the first explosion. The ground under his feet rocked and Gabe stumbled sideways. Brick and timber were blasted off storefronts, landing hard on those unfortunate enough to be in the way. Windows on both sides of the street shattered and trees near where the dynamite landed blew apart, dropping more debris onto the crowd. The air filled with the smell of burning cloth and wood and flesh.

The tenor of the mob's screams changed with the explosion. Anger evaporated and gave way to terror. People who'd refused to budge a minute earlier ran now, frantic to get away. Gabe fought the surge of people, struggling to keep the men on the rooftop in sight and make his way toward the building.

He caught up with Jack and pointed. "There are two of them on the roof. We need to get up there, but I'm guessing they were smart enough to barricade the door on the way in. Find two or three of our men in case we need to break the door down."

Another small explosion went off behind them. Instinct made them both duck and cover their heads with their arms, but nothing more than a fine rain of pulverized paving stone and dirt fell.

Jack stood first. He gripped Gabe's shoulder briefly, his grim expression at odds with his flip tone. "Stay low, Captain Ryan. If you get yourself killed, Sadie would never let me hear the end of it."

"You do the same, Lieutenant Fitzgerald. I'm too old to break in a new partner." Gabe rolled up his fedora, stuffing it in an inside overcoat pocket. He was fond of the familiar hat and didn't want to chance losing it. "Let's go."

Both of them moved toward the building in a crouching run, brushing aside the clinging hands of panicked civilians. Jack broke away to intercept two officers in uniform, both of them rookies with semi-panicked expressions. Parade duty was supposed to be an easy assignment. Gabe shoved away guilt and kept running.

The man on the roof tossed off two more thick bundles of dynamite, lobbing one as far as he could to the left and the other to the right. A parade float flipped end over end and skidded across the intersection on its side. More windows broke and a building caught fire. The wind picked up and gusted down Market Street from the Bay, twining between buildings and howling under the eaves with a lost, mournful sound. Gabe shivered as the wail grew louder and hung in the air.

Smoke and ash swirled around him now, mixed with brick dust, and made it hard to see. Shapes moved in the murk, half-glimpsed figures riding the wind and reaching toward the fleeing crowd, fingers hooked into long, grasping claws. Gabe wiped his eyes, willing the apparition out of existence and refusing to acknowledge the queasy feeling in his middle. Delia and Isadora knew how to deal with spirits or creatures drawn to death and misery, but he didn't. Ignoring them was the best he could do on his own.

Gabe dodged around a pile of burning timber. His mind registered the small hand sticking out from underneath, but reacting—feeling—could get him killed. He heard the rifle shots now, each one a muffled crack that sounded far away underneath the ringing in his ears, but he could count them off. With people more scattered, the gunman had clearer shots and took his time, picking his targets off slowly.

That the man on the roof hadn't shot him or Jack, or any of the uniformed officers, baffled Gabe. He picked possible reasons apart as he ran, each smoky breath burning his throat and eyes.

A hunch became conviction as the wind wailed again, feeding his imagination. Cops dressed in bright blue uniforms or with their badges reflecting the sunlight were easy to spot in the crowd, but the gunman had no interest in picking them off. Only one target mattered to the men on the roof. The explosions and shooting people at random were a diversion, a way to flush someone from hiding. Whoever the gunman was looking for, he hadn't found them yet.

The next bundle of dynamite fell short of landing on the roof of the *Examiner* building and went off before hitting the ground.

Chunks of brick blasted off the front, tearing through canvas sunshades on ground floor windows and falling onto the sidewalk. An older couple and a young woman who appeared not far out of her teens dashed away from the shelter of an awning, and into the open. As soon as the men on the roof were able to see the terrified family running below them, the shooting stopped.

Gabe's gut told him the hunter had finally flushed his prey. He waved his arms over his head and yelled, trying to attract the old couple's attention. The space between his shoulders itched, waiting for the crack of a rifle and pain. "No, stay there. Stay there!"

The wife said something to her husband and slowed down. Her husband glanced back to see brick and masonry crashing into the awning, tugged his wife back into motion, and kept going. They'd almost drawn even with Lotta's fountain when the old man fell, clutching what was left of his knee and writhing in pain. His wife and daughter grabbed the collar of the old man's coat and an arm, trying to drag him behind the fountain. The gunman shot the old man a second time and immediately fired again, hitting the old woman in the chest.

"Move, damn it! Move!" Gabe shouted again, but the girl didn't react. She stood stock-still in the middle of the street, staring at the dead couple, chest heaving and face blank with shock. Safety and cover were only a few steps away, but they wouldn't do her any good if fear froze her in place. And Gabe would never reach her before the gunman killed her too.

He knew, but he ran toward her anyway. "Get behind the fountain! Run!" A bullet hit the paving stones at her feet, sending up pointed shards of rock that nicked her cheek. Blood mingled with the tears sliding down her face. She stumbled backwards, but still didn't try to get away.

Another bullet slammed into the paving stones, driving the girl back a few more steps. The gunman hadn't missed any of his targets up until now. He was deliberately tormenting her, hoping she'd break and run. She set her shoulders and lifted her chin, staring at the men on the rooftop, and held her ground.

Gabe was completely focused on the young woman and hadn't seen Sam Butler until the tall reporter moved. Sam was much closer, his long legs adding speed to his sprint that Gabe couldn't match. Of the two of them, Butler had the best chance of reaching her first. He also had the better chance of dying.

Sam reached her seconds after the next round slammed into the ground, looping an arm around her waist and dragging the young woman into cover behind the fountain. The gunman's angry shout echoed, harsh and distorted. Bullets pinged against the brass in rapid succession, but the base of Lotta's fountain was wide enough to keep Sam and the girl out of the field of fire.

A quick glance to the left and right brought back the itch between Gabe's shoulders threefold. Only a handful of cops slunk along the edge of buildings, hugging cover while trying to work around to the shooter's building. Other officers helped the injured to safety, staying low and moving quickly. The empty square was littered with smoking debris and lifeless bodies. Gabe was the only person standing.

Shots still pinged off the fountain, but he didn't trust the gunman not to turn his frustration on other targets. Gabe ducked behind a small mound of bricks and a partly buried ice cream vendor's cart, imperfect cover at best. He quickly searched the street for Jack. His partner had reached the building harboring the gunman and the man throwing dynamite. Jack and the two rookie officers were swinging a cast-iron bench from a trolley stop between them and trying to break down the front door.

Two more uniformed officers approached Jack from an alley between buildings, accompanied by a third man dressed in street clothes. A large badge was pinned to his coat, marking him as a detective. Gabe didn't recognize him from a distance, but the chief would have called in other squads by now.

The strange detective said something to Jack as he pulled a .38 Smith & Wesson with a six-inch barrel out from under his overcoat. Very few cops carried that kind of service revolver. Those who did were usually ex–army officers who'd been issued the pistol during the war. The detective stepped back to the curb and fired at the men on the roof. Jack yelled, but it was too late.

Gabe barely had time to huddle tight against the ice cream cart before bricks and broken glass, hunks of wood and shingles began to pummel him. Small impacts drew involuntary groans and grunts. A few larger, heavier pieces hit his back and pried loose cries of pain, pain that lingered and let him know he'd been hurt. The cart took the worst of the punishment, his sole bit of luck in the midst of an unlucky day.

His ears rang to the point he could hear little else when the deluge stopped. Dust caked his face, plugged his nose, and the taste of gunpowder sat on the back of his tongue. Blood matted his hair. Gabe groaned and dragged himself up to his feet, bracing an arm against the cart and keeping his eyes closed until the world stopped spinning. Waiting, as well, to dredge up the courage to view what might have happened to Jack and the officers with him, to Sam and the young woman.

He turned in time to see Sam help the girl to her feet. Both of them were filthy, covered in brick dust and powdered glass, but they were alive. She looked stunned, barely responding to what Sam said, but Gabe couldn't blame her for that.

Dust settled rapidly, clearing some of the haze from the air. Most of the force of the explosion had gone straight up or down into the building, an unexpected blessing. If the blast had traveled a different path, Gabe, Butler, and the unknown young woman would all be dead. Even so, how far masonry and framing timbers had traveled across the square was sobering.

The top floor at the front of the building was gone, a gaping hole that allowed the heaped rubble inside to show. Patrolmen who'd lurked down side streets and alleyways to avoid the gunfire rushed back, picking their way through rubble toward the front of the building. Toward the last place he'd seen Jack.

Their squad worked together to shift piles of brick and wood, passing the pieces from hand to hand before tossing them out of the way. Gabe stayed where he was, too dizzy and nauseated to be of any use. His men dug quickly, looking for survivors, but the first two bodies they uncovered were broken and lifeless. Relief that neither man was Jack left him light-headed.

Shouts and cheers went up from the rescuers as they heard voices calling for help, and they dug faster. Gabe's fingers curled around the broken and twisted pushcart handle. He'd lost too many people he cared about to think prayer offered any help or hope of survival. The hope he felt sprang from not being able to imagine a world without his best friend. "Come on, Jack, come on. Sadie and the kids need you. Crawl out of there."

Most of the explosion wreckage had fallen back inside the building, not onto the sidewalk and street out front. That, and his own piece of luck, was what saved Jack and the men with him. One by one, they pulled three uniformed officers out of the bricks and rubble heaped against a wall, battered and injured, but alive.

Jack was the fourth and last man out. He clutched the front of Maxwell's coat, peering into the patrolman's face and asking questions. Maxwell pointed toward Gabe.

He waved and the tightness left Jack's face and shoulders. Bruised and bleeding, Jack leaned on Maxwell and limped toward Gabe.

Gabe sat down hard, his back against what was left of the ice cream cart, and waited for his partner. He and Jack would go to meet their wives at the Palace Hotel, holding each other up if need be, but finding Delia and Sadie came before anything. The job would still be there when they got back.

He watched Sam Butler tend to the grieving young woman. Sam wet a handkerchief in Lotta's fountain and washed blood and dirt from her face, talking the whole time. Knowing Butler, he was telling her stories about places he'd traveled, hunting for a headline, or what it was like to be a reporter in a big city. Sam Butler was good at telling stories. Some of them were even true.

Listening to Sam would keep her from thinking too hard or sinking deeper into shock. Listening would keep her from running. She would run, given half a chance—he was sure of that—and Gabe couldn't afford to lose track of her.

An icy breeze found its way down the back of his neck, making him shiver. Gabe flipped up his collar. The odds of Dominic Mullaney's fledgling labor union's having anything to do with the riot starting were slim, and any connection between the union and a gunman picking people off from a rooftop even more farfetched. He'd bring Mullaney in for questioning, but that was a dead end.

No, the real reasons, whatever they might be, had to do with the girl sitting on the curb next to Sam. Gabe would wager a month's salary on that.

Delia

Quiet followed a small explosion on the far side of the square. We took a risk and dashed into the hallway leading to the private portions of the shop. Even if we went no farther, the windowless rooms in the rear were far safer. Still, I couldn't shake the feeling that staying here was a mistake. We needed to keep moving.

An unlatched door swung back and forth in the shop's rear wall, giving glimpses of dustbins and a sunny alley. The prim clerk and the owner, Mr. Perkins, appeared to have fled in panic, leaving the shop to us. I smelled smoke, and the light outside the door appeared slightly murky, but it didn't appear that the fire was close enough to be a danger.

That the clerk and the shop owner were gone was for the best and a blessing. I was reasonably certain that Libby wouldn't panic, and Sadie could be counted on to keep a cool head. The sense that something wasn't right still itched along my skin, something that went far beyond dynamite explosions and rifle fire, or people rioting on San Francisco streets. We weren't out of the thick of things yet.

I gestured toward the door. "We can follow the alley to reach the hotel. It should be safe enough with the buildings between us and the street. The thought of staying here makes me nervous."

Libby brushed at the dust on her jacket, a futile gesture considering, and nodded. "I agreed, Delia. More people around and being inside a larger building would make me feel miles safer."

"Oh yes, let's do go, Dee. The sooner, the better. Jack and Gabe expect to find us at the Palace." Sadie stood with her back against the wall and arms wrapped around Stella, rocking her little girl back and forth. She trembled visibly and her face was flushed, but no one could fault her for that. "If we're not there, they'll imagine the worst. Do you think the explosions took down the telephone lines? I'd like to let Annie know all of us are safe. She's bound to have had a call from the station summoning Jack for duty by now. She'll be worried sick."

"We won't know about the telephones until we reach the hotel. If Gabe and Jack weren't set on meeting us there, I wouldn't go to the Palace at all. I'm not sure there's safety in greater numbers, or any safety at all, for that matter. People were far too eager to fight with total strangers. It all makes my skin crawl, but we can't stay here either." I pushed sweat-soaked hair off Connor's face and kissed his forehead. He'd stopped screaming in fright, but he was still lying wide eyed and stiff on my shoulder, staring at ghosts. New haunts appeared as soon as I sent others away, fresh victims who'd died at the hands of the gunman or in the explosions. "If the telephones are working, we should ring Dora too. Randy will have gotten the same call to come in before his shift. I don't want her to worry needlessly."

Randy and Isadora were devoted to one another, best friends as well as lovers. They'd lived together more than a year and a half now, and Randy asked her to marry him at least once a week. I suspected that Dora would say yes one day soon. She'd admitted to me that the only thing holding her back was fear. The last two men she'd been involved with had both been murdered. Their deaths weren't remotely connected to her relationship with either Daniel or John Lawrence, but Dora still saw herself as somewhat cursed.

"Let me check that the alley is clear before we start. I'd hate to get stuck partway there and have to come back." Libby cautiously stepped out the open door and moved away. She returned quickly. "I've been down lanes in other parts of the city that weren't so wide or so clean. The alley continues through to the end of the block, and the buildings on the street side are packed pretty tightly. We should be safe making a run for the back of the hotel."

Another large explosion shook the walls, and the ceiling groaned, spawning clouds of paint dust and plaster. Ghosts filled the hallway in large numbers, men and women and a scattering of children, all crowding in as near as possible. Connor buried his head in my shoulder, whimpering. I hugged him tighter, whispering banishment charms to scatter gathering spirits and building layers of protection around him as quickly as I could.

Ghosts often sought out people sensitive enough to detect their presence, drawn to their life force the way moths swarm a streetlamp. That was especially true of the newly dead who often didn't remember dying. I prayed that I was the beacon that drew spirits in such numbers, not the tiny child in my arms. He was too young to understand what ghosts might want from him, overwhelmed and defenseless in the face of their emotions.

I'd suspected Connor watched ghosts, but I hadn't realized how sensitive he truly was. At his age, possession was a very real danger. I added one more worry to the immediate list. Now I was the one whose heart beat too hard and too fast, exhausted from keeping the ghosts at bay and eaten by guilt that I hadn't done more for Connor before now.

Libby peered at me quizzically as I stepped into the alley. "Delia?"

I held tight to calm and managed a smile. "Connor's heavier than you'd expect. I'm fine. Lead the way."

The alley was a smoky canyon overlooked by the unadorned back walls of millinery shops, gentlemen's haberdasheries, and boot makers. Small placards marked doors for tradesmen to make deliveries, some nearly as faded as the weathered brick they hung on. Very few ghosts moved through the alley, and the ones I saw were long dead, old and thin to the point of nearly vanishing. Connor lay limp against my shoulder, exhausted from crying and fear, but he still watched each ghost's passage. I'd worry less once we got him home. The protections I'd put in place around Sadie's house more than four years before were worn with time, but they'd still help protect him. Dora and I would work on new barriers tomorrow morning at the latest, tonight if possible.

And I'd find a way to break the news to Sadie just as soon as we were home and safe. I'd already waited too long.

Gunshots still echoed from the other side of the buildings, faint and sounding far away. Time flowed slowly, an odd feeling, almost as if we were fated to run down this alley for eternity. While I knew that wasn't really true, reaching the door of the hotel took longer than I'd thought it should.

A young, freckle-faced patrolman I didn't know guarded the back entrance to the Palace, ushering in stragglers seeking refuge just as we were. That sense of dread and disquiet—and a compulsion to keep looking over my shoulder—stayed with me even once we were inside. I couldn't find the source or see any danger, but I couldn't shake the need to be wary either. We were safe from gunshots and explosions, at least for the moment. I tried to take consolation in that.

Enormous crystal chandeliers chased away shadows in the passageway leading from the alley entrance to the lobby. The lobby itself was crowded with overly polite people determined not to tread on toes or jostle the person walking past. Nearly everyone I saw was covered in dust, their clothing torn and faces sometimes bloodied. No one looked at us; no one smiled or made an effort to be social, or asked if the children were all right.

These quiet, subdued people had been eager participants in the riot on the square; I was sure of that. I'd pushed past them or people just like them as we fought our way free. Now they milled around the lobby not speaking to anyone, sleepwalkers with blank expressions. The source of my disquiet was all around me. I'd just not known where to look.

On another day, I might have believed shock over watching people gunned down in the street and bombs going off were to blame, or that guilt over rushing to join a riot had left them ashamed.

But the need to be cautious and shy away from these people grew stronger each moment, causing me to pay more attention. Some other influence was at work, a force that set respectable people at each other's throats and left them drained afterwards.

I'd spent the last four years working with Isadora, learning about the spirit realm and a myriad of dank, unpleasant creatures and forces that moved through the world. Most people never encountered those creatures or felt the touch of influences that could only be described as evil. Knowing these things existed and what to look for was decidedly a mixed blessing.

Above all, she taught me to trust my instincts, to believe the revulsion settling in the pit of my stomach was a warning I should heed. If I was the least bit unsure or didn't understand what I was dealing with, I should back away.

Whatever was going on here had the feel of something best left undisturbed. Under other circumstances, I'd have taken Sadie by the hand and fled.

"Sadie . . ." I touched her shoulder. "Wait."

Sadie stopped right where she was, shifting Stella to the other arm and looking only a little frightened. She'd known I could see ghosts since we were children, and took it on faith that strange requests from me had to do with spirits. Most things she took in stride, but given the day we'd had, I'd have forgiven her a little panic. "What's wrong, Dee?"

"I wish I knew." I patted Connor's back and rocked side to side, trying to keep him calm and sort out how best to explain. "A crowd of ordinary men and women came to watch a parade and ended up willingly joining in a riot. I'd wager that behavior would horrify them in normal circumstances, but nothing about today has been normal. Now I look around, and those same people are still acting strangely. I can't pin down exactly what I'm sensing, but it's real and makes me extremely uncomfortable."

"We can't go back out there. It's not safe." Sadie's eyes widened as she watched people wandering the lobby, really seeing them for the first time. She turned back to me, weary and scared, but not coming apart. Hidden under her sometimes frivolous exterior, Sadie Fitzgerald had a core of iron. "I assume you'd know if this was a ghost."

I shook my head. "No, it's not a ghost. So far, whatever this is has taken no notice of us. That's puzzling in and of itself, but I'd like to keep matters that way without wandering too far. I know you had your heart set on phoning Annie, but I think it best to wait. Gabe and Jack will still look for us here when they can. Sam too."

"I hope that's soon. I can't help but worry and imagine the worst." Sadie's eyes were bright with unshed tears. "I keep praying I'll turn around and Jack will be standing there."

"Jack and Gabe are all right, I promise." Libby looked between me and Sadie, clearly bewildered but silent. I was grateful she didn't ask a hundred questions. "Give me a moment to find the best place to wait."

I turned in a slow circle, arms beginning to ache from carrying Connor. Searching the cavernous lobby didn't take long and I found what I'd wanted, a place to hide in plain sight. Comfortable-looking sofas, with large plush throw pillows, filled an otherwise unadorned alcove set apart from the main room by tall rattan screens and potted palms. Not a single painting or ornament to attract attention hung on the walls, a strange thing in the lavishly decorated lobby, but that made the alcove ideal for my purposes.

The space was sheltered and less exposed, but Gabe and Jack could still find us easily. I pointed. "Over there, between the pillar and the bellboy station. It's the perfect place. We can rest until Sam and Jack and Gabe arrive."

Libby brushed long strands of dark hair off her face and started for the alcove, trusting Sadie and I would follow. "You sound so sure they'll survive, Delia. What with guns and explosions . . . I wish I had your faith."

"I'd know if anything happened to them. I promise you, the three of them are all right." "Skeptical" was the kindest word I could think of for the expression on Libby's face, but I let it pass unremarked. This wasn't the time to explain the strangeness in my life to Libby Mills.

I laid Connor on one of the sofas, his head cushioned by a green velvet throw pillow, and settled next to him. He'd finally fallen asleep and I chose to think of that as a good sign. Sadie settled into one corner of the second sofa with a drowsy Stella, while Libby sat in a wicker chair angled to face the lobby.

The interior of the hotel was brightly lit, a combination of the numerous crystal chandeliers reflecting and magnifying each other's light, and the mirrored sconces set into every wall. I was able to see people in the lobby by peering through palm fronds and the loosely woven rattan screens. Anyone looking our way would see nothing more than shadows or indistinct shapes, something that should have made me feel safer and didn't. Huddling in the darker alcove didn't stop the wariness grating over my skin, nor silence the voice telling me to stay still and quiet. I imagined this was what a rabbit felt while eyeing the circling hawk overhead.

Two men came into view, visibly angry and arguing at the top of their voices. The man shouting loudest didn't appear to care who heard or notice that none of the people wandering aimlessly through the lobby so much as looked in his direction. His disagreement might as well have been conducted in pantomime, for all the attention people paid.

The second man was keenly aware of the total lack of reaction by the strangers around him. He took furtive glances over his shoulder, watching the women and men milling about with a nervous expression I found all too familiar.

"Dom, stop and listen to me!" The first man, still shouting, grabbed Dom's arm, forcing him to halt on the other side of the rattan screens. I saw then he was yelling at Dominic Mullaney, head of the fledging labor union. Mr. Mullaney had been on the receiving end of the fighting in the square. His face was scratched, bruised, and dried blood caked one corner of his mouth. Broad through the shoulder, with a square chin and broad nose, he was easy to picture as a boxer. I imagined he'd given as good as he got.

Sadie and Libby gave me owl-eyed looks, but didn't make a sound. I put a hand on Connor's back, hoping he wouldn't cry and draw attention to us.

"Going to the police is a stupid thing to do. You'll make yourself look guilty and destroy the work you've done. Don't do the policeman's job for him, Dominic. Make him come to you."

"The police already think I'm guilty, Aleksei! Running will only make things worse." Mr. Mullaney yanked his arm free and wiped a hand over his mouth. "Father Colm tried to talk me out of this, but I wouldn't listen. I promised him we'd march and go home, that there wouldn't be any fighting or trouble. Some of the men brought their wives and children to watch the parade. None of this was supposed to happen. Mary and Joseph . . . all those people hurt or dead."

Gray frosted Aleksei's temples and his neat, light brown beard. Deep lines around his pale blue eyes and mouth made him appear older, but I guessed him to be no more than forty. His slight Russian accent was difficult to detect, a harshness rolled around his words and into the rhythm of his speech. I'd known a friend at school who spoke the same way, but she'd grown up speaking both Russian and English at home.

"I've known idealists like you before. You want a bloodless revolution." Aleksei slipped his hands into his coat pockets and shrugged. "Not everyone involved with the unions agrees. They want change now at any cost."

Dominic clenched his fists and took a step back. "Those aren't my men on the roof. I swear on my mother's grave, Aleksei, the unions had nothing to do with this."

Aleksei studied him, face expressionless. "Someone set *you* up, my friend. If your enemies bring you down, the union will fail. Whether you were involved or not makes no difference. You're the leader of a loyal band of revolutionaries, and that makes you guilty."

"Stop calling us revolutionaries. This isn't Saint Petersburg or Moscow." Dominic glanced over his shoulder, nervous. "You spent too much time running from the Bolsheviks."

"The point remains. People will accuse you." Aleksei brushed at the front of his coat and scowled. "Your own people may be the first to lay blame. Prepare yourself for that, Dominic."

A huge explosion outside echoed against the ceiling, causing the floor to rock and the chandeliers to sway violently. We were at the back of the hotel, far from the street or the danger posed by breaking plate glass windows, but I still curled over Connor protectively. Sadie did the same with Stella.

One of the rattan screens shielding us tipped to one side, taking the other screen down as well. Huge porcelain vases full of early spring flowers rocked off the edge of tables, shattering. Paintings slid off walls, landing facedown and cracking the frames. Individual crystals fell from swinging chandeliers, the ping they made hitting the floor drowned by the screams of frightened people. The sleepwalkers were fully awake now, no doubt reminded of earthquakes and the destruction left behind.

But the explosion's aftershock passed quickly, leaving shaken nerves behind but very little real damage. I sat up and pulled Connor into my lap. He was shaking and staring at the ceiling with frightened, solemn eyes, but he didn't cry. I smoothed his hair, rocking him and trying not to be obvious about watching Dominic and Aleksei. The two men couldn't help but see us now or know we'd heard every word. That concerned me a great deal.

Mr. Mullaney glanced our way, but something else, a noise or a movement I'd missed, caught his attention. He stared at the ceiling for an instant, eyes growing wider. "Mother of God . . . look out!"

Dominic Mullaney shoved Aleksei hard, sending him flying to one side. He dodged in the opposite direction, hitting the floor and rolling. A chandelier crashed to the ground between them, missing Aleksei by inches.

Connor stared at the fallen chandelier, quiet and unnaturally calm. A thousand shards of shattered crystal littered the floor, and a thousand more unbroken crystal prisms still clung to the chandelier's frame, or had rolled into the alcove. I looked out across the lobby at the mirrored sconces set into walls, the remaining chandeliers, broken vases and crystal prisms scattered on marble floors.

The princess ghost looked back from each one.

CHAPTER 3

Gabe

Picking their way through the debris in the square took longer than Gabe had planned, but both he and Jack were unsteady on their feet and ready to collapse. By the time they limped into the damaged lobby of the Palace, Gabe knew neither of them was in any condition to run an investigation. Only sheer stubbornness and the need to see their wives, to make sure Libby and the children were safe, had gotten them this far.

One small window on the front of the hotel building had shattered, but the rest were crazed with spiderweb cracks and would need to be replaced. Distance from the blast was the only reason Gabe could come up with for why they hadn't all broken. Hotel staff rushed around the lobby, doing their best to clean up the wreckage caused when the dynamite cache exploded. Fragments of broken porcelain vases crunched underfoot and flowers lay dying in puddles of water, but the damage was only an annoying mess, not anything life threatening or that would bring the building down.

Sending Dee and Sadie to the Palace had been the right thing to do. Still, he wouldn't relax until he saw them.

"Delia said they'd wait near the back of the lobby." Jack was flushed and winded, his limp much worse. "Don't let me fall over before we find them."

"Not a chance. Sadie would never forgive me if I left you behind." Gabe got a shoulder under Jack's arm and took more of his weight. He ignored the stabbing ache in his side. "Sam's got his hands full and I'm too tired to drag you the rest of the way. Let's go."

More cops were already arriving on the scene, including the rest of their squad. Both Sergeant Rockwell and Marshall Henderson were more than capable of taking over, questioning any witnesses that hadn't fled and making sure nothing was overlooked. Unless he missed his guess, Henderson had already started the squad searching the rubble for the injured and laying out bodies of those who'd died.

Gabe wouldn't need to argue his partner away from duty and into going to the hospital; Sadie would see to that. She'd take one look at Jack, and the battle would be over before it started.

A glance over his shoulder let Gabe know Sam Butler and the girl were still right behind them. She was leaning heavily on Sam, his arm around her shoulder all that kept her moving. Shock and reaction to everything she'd seen left her with a disbelieving expression and a glazed look in her eyes.

He'd seen that same numbness on the face of survivors trapped in their own heads, reliving the horrors they'd witnessed again and again. Guilt over being spared while others died made the pain worse. Some never found the strength to put guilt aside and go on with their lives. He didn't know this young woman. He couldn't say which way the pendulum would swing.

Sam had figured out on his own that leaving the girl unprotected was a bad idea. He'd insisted she come with them, and she hadn't had the strength to put up more than a token protest.

Butler was doing a good job of trying to distract her, keeping up the same steady stream of banter and stories he'd started at Lotta's fountain. She responded to Sam's occasional question with a nod or a shake of the head, but didn't speak. That she responded at all gave Gabe hope she'd be all right in the end; if he and Jack could keep her alive.

Every instinct he'd honed during his years on the force told Gabe the men shooting and tossing dynamite off the roof weren't the ones giving the orders. Someone else wanted her dead. That the men trying to kill her had failed once didn't mean they'd stop trying. One way or another, he needed to find a way to protect her.

"Jack!" Sadie saw them first and called out; otherwise, Gabe wasn't confident he would have found them easily. Dee, Sadie, and the children were waiting with Libby in a dim, semi-hidden alcove set back from the main lobby. There were dozens of simple reasons Delia might have chosen this spot, but very few things in their lives were simple. He didn't miss the way Delia watched the lobby with anxious eyes, ready to run. That she didn't come to meet him halfway said even more.

"Oh God, Jack . . . Jack." Sadie thrust Stella into Libby's arms and rushed toward them, dodging around the fallen chandelier in the middle of the floor. She gently cupped Jack's face in her hands and kissed him. Tears streamed down her face as she babbled. "I can't believe you're here. Dee said you were all right, but I was so afraid I'd never see you again. You're bleeding! There's . . . there's blood all over your shirt. How badly are you hurt? We need to get you to the hospital right now."

"I don't need a hospital." Jack coughed hard, his face screwed up with pain. "I'll be fine once we get home."

"Most of that mess isn't his blood, Sadie, but don't let him try to talk you out of the hospital." Gabe gritted his teeth and shifted his grip. "Help me get him onto the settee. I can't hold him up much longer."

"Alina needs to sit down too." Sam spoke from just behind Gabe's shoulder, raspy and hoarse. Butler had managed to learn the young woman's name, a surprise Gabe welcomed. That she already trusted him that much was a good first step. "Do what Gabe asked, Sadie. I promise we'll get things sorted and everyone will be taken care of."

For the first time since she'd spotted them limping across the lobby, Sadie saw something other than Jack's face. Belatedly, she took in the state of Gabe's clothing and how Sam was struggling to keep the young woman—Alina—from sliding to the floor.

"Oh Gabe, I'm so sorry!" She rushed to get Jack's other arm around her shoulder. "I should have known better. What was I thinking? You're hurt too."

"I'm a little beat up, but you were right to worry about Jack first. He's a lot worse off." They eased Jack down onto the sofa, slow and careful. He didn't think he'd be able to manage getting Jack on his feet again, but most of their squad was outside the hotel. Finding men willing to move Jack when the time came wouldn't be a problem.

He had other things to worry about. Not the least of those was that he became more aware of his own injuries with each second. Gabe pressed a hand to his side and prayed the pain each time he moved too quickly was a sign his ribs were bruised, not broken. "Taylor and Maxwell will be here soon with a car. Some of the men were hurt more than either of us. I wanted them taken to the hospital first."

Libby patted Stella's back and set her down. "Sit with your papa, sweetheart. Be very careful not to bump him. I need to help Sam."

Gabe managed to sit next to Delia without jarring his ribs too much. Connor sat on her lap, fully awake and watching everything. There was something fiercely protective about the way Dee held Connor, something that went beyond offering comfort to a scared little boy. Given how badly the day had gone, he couldn't blame her for holding on extra tight.

But Gabe knew his wife too well to let it pass as a simple case of nerves. Delia had reason to worry about Connor, a reason that went beyond events in the square. She wanted to hide how deep that worry ran from Sadie. What he didn't know was why.

Delia's lip trembled and tears filled her eyes, but she managed a smile before leaning her head against his shoulder. "I knew you were all right, but I'm still awfully glad to see you. The same goes for Jack and Sam. It's been a difficult afternoon."

He laughed, regretting it instantly. No matter how much he wanted to pretend otherwise, his ribs were almost definitely cracked or broken, and that meant getting a doctor to tape them before he went back to work. "'Difficult' is the perfect word, Mrs. Ryan. I can't think of a better way to describe it. Unfortunately, the day's not over yet. I have to go back to work once Jack's on his way to the hospital."

Libby looked up from fussing over Alina and frowned. "I'll never understand why men can't be sensible about these things. You need a doctor as much as Jack does, and I wouldn't be surprised if Sam doesn't need to be seen as well. The only place any of you should go is home to bed. I'm positive Delia agrees with me."

Gabe agreed with her too. All he wanted was to go home, to lie propped up in the corner of the sofa with an arm around Delia and the smell of her hair surrounding him. But he couldn't dismiss the cold itch on the back of his neck nor silence the half-heard whispers in his ear about how the men on the roof had died. He needed to discover who the strange cop with the army revolver had been.

Above all, Gabe had to find a safe place for Alina to stay before he went home and collapsed. A place no one would think to look for her.

Delia twisted in her seat to peer at him, her arms still wrapped tight around Connor. "Libby's right, you should go home. But I know you, Gabe Ryan, and you'll do nothing of the sort. What haven't you told me?"

He briefly outlined the story of the strange cop setting off the dynamite on the roof, killing the two men sowing death amongst the crowd of parade spectators. A glance at Sadie made him leave out details of the building's partial collapse, a collapse that had almost buried Jack alive. He was mindful of Stella listening as well.

"Five officers died when the dynamite on that roof exploded." Gabe shut his eyes briefly, but that was a mistake. All he saw were his men's broken bodies and their startled expressions. He eased himself up straighter in the seat. "Two of them were rookies from my station. I'll likely have nightmares about that. And the way the explosion happened—something's not right. I can't walk away, Dee. I need to at least try to find some answers before the trail goes cold."

Delia rested her chin on the top of Connor's head, chewing her bottom lip. "Nothing about this afternoon feels right, and I don't understand it any more than you do. That bothers me a great deal. But the thought of you going back out there without Jack gives me the willies. You've already been hurt."

"Pardon me." Sam cleared his throat and traded looks with Gabe. "I understand why Gabe doesn't feel he can leave this mess for someone else to clean up. Since I might be the only one who doesn't need a doctor, I'll stay here to watch his back. Gabe can supervise and I'll do the hard parts."

Gabe saw more questions and doubts in Delia's eyes, but she kept them to herself. Instead, she sat back and nodded. "I'm holding you responsible for him, Sam Butler. Don't let him stay longer than absolutely necessary. And don't let him do more than he should."

Sam put a hand over his heart and bowed his head. "You have my solemn word. I'll get him home as soon as possible."

"You've got my promise too." Gabe took her hand. "I'll be careful."

Alina cried quietly, arms wrapped across her chest and rocking. Gabe would never forget the days just after his father was killed and how for a time, grief was his whole world. He imagined the initial shock of watching people die and being shot at herself was beginning to wear off. He pitied her that. Pain would rush to fill the emptiness, razor edged and unrelenting.

Libby gathered Alina into her arms, letting the brokenhearted young woman sob against her shoulder. "There, there, it will be all right. Cry it all out if you need to, but the worst is over. You're safe. I promise, no one's going to hurt you."

"She just watched her parents die, Libby. Then they tried to shoot her too." Sam wiped a hand over his face, suddenly looking much older than twenty-five. "I don't think things will be all right for a very long time."

Tears filled Libby's eyes and she hugged Alina tighter. "Then it's best she cry it out. Keeping the hurt inside will only make it last longer."

"Excuse me, Captain Ryan. Can I have a word with you?"

He looked up to see Dominic Mullaney standing at the entrance to the alcove. Mullaney was nervous, sweating and fidgeting, and toying with the brim of the hat in his hands. Dominic's face showed just how much punishment he'd taken in the fight outside. Gabe was oddly relieved to see he hadn't been hurt worse. Business owners might not like Mullaney, but he didn't see much wrong with Dominic's goal of making sure his men were paid a decent wage. As long as the union stayed on the right side of the law and off private property, Gabe saw no reason to stop them from recruiting new members.

That Mullaney came looking for him confirmed his opinion of the union leader's character. And he'd wager Jack coffee and cookies for a week that his growing hunch was right; Dominic Mullaney had nothing to do with the violence and destruction surrounding Lotta's fountain.

Not that Gabe could say that to anyone but his partner, not without proof. He couldn't cross Dominic Mullaney off his list of suspects just yet.

Movement in the lobby caught his eye. An older man, nattily dressed in an expensive serge suit and with a neatly trimmed beard, stood a few yards back. The scowl on the stranger's face made it clear what he thought of Dominic speaking to the police. As soon as the stranger noticed Gabe watching, he spun on his heel and quickly walked to the other end of the lobby. He loitered there, apparently waiting for Mullaney.

Not everyone was fond of police officers, and even honest people went out of their way to avoid cops. All his years of experience said that wasn't the case here—the stranger had something to hide. Gabe put finding out exactly who this man was and his connection to Mullaney on the list of things he needed to know.

Gabe glanced at Jack, but his partner's eyes were closed tight. Sadie leaned over him, whispering in his ear and brushing the curls back from Jack's face. Stella sat still and quiet at her father's side, holding his hand. His stomach lurched, the specter of losing his best friend looming large again.

He prayed Taylor and Maxwell would bring the car soon. Gabe cleared his throat and turned his attention back to the young labor leader. "What can I do for you, Mullaney?"

"I needed you to know that my men and I, we didn't have anything to do with what happened." Dominic waved his hat toward the square. "The fighting, the guns and the explosions—the union didn't have a part in starting any of that. Our families were here watching the parade. No matter what the ship owners claim, the union's not cold blooded enough to set off bombs around our kids."

Gabe studied Mullaney's face. Even if that wasn't true for all the union men, Dominic believed what he'd said. "All right, fair enough for now. I don't know you very well, but Father Colm speaks highly of you, and I respect his opinion. But that doesn't mean I won't keep asking questions. Any idea who might have set this up?"

"I swear on my mother's grave, Captain Ryan, I don't have any notion of who was on that roof. I'd like to find out." Mullaney crushed the brim of his hat in a fist and scowled. "And I want to know what trick they used to get friends fighting each other and seeing things that weren't there."

Delia had stayed silent and listened to everything said, but now she leaned forward, suddenly more attentive. "Seeing things, Mr. Mullaney? What did your men see?"

Dominic glanced over his shoulder and lowered his voice. "All the men I talked to said there were monsters and angels reaching for them. That's who they thought they were fighting or trying to drive away from their families. If twenty men weren't all telling the same story, I'd think the whole lot of them were lying."

"I agree, Mr. Mullaney. The odds of twenty men concocting the same story are very slim." Dee chewed her bottom lip, thinking. "Did you see these angels and monsters?"

Mullaney slapped his hat against his leg, a nervous rhythm that said he was as confused about what had happened as any of them. "No, missus. I didn't see anything myself, but I heard the wind keening like a banshee. All my men heard the wailing and made a point of saying so. I can testify to that part being true."

The urge to move, to walk away while he thought things out swept over him, but Gabe forced himself to be still. He'd been too young before his grandmother died to hear her stories about banshees, but his mother had repeated the tales for him once he was almost grown. Gram's stories said banshees could appear as ugly old hags or as beautiful women, and that anyone who heard them wail knew death stalked the household. If several banshees appeared together, it foretold the death of someone important or holy, a nobleman or a priest. Another of his grandmother's tales said a banshee was the ghost of a murdered woman.

"Monsters and angels . . . Mother of God." Gabe wiped a hand over his mouth. Those stories belonged to the Irish countryside where his grandmother was born, not San Francisco. "I saw something in the smoke, but I thought it was my mind playing tricks."

"Then my mind was playing tricks on me too. I've never heard anything like the voices riding on that wind." Sam crossed his arms over his chest and stretched out his long legs. "But I didn't feel the need to take a swing at anyone after hearing them, other than in self-defense. Neither did Gabe or any of the uniformed officers. From what you say, Mr. Mullaney, the same holds true for you. I wonder why that is?"

"You're right to wonder, Sam. None of it makes sense." Delia met Gabe's eyes. She didn't need to tell him that the faces in the smoke were phantoms of some sort. That much was clear. Over the years, he'd learned enough from Delia and Isadora to understand that spirits were limited in what they could do, and who they could influence. Not even the strongest ghost could incite an entire crowd to riot.

From where he sat right now, that looked to be exactly what happened. That was a terrifying thought, but so was the possibility that something else, something entirely outside his experience, had happened.

Maxwell and Taylor came into view, hurrying through the lobby, looking for Jack and Gabe. The two patrolmen were followed closely by four other men carrying canvas stretchers. Taylor saw Gabe and pointed the alcove out to the stretcher-bearers before trotting over himself.

"Captain, the hospital sent an ambulance for the lieutenant." Taylor spoke quickly. "Dr. Jodes insisted and said for us to hurry. He's worried the lieutenant might have a concussion."

"I'm going with him. Sit with your aunt Delia, Stella." Sadie kissed Stella's cheek and moved her to the other sofa near Gabe, giving the ambulance attendants room to work. She stood out of the way, clutching her handbag tight as the four burly men eased Jack down onto the stretcher. "Dee . . . would you mind getting Stella and Connor home to Annie? I'll call from the hospital as soon as I have news."

"Of course I don't mind! Don't worry about either of them for an instant." Delia stood, putting Connor on her hip so she could hug Sadie. "You tend to Jack and I'll look after the children. Everyone will be fine, I promise."

Gabe managed to get to his feet without too much trouble and stood with Delia. All Jack's friends watched the ambulance attendants carry him away. Sadie walked right next to the stretcher, never taking her eyes off Jack's face. Stella sat on the edge of the sofa as her parents left, swinging her legs and singing quietly. She was too young to understand.

Too young to worry.

Taylor cleared his throat. "Captain, the car's waiting at the side of the hotel. Now that Lieutenant Fitzgerald's seen to, I can drive Mrs. Ryan and the children to the lieutenant's house."

"Yes, that would help a great deal. Is that all right with you, Dee?" He tucked a strand of brown hair behind her ear, fighting back the pang of loss and longing that always surfaced when he saw her holding Connor. She'd made her peace with not having children, but there were times he still struggled. "I'll feel better knowing you're all with Annie."

"That's more than all right. I think I've had enough adventures for one day." Dee leaned against him for an instant, eyes closed. She sighed and stepped back. "We weren't able to telephone the house. Annie's likely worrying herself into a fine state by now. If we leave her to her own devices for too long, she's likely to come down here and take command. She's put them to work in her kitchen often enough, I don't think there's a man on the squad who wouldn't obey her orders. We should likely avoid making the men choose between her cooking and you."

He smiled. "You're right. It wouldn't be a fair contest."

"Gabe, I've got an idea." Sam gestured at the sofa, his expression pleasant and carefully bland. A public face, designed to hide secrets from Mullaney and anyone who might be watching. "Send Libby and Alina with Dee. That would solve the immediate problem of making them wait until I could escort them home. We can work out the rest later."

Alina had stopped sobbing, but she kept her head on Libby's shoulder and her face turned toward the wall. She was likely both hiding and listening to everything that was said. The young woman didn't know any of them, and given what had happened, she'd good reason to be cautious.

At Jack's they'd all be safe, at least for the moment. He didn't have many men to spare, but he'd find two or three to stand guard over the Fitzgerald house. Gabe wasn't willing to take any chances. "That's an excellent idea. Libby and Alina will be more comfortable and Annie will worry less if she has someone to fuss over until Jack comes home. Square things with Libby."

Butler moved to kneel next to Libby, keeping his voice low and talking quickly. Libby glanced up, meeting Gabe's eyes, and nodded.

Gabe took Taylor aside and gave the patrolman his orders. His estimation of Libby Mills went up a notch when she took off her shawl and draped it around Alina's head and shoulders, swaddling the girl so that her face was almost completely hidden. Libby helped her to her feet, wrapping an arm around Alina's waist. "That will help warm you up and keep you from taking a chill. Come along, now. We're going someplace you can rest."

Delia watched the whole exchange, but didn't say anything. She kissed Gabe's cheek and took Stella's hand. "Let's go home to Annie. She must be lonely without us. Wave good-bye to Uncle Gabe."

Mullaney stood awkwardly off to one side as they left, still toying with his hat and obviously torn about whether to leave or stay. Exhaustion tugged down the corners of his mouth and made his shoulders droop. Gabe took pity on him.

"Go home, Dominic. It's been a rough day for all of us. Just don't get the idea that I'm finished with you. I want you in my office to answer questions tomorrow morning." Gabe fished his fedora out of an inside pocket and combed fingers through his hair before putting the hat on. Lifting his arms that high still hurt like hell, but he wasn't going to let Mullaney see. "If I don't hear from you by noon, I'll issue a warrant for your arrest."

"I'll be there." Mullaney looked Gabe in the eye. "I've got nothing to hide, Captain. I'll answer any question you want."

"I'll hold you to that. Answer one for me now, and then you can leave." Gabe stuffed his hands into his overcoat pockets, surprised to find they weren't filled with debris. He nodded toward the far side of the lobby. "That man's been watching us since we started talking. Who is he?"

Mullaney glanced over his shoulder. "A friend, Aleksei Nureyev. He's one of the union officers. Why?"

"Curiosity. I like to know who's watching me." He shrugged

and gave Dominic a fleeting smile. "Don't forget. Tomorrow before noon."

"I'll be there." Mullaney slicked his hair back before walking away. "Get some rest, Captain. You look like you need it."

Butler came to stand next to Gabe, arms folded over his chest. Together they watched Dominic cross the lobby and join Aleksei Nureyev.

"Sam, I need to ask a favor."

"Let me guess. You want me to dig something up on Nureyev." Sam gave him a sideways glance. "Consider it done. Any special reason?"

"Call it a hunch. Something about him rubs me the wrong way. And I really do like to know who's spying on me." Gabe stared across the lobby, watching Dominic talk to Nureyev. Aleksei was angry and red faced, holding tight to Mullaney's arm and speaking rapidly. The only thing that kept him from yelling was that Gabe and Sam were watching. At a guess, Aleksei knew he'd been seen skulking and trying to eavesdrop, and that Dominic had given the police his name. Mullaney might not have anything to hide, but Aleksei Nureyev did.

Nureyev's secret was the top question on Gabe's list. He doubted that Dominic knew the answer.

CHAPTER 4

Delia

I tucked another blanket around Connor, relieved and grateful that he could relax at home and had fallen asleep so easily. The wards and boundaries on the house were stronger than I'd hoped. Even after four years, they still served well to keep all but the most determined spirits from entering his bedroom.

"Determined" was the only word to describe the princess ghost. She'd followed me here, just as she'd followed me all day. I'd discovered her image in the corner of a silver picture frame and in the small mirror hanging near the door. She watched as I got Connor settled, interested and aware, and noting my every move. As long as she didn't disturb his rest, I was content to let her be, at least for now. Mustering the energy necessary to send her away would be difficult at best.

I sat in the rocker next to Connor's small bed, one hand resting lightly on his back, and studied her. Whether it was a mask donned to show the members of court I couldn't say, but she carried herself with a confidence instilled in royals from birth. She'd been sure of who she was, of her future and the path laid out for her. I didn't sense any arrogance, or any hint that the princess had looked down on people of a lesser station. Death had come for her suddenly, a surprise, cutting short the dreams she'd had for herself.

That was a sad thing to realize. We all had hopes and dreams.

The princess observed me in turn, calm and placid in a way I'd rarely seen in such a strong ghost. Normally strong spirits were disruptive, inserting themselves into the world of the living and imposing their will on anyone unable to resist. People had gone mad under the combined onslaught of a ghost's focused anger and pressure to do as the spirit bade. Some minds had never recovered after being broken. I counted it a blessing she appeared to have no interest in Connor.

But it occurred to me that the princess wasn't here because of Connor's sensitivity to spirits. I became more sure of that the longer I looked into her eyes. She wanted something of me, desired I deliver a message or fulfill a task she couldn't perform herself. I'd learned through hard-won experience that the princess, like all ghosts, would persist until I found a way to banish her or the task was completed.

I was nothing more than a means to get what she wanted, a tool to be used and discarded. The truth of that nestled into my bones. She'd warned me before the shooting started not out of any sense of altruism or concern for my welfare, but for reasons of her own. Not the least of those reasons was that I'd be useless to her dead.

"Who are you, spirit? Where did you come from?" My words were little more than a whisper, but I knew she'd hear. I'd no hope she'd answer. "And why come to me? I can't imagine what use I'd be to royalty. Those who knew you or might have cared for you are on the other side of the world. Europe is a long way from San Francisco."

Curiosity about who the princess had been and where she'd

lived warred with my good sense. Much as I wanted to know why she'd sought me out, I couldn't take the risk of letting down my guard. She'd shown no interest in Connor as of yet, but that couldn't last. His safety was more important than seeking answers to my questions.

The flurry of Dora's arrival sounded from downstairs, complete with flirtatious greetings for the officers on guard. Living with Randy Dodd had ended her quest to conquer the hearts of all the officers in Gabe's squad, but nothing would keep her from flirting. Still, I heard the strain in her voice.

"Be a dear, Charlie, and hang up my coat. Where is Mrs. Ryan?"

Officer Finlay's voice echoed in the entryway. "She's upstairs with the lieutenant's little boy. Any word from the hospital?"

I could imagine Dora shaking her head and touching his arm before answering. "No, nothing yet. I'd hoped someone here would know."

Rapid footfalls sounded on the stairs, reaching the top so fast, Dora must have taken the steps two at a time. She hurried down the hallway just as quickly.

I glanced at the princess ghost to see how she'd react to Isadora's arrival, wondering if she'd vanish or her expression would change. Instead of reacting as I'd imagined, the spirit had turned to watch the door, calm and seemingly unconcerned.

That puzzled me and added another layer of worry, not that I needed more. Most ghosts had the self-preservation and good sense to avoid Dora. I'd learned a great deal about the spirit realm and the occult world from Isadora Bobet over the last four years, but her abilities still far outstripped mine. Spirits feared what she could do in terms of driving them from the world of the living.

They had good reason to be afraid. No spirit had ever stood for long against the force of Dora's will.

I didn't think for an instant the princess was ignorant of

Dora's power. The question was whether her willingness to face Dora came from arrogance or some arcane knowledge that nothing could touch her. Gazing at the spirit's serene expression, I wasn't sure it mattered. The princess ghost meant to stand firm.

Dora appeared in the doorway, flushed and uncharacteristically teary eyed. She hurried across the room and pulled me up out of the chair, folding me into a fierce hug. "I've never been so glad to see you, Dee. I drove Randy over to the Palace Hotel. I couldn't get very near the square or the fountain. They . . . they were still uncovering bodies in the rubble. Are you all right? And Gabe? I haven't heard a word from anyone about him."

"I'm shaken and a bit frightened, but otherwise fine. Gabe admits to being sore and bruised, but he's not letting that stop him from working. He refused to go to the hospital with Jack. Sam's looking after him for me." I hugged Dora in return and stepped back to see her face. "Sadie and the children, and Sam and his friend Libby all escaped unhurt. It was a near thing for all of us, but we made it home in one piece."

"I was half-frantic when I first heard what happened, and after seeing the wreckage . . . I was beside myself. Noah Baxter told me you were all right, but I needed to see for myself. But your husband is the most stubborn, obstinate creature I've ever known, and I plan to tell him so. Gabe should have seen the doctor." Dora gripped my hand tight, steeling herself for the next question. "I know Sadie went with Jack to the hospital. How much should I worry?"

"Jack was terribly pale and quiet, but he managed to walk to the Palace lobby before he collapsed. Scott Jodes is taking care of him, so I'm not so worried as I'd be otherwise. Sadie promised to call as soon as she knew anything. All we can do is wait." Connor stirred in his sleep, stretching and kicking at the blanket, but didn't wake. I patted his back and went on. "I'm just as glad to see you, maybe more so. This has been a very strange and trying day, and a lot of what happened baffles me. I'm hoping you might know what to make of things. Men tossing bombs off a roof and shooting into the parade crowd aren't near half of it."

"Really . . . I thought escaping bombs and rifles was more than enough. I should have learned by now to set my standards higher." Dora sat on the end of Connor's bed, leaning back on her hands. "Start at the beginning and tell me everything. My guess is that at least part of this involves Connor, or you wouldn't be hovering over him."

"A great deal of it involves Connor. We were right about him being able to see ghosts, but his sensitivity goes far beyond that. I can't put off speaking to Sadie another day." I recounted my fight to keep an ever-growing number of ghosts away from him, the way dead kings and other royals watched him with knowing eyes, and how near I'd come to being overwhelmed by the sheer number of haunts seeking him out. Relating the story of people who'd never dream of committing violence eagerly joining a riot, phantoms reaching out of the clouds and banshee screams earned me a raised eyebrow.

At the last, I told her about the princess ghost. By the time I'd finished, Dora was on her feet, pacing the room and scowling.

"You've quite the talent for bringing me pretty problems to solve. First things first. We do need to speak with Sadie and Jack, but she has enough on her plate for today. I'm going to ask you to put it off until after Jack's home and on his feet. That will give me a day or two to come up with a solution to the problem of protecting Connor. When the time comes, we'll both talk to them." She stopped next to Connor's bed and stared down at him, her face a study in regret and sorrow. "Poor little boy. I'd never have wished this on him."

"Neither of us would." I'd been drawn to Connor from the day he was born, my bond with Sadie's son much stronger than it had ever been with her daughter. Now I understood why. "And I know it's silly, but I can't help but think this might be my fault somehow, that . . . that Connor's being with me pried open a doorway. He's so young and I spend so much time with him."

"You are being silly, but I'll forgo teasing you this once. It truly isn't your fault." Dora draped an arm around my shoulders. "Spiritual talent can't be transferred or awakened by associating with a practitioner. A person is born with the ability or they're not. We both know Esther saw ghosts, but I'd thought that was a result of age and illness. Many times the ability to pierce the veil between worlds skips a generation or two. When the talent surfaces again, it's almost always stronger."

"You're saying someone in my family saw ghosts as I do." I twisted my fingers in the soft wool fabric of my skirts, trying to imagine what growing up might have been like if I'd known I wasn't alone in how I saw the world. Connor wouldn't be alone. I took comfort in that. "I know neither of my parents saw spirits. A grandmother perhaps, or one of my grandfathers."

"That's precisely what I'm saying." Dora beamed at me for my cleverness and gave my shoulders an affectionate hug. "Talent runs in families, though it's not entirely unheard of for it to manifest on its own. I don't think that's the case with Connor. Esther is the most likely candidate, but we can't rule out his having inherited his sensitivity from Jack's mother either. Aileen Fitzgerald was an extremely powerful spirit."

Aileen's ghost was the first to truly haunt me, strong willed and determined. Without Dora's help and tutoring, I might have succumbed to the same ghost-induced madness I feared for Connor. "I haven't forgotten Aileen. There's little chance of that."

She sobered and hugged me again. "No, I don't imagine you would. We'll tackle the question of what influences were at work near Lotta's fountain later. This new spirit is the more immediate problem. Can you summon this princess ghost?"

"No need to summon her." I gestured toward the small mirror holding the ghost's image. That Dora hadn't known the ghost was watching surprised me. "She's already here."

Dora looked where I'd pointed, her expression changing from interested to horrified. "Oh dear God no . . . Sunny." She moved closer, still staring. "I can't believe it. This girl seems too young, but she looks so, so much like Sunny."

She brushed trembling fingers across the ghost's image, a startling gesture from Isadora. That she didn't immediately faint was a bigger surprise. I'd felt the moment of a person's death, known the pain of their last seconds and struggle to cling to life, but those were fleeting things for me. I could grit my teeth and go on.

Powerful emotions and the pain of others—both living and dead—sought Dora out, lingered, and grew stronger. Being swept away was a real danger, one she couldn't take lightly. Seeing her willingly touch a ghost was a shock.

"I don't have the vaguest idea what you're talking about, Dora." I stood shoulder to shoulder with her, watching the ghost who'd shadowed me all day and ready to catch Isadora if she did faint. "You need to explain it to me."

"I was married for several years while I lived in Europe. My husband, Mikal, was killed while on a hunting trip with friends. A rock slide is what I was told." A shadow of old grief, old sorrows, moved across Dora's face. "Losing Mikal is why I left the Continent and moved to Atlanta."

"I didn't know." I touched her shoulder. My understanding of why Dora felt her relationships were cursed became painfully clear. "I'm sorry."

"That was a long time ago, Dee, and I rarely talk about it. But this ghost of yours looks a great deal like a cousin of Mikal's.

Everyone in the family called her Sunny and I took up the practice once we became friends. How much the two of them look alike took me by surprise, but Sunny was much older than this girl. I haven't seen her since I left Europe. That's more than twelve years now." She touched the ghost's face one last time and stepped back, folding her arms over her chest and shivering. "You won't be able to banish this ghost or shut her out of your life, not unless she leaves willingly. There are haunts that some of the old texts refer to as memory wraiths. Other old stories call them mirror ghosts, for obvious reasons. Memory wraiths are extremely rare. I've never seen one before today."

I followed Dora's lead and touched the mirror. Cold glass was all I felt, no sense of who the princess had been nor any lingering trace of how she'd died. I'd felt far too many ghosts die in the past to think of this as normal. "I can see her, but she's not really there."

Dora studied the princess in the mirror. She was more thoughtful, working out the puzzle, now that shock had worn away. "No, she's not. The grimoire I studied maintained that mirror ghosts are never fully in the world of the living or the spirit realm. They exist in a kind of limbo between life and death. They are reflections of a memory, frozen in time exactly as remembered."

"A reflection of a memory." I turned to check on Connor, somewhat surprised our conversation hadn't woken him. A part of me wondered if the princess had a hand in that. "Then the question becomes whose memory does she belong to? We've established it's not one of yours. And I've never seen her before this morning."

"No, definitely not a memory of mine or yours. The memory of this princess belongs to someone else. That she appears to have attached herself to you is really rather confusing." Dora paced a few steps to the left to stand next to Connor's bureau, never taking her eyes off the mirror and the image of the princess. "Come stand over here, Dee, but don't block my view of the mirror as you move."

Dora always had reasons for her requests and I'd learned not to question. I did as she asked, making a wide circle so she never lost her view of the ghost. Once I was standing next to her again, Isadora looked away from the mirror.

"Fascinating. There's no question she's attached to you." She drummed long nails on the top of the bureau and frowned. "Her eyes follow you and she shifts position as you move. She's very lively for a memory. Everything I remember reading about mirror ghosts conflicts with what I see. But as I said, they are rare and the literature on them is rather sparse."

"So what do we do now?"

Isadora hooked her arm through mine. "We go downstairs and wait for Sadie's call. I plan to occupy my time raiding Jack's liquor cabinet and listening to you tell me more about what the union men saw. Much as I tease, you don't go actively looking to get tangled up with unusual occult activity or ghostly manifestations. You seem to be some sort of lodestone for obscure denizens of the spirit realm. Damned if I can figure out why."

"At least you allow that it's not my fault. That's progress of a sort." I looked back at Connor, torn about leaving. "Will he be all right alone?"

"This used to be your room, as I recall." She tipped her head, peering into the corners of the room. "We layered enough wards and charms and protections on this room to last a millennium. Don't fret about Connor. He'll be fine."

We went toward the stairs, still arm in arm. I did my best to ignore the face of the princess looking back at me from every shiny surface. Dora paid her no attention. I wasn't at all sure she saw the ghost.

"So tell me about this friend of Sam's. I think you said her name was Libby?"

"Yes, Libby Mills, the social worker. The papers have written several articles about her obtaining employment for soldiers' widows. I like her a great deal." I gave Dora a sidelong look, but her eyes were crinkled up in concentration, and not a trace of mischief showed on her face. She was paying more attention to the ghost than I'd thought. "Libby's not at all subject to panic in a crisis. She's downstairs right now, helping Annie tend to the poor young woman Sam rescued."

Dora stopped to stare at me. "Really? Our Sam is a hero?"

I nodded. "Very much so. He saved Alina from being shot."

"Well, well . . . Sam is always full of surprises. I suppose displaying full-blown heroics was just a matter of time and circumstance." Dora patted my hand. "Raiding the liquor cabinet can wait a bit. I want to meet Sam's friend Libby and his damsel in distress. What did you say her name was?"

"She told Sam her given name is Alina, but she's said little since. The poor thing had just seen her parents gunned down and he was lucky to get that much from her."

"Alina . . . Sam's sure that's the name?" I nodded. An expression I couldn't read crossed Dora's face. She glanced at the princess ghost and frowned. "Imbibing can definitely wait a little longer. A clear head is always best when meeting new people."

"Tell me what's wrong, Isadora Bobet." I dug in my heels, facing her straight on and refusing to go any farther until I got an answer. "And don't try to pretend it's nothing. I know you too well."

She started to pout and make light of it, but thought better of games after a good look at my face. "I can't absolutely say that anything is or isn't wrong. Let's just say I have a hunch."

"A hunch?" Dora had surprised me for a second time. I couldn't keep myself from staring openmouthed. "I don't think I've heard you use that word before, not once. Is this a new thing for you?"

"Mock me if you choose. Gabe doesn't have exclusive ownership of the word." She sniffed in exaggerated disdain, but the worry in her eyes ruined the effect. "A hunch is just a milder form of a premonition. I've had more than my share of those. Now, let's get downstairs. I'm eager to meet Libby and Alina."

Dora strode down the stairs, head high and moving with that same ingrained confidence I'd attributed to royalty. I followed, thinking hard.

She hadn't fooled me; something was wrong. I'd just have to wait to discover what.

Gabe

Gabe stayed in the area surrounding Lotta's fountain long enough to make sure all the bodies had been recovered and survivors accounted for. Shifting rubble and exploring damaged buildings took hours, a grim task for everyone involved. Smoke still clouded the air, a result of smoldering fires. The search was further complicated by trying not to bring down teetering skeletons of charred timber and brick on the searchers' heads.

One of the deputy coroners, a young doctor named Jefferson West, gave him a tally when they'd finished. They'd found five people trapped in a ruined storefront, all of them frightened and with minor injuries, but still alive. He counted that a victory, considering. More than a hundred and twenty bodies went to the morgue. West didn't say how many of the dead were children, and Gabe didn't push for an answer. He didn't want to know.

What he did know was bad enough. Nine of those bodies were cops, two of them the frightened rookies from his squad who had gone with Jack. Guilt dug its hooks in deep as Gabe watched their bodies carried away. The death of any man under his command always felt like his responsibility, his failure.

He made sure the deputy coroner had all the dead officers'

names before the stretchers were loaded into the vans and taken away. There were enough officers on the scene from all over the city that finding out the names Gabe didn't know right away wasn't difficult.

That held true until they tried to identify the unknown cop who'd set off the dynamite cache. Gabe had stared at the face of the strange detective with the long-barreled Colt, memorizing his features. Older with thinning brown hair, the dead man's features were unremarkable. Forgettable. Even after spending time studying him, Gabe wasn't sure he'd know the dead man again if they passed on the street.

No one else recognized him, knew his name, or could say what squad he came from. A sick feeling took root in Gabe's gut as patrolman after patrolman claimed not to know the stranger. He asked the coroner's men to wait and tugged off the blanket covering the body.

The stranger's pockets were empty, as if the suit and overcoat were brand new and he hadn't gotten around to filling them with spare change, trolley tokens, or sales slips from the tobacco shop. Gabe kept searching, but there was nothing for him to find. Nothing to tell him who this man might have been.

Pulling the dented, bloody badge off the dead man's overcoat and wiping it clean provided the only clue. The words engraved on the brass shield read *Chicago Police Department, number 687.* Gabe shoved the badge deep into his trouser pocket. No one recognized the dead man, because he wasn't a San Francisco cop.

Cold fingers caressed the back of his neck. Gabe thought hard about what a Chicago detective was doing in San Francisco unannounced and carrying a gun. More wind off the Bay swirled past, whispering in his ear. This stranger hadn't been a cop at all. The explosion, the death of the gunman and his partner, were all part of a bigger, deliberate plan.

Gabe straightened up much too quickly, gasping at the stab of pain in his side. Black spots skittered in front of his eyes. He took shallow breaths to keep from being sick and waited for the dizziness to pass.

Sam materialized at his side, eyeing Gabe. Butler was a good nursemaid, allowing him to do his job and still keeping his word to Delia. "Are you all right? Maybe we should leave now."

"Give me another minute." He caught Marshall Henderson's attention and motioned him over. The tall, red-haired officer's face was streaked with soot, masking his freckles. Marshall said something to the patrolman working with him and started toward Gabe. "As soon as I give Marshall some instructions, you can take me to the hospital. I want to check on Jack."

"Excellent idea, Captain Ryan." Sam pulled a handkerchief from his inside pocket and wiped his face. "While we're there, Dr. Jodes can look you over. That will make Delia happy."

He wasn't going to argue. Arguing took too much air.

Marshall nodded at Sam before giving Gabe his full attention. "Something I can do for you, Captain?"

"I need you to send a telegram for me." He fingered the badge in his pocket, but thought better of pulling it out. "Have it delivered to the chief of police for the Chicago City PD. I want to know if they have an officer with the badge number six hundred eighty-seven and what his name is. If there's anything else they can tell me about him, I'd appreciate knowing. Request the information be sent back as soon as possible. Make sure to thank the chief for his cooperation and his help."

"Yes, sir." Marshall scribbled notes in his notebook, a habit two-thirds of the squad had picked up from Jack. He glanced up. "Anything else?"

Gabe adjusted his hat, taking pressure off the bump on the back of his head. He was grateful the world stayed relatively steady afterwards. "Go send it off now. If we're lucky, we might have an answer tomorrow."

Butler's hands were stuffed into his pockets and he whistled softly as he watched Henderson hurry away. He waited until Henderson reached a patrol car on the far side of the square before taking hold of Gabe's arm. Sam waved at Taylor, giving a prearranged signal to fetch the car.

They turned their backs on ruined buildings, coroner's vans, and blanket-covered bodies lined up on the pavement, picking their way across the debris-strewn square. Gabe moved slowly, the pain in his side worse, and Sam let him set the pace. By the time they reached the edge of the rubble, Taylor was there with the car. Getting into the backseat wasn't easy, but at least he didn't need to hide how much he shook or that he was in pain. Butler already knew.

Sam slumped against the opposite door and toyed with his straw boater, picking at sections of the damaged brim and frowning. Gabe leaned back and shut his eyes. After two years of friendship, he knew Butler fairly well. The young reporter wasn't mourning the loss of his hat; he was mulling over everything that had happened and trying to make sense of the chaos. Once Sam had things figured out, he'd offer an opinion.

Butler's silence lasted until the car pulled up in front of the hospital. "Be honest with me, Gabe. My guess is that you don't really think the dynamite explosion on that roof was an accident. Am I right?"

"You should have been a detective, Sam." Gabe eased himself up in the seat. Getting out of the car was going to hurt like hell. "I don't think there was anything accidental about what happened. Blowing up that dynamite was outright murder. Someone didn't want those men on the roof caught. The man with the Colt was another loose end they couldn't afford to leave lying around, but I don't think he planned to die. Not like that."

"Agreed. That's a brutal way to commit suicide. Sit still another minute." Sam stuffed his ruined hat into the dustbin on the curb and came around to open the door. He got Gabe to his feet. "You're going to need some help with this one, at least until Jack's back up to snuff. I'd like to volunteer."

"You know I can't let you work a murder case." Those were his father's words, and the firm ideas he had about what a good cop would do. But the world had changed since Captain Matt Ryan's day. His dad never had to deal with the kind of cases Gabe did. He gave Butler a sidelong glance. "Not officially. But the department always welcomes information from a concerned citizen."

"I like the way you think, Ryan. That's all I am, a concerned citizen. Finding out why those men were shooting at Alina is the number one thing I'm concerned about." Sam held the door open so Gabe could hobble through. "First we'll check on Jack and get you looked at. Then I can hit the street. You take the night off."

"This could be dangerous, Sam. Whoever is behind what happened today means business."

"I've been in dangerous spots before. This wouldn't be the first time." Butler shrugged and shifted his hold to take more of Gabe's weight. "No one should watch their parents be shot down that way and not know why. She deserves to know why. I'd like to give her that if I can."

Gabe concentrated on putting one foot in front of the other and stopped attempting to talk Sam out of trying to find answers for Alina. She did deserve that much and more.

Maybe between the two of them they could find her a little peace as well.

CHAPTER 5

Delia

The click of Isadora's heels on the entryway tile summoned Stella from hiding as effectively as any charm. She ran out of the sitting room as quickly as she could, meeting us before we'd gotten too far from the base of the stairs. Stella flung her arms around Dora's legs, hanging on tight and words pouring out in a rush. "Aunt Dora, Aunt Dora! Are you staying for supper? Annie said that Libby could stay. She knows how to make paper dolls just like Mama."

"Hello, poppet. I'm glad you and Libby are having fun." Dora scooped the little girl up, smiling broadly. "I'll talk with Annie and ask if it's all right that I stay for supper too. I don't want to put her to extra work."

Isadora Bobet and three-year-old Stella Fitzgerald were fast friends, something I'd never have credited when Stella was a baby. Dora appeared to have infinite patience with her, holding long conversations on a wide range of subjects or discussing picture books at great length. Given that Dora looked upon most small children as creatures to be avoided at all cost, watching her friendship with Stella grow was both amusing and touching.

"Mama's not home. She took Papa to see the doctor. He got

hurt when the bad men were shooting guns." Stella solemnly told Dora all about her father lying on the hotel sofa and how scared she'd been when Jack didn't talk to her. Listening twisted my stomach. Young as she was, Stella understood much more than I'd thought. "But Annie says Papa will be all right and I don't need to worry. You shouldn't worry either, Aunt Dora. God's taking care of Papa and will make him well. Then he can come home again."

Dora's eyes met mine over the top of Stella's head. Those were Annie's words, Annie's heartfelt beliefs. Hearing Stella repeat those same thoughts to keep Dora from worrying about Jack was an odd, uncomfortable feeling. She was only a child and believed the people she loved—believed Annie—knew everything.

"I shan't worry, then. Everything will be fine." Dora hugged the little girl tight and set her on the ground. "Now, run along and find Annie. Delia is going to introduce me to your new friend Libby and to Alina. We're going to talk about boring grown-up things and I promise it won't be any fun at all. But if you ask nicely, Annie will let you help with supper. Go on now. I'll find you later."

"All right. I'm going." Stella sighed, her expression every bit as dramatic as I'd expect from Sadie's daughter. "I almost forgot. Annie said we should be extra nice to Alina. Her heart is broken."

"I will do my very best, poppet." Dora smoothed curls back from Stella's face. "Promise."

A promise was all she needed. Stella dashed through the dining room and shoved open the door into the kitchen.

Dora watched her go, mouth pulled into a tight, thin line. "I don't like lying to her about Jack, even if she won't be four for months yet. Children are better served by the truth, even uncomfortable and frightening truth. If anything bad happens to Jack, she'll remember I said everything would be all right and blame me. I can't stand the thought that Stella might end up hating me."

"She'd never hate you. She adores you." If I said the words to Dora with enough conviction, maybe I'd banish my own fears about damaging my friendship with Sadie. "And Jack will be home soon, that's not a lie. He's a strong man and Dr. Jodes will take excellent care of him."

Dora waved her hand in dismissal, the lines around her eyes pulling tighter. "Yes, yes, that's all well and good. But knowing the probable outcome doesn't make me feel any easier. This entire day has been unsettling. Let's go in and get these introductions over with."

Libby sat cross-legged on the floor in front of the low table between sofas, her skirts spread around her. Annie's sewing shears, scraps of fabric and lace, a pot of glue, and small figures cut from heavy paper littered the top of the table, evidence for Stella's claim of manufacturing paper dolls. Soft, dark waves hung around Libby's face, making her appear ridiculously young and not far past the age of playing with paper dolls herself.

She looked up at our entrance. Libby's eyes showed how tired she was after our adventures, but she did her best to be pleasant. "Hello, you must be Miss Bobet. Sam's told me all about you. I'm Libby Mills."

Dora put on her most dazzling smile and stuck her ungloved hand out. She rarely touched strangers, another surprise in a day where I'd given off counting. I saw a small wince as she shook Libby's hand, but only because I was watching for a reaction. Libby didn't notice. "Assume anything Sam says about me is a lie, Libby. Please, call me Dora."

"Pleased to meet you, Dora." She craned her neck to look past me and into the entryway. "Where did Stella go? She asked me to make a princess doll."

"Stella's helping Annie with supper. That will give us a chance to talk about what happened today." Dora's eyes darted to the small, quiet figure huddled in a corner of the larger settee. Alina was wrapped in one of Annie's hand-stitched quilts, her knees drawn up to make herself smaller and face turned toward the back cushion. She was the picture of utter misery. "Delia told me all about the strange creatures and phantoms the union men claim to have seen. That and the behavior of the crowd concern me a great deal. Did you see anything out of the ordinary, Libby?"

"No ghosts or ghoulies, or other such rot. No offense intended, Dora. Sam did tell me what you do." Libby's mouth screwed up in distaste. "But I'm not a believer in spiritualism or any of the occult nonsense so popular these days. Although I suppose mothers abandoning babies in their prams and total strangers starting fights with each other qualifies as out of the ordinary. I keep trying to think of a logical reason for that kind of behavior."

"No offense taken. Most people have to come face-to-face with the unexplainable before they believe such things exist." Dora's smile was tight and brittle, but she did smile. I took that as a hopeful sign. "But what you consider a logical reason for how people behaved today may not exist. What you think of as occult nonsense may indeed be involved. People don't change their normal behavior quite so drastically unless an outside influence is at work. Try to keep an open mind."

Libby gave her a dubious look, but didn't say more. Dora settled herself in the center of the settee, near enough she could reach out and touch Alina if she chose. She folded her arms and crossed her legs, one foot bouncing rapidly in an odd, jerky rhythm. Dora studied Alina, eyes narrowed. She sought to see below the surface world and into the spirit realm, but I'd no idea what she looked for.

I leaned against the doorframe and studied Alina as well, shifting the way I looked at her. Her aura was muddied, the colors muted to a dull, flat brown. Once those colors had been bright golden yellows and soft reds, and I still saw flashes of her old life mixed in. Grief might have that effect, but not that strongly. My instincts all said there was more wrong with Alina than could be accounted for by witnessing the death of her parents.

The bouncing of Dora's foot came to a sudden halt. She scowled and glanced at me, as if she wanted to say something but didn't deem it wise to speak. Instinct became belief. Isadora and I saw spiritual energy differently, at varying levels and depths. What I saw as a muddied aura might be much more to her. I wasn't at all surprised that she'd seen something I'd missed.

Dora extended a hand toward the girl, but carefully avoided touching her, a marked contrast from how she'd greeted Libby. "Hello, I'm Isadora. You told our friend Sam your name is Alina. That's really a lovely name and not one I've heard in a very long time. Has it always been yours or did you have another? Do you remember?"

Alina squeezed her eyes shut and slid farther under the quilt. She didn't answer nor look in Dora's direction, but instead curled into a tight ball. If wishing herself invisible were possible, I felt sure she'd have done so.

I'd lingered near the doorway, but now I moved to stand near the settee. The air in the room was heavier, thicker, a barrier thrown up between me and Alina. I couldn't say what stirred, but Dora had roused something with her questions.

Libby looked between me and Isadora, puzzled, but she didn't let being baffled stop her from speaking up. "Alina's had a terrible, tragic day, Dora. Her parents were shot right in front of her and if not for Sam, she'd have died too. Perhaps we should leave off asking questions until later."

Dora was completely focused on the girl, coiled tight as my cat Mai waiting to leap on an unwary grasshopper. She never looked away from Alina. "Normally I'd agree. But I'm afraid that waiting too long may cause her to forget more than she has. Learning her real name would be a huge stride in the right direction. Dramatic as it sounds, remembering what she knows and who she is could help save her life."

"Are you joking?" Libby's face flushed with anger, stripping away the impression of youth. "Those men on the roof were either madmen or anarchists, likely both. And they're dead, Dora, blown to bits. Those men can't hurt her, not ever again."

"Are you absolutely sure of that, enough so to risk her life? Because I'm not. Her aura is suppressed in a way that appears quite deliberate, and so is her memory. I can't begin to imagine what the long-term consequences of that might be. Nor can I understand why someone thought it necessary." Dora lifted an eyebrow, looking at Libby with a calm, almost deadpan expression that was at odds with the snap in her voice. "I know you have the best of intentions. What you don't have is knowledge of the spirit world or experience dealing with murderers. Unfortunately, I have both. Please stay out of this."

"Stay out of what?" Libby braced her hands on the edge of the table. The color in her cheeks burned brighter and her jaw set in stubborn lines. "An attempt to convince this poor girl that the nonsense you're spouting is the truth? She's been through enough and doesn't need your mumbo jumbo confusing her. Leave her alone."

"Mumbo jumbo?" Dora's calm expression stayed in place, but the rhythmic bobbing of her foot began again, a sure sign she'd reached the end of her patience. "My, my . . . now that the insults are out of the way, perhaps I can get back to helping Alina."

I'd wanted Libby and Isadora to be friends, but the conversation had taken a nasty turn. That I knew Dora was right made it all worse. The thick, expectant feel in the air was stronger, the pressure more noticeable. Two men had died on that roof, but death was no guarantee the people after Alina would stop pursuing her.

"Please . . . don't argue. I can't remember being anyone else."

Alina peered out of the cave she'd built of sofa cushions and quilts, eyes brimming with tears. Her soft voice held the remnants of an accent—an accent I couldn't place—but likely Dora would know. "Aunt Mina and Uncle Fyodor always called me Alina. That must be my name."

I traded looks with Isadora. The barest of smiles was all Dora gave me, but it was enough. She'd known somehow.

Some of the heaviness left the air and moving toward Alina grew easier. I knelt next to her and took her hand. Her skin was soft, unmarked. "The older man and woman with you . . . those weren't your parents?"

She angrily wiped away tears on a sleeve. "No, my aunt and uncle. They took care of me, protected me."

A flicker of movement caught my eye. The princess ghost shimmered into view on the glass door of a curio cabinet near the fireplace. I glanced around the room, finding her face looking back at me from picture frames, silver candlesticks, and a crystal candy dish. She wasn't watching me this time. Alina commanded all of the princess's attention.

Libby scowled and gave me a handkerchief from her pocket. I handed the plain square of cotton to Alina. "Who were your aunt and uncle protecting you from?"

"They never told me." Alina wiped her eyes and sniffled. "Aunt Mina said I didn't need to know and wasn't to worry, they would keep me safe. America was a big place and no one would find us here."

Dora twisted in her seat so that she sat facing Alina. Compassion and sympathy were all she let show, but her fingers dug deep into the seat cushions. "Do you remember your parents at all? Or where you lived before you came to San Francisco?"

Alina leaned forward, balling the handkerchief in her fist and rocking slightly. "Sometimes I dream of Mama reading poetry, or of playing with Papa in the snow. But I never see their faces or remember their names. Uncle Fyodor said I was very young when they died and that it was natural I'd forgotten."

"And your aunt and uncle never told you who your mother and father were?"

"No." Her voice was barely above a whisper. "Aunt Mina said it was safer if I didn't know."

Isadora moved the quilt away, uncovering Alina's face. She stared, searching for something familiar, something she recognized in Alina's features and bright blue eyes. Dora's expression was unreadable to those who didn't know her, emotions tucked away and hidden. But I did know her, and far too well to be fooled. She saw something that troubled her a great deal.

Dora's gaze shifted, moving to a spot behind Alina's shoulder. I'd no idea what she watched so intently, not at first, so I moved to where I could see as well.

The princess ghost looked back at me, calm and serene. Just how much Alina resembled this strange ghost was startling. Alina was a little younger, her features softer, but they had the same blue eyes and thick chestnut hair, the same slant to their chin. Imagining the two of them were related somehow would be an easy trap to fall into.

Resemblance didn't equal kinship, a fact I reminded myself of firmly. This ghost was made of memories, memories that didn't belong to me or to Dora, and undoubtedly not to a girl with no memory at all of who she was, of her family or where she'd spent her life. Looking somewhat alike didn't change any of those things.

And ghosts had been known to alter their appearance in order to gain what they wanted from the living. Dora had been taught that a mirror ghost was a moment frozen in time, unchanging, but the princess had already behaved in unexpected ways. How she manifested and the face she showed could be a trick. I'd be foolish to forget that.

Dora glanced at the ghost. She'd come to the same conclusion, but she still braved the depths of Alina's grief and took the young woman's hand. "Forgive me, but I disagree with your aunt and uncle. I'm not entirely sure how it was done, but someone made you forget deliberately. You're far safer with your memory whole, Alina, and with knowing why people are set on harming you. Dealing with your enemies is much easier if you know who they are."

Libby cleared her throat. "There's no delicate way to say this, Alina. I don't agree with everything Dora's said or her methods, but she's right about one thing: Not allowing you to know the names of your own parents is very odd. Are you sure your aunt and uncle told you the truth?"

The question was indelicate and bordered on being outright rude, but I understood why Libby asked. She needed a reason for everything that had happened to Alina, a reason not grounded in mysterious enemies or someone stealing Alina's memories by arcane methods. Libby Mills was convinced she knew how the world worked. Shaking her faith in that belief would take a lot more than Dora's word.

If nothing else, the question woke Alina from her shocked haze. She glared at Libby, clearly angry. "Why would they lie?"

"Frankly, to control you." Libby folded her hands on the table, looking for all the world like a rumpled schoolteacher preparing to give a lecture. Dora rolled her eyes at me, but she'd let Libby have her say. "You're very young. Keeping you afraid ensured that you'd be obedient and not question their decisions. It's not unheard of, especially if they had something to gain."

Alina's chin came up defiantly, her voice growing rough with emotion. "No, you're wrong. You didn't know them. They gave up everything for me, and you make them sound like thieves."

"That's quite enough, Libby." Dora squeezed Alina's hand, but didn't let go. "That someone was willing to go to such lengths to drive Mina and Fyodor out of hiding should be proof enough they told Alina the truth. Unfortunately, their secrets died with them, and finding answers will be that much harder. But first things first. Alina needs a safe place to stay while we sort this mess out. The rooms she shared with her aunt and uncle will be watched. She can't go back there."

"She's right, that wouldn't be at all wise." I hadn't thought before Dora spoke up, but Alina didn't have anywhere to go. From the stricken expression on her face, I was sure Alina hadn't looked beyond the next minute. My mind raced, trying to think of suitable lodgings. "Normally I'd suggest putting her in a room at Katie Allen's boarding house, but I don't think that's a good idea."

"Nor do I, Dee. That Gabe's sent people to stay with her in the past is too well known. As determined as the people after Alina appear to be, they'd locate her within the hour." Dora tapped a long, slim finger on her knee and frowned. "And I don't feel at all easy about placing Katie or her tenants in harm's way. Ideally, I'd like to find a hiding place with little or no connection to any of us, but we're unlikely to come up with an ideal solution. My house would be much safer, especially with Randy living there, or yours and Gabe's, for that matter."

We sat in silence for a few seconds, both of us attempting to come up with a solution, before Libby spoke up.

"She could stay in the settlement house with me. I don't think anyone would think to look there, it's far too public." Libby looked from me to Dora, and on to Alina, her expression eager and seeking approval. "No one will connect my work to Jack and Gabe, and they won't connect me to Alina. Women come and go all the time. A new face in the house won't cause any comment."

"I'm not keen on the idea. But a place in public view will throw these people off track until we can come up with a permanent solution. At the very least, it will buy us some time. Her pursuers will no doubt search every shadowed corner in the city before looking right under their noses." Dora glanced at me before turning all her attention on Alina. "Assuming, of course, that Alina agrees. I won't treat her like a child. She has a say in her fate and what happens to her."

The princess ghost smiled softly at that and faded from view. I didn't know what that meant, not for sure, but I guessed that she approved of Isadora's letting Alina choose. Why she cared was a question I couldn't answer. Almost everything about this ghost was a puzzle waiting to be solved.

Alina held tight to Dora's hand, an anchor against the ambiguity in her life. "I'm grateful for the offer, Libby, but I need to be sure you understand. Helping me is dangerous." She hesitated, a flash of panic in her eyes. By trying to make Libby see the risk she took, Alina fully understood herself, maybe for the first time. "The people who murdered my family, my—my aunt and uncle, and killed all those strangers watching the parade—killing you won't mean anything to them. Those men won't give up until I'm dead too. I—I don't want anyone else to die protecting me."

Libby's bright smile was heartbreakingly innocent. She didn't understand; that much was very apparent to me. "No one is going to die. Gabe and his men will find these people before they find you. You'll be safe with me, I promise."

I had a harder time believing that Alina was truly safe anywhere or with anyone, not until we discovered why she was being hunted. Dora felt the same way; her expression made that clear. We'd both lost our innocence about the world years ago.

The bell on the parlor phone jangled, two long rings and one short. Dora jumped to her feet. "That's Sadie calling from the hospital."

She dashed from the sitting room. I heard Dora answer and muffled fragments of the conversation, heard Annie come out of the kitchen to stand in the parlor door and wait to hear the news about Jack.

I waited as well, barely able to keep from rushing to the other room and hovering at Dora's shoulder. My stomach knotted, pulled tighter with each tick of the clock. The longer Dora spoke with Sadie, the more I imagined bad news. By the time she hung up, I was braced for the worst.

"Dee! He's going to be all right!" Dora's relieved smile as she came through the door was a welcome sight. She wrapped me in a tight hug. "Sadie says it took forever for them to develop the X-ray films or she'd have called long ago. Jack broke three large bones in his foot and has a moderate concussion, but all the rest is scrapes and bruises. Dr. Jodes is going to keep Jack overnight, just to be safe and make sure nothing else is wrong. Sadie gets to bring him home in the morning."

"That's such good news!" I laughed and hugged her back. "Sadie must be so relieved."

"She went on at some length about that. I'm sure you can imagine." Dora smiled and touched my face. "And I'm to tell you that Sam Butler took Gabe in to see Dr. Jodes. He cracked two ribs, but the doctor taped them tight, and Sam is taking Gabe home. Sadie says you're not to scold Gabe overmuch when you see him. I told her I couldn't guarantee that last part."

"Sam's a good man." The worried knot in my stomach unraveled completely. Gabe and Jack would both heal. I brushed away a tear. "I knew I could count on him. But what about Connor? I can't leave him alone."

"Connor will be fine. I'll strengthen the wards around his bedroom and the house before Sadie gets home. Trust me to take care of things here. Your job is to go home and fuss over your husband."

Dora patted my shoulder and went to sit with Alina again. The young woman rested her head on Isadora's shoulder, grief shattered and numb, trusting that she was welcome. How she knew, I couldn't say, but Dora folded Alina into her arms, protective and tender.

I'd never have imagined Isadora letting a total stranger get inside the barrier she kept between herself and the world. Protecting herself from the pain and emotions of others helped keep her sane, but I couldn't deny what was right in front of me. That sense there were things left unsaid, things Dora didn't want to believe might be true, came back tenfold.

When the time was right, or when she was very, very sure of the truth, Dora would tell me. Until then I'd savor my luck and Sadie's luck too, and thank Providence that Jack and Gabe were coming home to us. We could have lost everything today, all we held dearest in the world.

If I doubted the truth in that, I'd only to think of all the new-made ghosts wandering near Lotta's fountain, or look at Alina's tear-ravaged face.

I went home and did exactly what Isadora said; I fussed over Gabe. That he let me fuss worried me at first, but he was tired more than anything. The pain medicine Dr. Jodes had given him added to his fatigue. By the time we'd finished supper, Gabe could barely keep his eyes open. Going to bed early seemed the wise thing to do.

Exhausted as I was, I couldn't bring myself to fall asleep. Listening to the small noises Gabe made in his sleep, feeling him next to me alive and safe, was much more important than rest. And the truth was that I was too frightened to close my eyes, afraid I'd have nightmares about explosions, the screams of people dying, and the struggle to defend Connor as ghosts crowded me against a wall. The calmness I'd felt at the time had totally deserted me, growing more distant hour by hour. Reliving the day, even in dreams, might undo me.

Sleep always wins in the end. That the dream I fell into wasn't about the parade or the aftermath didn't make the nightmare less horrifying. I was trapped in the ruin of another woman's life, watching events unfold through her eyes.

The guards moved the three of us to new quarters every few weeks, always with very little warning and always at night. No one would see my sisters and me in the darkness, or wonder why men with rifles herded us into the back of a truck. We'd stopped unpacking all but one small bag for fear of leaving something important behind. Once we'd left one isolated prison for another, there was no going back.

This day wasn't any different. Men came to our room just after supper and gave us a few minutes to gather our belongings. My younger sister slipped on the stairs while struggling with the heavy cases, but refused to let any of these men help her. We'd already been told that anything we couldn't carry would be left behind. The guards tossed the satchels into the back of a truck before ordering the four of us inside and tying the canvas flap shut.

The inside was dark and stuffy, a canvas box without windows to let in a scrap of moonlight or let us see where we were going, or allow us a whiff of air that didn't smell of gasoline. Empty wooden crates were all the seats we had. A scowling guard sat in the back, a rifle cradled in his arms. He was bald and looked older than our father, and his coat reeked of fish and boiled cabbage.

Hate glittered in his eyes. I'd never get used to being hated by strangers.

My sisters and I held hands, but didn't speak. None of us

wanted to risk being sick in the closed-up truck or give the guard reason to shoot us.

Closing my eyes was easier than seeing his face. I braced myself against the side of the truck as it lurched around mountain curves and gears slipped on steep inclines, reciting to myself all the little things I wanted to remember to tell Mama and Papa when I saw them.

I would see them again. I had to believe for the wish to come true.

The light was rose colored with dawn when the truck stopped. Men shouted, giving orders and instructions on where to park, to get the gate closed as soon as the truck passed through. The air was colder and I guessed we'd moved higher into the mountains, farther from cities and people who might know us.

New guards, strangers, untied the door flap and began grabbing satchels. The man who'd guarded us all night eyed us, fingers flexing on his rifle and licking his lips. My sisters and I sat still, waiting for the order to climb down.

A new face appeared in the opening, an officer, younger than the man who'd watched us all night. He touched his cap in greeting and nodded. "Don't just sit there, Private. Get out and help them down."

The man who reeked of fish and cabbage didn't move. I wouldn't look away from him. If he meant to shoot me, he'd do it while looking into my eyes.

"Did you hear me?" The young officer scowled. He smacked the old man on the back of the head, hard. "Get out. Now!"

Our jailer clambered out of the truck, muttering curses, and stalked away. The officer watched him go, clearly angry. He waved to the group of guards who'd taken our bags. "You and you, help the ladies down and take them to their rooms. The rest of you carry their bags."

The men helping us down had pistols in their belts, not rifles, but I'd grown used to guards with guns. My sisters followed the men carrying our belongings into the house, into our new prison. I looked back before going inside to see the officer watching. He touched his cap again and smiled. I turned away quickly, heart pounding and tears burning my eyes.

His kindness was a trick to make us trust him. I couldn't allow myself hope or to think we might have a friend here.

The hurt would be all the worse when hope was yanked away.

The parlor clock's chimes woke me at midnight. I bolted out of bed, running down the hall to the kitchen for a glass of water. Washing the taste of fish and gasoline out of my mouth was all I could think of. I'd be sick otherwise.

Moonlight spilled into the kitchen over the top of the shutters, allowing me light to see. My hand shook while filling a glass from the tap, but I managed to rinse the taste from my mouth without dropping anything. I filled the glass again and sat at the table, thinking and trying to make sense of it all.

I'd had this dream before, seen these faces. The difference was that this time I'd remembered each detail, clear and vivid. Not knowing their names, or who these four sisters were, didn't make the echoes of their fear any less real. The one thing I knew without question was that these young women were dead in some far-off land. Ghosts.

All the strange and unexplained things in my life came back to ghosts and what they wanted from me.

Gabe still slept when I got back into bed, quiet and at peace. More than anything, I wanted to tell him about what I'd seen, to have him help me puzzle out what it meant, but I couldn't be selfish enough to wake him. Morning would be soon enough. In the morning I'd tell Dora as well.

I turned away, staring out into the darkened room. The princess ghost watched me from the dressing table mirror, her image crisp and bright in the dim light. Looking into her eyes, I knew that what I'd dreamed was true, a memory of something real.

The princess knew too. I drifted off to sleep, wishing she could tell me everything.

CHAPTER 6

Delia

I rang Dora's house early the next morning, knowing she'd probably still be sleeping, and spoke with Randy. He promised to give a message to Dora and readily agreed to pick Gabe up on the way to the station.

Stiff and sore to the point of hobbling, Gabe still insisted on going in to work. Nothing I said managed to change his mind. He was as stubborn as Isadora maintained and twice as obstinate, so I soon gave up trying. But if I couldn't convince Gabe to stay home, I wasn't above recruiting others to watch over him for me. I'd feel easier about his going if Randy or Marshall were with him. Sam would take over sometime in the afternoon and bring Gabe home for supper.

The truth was that I understood his need not to let the case grow cold. Even a day away from the investigation would let memories turn vague, leads grow faint or vanish completely. Gabe didn't need to say that finding the people responsible for the riot and massacre at Lotta's fountain ate at him. I knew my husband well. He wouldn't rest until he found them.

Neither would I. Too many oddities, arcane and rooted in the world of the living, revolved around events in the square. My hope was that solving one puzzle might be the key to unlocking them all.

Once Gabe and Randy left, I washed dishes and tidied the house. The princess ghost shadowed me from room to room, her image reflected in every windowpane and mirror, each shiny white tile around the tub, and every piece of cutlery in my kitchen. Seeing the ghost's face peering up from the surface of my tea was an odd experience, but I drank lemon-laced chamomile down in any case. She wasn't really there.

My cat, Mai, followed me as well, batting at the princess and trying to pry her loose from wherever she appeared. Mai soon grew bored with hunting a ghost she couldn't catch and gave up. She stalked back to the bedroom with her tail held high, the picture of wounded pride.

One ghost made me think of the others. I'd recounted my dream of the four sisters to Gabe, but he'd no better guess of what the nightmare meant than I did. Now all I could think of was the unfamiliar style of the house they were taken to, the clothes these young women wore, or the scent of snow riding the wind as they climbed out of the truck. Ghosts came to me for reasons of their own. Clues as to what these four wanted from me lurked in the images I remembered.

Gabe had his mystery to solve and I had mine. The idea that the two were related in some strange way wouldn't leave me alone but going over what I knew failed to turn up a connection. I couldn't help thinking Gabe's might be the easier task.

Shortly before noon, the front bell rang. Dora swept in the instant I opened the door, already tugging off her black driving gloves and stuffing them into her handbag. Her roadster was parked at the curb. The dress under her fur coat had black silk full skirts, a white lace collar, and pearls scattered over the white silk bodice.

Her clothes were far too stylish and elegant for tea in my kitchen. My call had disrupted her plans.

She shrugged out of her full-length beaver coat and passed it to me. "Forgive me for not being here sooner, Dee. I thought I'd given Randy sufficient instruction on when to wake me and under what circumstance. And yet he persists in believing that waking me before ten is dangerous. I haven't the faintest notion where that idea came from."

I hung her coat on the hall tree, all the while struggling to keep a straight face. "Perhaps the time you threw a bedside lamp at him left an impression."

Dora waved a hand dismissively, but the corners of her mouth twitched. "Randy overreacts to my moods. All that aside, he still should have told me you'd called right away, not waited to ring me from the station. I was already dressed and leaving to meet an acquaintance of Sadie's downtown for lunch. Melba something or other."

I led the way to the kitchen, aware that Dora kept an eye on the princess as we walked. The ghost kept pace, her reflection shimmering in and out of view on vases and picture frames. I suspected she was eavesdropping on our conversation. "Melba Andersen? I'm sure I read something about her heading up the local ladies' temperance union. I don't picture a teetotaler as your ideal lunch companion."

"Nor do I." Dora's nose crinkled up. "She wants to hire me. Apparently Melba needs me to perform an exorcism."

I stopped just inside the kitchen door and stared, not at all sure I'd heard right. "You can't be serious. Melba attended one of Katherine Fitzgerald's charity functions a few weeks ago. Sadie dragged me along for company. Melba decided to begin holding forth about the evils of spiritualism over the soup. She didn't conclude until well after dessert."

"I'm completely serious. From what Sadie said during our phone call, Melba is quite earnest and very frightened. I'm taking this seriously as well, at least until I have all the facts." Dora took her customary place at the table, retrieving a cigarette case and matches from her handbag. "I rescheduled our meeting for half past two so I could come see you. Why don't you fix us some tea?"

I did as Isadora asked and refilled the teapot with hot water from the kettle, gathered clean teacups, applesauce muffins, saucers, and a dish of sugar cubes, and set them on the table. Dora stirred sugar and lemon into her tea, but her whiskey flask wasn't anywhere in sight. That she drank less was another sign of Randy's influence and that she was happy with him, something I was thankful to see.

The princess ghost watched us from the window above the sink, a vantage point that gave her full view of the kitchen. Her image filled the entire window, partly veiled by lace curtains and sunbeams. She appeared bright eyed and eager, as if she'd waited for Dora's arrival and for me to tell about my dream.

Perhaps she had been waiting. I glanced at the ghost before sitting across from Dora and pouring tea for myself. Not for the first time, I pondered what role the princess played in the events of the last few days. That she'd saved my life, as well as the lives of Libby, Sadie, and the children, outside the jewelry store was clear. But that was all I knew, that she'd wanted me alive.

I shook off my concerns about the ghost and plunged into telling Dora about the dream. Holding off the fear was easier in the light of day. I let Dora's bright blue eyes be the anchor that held me here, in my own life, and kept me from drifting into another. It wasn't me shut into the back of a truck between my sisters, or marched into a strange house, unsure if I'd live to see another morning. Looking into Isadora's eyes, I could remember that life belonged to a stranger.

Dora sipped tea and, other than a raised brow, refrained from comment. Once I'd finished, she stared into her teacup, swirling sodden black leaves so that they clung to white china in delicate patterns. She set the cup aside and looked me in the eye. "You never heard names, never caught a glimpse of the fourth sister's face?"

I shook my head. "No, no names. I only saw the women sitting on either side, and for the life of me, Dora, I can't remember what they looked like. I never saw me . . . who I was."

"I thought that might be the case." She turned to watch the princess in the window, long lacquered nails tapping a staccato rhythm on the tablecloth. "Even minor royalty generates the kind of hate and secrecy you described, especially in time of war. The temptation is to say your new ghost is the fourth sister, but that isn't possible. She's formed from old memories, and no matter how strangely she behaves, that fact remains unchanged. We've established those memories can't be yours or mine. There's someone else involved, a person we're not aware of yet. That person is still very much alive or the ghost would vanish."

"Maybe that's why she came. To make me aware so I can find the person who remembers her." I picked apart a muffin, mounding the crumbs on a saucer. What disturbed me was the very real possibility I might already have found that person. The pain that might cause Dora if the ghost was somehow related to her friend Sunny didn't bear thinking about. "And don't bother to lecture me on assigning benign motives to the dead. I do know better. If the princess wasn't such an unusual spirit, I wouldn't be thinking along those lines."

Dora beamed at me fondly. "I've spent four years teaching you to think on your own and follow your instincts. Far be it from me to scold when you do." She patted my hand before pouring more tea for both of us. "Besides, I don't lecture, I advise. But if it's any comfort, in this case, I think you're right. I wouldn't be at all surprised if the ghost and your dream all arise from the memories of the same person."

"The fourth sister." I studied the princess ghost, struck by how her appearance had altered in a few short days. When I'd first seen her, she'd been stiffly posed to the point of being wooden, with almost no expression at all. Now her face was animated, her eyes bright and aware. I gestured toward the window. "I think I'd remember seeing the princess, but I don't. I can't say if she was part of the dream or not."

"She may never have visited that house or ridden in that truck." Dora sat back and cradled her teacup in both hands, her expression troubled. "You need to keep in mind that this is how someone close to the princess remembered her, an old memory that likely hails from a happier time. There's no pain or sorrow associated with the way the ghost looks, at least none I can detect. She's dressed very formally, maybe for a portrait or an official function. I keep thinking I should recognize the court style of her clothing, but I've been away almost twelve years. I've forgotten more than I thought."

"Knowing what court she was part of would make it easier to discover her identity." My tea had grown cold. I crossed the room and poured the dregs into the sink. Leaning against the drain board put the princess behind me. I'd grown used to her watching, but not having her looming in the background made it easier to think. "And please don't take this as me being flip, but I'd assume a limit to the number of princesses in Europe."

Dora retrieved a cigarette from her case, lighting it and dragging smoke deep into her lungs before answering. She kept staring at the ghost behind me. I saw the same faraway, troubled look in Isadora's eyes she'd had while watching Alina.

"You might be surprised, Dee. Even a minor province would have had a ruling prince before the war." She forced her gaze away from the princess and back to me, her smile wistful and melancholy.

"There's not quite the limit on princesses you might think, but narrowing things down a bit would still help. Now be a dear and get dressed to go out. You're coming along with me to meet Melba. Not that I suspect trickery or anything underhanded, but I want your opinion on how genuine her story appears. We're going to a cozy new café on Belden Lane in the French Quarter. Wear your red shantung and that little white hat you bought last month."

"Go ahead and admit it, Dora. You'd planned to fetch me all along. I should have known." I untied my apron and hung it next to the back door. Most days I'd jump at the chance of lunch in the French Quarter, but time with Melba was a steep price to pay for croissants and quiche. "What makes you think I can tell if Melba's telling the truth or not? Suffering through one evening of her company doesn't make me an expert. I barely know the woman."

"I wouldn't ask you to endure her again, but you have a level of expertise I lack. And if you're going to blame anyone, blame Sadie for suggesting I speak with you before my meeting." Dora ground her cigarette out in an old saucer I kept for just that purpose. "You heard Dominic Mullaney's story firsthand about what his men saw during the riot. I recall you saying his men saw angels and monsters reaching out of the clouds. What Melba describes as demons gathered outside her house sounds very much the same."

"Angels and monsters, riding the wind." I gripped the chipped and worn lip of the drain board, edges biting into my palms. "Banshees."

"I hesitate to jump to that conclusion just yet. For one thing, this is San Francisco. We're not in Galway or Kilkenny." Dora's mouth puckered in distaste. "But I'm hard-pressed to think of another explanation, not one that doesn't terrify me a great deal more. San Francisco does have a large Irish population. Magical creatures and spiritual beings have followed the people who believe in them to other lands since the beginning of time."

Rain-swollen clouds had begun to fill the sky, blotting out the sun and piling up against the East Bay hills. I went to stand behind my chair and folded my arms over my chest, suddenly chilled. "So you're saying this really could be banshees."

"There is a chance, yes. I'd be foolish to dismiss the idea out of hand, Dee." Dora poured the last of the tea into her cup, grimacing as she took a sip. The tea must have been lukewarm at best by now. "Stories about black dogs, veiled and shrouded women on horseback, and even tales about a hearse pulled by two headless white horses are very common in the South and throughout the Appalachians. Every small mountain town and isolated hollow has stories of a family member hearing a banshee wailing before someone in the household died."

"We take Melba and the union men at their word, then, at least for now." I brushed a finger along the top of the chair, noting the alternating smooth and rough patches. "And if banshees are roaming the streets of San Francisco and inciting riots in their off hours, what then?"

"Don't be absurd, Delia. Banshees can't change their fundamental nature any more than your cat could sprout wings. I'd be more inclined to think Melba is right and she is seeing demons." Dora smiled brightly and shooed me toward the kitchen door. "Now, go get dressed. I'd like to arrive before the rain starts in earnest. On the way back, we'll stop in to check on Connor and Jack."

I left to change, thinking hard and searching for answers. All I found were more questions.

More puzzles.

Newcomers to San Francisco were often confused when the short stretch of Belden Lane was spoken of as being the heart of the French Quarter. I was never sure if the confusion arose from not knowing the city had a French Quarter, or that such a short, narrow street was its heart. Both things were true, no matter how strange they appeared to outsiders.

I couldn't imagine the city without the cafés, the bakeries, and dressmaker shops of the French Quarter. The first three thousand French settlers had arrived in 1851 at the end of the Gold Rush, their journey to settle in California sponsored by the French government. Those early French settlers held their place through waves of Chinese, Irish, and Italian immigrants, coexisting with all of them. The enclave still existed, changed as all the city had changed, but still thriving.

The sky had cleared, taking away the threat of rain. Dora parked the car less than a block from the entrance to Belden Lane. Men smiled and tipped their hats as she climbed out of the car, or boldly said hello. Many women would have shied away, or pretended they didn't see, but Dora, being Dora, smiled right back. She wasn't at all shy, but she wasn't flirting either.

Dora fussed with the drape of her coat before tucking her black leather handbag under an arm. "The café isn't right on Belden proper, but a few doors down in this direction. We can walk from here." I pretended not to notice the shimmer in a shop window and the image of the princess ghost that immediately followed. She'd ridden along with us, her face occupying a lower corner of the windshield. If I'd harbored any doubts she was attached to me and not a specific place, those were gone. "Will Melba be waiting inside or on the walkway?"

"She didn't say." Dora looped her arm through mine and we set off. She was smiling and extraordinarily cheerful, a combination I normally welcomed. But there was an edge to her cheerfulness, a wariness in the way she watched people, that put me on my guard. "Remember, Dee, I've never met Melba. I'm counting on you to prevent me from questioning a complete stranger about the demons outside her window."

"I can see how that might grow awkward." I patted her arm and laughed, maintaining the cheerful façade for passersby. "I promise to point Melba out if you tell me what's wrong. And don't try to put me off, Isadora Bobet. I can tell something is bothering you. You might as well come out with it."

She gave me an exasperated sidelong glance, but her smile never faltered. "If I knew exactly what was wrong, I'd tell you. All I'm sure of is that we're being watched and have been since shortly after we left your house. What bothers me most is I can't tell *what* is watching us. I should at least be able to tell if we're drawing attention from the living or the dead, but I can't. Each time I attempt to determine where the attention comes from, things become fuzzy. That I can't be sure one way or the other makes me doubly cautious."

"Let me try. Maybe I can at least sort out who or what is spying on us. We both know spirits hide from you." I tugged Dora toward a dressmaker's window, pointing out embroidered cotton-lawn collars. She chatted on about workmanship and stitch patterns. That freed me to look inward and cast about for anything out of the ordinary.

I found the watcher in an instant and immediately regretted that I had. The weight of ages come and gone filled its eyes and pinned me where I stood, a presence cloaked in shadows and the dry smell of death. That the sun shone and people were all around didn't lessen my fear. I couldn't move, couldn't breathe, until the watcher released me and slithered away.

Old haunts, Gold Rush miners and dance hall girls, Russian fur trappers and long-dead sailors, occupied the space where the watcher had been. These ghosts belonged here; they were a part of this city and its past. The presence I'd sensed was older than any of San Francisco's ghosts, but the watcher was an intruder.

Dora loosened her grip on my arm and peered at me. "My, my, Dee . . . how interesting. I couldn't see anything, but I definitely felt it leave. What exactly did you do? You seem to have scared whatever that was away."

A quick glance showed me the princess ghost had vanished from the window. Instinct, or that second sense that told me what to expect from ghosts, said she'd return eventually. She wasn't afraid of me, I knew that, and nothing I'd done had persuaded the ghost to leave. That she left with the watcher was puzzling.

"I didn't do anything." I struggled to calm my racing heart, no longer panicked but desperate to banish the feel of drowning. "I absolutely wasn't responsible for that—that creature leaving. Whatever that was left of its own accord. Either we got a passing mark or the watcher grew bored waiting for us to do something worthy."

"Judgment? Are you sure, Dee?" Isadora's eyes took on a faraway look, a sure sign she'd half remembered something and searched for the missing piece. She gripped my arm again, rushing me away from the shop window and toward our meeting with Melba. "Take your time deciding if need be."

I didn't have to think; the answer came easily. "I'm sure. Do you have any idea what that was?"

She frowned. "No, only bad guesses, and those are likely to be more dangerous and harmful for being wrong. Very few spirit beings judge the living—family or land guardians, for the most part, or individual keepers charged with the safety of an heir. These are old-world creatures, tied to ancient dynasties, and I've not heard of them existing on this continent. Knowing what guardian has taken such a keen interest in the two of us might be the missing piece to a puzzle or two."

We sidestepped around a young couple. They walked arm in arm, deep in conversation and blind to anything but each other. Seeing the two of them together awoke all my worry for Gabe and how he was weathering the day at work. Changing things for him, good or ill, wasn't within my power. That didn't stop me from fretting.

"Banshees appear to have taken up residence in San Francisco. I'd assume old-world guardians aren't outside the realm of possibility, especially with the number of refugees living here." Speculation flickered across Dora's face, crystalizing mine. "Alina is a refugee. I can't think of anyone more in need of a guardian."

"You may be right, Dee. That Alina doesn't remember who her family is may be a guardian's attempt to protect her. My guess is that she isn't able to handle the memory of what happened to her family. That is only a guess at this point." Dora smiled sadly and patted my arm. "Perhaps we dismissed her resemblance to your new ghost too easily. Sending a telegram to an old friend in New York might help provide answers. Trevor has special access to all the closed and restricted areas of the New York Public Library. The materials I need aren't available to just anyone."

"And what do we do if the watcher comes back?"

"I'm not at all sure the creature is really gone. My guess is it's taking more care to stay hidden now that we've discovered it exists." Dora's steps slowed as she checked signs and read addresses. "The café should be very close by. It's called Moulin de Provence. Do you see it?"

"No, but there's Melba." I pointed to a set of overgrown hydrangea bushes on either side of a doorway and the woman half hidden behind pink bubble-shaped blossoms. Melba Andersen had been thin to the point of appearing ill since the day I met her. A pale, almost pasty complexion added to the impression of someone slowly wasting away. That Melba wasn't riddled by consumption came as a shock to people meeting her for the first time. "I wonder if she wore that shade of green to blend into the scenery."

"Try to be kind, Delia, and remember she's genuinely frightened." I rarely saw pity in Dora's eyes, but her expression softened as she watched Melba. "Given Melba's opinions on the occult and prohibition, consulting with me could destroy her reputation. Can you imagine the scandal if word gets out? It took a great deal of courage for her to come at all. Introduce me and we can get on with this."

"Melba?" She jumped at her name, startled to the point I thought she'd bolt down the street. I put on a friendly, social smile, burying the lingering distaste generated by memories of my last encounter with Melba Andersen. Dora was right; Melba appeared genuinely terrified. "We've found you at last. I'd like to introduce my friend Isadora Bobet. Dora, this is Melba Andersen."

"I didn't expect to see you, Delia." Melba clutched her handbag to her chest, fingers digging into brown leather and bled white from holding tight. "I've made a mistake. Forgive me for bringing you out for nothing, Miss Bobet, but I think I should leave now."

"Mrs. Andersen, please stay." Dora smiled and stepped up to block Melba's way, lightly touching her arm. Melba wouldn't notice the wince or the tightness around Dora's eyes, but I saw. "I apologize for not warning you in advance that Dee would be joining us. Delia is a colleague and knows nearly as much about these matters as I do. Since we'll be working together I thought it best if she heard your story, too. Let us help you, Melba. Please."

Melba looked between us, searching our faces for a trace of mockery, hoping to find the truth in Dora's words. I knew the instant she'd decided. All the wariness vanished from her eyes and tension bled from her stance. "There's a small private dining patio in the back. I've made arrangements for us to have lunch there if that's all right with you."

Dora gave Melba her brightest, most charming smile and took her arm. "That sounds perfect. Lead the way."

The entrance to a narrow brick pathway lay just past the largest of the hydrangea bushes. Johnny-jump-ups, pansies, and dianthus filled flower beds on either side, making the trip to the back patio both colorful and fragrant. Dark green moss grew in the cracks and spaces between the broken flagstones that formed the patio, adding a splash of color to the gray and white stone. Flowering plum trees grew around the margin, casting leaf shadows that skittered and danced with each passing breeze.

All in all, it was a beautiful, secluded spot, out of sight of the street as well as the café patrons inside. Melba couldn't have chosen a more perfect place for a clandestine meeting. Still, she fidgeted in her chair until the waiter had taken our order and gone back inside. This was more than a mere case of nerves or the fear someone might see her with Isadora.

Dora pulled out her cigarette case and matches, holding them up to Melba. "Would it bother you if I smoke? I imagine the waiter won't bring the soup for some time."

"Go right ahead." Melba tugged off her gloves, tucking them into her bag and snapping it shut. She folded her hands together, no doubt hoping to hide they were as unsteady as her smile. "My husband delights in filling the house with cigar smoke. I'm quite used to the smell of tobacco."

"Sadie told me the little that you'd confided in her. Your husband is the person you're worried about, if memory serves." Dora leaned back in her chair, one arm folded over her stomach and a lit cigarette dangling from the other hand. She smiled, but watched Melba with slightly narrowed eyes. "Why don't you explain what concerns you while we wait? That way Delia and I will have an idea of what we're facing."

I sat back and observed as well, searching for those things not visible in the surface world. A smoky fog surrounded Melba, obscuring her aura and making it difficult to see beyond pearly gray swirls. The haze grew thicker as I stared. Dora's gaze flickered to me, making sure I'd seen.

"What Sadie didn't tell you is that Gregor is my second husband. My first, Timothy Andersen, died of the black flu just after New Year's in 1917. I keep his name for social reasons." Melba shifted nervously in her chair, fussing with the collar of her dress and smoothing down the tiny pleats marching across the bodice. "Gregor and I were married in Holy Trinity Cathedral on Green Street a few days before Christmas."

Dora leaned forward, her attention even more focused. "Isn't that the Russian Orthodox church?"

"Yes, do you know it?" Dora nodded. Melba stared at her hand, a small smile softening her features, and ran a finger along the double row of diamonds and rubies set in her wedding band. "Gregor wanted to be married in his faith and to have his priest's blessing. He never said, but I think the ceremony made him feel he hadn't left everything behind. This ring is the only possession he had that wasn't lost or stolen when he fled Russia. It belonged to his grandmother."

Dora flicked her cigarette into the ash stand behind her chair. She reached across the table to take Melba's hand, flinching noticeably but hanging on nonetheless. More than Melba's distress resided in that ring. "I'm guessing the trouble all started not long after you were married."

"We had a month of peace before the nightmares started. He'd wake screaming and pleading with someone in Russian, and Gregor could never remember why, or what he'd said. That was terrifying enough." Melba brushed away a tear and cleared her throat. "Then Gregor became convinced he'd heard someone, a woman, crying and wailing outside our windows. I couldn't hear anything, but this went on night after night. And Gregor kept insisting this was real, so one night I—I pulled back the curtains."

She stopped speaking, staring blankly across the patio, her eyes focused on things only she saw.

"Melba, what did you see?" Dora leaned forward, a patient, coaxing tone in her voice. She squeezed Melba's hand, trying to regain her attention. "Talk to me. We can't help you otherwise."

Melba jerked her hand away and folded her arms over her chest. Her gaze darted from object to object, lighting anywhere but on Dora. "At first I thought they were angels. They were so beautiful, their faces kind and gentle. But I thought to myself, why would angels be weeping outside our window . . . and they *changed*." Her voice grew stronger and Melba looked right into Dora's eyes. "I didn't need to be told they'd come for Gregor's soul. Please, Miss Bobet, I need you to send them away. I don't care what it costs. Just keep them away from Gregor."

I'd never have imagined feeling sorry for Melba Andersen. The few times I'd encountered her, she'd been petty and spiteful, and more than a little self-righteous about her opinions. But now I was moved to pity. She looked older, defeated, and utterly lost.

Dora's frown grew darker, and her long red nails drummed rapidly on the tabletop. I was all too aware that what Melba described was the same type of spirit as the union men claimed to have seen during the riot. Banshees or ghosts, they'd already demonstrated they had the power to turn friend against friend. If these spirits were after Gregor, I prayed they couldn't turn husband against wife.

When her nails ceased tapping on the table, I knew Dora had reached some kind of conclusion. "Bear with me a moment longer, Melba, and answer one last question if you will: Did your husband leave Russia before or after the revolution?"

She looked up, as startled and mystified by the question as I was. "Not long after. Gregor's mother was distantly related to the emperor, a cousin or some such, and it wasn't safe for him to stay. His escape was rather harrowing, but he was able to follow friends to California. There's a sizable community of Russian refugees in San Francisco. What does it matter?"

"Likely not at all." Dora's smile was guileless, but I knew her too well to be fooled. She didn't ask meaningless questions. "But more information increases the chances of a good outcome. For now, I can put your mind to rest as far as possession and the need for an exorcism. I'm convinced that isn't what's happening in Gregor's case, but something else entirely. It's not unheard of for unscrupulous practitioners of the arts to conjure up phantoms much like you describe. Nightmares are all part of the same incantations. The sole purpose of these apparitions is to frighten an intended victim."

Or flush them from hiding. Dora glanced at me and I saw the same thought in her eyes. The phantoms at the parade were meant to panic the crowd and strip away Alina's concealment. Jack and Gabe, Sam and the patrolmen on duty, never saw anything because they weren't supposed to see.

But Gregor wasn't hiding, or at least not very well. My mind cautiously circled the question of possible connections between Alina and Melba's new husband. The truth was, I didn't know enough about Alina to find an answer. Not yet.

Melba gaped, eyes wide with shock. "But why? Who would do such as terrible thing?"

"Someone with either a grudge against your husband or a vendetta against his family. My guess is the latter, but that's only a guess. As for who the practitioner is creating these phantoms?" Dora shrugged and gathered up her cigarettes, stowing them in her bag. She surprised me by shoving her chair back and standing, a sure signal we were leaving. I did the same, ready to follow her out. "I don't have the first notion. A person with enough money and determination might find a conjurer for hire, but not in San Francisco. No one living here would take such a commission. The rest of us wouldn't allow it. I will make inquiries, but I don't expect much will come from them."

The waiter started out the café door, heavy tray carrying soup bowls, a lidded tureen and a basket of sliced sourdough bread balanced on one arm. Dora held up a hand and smiled an apology, sending him back inside.

Melba worried at her bottom lip with her teeth, thinking. "So what do I do? Things can't go on as they are."

"I agree." Dora tugged on her gloves, casting glances past me and toward the path to the street. "Explain everything we've talked about to your husband. Often knowing what's going on weakens the apparition's power. But I'm afraid my primary recommendation is that the two of you should leave San Francisco, at least for the foreseeable future. Don't tell anyone where you're going. Simply vanishing is best."

"All right." Melba stood and held her hand out to Dora, more upset and unnerved than before. "Thank you, Miss Bobet. A messenger will deliver your check by this evening."

Dora barely touched Melba's hand before turning on her heels and striking out for the front sidewalk and the street. I wasn't nearly so sensitive to emotion as Isadora, but I couldn't avoid feeling anger rise off her in waves. That she didn't wait for me was a measure of how upset she was.

By the time I caught up with her, Dora was sitting in the car, talking to herself in a language I didn't know, and scowling. Getting into the car earned me a scowl as well, but I'd weathered other storms of Isadora's temper. I folded my hands in my lap and faced her calmly. Most of her foul moods passed quickly. This one proved to be no exception.

Dora had tossed her handbag onto the front floorboards. She

reached down to retrieve it, her expression a bit sheepish. "In case it wasn't clear, I'm not angry with you, Dee. Discovering Gregor is Russian sheds a new light on things. Needless to say, this isn't a case of banshees taking up residence in the city. I thought I'd left these loathsome vendettas and practices behind when I left Europe. And I'll be damned if I'll let that kind of filth take root or flourish in San Francisco."

"All right. That's perfectly understandable and I'm more than willing to help." I gestured toward the people and the buildings around us. "This is my city as well. But perhaps you could explain in more detail before we embark on a grand crusade. I'm much better at cunning schemes if I have time to prepare."

She rolled her eyes and started the car, barely checking oncoming traffic before pulling out and speeding away. "Don't worry, I'll make sure you're prepared. Much as I hate to push it back another few days, we need to postpone our visit to Sadie. Connor is as safe as we can make him for now. And springing this on her just as Jack comes home might be even more unkind. I won't rest easy until we check in on Alina at the settlement house. I need to make sure everything is quiet."

"Putting a few wards around Libby's place might be wise as well. Just in case." Alina was in more immediate danger, I knew that, but that didn't stop guilt weighing on me. Connor was my godson, my responsibility. "I'm guessing that whoever is after Gregor is involved with the people hunting for Alina."

"Or the culprit in both cases is one and the same. That's the more likely explanation." Dora rolled to a stop at the intersection, waiting for a heavily laden truck to creep up the steep grade. Her finger tapped an impatient rhythm on the steering wheel. "Don't think me cruel if I push Alina a bit harder about what she remembers. I may need you to keep Libby occupied when I do. This may take more force than Miss Mills is comfortable with."

I shook off my guilt over Connor and keeping secrets from Sadie, concentrating on the matter at hand. "I'll do what I can. Alina needs to remember."

Dora inched the car around the back of the truck until we were in the clear, her expression grim. "Yes, Dee, she does. I suspected before that something, or someone, had buried her memories purposely. Now I'm convinced that's the case. There's too much evidence of arcane intrusions into her and Gregor's lives to believe otherwise."

I braced myself against the dash as Dora accelerated up the hill. Years of driving with her hadn't hardened me to her sudden bursts of speed. "And if pushing her to remember doesn't crack the shell around Alina's memories, what then?"

"I haven't planned that far ahead yet." Dora's expression was decidedly sour. She grimaced before sending the car careening around a corner. "I'm sure I'll think of something. But purely as a precaution, it might be wise to have one of your cunning schemes in reserve."

"I'll do my best, given the short notice."

We'd reached the top of the hill and began hurtling down the other side, driving all thoughts of plans and schemes from my mind.

Instead, I shut my eyes and concentrated on holding on.

CHAPTER 7

Gabe

Gabe spent the morning at his desk, reading files full of witness reports and what little information they'd been able to gather at the scene. Honesty made him admit, if only to himself, that sitting still was all he was capable of doing. At least sorting through reports was useful.

Hours of squinting at page after page of cramped handwriting was giving him a headache, but Gabe kept working. Detective work wasn't glamorous or exciting. Most days consisted of sifting conflicting information, searching for a nugget of truth. A witness statement, or something a patrolman picked up at the scene, could be the key that led him and Jack to the people behind the massacre.

But he'd never know unless he kept looking. A headache was a small price to pay.

A complete roster of the dead was included in one of the coroner's reports. The list was longer than Gabe expected. Victims who'd died on the way to the hospital, or didn't make it through the night, had been added to those declared dead at the scene. The new deputy coroner must have spent all night and most of the morning putting the list together. Each victim's name and age were noted, as well as how they'd died.

He paid particular attention to people the gunman on the roof had singled out. Gabe hadn't found a pattern yet, but that didn't mean there wasn't one. If there was anything to tie these people together, he was determined to find it.

A dozen times or more he stopped himself from thinking that Delia's name could be on that list, or Jack and Sadie, that any of the dead children might have been Stella or Connor. He wanted to be grateful that none of the people he loved had died, but gratitude felt selfish. Others weren't so lucky.

Gabe sighed and forced himself to continue reading and jotting down notes. Gratitude was selfish. He couldn't bring himself to be sorry.

A heavy knock on the pine frame rattled the glass in his office door. He eased back in his chair, moving slow and taking care not to jar his ribs. "Come in."

"Captain?" Marshall Henderson opened the door and leaned inside. "Dominic Mullaney is here to see you. One of the union officers is with him. Do you have time to see them now?"

He glanced at the clock above the door. Dominic was right on time. "Show them in, Marshall. And I'd like you to stay and take notes if you don't mind. That would be a big help."

"Yes, sir." Marshall patted an inside pocket. "I'll just stop at my desk first to get a pencil and notebook."

Gabe managed to gather up most of the files and stuffed them into his lower desk drawer. Files that interested him most or needed a second look went into the narrow top drawer.

The effort left him sweating and woke the ache in his side. He shut his eyes and concentrated on forcing the pain into the background again. By the time Marshall ushered Mullaney into his office, he'd recovered.

He was only mildly surprised to discover the union official with Dominic was Aleksei Nureyev.

"Glad to see you took me seriously, Mullaney. Have a seat." Gabe leaned forward enough to rest his forearms on the desk, and toyed with a pencil. He thought about hiding his injury, but changed his mind. "Forgive me for not standing. I cracked a few ribs yesterday, and the doctor ordered me to take it easy. Officer Henderson has agreed to sit in and take notes for me. Lieutenant Fitzgerald is still in the hospital."

Dominic leaned forward in his chair, startled and slightly anxious. "Will the lieutenant be all right?"

"He needs some time, but he'll be fine." Gabe studied the young union leader's face. Mullaney wasn't faking concern; he'd wager his badge on that. "Jack broke his foot and has a slight concussion. Nothing that won't heal."

"Good to hear." Dominic's relief appeared genuine too. "The lieutenant's always played straight with me and my men."

"Is having another person take notes standard practice for American police officers, Captain? Policemen in Russia seldom want witnesses." Nureyev smiled and unbuttoned his heavy wool overcoat before taking his seat. The overcoat looked expensive, with jet buttons and the type of tailoring Gabe associated with Nob Hill bankers, not labor union officials. His curiosity about Nureyev rose another notch.

"It's standard for me, Mr. Nureyev. I find it helps avoid misunderstandings." Icy fingers stroked the back of his neck, urging him to pay extra attention. Gabe kept his voice professional and stripped of emotion. "You're free to go if that bothers you, Mr. Nureyev. Dominic has to stay."

Aleksei laughed and gestured toward Mullaney, totally unshaken and at ease. His confidence grated on Gabe. "That's why

I'm here, Captain, to ensure there are no misunderstandings between my friend and the police."

"Let me handle this, Aleksei." Mullaney leaned forward in the visitor's chair, hands on his knees. "Ask your questions, Captain Ryan. I've nothing to hide."

Gabe believed him, but he wasn't going to say so in front of Aleksei Nureyev. The man woke every cop instinct he had, every one of which said not to trust Nureyev or let him get too close.

Instead, he opened his top desk drawer, rooting through the papers until he came up with the list of people killed at Lotta's fountain. He passed the list to Mullaney. "These are the bodies we've identified from yesterday. How many of these names do you recognize?"

Dominic began reading and blanched. "Christ . . . I know at least thirty of these men. Maybe another twenty or so sound familiar if you're counting wives and children, but I'm not that sure of all the names."

Mullaney dropped the paper on Gabe's desk abruptly and stood. He paced to the office door and stood there, both hands on top of his head, staring at the frosted glass. Henderson started to say something, but a look from Gabe stopped him.

They'd wait Dominic out. In the meantime, Gabe took the opportunity to watch Nureyev. That Aleksei knew he was being observed and didn't care made the man all the more interesting.

What struck Gabe hardest was how bored and disinterested Aleksei appeared. He claimed to be one of Dominic's friends as well as his union second-in-command, to care about Dominic's welfare. Yet not a trace of emotion showed on Nureyev's face or in his eyes. Dominic's distress didn't touch him at all.

Gabe suddenly remembered a boy he'd met the summer he was ten. His father was granted one of his rare weeklong vacations and his parents had booked a cabin in the Santa Cruz Mountains. Harold was the same age and the only other boy in the campground, but after the first day, Gabe wanted nothing to do with him.

Harold's idea of fun was catching turtles in the pond and flipping them onto their backs in the middle of the hot, dry gravel road. If a turtle did manage to right itself, Harold tipped it over again. Gabe's angry attempts to stop the larger boy's cruelty resulted in Harold giving him a split lip.

As soon as Gabe told his father, Matt Ryan went straight to the campground director. The next morning, Harold's family packed up and left.

Gabe had never forgotten the look in the other boy's eye as he watched the poor turtles struggle. The same cold, blank look sat in Aleksei Nureyev's eyes as he watched Dominic Mullaney.

"Dom, you're wasting the captain's time." Aleksei's dispassionate stare never wavered. "Pull yourself together."

Mullaney came back to his chair. His voice sounded rough, choked. "I'm sorry, Captain. My friend Shawn is on that list. I was best man at his wedding not more than a month ago."

"No need to apologize." The only Shawn on the list was a Shawn Fitzhugh, a twenty-four-year-old dockworker. Fitzhugh had been shot. Gabe put a mark next to Shawn's name. "Do me a favor if you would. Read aloud all the names of union men you recognize so Officer Henderson can write them out. We'll leave the wives and children for another time."

Dominic went through the list a second time, reading off names. He found four men he'd missed the first time. Henderson dutifully added their names to all the rest.

A quick comparison of Henderson's list and the coroner's report showed Gabe that only Fitzhugh had been shot. The rest of the union men died as a result of explosions, either caught too close to a blast or as a result of being struck by flying debris. That

Mullaney's best friend was the only union member to be shot might be a coincidence, but Gabe didn't believe in coincidence. Not when it came to murder.

"We're almost finished, Mullaney." Gabe tucked the two lists into the drawer and eased back into his chair. "I don't believe you were responsible for what happened at the parade. You're too much of an idealist. But what I believe doesn't matter. The mayor's office and the press are already looking for someone to blame."

"And the most convenient person to blame is Dominic Mullaney." Nureyev stood and took his coat off the back of the chair. "I told you coming here was a mistake, Dom. Let's go."

Anger glittered in Nureyev's eyes, and Gabe's budding hunch became firm conviction. Aleksei had reasons of his own to keep Dominic from talking. He meant to find out what those reasons were.

"I'll tell Dominic when he can leave, Mr. Nureyev." Gabe put the steely tone of command into his voice, a tone reserved for only the most reticent rookies. He had no qualms about using it on Nureyev. "But since you appear to be in a hurry, I'm going to help you along. Officer Henderson, please escort Mr. Nureyev to the lobby. Make sure he stays there."

"Yes, sir." Marshall moved from his spot next to the file cabinet and opened the office door, eyeing Nureyev. "You heard the captain. We're going to the lobby."

"So much for your principles and avoiding misunderstandings, Captain Ryan." Aleksei's lip curled. "I understand all too well. All policemen are alike. You intend to hang Dominic with his own words."

"I've already said I don't think Dominic was behind what happened. Your low opinion of policemen aside, I meant that." Gabe leaned forward, his smile cold. He didn't want Nureyev to mistake his intentions. "Perhaps we should talk about why you're so determined to keep him from cooperating. That interests me a great deal."

Gabe wasn't sure if Nureyev understood or not, but Dominic did. Mullaney glanced at Gabe and frowned. "Wait outside, Alek. Everything will be all right."

"Since you insist, I'll go." Aleksei strolled to the door, the picture of wounded dignity. "I'll wait for you at the car, Dom."

Gabe hadn't realized how stiff and tense he was, or that he'd sat up ramrod straight in the chair, until the door shut behind Henderson. The renewed ache in his side let him know. He sat back gingerly. "Look, Dominic, the truth is your union isn't very popular with the shipping companies or the hotel owners. People will try to blame you and your men for starting the riot. They'll try to say you hired the men on that roof too. Things will go easier for you if you help me figure out who tried to set you up."

Dominic wiped a hand over his mouth and glanced at the office door. "Alek's been saying since the start that someone set me up to take the fall. Much as the business owners hate me, I can't see them murdering women and children in cold blood. One of my men heard a rumor that anarchists were behind it, like those fellows back in 1916. A few of the hotel waiters were in a bar last night and heard people going on about the Bolsheviks bringing their war here. Could be either of those or something else entirely. I wish I knew who to set you on, but I don't."

Gabe tapped his pencil on the desk, but stopped abruptly. The sound reminded him that Jack wasn't here. He was on his own. "I agree on one point: The chances of any business owners hatching a plot like this are pretty long odds. And from what I've read, anarchists support the labor unions. My guess is that if they were to toss bombs, they'd target the shipyards or the hotels."

"You're dead right about that, Captain. I heard Emma Goldman speak a few years back, before she went to prison." Dominic folded his arms over his chest and shrugged. "I'm not keen on this propaganda of the deed Goldman and some of the other anarchists talk about, but they do back the unions. I'd have a hard time believing anarchists had a hand in this."

"But they're easy to blame. If you read the papers long enough, anarchists get blamed for just about everything." Gabe frowned, trying to pin down what bothered him about the other rumor. The back of his neck itched as he chased after the thought, a sure sign to keep pushing. "This is the first I've heard of people worrying about Bolsheviks. Why is that?"

"More White Russian refugees are arriving, and the truth about the Bolsheviks' revolution is starting to spread. People with even a hint of noble blood in the family left because staying meant being rounded up and shot. A lot of the hotel workers are Russian, and the stories they tell are horrible." Mullaney scowled and hunched his shoulders. "Entire families were killed, from gray-haired grams to wee babes in arms. Rumors have started making the rounds that people who made it out are turning up dead in New York and Seattle. That has the Russian community afraid the Bolsheviks are hunting for people who escaped them. People who came over earlier don't know who to trust."

"I don't doubt your word, but why keep chasing someone after they've left the country? Once out of Russia, they wouldn't be a threat." Gabe rubbed the back of his neck, trying to erase the feel of cold fingers, but that didn't help. It never did. "Explain that to me, Dominic, and make me understand why the Bolsheviks would follow anyone to San Francisco. From where I'm sitting, that doesn't make any sense."

"I'm not surprised. Alek is convinced Lenin is mad as a hatter." Dominic braced his hands on his knees and stared at his boots, studying the patterns of dust on creased black leather as if they held all the answers. He straightened up and looked back at Gabe. "The tsar and his family haven't been seen since the Bolsheviks took them into custody two years ago. Lenin probably had them killed, but the government still starts rumors about the tsar quietly going into exile or retiring to the mountains. Now Lenin's working to wipe out even the memory of the monarchy. If his followers kill anyone with even a distant blood tie to the throne, the Royalists won't have anyone to rally around."

Gabe sat quietly, letting what Mullaney had said mix with what he already knew. Thinking. Putting scattered pieces of the puzzle in place.

A part of him wanted to scoff at Mullaney's story. The idea of Lenin or anyone else sending men to San Francisco to hunt escaped nobility was laughable. Still, no matter how he circled around Dominic's story and turned the events surrounding the parade inside out, he always came back to how the gunman had singled out Alina. That was a fact he couldn't disregard or put aside. He'd watched it happen.

In the end, all he could say was that someone wanted her dead. He could guess or invent reasons based on Mullaney's story, but he needed to *know*. Cases were solved with evidence, things he could touch and prove. Right now he couldn't say who was behind the shootings or even what part of Europe Alina came from.

That Alina couldn't remember anything about her life or her family made this case more difficult. Dee was convinced that some arcane, and likely sinister, influence was involved in the young woman's memory loss. With luck, Dora and Delia would find a way to help her.

The new ghost haunting Delia suddenly came to mind. A princess, she'd said, pretty and chestnut haired, one who bore a strong resemblance to Alina. Maybe there was something to this idea of Lenin's men turning Gabe's city into a hunting ground. That was a disturbing thought, one he couldn't dismiss out of hand. The touch of cold fingers on his face grew stronger, joined by indistinct whispers he struggled not to hear.

Gabe cleared his throat. "I'd guess about half or more of the union is made up of hotel workers. How many of those men are Russian?"

"Damn near all of them, Captain. That was the first reason for making Alek a union officer. Most of the waiters speak English, but not the kitchen workers. I probably wouldn't know about any of this if the men didn't trust me." Mullaney glanced at the door again, his expression troubled. "Alek trusts me too, and he'd be angry if he knew I was talking this much. But I owe it to Shawn to do what's right. If you're going to catch the people responsible for Shawn and all the rest dying, you need to know, Captain."

"You did the right thing." Gabe braced himself on the edge of the desk and stood. Stiff and sore, he knew that sitting much longer meant getting up under his own power would be impossible. "One last question and then you can go. Did Nureyev have a reason to run from the Bolsheviks?"

Dominic smiled, but the smile didn't mask the grim, sober look in his eyes. "If you mean was Alek part of the Russian nobility, the answer's yes, Captain. He lost most of his family. Red army soldiers herded his parents, sisters, his wife, and two wee daughters out of their house in the middle of the night. Lined them up against a wall and shot the lot of them."

"Mary Mother of God. No wonder he thinks Lenin is mad." Gabe ran fingers through his hair. He couldn't imagine what coming home and finding your family slaughtered was like. "You said he lost most of his family. Who escaped with him?"

"His son. The boy was only six weeks old when Alek ran. I don't know how he managed to keep a baby alive on that trip." Mullaney frowned, his fists opening and closing as he told the story. "Alek came home the next morning to find his family lying where they fell and strangers looting the house. All the servants had gone except the baby's nursemaid. She'd taken the baby to bed with her that night, and the Reds believed her saying the boy belonged to her. Alek managed to get the three of them to San Francisco."

Gabe's opinion of Nureyev shifted a little, but didn't entirely change. The man was aloof and arrogant, and extremely distrustful, but it appeared that Aleksei had good reasons not to trust everyone. Still, Gabe couldn't shake the feeling that Aleksei deliberately put people off to keep them at a distance. Nureyev had something to hide. The question was what.

"Thank you for coming in, Dominic. I'll let you know if I have more questions." Gabe offered his hand, a gesture he hoped would reassure Mullaney. He'd never shake hands with a man he considered a suspect. "Keep your head down. Whoever set you up is still out there."

Dominic rubbed his palm on his jacket before taking Gabe's hand, a habit he'd seen in other men who worked with their hands. Mullaney's fingers were callused, his grip strong. "I'll be careful. You do the same, Ryan."

He spoke up before Mullaney had the door all the way open. "Dominic, one last thing. Where was Alek the night his family was shot?"

"Making contacts to smuggle them and a few friends out of the country. His father refused to leave Russia, but his sisters were going to go with him." Mullaney's tone was brusque, annoyed. He looked Gabe straight in the face. "He'll never forgive himself for not sending his family into hiding until after the arrangements were made. Alek is a good man. I wouldn't have him as a friend if he wasn't."

Gabe stared at the door after it closed, thinking. Nureyev might be a good man who mourned his family and regretted his choices, but he'd wager Jack lunch for a month there was more to the man. More Aleksei was determined to keep hidden.

All his instincts told Gabe he needed to find out what Nureyev was keeping secret and why. More people, including Dominic Mullaney, would die otherwise.

He wasn't sure of much in this case, but Gabe was sure of that down to his bones.

CHAPTER 8

Delia

The streets were oddly empty of spirits. A drive from the French Quarter to Libby's settlement house downtown passed through older sections of the city, including areas leveled by the 1906 quake and fire. On a normal day, the sidewalks were thick with ghosts and I might see anything from the haunts of shopkeepers who'd died in the quake to Spanish padres leading heavily laden mules, and everything between. Today only the palest, oldest ghosts walked unseen pathways, and there were few enough of those.

Once I'd desired nothing more than to be free of ghosts, to never see one watching from the edges of a room or moving through the walls of a pleasant café. Now a lack of spirits unnerved me, as if the natural order of things had been unbalanced. Fair or unfair, I placed the blame on the watcher. I couldn't sense its presence, but that didn't mean the guardian hadn't followed along with us.

Isadora had slowed the car considerably, frowning and glancing left and right as we crept along the street. "How very odd. This guardian, or watcher as you call it, displaces all the local spiritual activity. I don't think I've ever encountered anything quite like this, Dee. Not to this extent."

"I know that I haven't." The princess ghost still hadn't returned to her place in the corner of the windscreen, giving more credence to my feelings. "It's not that the other ghosts are gone, they've . . . they've been pushed aside. The watcher doesn't leave enough space for them."

She gave me one of her small, approving smiles. "Very good, Dee. You've summed the effect up perfectly, but I'd feel easier about all of this if I understood the forces at work. Not knowing makes me nervous; especially since the guardian's influence increases the closer we get to Libby's house."

"Then coming here was the right decision. This must have something to do with Alina." I sat back in the brown leather seat, trying to relax. The car continued to creep along slowly, almost as if the engine labored to move the automobile through the same space occupied by the watcher. That was silly and I knew it, but I couldn't think of a better explanation. I couldn't blame a newfound sense of caution on Dora's part.

We rounded the corner onto Battery. Libby's settlement house was the fifth building on the left, and Dora was able to park reasonably close. A plain three-story brick-front building, the house looked more like a crumbling warehouse than a home for displaced women and children.

Stunted red and white geraniums grew in planters on either side of the front door, an attempt by one of the residents to bring a bit of cheer to her new home. Curtains fluttered on open top-floor windows, and the sound of children playing carried down to the street. The wide ground-floor windows were painted over on the inside, blind eyes staring out at the world.

Dora came around to where I stood on the sidewalk. She slipped her arm through mine and eyed the building with a degree of distaste. "Cheery place, isn't it? Come along, Dee. Perhaps things will improve once we're inside."

Five stone steps led up from the sidewalk to the front door. Dora knocked and I took the opportunity to look around. A man stepped out of a shadowed doorway across the street, giving me a start. Officer Perry tipped his hat back so that I could see his face and pulled a pack of cigarettes out of an overcoat pocket. He took his time lighting his cigarette, making sure I'd seen him. I relaxed a little, knowing he was watching us.

The door opened a crack after Dora knocked a third time. "Delia? Isadora?" Libby pulled the door wide and stepped out, her expression a mix of nervousness and surprise. She was dressed plainly, wearing a pleated dark skirt and pale gray blouse, an outfit that wouldn't look out of place on Katherine Fitzgerald's chambermaid. "Come in, both of you. I didn't expect to see you here. Is something wrong?"

The entryway was less dreary than outside, but not by much. All the furniture was mismatched, used hand-me-downs that had seen better days, most likely donations from some well-meaning soul. I shied away from imagining Libby hauling home furniture she'd found on the curb. The air inside wasn't stale or unpleasant, but the prevailing scent reminded me of delving into my grandmother's linen cupboard. A few outdated paintings and lithographs in gold-leafed frames hung on the walls, adding to the overall sense of tattered grandeur.

Dora wandered the large entry hall, a smile pasted on her face. She didn't speak or comment on Libby's greeting. The tightness around her eyes and the stiff way she carried herself were a warning and a sign. She was in pain, I saw that, I just didn't know why. Why was likely important.

Libby watched Isadora, her frown growing darker. She didn't believe in the occult or the spirit realm, and wouldn't understand if I tried to explain.

"We felt honor bound to check on you." I stuffed my gloves into my pockets and unbuttoned my coat. "Yesterday was trying for all of us. I wanted to make sure everything is going smoothly."

"Trying days are meant to be survived and overcome." Libby took my coat and hung it on a rack near the door. She turned to face us, hands held primly at her waist and expression perfectly composed. "I'm not one to indulge in hysterics, no matter what the circumstances. I couldn't be better."

"That's all very nice, Miss Mills." Dora turned from the painting she'd been studying, her smile brittle and strained. "I imagine you could endure almost anything and emerge unscathed. To be brutally honest, Alina is the one we're concerned about."

I stepped between the two of them, determined not to let the sniping continue or allow them come to blows. Given the scowl on Libby's face, blows were a very real possibility. "Yes, how is Alina? She was so completely shattered, I worried about her all night. Has she remembered anything more?"

"Alina is doing as well as can be expected." Libby gave Isadora a spite-filled look and turned her back, dismissing her. Dora rolled her eyes and began restlessly stalking the entry again. "I sat with her a large part of the night. She kept starting awake, or sitting up and talking in her sleep. Alina didn't really settle down until nearly four. Last I looked in, she was still sleeping. I saw no reason to wake her."

I traded looks with Dora. Sleep might relax the walls around her memory. "Do you remember any of what she said, Libby? It might be important."

"I'm afraid not." She frowned and brushed at a spot on her blouse. "At times I thought she was calling out names, but I can't say for sure. She wasn't speaking English."

A barefoot, tow-haired little boy of not more than three or four dashed into the entry. He ran as quickly as he could and hid behind Libby's skirts. She scooped him up, giving him a hug and ruffling his hair. "We have company, Jake. Mind your manners and say a proper hello to Mrs. Ryan and Miss Bobet."

Jake laid his head on Libby's shoulder and smiled shyly. "Hello."

"Hello, Jake." I gently tapped the tip of his nose, earning a grin. "Pleased to meet you."

Libby hugged him again and set him down. "All right, you've seen who came in, nosy boy. Now back to the kitchen with you. Tell Patty I said to give you some bread and butter. That should keep you busy for a minute or two."

He ran back the way he'd come. Dora watched him go, her expression an odd mix of tenderness and sadness. "He misses his mother. Each time the front door opens, he hopes she's come back again." She turned to Libby, all trace of impatience and anger gone. "Does he talk about what happened?"

"How did you—?" Libby stared, her already fair skin losing what little color it held. She wrapped her arms across her chest, holding tight to herself and what she believed. "Please stop pretending some spirit guide or magic power tells you things. The only way for you to know about my sister is from Sam. Since you asked, no, Jake doesn't remember anything about that night. He's even stopped asking for Miranda. She wouldn't have wanted how she died following him the rest of his life."

Dora looked the way Jake had gone, one long lacquered nail tapping against the clasp of her handbag. She glanced at me and moved closer to Libby, stopping short when Libby took a step back. "Take this advice to heart, Libby, for Jake's sake. He remembers much more than you think about his mother's death. Get him to talk about the happy things surrounding his mother's memory. Right now, all he associates with your sister is the horror of watching her die. Believe me when I say that will do far more damage in the end."

"And you know all this after one minute with my nephew?"

"Children haven't learned to build walls around their feelings." Dora rummaged in her bag and immediately snapped it closed again. She'd taken to always leaving her flask at home, a newly reached compromise with Randy, but at times she still looked for it. "They leave that to the adults in their lives. He's confused and afraid, but doesn't think he can tell you. Somehow Jake's gotten the idea he should pretend all's well."

Libby's lower lip trembled, the first crack I'd seen in her armor. "I'd never do anything to hurt Jake. Sam told me to trust you, so I'll trust you on this. That doesn't mean I believe in spirits or all the rest."

"Of course not." Dora grimaced and massaged her temple. "Now, be a dear and tell us where to find Alina."

"Her room is on the second floor." Libby brushed a hand over her eyes. "I'll take you up."

She led us down a short hallway to the foot of the stairs. The air of age and faded grace that surrounded the house grew stronger as we climbed. Wallpaper in the stairwell had faded to nothing but hints and shadows of rosebuds, and each stair creaked alarmingly under our weight. Libby didn't seem to notice the way the banister wobbled, but I did.

Dora gripped my arm tight and trailed a hand against the wall, her bright smile firmly in place each time Libby glanced back. I'd have to be made of wood not to feel her tremble, or hear how her breath rasped with the effort of taking each step. Why she felt the need to put up a brave front for Libby I couldn't say. "Are you all right?"

Her smile wobbled as badly as the banister, but the amusement in her eyes was reassuring. "We've known each other more than four years, and yet you still feel the need to ask. I'm touched." Dora fixed her gaze on the second-floor landing. "No, I'm far from all right, but I'll survive. There is so much pain in this house, Dee, so much pent-up sorrow. I'd no idea or I'd have insisted on making other arrangements for Alina. She'll be much better off coming home with me."

I leaned close. "Libby won't take that well. Convincing her will be difficult."

"I've no intention of convincing her of anything. Disabusing her of the notion she's Alina's savior is much closer to the truth. I'll force the issue if need be. Gabe will listen to reason even if Libby refuses." Children's voices drifted down the stairs, singing and playing games. Dora glanced up at where Libby waited on the landing. "I didn't realize so many children lived in the house. Not asking was foolish and compounds my mistake, but it's another reason to take Alina out of here as soon as possible. I doubt Libby realizes the great risk she's exposed these children to by taking Alina in."

"I share at least half the blame. I never thought to ask, and I knew the kind of work she does." Libby was young and idealistic, eager to save the world and with no real belief in evil. She saw everything in terms of obstacles to be overcome. I'd been like Libby Mills once, naïve and convinced there was nothing in the world I couldn't handle on my own. "Libby has no idea of the danger. She thinks it's safe here because it's always been safe."

Dora squeezed my arm. "Let's hope she's right. Moving Alina will go a long way toward making that so."

We topped the stairs and Libby gestured toward the end of the corridor. "I gave her the bedroom near the end on the right. The room is small, but it's away from the younger children and very quiet."

I locked arms with Dora, letting her lean on me more heavily. "I'm sure you did your best, Libby. Lead the way."

We'd only just started down the hall before the sound of pounding on the front door echoed in the front entryway. Libby turned, startled. "The two of you go on. I have to get that."

Dora grabbed her sleeve. "Are you sure that's wise?"

Libby stared pointedly at Dora's fingers until she let go. "I know what I'm doing. There's a peephole that gives me a view of the whole porch. I won't open the door unless I can see who is there." She started down the steps, calling back over her shoulder. "Besides, Gabe has men watching from across the street. I'll be safe enough."

The corners of Dora's mouth twitched, edging toward a smile. "Touchy, isn't she? Let's go wake Alina."

Alina's door stood open a few inches, giving us a view of her sleeping face. Her hair pooled on the pillow, framing her face and rendering her beautiful as a storybook princess. I started to push the door open wide, but Dora stayed my hand.

"Wait, Dee." Isadora shut her eyes and cocked her head to the side, face screwed up in concentration. "Do you feel that?"

I concentrated as well, reaching out beyond the surface world. The sensation of falling into the watcher's eyes was stronger this time, more intense, as was the sense of being judged. Release came faster as well, but this time it hadn't let go of us completely. We were on a tether. "The guardian."

"Yes. Your watcher isn't hiding any longer, at least not from us." She pinched the bridge of her nose and sighed. "I do wish spirit creatures could master the art of introducing themselves without giving me a splitting headache. I suppose I should be grateful we're not barred from entering. Open the door, Dee."

I'd half expected the hinges to creak, but the door swung open without a sound, a detail I almost failed to notice. Alina's room was full of ghosts, an assembled choir of dead royalty much like I'd seen on the streets before the parade. They stood around Alina's bed in a half circle, ranged in neat rows that melted into the walls and continued beyond the boundaries of chipped paint and torn wallpaper. Kings in velvet tunics and queens in silk gowns, princes and princesses in rich court dress, and minor nobility I couldn't name, they all stood guard while she slept.

The assembled dead royals turned as one to stare as Dora and I entered the room. They were all faceless, unrecognizable as having once lived, or ever being human. A macabre mask of writhing mist replaced their features, but that didn't stop the sensation of scores of watching eyes that slithered over my skin.

"Oh dear God . . . Dora." I recoiled and took a step back, not knowing why the spirits were there or what kind of ghost manifested as a faceless wraith. "What are they?"

"At a guess? Adjuncts to the guardian. They don't mean her any harm or they wouldn't be allowed so close. Now, hush a moment and let me think." Dora leaned against the doorframe and studied the ghosts through narrowed eyes. That she didn't seem overly concerned calmed my nerves. "Do you remember what Alina said about dreaming of her parents?"

The answer came back to me right away, leaving me to wonder how I'd ever forgotten. I stared at the faceless haunts filling the room. "She said that she could never see their faces."

Dora had moved farther into the small room, edging carefully around the outer line of spirits. I followed on her heels, even more careful not to brush against a ghost. The agony would pass quickly, but the thought of experiencing how any of these people had died was terrifying.

"Exactly." Isadora never took her eyes from the ghosts. "And now we find her deep asleep and surrounded by a host of faceless phantoms. The easy answer would be that these are her memories, and they well may be, but I don't think that's the entire story. Alina didn't wake when we came in or began talking, and frankly that concerns me. Whether these are avatars of her memories or not, I don't think we should start banishing ghosts willy-nilly. These manifestations are more than symbolic."

"Maybe all this is part of the watcher's protections. A way to cushion the blow of everything she's lost." I knew the words were true as soon as I'd said them. "Everyone Alina loves is still alive in her dreams."

Dora continued to edge around ghosts, leading me deeper into the room. "The same could be said for all of us, Delia. Dreams are the greatest bastion against losing someone forever. We can go on and pick up our lives with someone as if death or time had never interrupted."

"Do you often dream of Daniel?" The question was out before I stopped to think how it might make Dora feel. She stopped with her back to me, shoulders held rigid, and I was afraid I'd hurt her. Daniel had been dead two years, killed in Portugal during the war, but he and Isadora had been lovers and friends a long time. "I'm sorry, Dora. I shouldn't have asked you that."

"No, no, the question was fine. You just made me think for a moment. I sometimes dream about Daniel, but those dreams aren't about picking up our life again. All of them involve his leaving for Europe or saying good-bye in one form or another." Dora looked back over her shoulder with a small, hesitant smile and held a hand out to me. Her cold fingers gripped mine tight. "When I dream of the past, and losing someone, I dream of John and Atlanta. John Lawrence is the one who haunts me. Now, let's see about waking Alina."

An old, scratched, and scarred chest of drawers sat against the wall opposite the bed. The small mirror hanging behind it had lost most of its silver around the edges, but the princess ghost brightened into view in the small shiny spot left in the center. She looked past Dora and me, out into the hallway.

I discovered why soon enough. The sound of raised voices, shouts, and feet pounding up the creaky stairs carried into Alina's room.

Stained chintz curtains on the small corner window fluttered frantically, each gust of wind that whipped the fabric carrying a hint of women's voices crying out in loss and sorrow. Thick black smoke billowed in the open window, filling the room with an acrid smell and burning my eyes. Flakes of papery ash rode the wind, drifting in to coat Alina's bed and settle on her hair.

Isadora leaned out the open window, searching for the source of the smoke. She pulled back inside quick enough and slammed the window shut. Smoke still leaked around the casement, and the muffled keening of the wind could be heard, but the drift of falling ash stopped. "Delia, we need to get Alina on her feet right now. The corner of the building is on fire."

Fire caught quickly in old buildings like this, sometimes spreading through most of a block before the fire brigades arrived. I was much more afraid of dying in a raging inferno than of plowing through the army of ghosts watching over Alina. That the spirits drew back from me, melting into one another and leaving a clear path to the bed, was a surprise and an unlooked-for blessing. Now wasn't the time to question why.

"Wake up!" I shook Alina hard and did my best to force her into sitting up. The princess ghost overlooked the room from the mirror, but she wasn't watching me. Her attention was still on the doorway, bright eyed with interest and eagerly awaiting the person running down the hall toward us. Dead kings and queens vanished, along with the myriad of lesser royalty. "Alina, wake up! We have to leave!"

She blinked rapidly and peered at me, confused by the smoke-filled room and my attempts to drag her off the bed. The wind moaned louder, rattling the windowpane. The fog of sleep vanished and Alina's eyes grew big. "They've found me."

"Delia! Dora!" Sam Butler ran into the room, accompanied by Officer Taylor. Other footsteps sped up the stairs toward the children on the third floor. "Come on, we're all getting out of here. The fire department is on their way."

I grabbed a shawl for Alina from the back of a chair and helped wrap it around her shoulders. Hunting for shoes and stockings would take too much time; time we didn't have.

Sam waved Officer Taylor back toward the stairs. "Taylor, go help Perry and Finlay with the children upstairs. We can get downstairs on our own."

Taylor left with no further urging. Dora and I flanked Alina, holding her up while Sam led the way downstairs. The smoke was thinner once we left the bedroom, making it easier to breathe and to see. Alina's jaw was set, angry and defiant, but tears streaked her ash-smeared face and she trembled under my hand. I couldn't fault her for either. She had an equal claim on both anger and fear.

The front door stood open when we reached the deserted entry hall. Fire sirens wailed in the distance, shrill notes that echoed between buildings and gradually grew closer. Voices of the assembled crowd across the street carried inside as well, both nervous adults who knew what fire meant, and excited children who hadn't yet learned. The smell of burning wood, paper, and cloth was stronger and clung to the back of my tongue.

Sam paused at the open door, holding a hand up for us to wait. He poked his head out, whether checking to make sure no one lay in wait, or looking for some prearranged signal, I couldn't say. A matter of seconds was all the time it took for him to be sure and motion us out the door, but those few moments stretched into an eternity.

A line of squad cars sat across the street. Sam hustled the three of us into the backseat of the lead car, leaving the door open. He leaned against the doorframe, half blocking the opening, and watched people on the street. I exchanged looks with Dora. Both of us knew Sam was standing guard, but I wasn't sure either Libby or Alina realized.

Libby was already perched on a small jump seat facing the rear when we arrived, arms wrapped tight around Jake and watching the front of the house. Relief at seeing us took some of the anxiety out of her eyes, but not all. "This is taking too long, Sam. I need to go back inside. They should have had the children out by now."

Sam frowned and tipped the brim of his straw boater up, glancing at the house and back to Libby. "Give them another minute. If they don't come out by then, I'll go back inside."

"You don't need to worry, I promise." I leaned and touched Libby's hand, ignoring Dora's raised eyebrow and the amused glimmer in her eye. No doubt she was hoping to watch me squirm when Libby questioned how I knew. The truth was I didn't know the how or why either, just that I was right. "All the children are safe and accounted for. The officers will bring them out any second."

An instant later, Officer Finlay and Patrolman Perry led eight children out the front door. Taylor was on their heels, an infant in each arm, and shepherding a girl of twelve or thirteen. The older girl carried a much younger little boy. From a distance, I might have mistaken him for Connor.

"Oh, thank God." Libby rested her cheek on Jake's hair and hugged him tighter. "Their mothers trusted me to take care of them. I don't know what I'd have done if anything happened."

"This is my fault. I put you all in danger." Alina curled forward over her knees, words catching in her throat. "I shouldn't have come here. I shouldn't have come."

"Nonsense. None of this is your fault." Isadora put an arm around Alina and held her close, petting her hair. Her eyes met mine, full of regret and resolve both. She meant to begin pushing Alina to remember. "Fires start all the time, for any number of reasons. There's nothing to suggest this has anything to do with you or the people looking for you. For the life of me, I don't see why you thought it did."

Alina's head came up and she jerked back. Her voice was a low, angry hiss. "Don't treat me like a child needing comfort, Countess, or mistake me for a fool. I heard the wind and I know what the voices mean. The hunters know where I am."

"I never meant to insult you." Dora's smile was small and tight, her expression guarded. "But now I'm curious. Why did you call me countess?"

"Because—" Alina stopped and stared, her mouth half open to speak. Her anger melted away. "I don't know. For an instant, I thought I remembered you. Are you a countess?"

Isadora looked away, fiddling with her skirt and crossing her legs, stalling for time before she answered. She'd unlocked one of Alina's memories, but she hadn't expected this memory. Dora rarely spoke of her time in Europe, waving any questions away and maintaining that time was long in the past. I'd never pressed her for details.

All I knew of her marriage to Mikal was that she'd lost him. Marrying Mikal might have bestowed a title on her. If so, I'd never known.

"Answer her, Dora. Let her know if that was a real memory or not." Sam still leaned against the open car door, hands in his trouser pockets. He looked pointedly at Isadora. "Are you a countess or not?"

Dora started to wave his question away, as she'd done with all of mine, but something stopped her. She studied Alina's face, searching for some memory of her own. "I was a countess once, but the title died with my husband Mikal. His relatives had scads of children, both boys and girls. There were always packs of cousins running wild when the family got together, but no one minded.

Mikal died a little over twelve years ago now. You would have been very young at the time."

"But I could have been one of those children. You could have known my parents." Alina's face lit up with eagerness and the hope she'd found a friend among strangers. She kissed the back of Isadora's hand. "And I remembered you were a countess. I must know you!"

Dora brushed strands of hair back from Alina's face while pain and sadness moved through her eyes in rapid succession. I knew then she couldn't bring herself to push Alina further. Not now. "Remembering that much is a good first step. When we leave here, you're going to come and stay with me. My house has special protections and I give you my word the hunters can't find you there. Once you're safe, we'll work on uncovering the rest of your memories."

"Just who do you think you are?" Libby's face flushed scarlet and her voice rose. "You don't have the right to make decisions for her. And I don't see how you can claim no one will ever find Alina at your house. That's utterly ridiculous."

Alina and I stared, startled by the outburst. She pulled back against the seat, wary at being caught in the middle and unsure how to react.

"I'm not making decisions for her, I'm offering her sanctuary." Isadora never lost her smile, but there was nothing friendly in her demeanor. That Libby didn't back down in the face of Dora's icy stare was a testament to either her fortitude or her foolishness. "Letting her stay with you was a mistake, one that put the children in danger and that I'm trying to make amends for. And despite what you think, Alina will be safer with me, Miss Mills. I'm not in the business of making spurious claims I can't support. Just accept the fact that I have means at my disposal that aren't available to everyone, and things will go swimmingly."

Sam had stayed quiet, as I had, but he spoke up now. "Don't take offense, Libby. Moving Alina to Dora's place really is best. If anyone can keep her hidden and safe, Dora can. I made the decision at the fountain to get between Alina and the people looking for her. Dora's making it now. No one else need be in harm's way." He looked deep into Libby's eyes. "You've done an outstanding job taking care of Jake since Miranda was killed. Let us take care of Alina. You can see the sense in that, can't you?"

I thought at first Libby was going to cry. She shut her eyes and kissed the top of Jake's head before rallying to face Sam, the stern set of her jaw at odds with the wistfulness in her eyes. "You know Dora better than I, Sam, and I can see you've thought this through. I didn't think at all. I owe you an apology, Dora. I spoke out of turn."

Libby never looked away from Sam's face, never so much as glanced at Dora while apologizing. I realized that Sadie's instincts hadn't failed her after all. Sam wasn't courting Libby, but she dearly wished he would.

"Apology accepted. No real harm done." Dora glanced my way and arched an eyebrow. She'd noticed as well. The only one who didn't see was Sam.

The smoke on the far side of the street was thicker now. Wind whipped dark, sooty clouds in circles and shot tendrils off in all directions. If I listened closely, faint sorrowful voices could still be heard on the wind, but they sounded distant, as if traveling from some far-off place.

I thought to wonder if the watcher had left as well. An instant's concentration set me straight. Alina's guardian filled my head as soon as I looked, greatly amused that I'd imagined it wandering far.

Fire engines had arrived. Limp lengths of canvas hose lay uncoiled on the street, held ready at the nozzle end by a line of strong men. Other firemen worked to open the hydrants. Water spurted out the nozzle, jarring the men fighting to hold the hose steady. Arcing fountains of water drenched the front and side of Libby's house from the roof to the ground floor. The children rescued by Finlay and Perry hung out of squad car windows to watch. They seemed disappointed that the fire died so quickly.

The princess ghost popped into view behind Libby's head, filling the center of the window closing off the driver's compartment up front. Faceless royals clouded the rest of the glass surrounding her, dimmer and harder to see, but there. I'd not seen them with the princess before, but maybe they'd been there all along, hidden. What I didn't understand was why I saw them now.

Seeing all these haunts clustered together shredded the last of my doubt about whose memories the princess ghost came from. She wasn't the cherished recollection of a stranger I hadn't yet found. She belonged to Alina.

The fire went out quickly, the damage to Libby's house minimal. A stack of wooden crates, many of them stuffed with old newspapers and creosote-soaked rags, was found against the outside wall near the kitchen. The fire had started there, whether by accident or deliberately none of us knew. Some of the older boys from the neighborhood had used a pole to shove the burning crates away from the building before the fire engines arrived. Libby would have lost the house for sure otherwise.

Gabe's men stayed to keep an eye on things and to help Libby clean up water that had seeped around the windows, and scrub soot from the kitchen. Sam drove me home before continuing on to Dora's. He'd volunteered to stay with Isadora and Alina until Randy got home.

Changing out of smoke-tainted clothing took only a few minutes. I lay down on the bed, meaning to do nothing more than rest for a short time before Gabe came home. The princess ghost filled my dressing table mirror, staring into my eyes with the endless patience of the dead.

I stared back, skittish about thinking too hard about how she might have died. What she'd meant to Alina in life and why she'd come to me were marginally safer topics for thought, but led me in just as many circles.

Asking the ghost outright was a sign of how desperate I was for answers. "Who were you, spirit? Were you a cousin, a sister? A friend? You meant a great deal to Alina or you wouldn't exist. Tell me so I can help her."

The ghost stayed silent, her voice frozen in the past in the same way her image was frozen in the glass. That wasn't unexpected. After all, memories spoke only in dreams.

I shouldn't have been surprised at falling asleep and into a memory. I'd asked her to tell.

The narrow beds were hard, our room always cold, but my sisters and I took comfort in each other's company. At night we wrote letters to Mama and Papa, telling them little stories about our day. A sparrow building a nest in a tree, or the first snowfall softening the edge of a stone wall—we wanted our parents to see what we'd seen while we were apart. Most of the letters we saved for the day we could hand Mama and Papa the ribbon-wrapped bundle to read.

Other letters we finished and tossed on the coal grate, poking at thin paper until it caught in a flash of heat and light. Those were letters written on the days we were most frightened.

We'd pushed two beds together as the nights grew unbearably cold, the four of us warmer and less alone sleeping together.

After the second night, we left them that way. I'd faced down a bleary-eyed guard who stank of beer and insisted we put them back in their proper places. He'd stomped away, returning not long after with the young officer who'd smiled at me the day we'd arrived.

I'd learned since he was a lieutenant and that his name was Dmitri. He'd come into our bedroom, hands behind his back, and listened carefully while the bleary-eyed guard explained that moving the beds was against regulations. All the while, I saw the lieutenant eyeing the frost on the windows, the heavy shawls the four of us wore, and the meager pile of blankets.

The guard finished reciting his list of our sins, and Lieutenant Dmitri turned to me. He touched his cap and bobbed his head. "Explain to the private why you're moving furniture, miss. He doesn't understand why you insist on pushing the beds together."

I stepped in front of my sisters, determined not to show fear. "This room is always cold. The blankets are too thin and there is never enough coal to last through the night. Sleeping together is warmer."

Lieutenant Dmitri nodded curtly before turning to the scowling guard. He clapped the man on the shoulder. "I told you there was a simple reason, Nikolai. No escape plots, just a desire to be warm at night. Leave the beds where they are."

The lieutenant paused in the doorway, his gaze taking in the sparse furnishings of our room. I'd have sworn I saw anger in his eyes, just for an instant, but he walked away too quickly for me to be sure.

I went back to playing cards with my sisters. Putting the lieutenant's visit out of my mind was best. We had no friends here, only jailers.

Mai was crouched next to me when I woke, green eyes gleaming in the half light and watching the princess ghost in the mirror. The princess had turned away, looking toward something I couldn't see.

I tucked the cat under my arm and went to the kitchen to start supper, thinking hard about what I'd witnessed.

That the story was true was never in doubt. What I didn't know was how to use what I'd learned.

CHAPTER 9

Gabe

Gabe climbed out of the patrol car gingerly, more stiff and sore after two days of sitting at his desk than he'd imagined. A new murder case in a well-off neighborhood meant his convalescence was over, like it or not. He stood next to the car for a few seconds to steady himself and look around.

He couldn't swear that he and Jack had been in this neighborhood before, but Gabe knew many just like this. Tall, compact two-story houses lined each side of the street, survivors of the '06 quake and fire. Neat box hedges or waist-high black iron fences separated front yards from the sidewalk. A few yards had beds of roses just starting to bloom, or window boxes full of bright-faced pansies and primrose.

From the outside, Marguerite DeVere's house looked like all the others on the block, but inside, her girls catered to men with lots of money and even more power. Gabe would be willing to wager that everyone in the neighborhood knew what went on inside. As long as Maggie's business didn't spill out into the street, people turned a blind eye. She ran a clean, quiet house and took care of her girls, refusing to allow anyone to hurt them.

News traveled fast when one of her customers turned up dead in a girl's bed. The combination of titillation and scandal was irresistible.

Sidewalks on both sides of the street were packed with neighbors and tradesmen. Shock was the overwhelming emotion on most faces, the result of a deep-seated belief that murder and other heinous crimes happened to other people, in other neighborhoods. A few onlookers craned their necks or stood on tiptoe to see over the people in front of them, no doubt hoping to catch a glimpse of someone important.

Anyone of any prominence was long gone, sent safely away before the police were called. Maggie wasn't going to risk exposing her clientele.

Gabe settled his hat and shoved his hands deep into his coat pockets, his face set in the calm, professional mask he wore while working. He let Randy Dodd and Marshall Henderson carve a path for him through a sea of respectable merchants and their wives, bankers, and frightened, wide-eyed servant girls. All of them backed away, still too stunned to shout questions or demand Gabe take action of some kind. That wouldn't last.

He let his guard down once he crossed the line of policemen shutting off the small front yard from the street. With his back turned, no one could see him wince as he climbed the front steps and went into the house. Good sense said he should have stayed confined to the office a few days longer, nursing his wounds until each breath didn't flirt with pain.

That was before Randy Dodd came into his office and described the beat cop's report. Good sense couldn't override the warning chill that spiked up Gabe's spine, or the inescapable truth that he had to see the scene himself. Why he was so sure was a question he never had an answer for, but Gabe had learned to pay attention. He couldn't sit by and let another detective handle this case.

The entry hall was full of cops, both men from Gabe's squad and neighboring precincts. Voices echoed off the high ceiling and black marble floor, adding to the noise. Two huge crystal chandeliers filled the entry with yellow electric light, pushing shadows into tiny spaces under round rosewood tables laden with flower vases. A pair of overstuffed chairs, upholstered in burgundy velvet and trimmed with neat rows of brass nail heads, sat on either side of the parlor door.

Noah Baker was the senior man on the scene. He'd taken charge and was doing Jack's job, handing out assignments and taking reports, making sure nothing was missed. In all the years Gabe had known him, Noah had never shown any interest in command. Baker was doing a good job under the circumstances, but Gabe never expected anything less from his men.

He saw Lon Rockwell coming down the staircase, hugging the wall to avoid interfering with Taylor dusting the banister for fingerprints. Lon looked right at Gabe and quickened his steps. "Marshall, see what you can do to help Noah. Sergeant Rockwell can fill me in on where we stand."

Rockwell had years of experience on some of the roughest streets in the city. The expression on Lon's face as he threaded his way through the crowded entryway told Gabe he'd been right to come. "Captain, I'm glad you're here. The victim's upstairs, a Mr. J. B. Rigaux according to Miss DeVere." Lon ran fingers through his hair and glanced toward the top of the stairs. "I wouldn't let the coroner's men move the body until you got here. You—you need to see this. He's in the last room at the end of the hall."

"All right. Lead the way." He caught Randy's eye. "Come with us. I want you to take notes."

He trudged up the stairs behind Rockwell, moving as slowly as a man twice his age. Gabe paused at the top and pressed a hand to his side, shaky and sweating. "The beat cop said a girl named

Trula May was found with the victim, but that the killer didn't hurt her. Did she see anything?"

Lon's neck flushed hot, and spots of color burned on his cheeks. "No, sir, I'm afraid not. Trula May was crying too hard to say much, but Miss Maggie explained. Mr. Rigaux liked to do special things with some of the girls. He paid extra for girls that were willing."

Randy looked up from his notebook, an eyebrow quirked and pencil poised over the page. "What kind of special things?"

"Ropes and blindfolds." Lon flushed deeper and waved Gabe toward an open door. "Mr. Rigaux liked to tie them up."

Baxter had set up the tripod for his new Speed Graphic and was busily taking photographs. Gabe stayed back out of the way. The photographs were important, a record they could come back to time and again. He still studied everything about the room and the placement of the body carefully, setting the details in his mind.

The room wasn't overly fancy, decorated more to set a mood than to impress. White lace curtains hung over the street-side windows, but heavy damask panels hung behind, shutting out light and the view from below. Red silk scarves covered bedside lampshades, softening and tinting the harsh electric light. Rigaux's clothes—an expensive shirt and collar, black jacket and black trousers—were folded neatly on a padded bench under the street-side window. Polished black boots sat on the floor underneath.

Short lengths of thick rope sheathed in soft satin were knotted to the headboard. Trula May wouldn't have been able to get loose on her own, and the cord looked to have had been hastily cut to free her. Small chintz and taffeta pillows in delicate pinks and mauve filled the corners of a settee. The pillows matched the torn, blood-splashed coverlet that had slipped half off the bed and onto the floor.

Breathing through his mouth was an old habit, helping to block out the worst of the smell of stale piss, the stench of blood and voided bowels. Rigaux had panicked when attacked and lost control, a common thing for someone who'd died suddenly and violently. Gabe guessed Rigaux had been somewhere between thirty-five and forty, and looked to be a few inches shorter than Jack. At one time, his thick brown hair had been slicked back with pomade, but now it stuck up at odd, grotesque angles.

Rigaux's naked body sprawled across the bed on his stomach, as if he'd attempted to crawl away. At first glance, Gabe thought the victim's throat had been cut, but he soon realized there wasn't enough blood. A closer look revealed a thin wire garrote wrapped four times around the man's neck. The first two fingers of one hand were trapped under a loop of wire and nearly severed.

Gabe walked around the edge of the room, viewing the scene from all angles. Discovering how the killer got in and out without being seen didn't take long. A window stood open on the far side of the room, away from the street and overlooking a back porch roof. Once out the window, the drop to the roof, and from there to the ground, was only a few feet.

He glanced at Randy and gestured toward the body. Dodd didn't have Jack's experience, but he was still a decent detective. "What does this tell you?"

Dodd didn't hesitate. "They came at him from behind. Since I can guess what he was doing, surprising him wasn't difficult. He fought and tried to get away, but he didn't stand a chance. See the dark patch in the small of his back? If I had to guess—I'd say the killer put a foot or a knee into his back for leverage. The poor bastard suffered. This was personal."

"It was personal. The killer scared the hell out of the girl, but he didn't hurt her. He wanted Rigaux." The truth in that settled under his skin, deep and unmistakable. "Let's go talk to Maggie and Trula May."

He found Maggie DeVere in a private sitting room on the ground floor. Two burly patrolmen stood watch outside the door. The room wasn't very large and didn't have any windows, but Gabe decided that was precisely why she'd chosen to wait there with Trula May. With only one way in, she'd see anyone coming at her. And unless Maggie had changed a great deal, she'd have a pistol within reach.

Maggie looked startled as Gabe and Randy came in, but promptly smiled. "Gabriel Ryan, as I live and breathe!" She stood and came to greet him, hands outstretched to take his. Rings glittered on every finger, stones scattering light. She'd bobbed her thick black hair since the last time he'd seen her, a fashionable style that flattered her. "I haven't seen you in years. Where have you been keeping yourself?"

Maggie DeVere had been born on a hog farm in Kansas, but anyone who didn't know would never guess. He and Jack had met her more than fifteen years ago, back when they were inexperienced rookies. Maggie was young and pretty and naïve, newly arrived in San Francisco and easy prey for the ruffians along the wharfs. She was also smart enough to know she didn't want to stay on the streets.

He'd been wise enough to walk away from her after Victoria died in the 1906 fire. Maggie wanted more than he could give.

Now Maggie DeVere was the picture of charm and good breeding, well dressed and well spoken. Years of effort went into perfecting that impression, years of living in the shadow of society and being sneered at. No one sneered now. Maggie had too much money, knew too many secrets.

Gabe hoped that made her happy. He smiled and took her hands. "Hello, Maggie. It has been a long time. I guess that means you've stayed on the right side of the law."

"I was always on the right side." Maggie leaned and kissed

his cheek. "Given the circumstances, I'm glad you're in charge of this case. Trula May and I can trust you. Trula May Wright, this is Captain Gabe Ryan. Don't be afraid to talk to him. Gabe will do his best to help you."

His first impression of Trula May was that her eyes were too big for her face, but that wasn't strictly true. "Fragile" was the word he settled on. Breakable. Her soft brown eyes appeared larger because of how fine boned and delicate her features were. She was very young, with olive skin and light brown hair that hung in waves over her shoulder. Dusky circles stained the paler skin under her eyes.

He doubted that she'd slept at all the night before. "Hello, Trula May. You can call me Gabe if you like."

Trula May tugged her silk dressing gown tighter over her chest, staring at the floor and refusing to look at Gabe. She was barefoot, a thick, woolen blanket covering her legs and her lap. Bruises darkened one ankle. From the looks of things, Maggie had rushed her out of the room containing Rigaux's body, not bothering with clothes or anything but getting away. Given the state Trula May must have been in when found, he wasn't surprised.

Maggie traded looks with Gabe and sat down again, taking Trula May's hand. "You need to tell Gabe what you remember, Trula. Once you answer his questions, we can get you cleaned up and Lemira and Jane will take you to the Sausalito house. Milton will drive the three of you and go with you on the ferry. You'll be safe in Sausalito and no one will find you. But you have to talk to Gabe first."

Gabe crouched down in front of her, putting himself at Trula's eye level. She looked even younger up close. "I'm sorry we have to do this now, but it can't wait. Not too many questions, I promise. Could you tell how many men came into the room?"

Maggie's girls weren't innocents or they wouldn't be here, but their experience didn't extend to witnessing murder. He waited patiently for his question to work its way through the thick fog of shock and fear that had left Trula numb.

"Tw-two. There were two." The slim hand clutching the dressing gown trembled. "One put his hand over my mouth and told me . . . he told me to lie still. He said . . . he said if I made any noise, I'd die too. The whole time I heard Jaret choking—and he kept kicking me and kicking me, fighting to get away . . . then he stopped moving."

Gabe couldn't keep from flinching. He couldn't imagine what that had been like for her, or what telling him now cost. "Did the man attacking Mr. Rigaux say anything?"

"He—he said prayers while Jaret died." Trula May stared, her huge brown eyes even larger with fear. Tears slid down her face, unnoticed. "And he'd stop for a second and I'd hear the wind howling . . . and the other man, the one with his hand over my mouth, he'd say Jaret's name and the wind got louder. They did that over and over. All I could think of is how Father Bryan half sings the Latin prayers during High Mass and—and the deacons answer."

His heart sped up, trying to outrace the ice threatening to freeze it solid in his chest. "Do you remember any of what he said?"

She hunched her shoulders, curling in on herself. "I couldn't understand him."

Randy cleared his throat. "Gabe—"

Gabe held a hand up, stopping him. Randy had recognized the give and take necessary for magical incantations. They'd both heard Isadora and Delia do it a hundred times or more.

A spell. Memories of hearing the wind howl during the riot around Lotta's fountain came back, strong and vivid. The way Gabe thought of this case twisted. "Did either one of these men say anything more before they left?"

"They warned me not to make any noise or they'd come back for me." Trula shrank into the corner of the sofa, sniffling. "I never even heard them leave."

"You were brave to tell me all of that. Thank you." Gabe didn't try to hide the wince as he stood. He had more important things to think of than his dignity. "Could I have a word in the hallway, Maggie?"

She peered at him quizzically, her expression not giving much of anything away. "Of course. Give me a minute with Trula first."

He reined in the impulse to pace while Maggie reassured Trula. Randy stood a few feet away, scribbling in his notebook, more silent than Jack would ever be, but that was for the best right now. Gabe needed to think, think hard, and he imagined Dodd did as well. Both of them knew the implications of Trula's story. Other than Jack, they might be the only cops in San Francisco who did.

Once Maggie stepped into the corridor, Gabe asked the two patrolmen stationed outside the sitting room to stand in the open doorway. Having them wait where she could see them might give Trula a feeling of safety. He took Maggie's arm and walked her a few feet away.

"I need you to tell me how Rigaux ended up in Trula's bed, Maggie. You wouldn't let him near her if you thought she might get hurt. I know you better than that." She stood with her arms crossed and stared at the floor, the pose reminiscent of Dora. Gabe glanced toward the sitting room and lowered his voice. "No games or dancing around the truth. I'm trying to keep that girl alive and catch the killers."

"I've no intention of keeping secrets, Gabe. My biggest concern is how to get Trula safely away from here and make sure those men never find her." Maggie rubbed her eyes. "What little I know about Jaret Rigaux may not be useful."

"Tell me what you can and let me be the judge of what's useful or not. If I have questions, I'll ask."

Maggie did pace while speaking, burning off pent-up energy in short loops that spanned the width of the broad hallway. "Jaret tended to boast and talk endlessly about himself, but Trula liked him. Despite appearances, he was . . . gentle with her. He was married, rich, and harmless, and seldom spoke about his wife." She turned and faced him, her expression stricken. "Oh, Gabe, I just thought. His poor wife. Finding out he's dead will be hard enough. Does she have to be told how he was found?"

"We have to tell his wife where he died and that he was murdered. That isn't a secret we can keep." Informing the next of kin was always a difficult, unhappy duty. The circumstances of Rigaux's death would add humiliation to his widow's grief once they became public knowledge. "I'll do my best, Maggie, but the papers are bound to catch wind of this sooner or later. I was surprised not to find a pack of photographers out front when I arrived. Reporters usually beat me to a murder scene."

She waved a hand in dismissal. "I called in a few favors. The press will hold off for a few more hours. Trula should be far away from here by then."

Gabe traded looks with Randy. He hadn't realized Maggie had that much influence. "All right, that explains the lack of reporters. Finish telling me about Rigaux."

"There isn't much more to tell. Jaret and his wife came to San Francisco from Europe just before the war ended. I know he was born in Belgium, but his mother was Russian. His wife's family is Russian too." Maggie shrugged and fingered the thin gold chain around her neck. "Like much of the nobility, they were forced to leave rather quickly. He bragged about their daring escape often enough, there might have been some truth in the story."

Randy spoke up, pencil poised over a fresh notebook page. "Did he say where they'd escaped from?"

"Not in detail." She frowned and sat on a small fainting couch placed against one corridor wall. Maggie pulled a red satin pillow into her arms, hugging it tight. The mirror above her head reflected the sitting room door and the two scowling patrolmen blocking the way inside. "All I know for sure is they abandoned an estate belonging to his wife's family somewhere near the Black Sea. Jaret fancied himself an aristocrat, but all his money came from his wife. She's the one with noble blood and titles."

"One last question, Maggie. How often was Rigaux in Trula's room at night?"

"Two or three times a week for the last six months." Maggie sat up straighter, understanding shining in her eyes. He'd expected nothing less from her. "Often enough to make him easy to find."

Gabe had stopped thinking of his hunches as nothing more than educated guesses years ago. Too many turned out to be leaps of faith that paid off, often bridging gaps in evidence and showing him new pathways to the truth. Strong pulls toward any bit of evidence or information were always worth chasing.

That pull grew stronger after he met Delia, and continued to strengthen the longer they were together. Isadora maintained that once he believed in what Dee was able to do, Gabe was able to believe in his own fledgling abilities. He'd stopped questioning why his hunches paid off so often and concentrated on the results.

He paid attention to that feeling now. The Russian waiters in Mullaney's union were frightened by stories of other immigrants who'd fled the Bolsheviks turning up dead in New York and Seattle. They were afraid the same thing would happen here.

The body upstairs made that fear reasonable and real. Rigaux fit that pattern, and Alina's aunt and uncle did as well.

Gathering the names of the people in Seattle and New York,

and discovering how they'd died, went near the top of Gabe's list. It occurred to him to ask the same question about Chicago, especially after finding a Chicago PD badge at the scene of the riot. Knowing who the dead were and where they'd come from originally might lead to connections here in San Francisco.

Before anything else, he needed to talk to Dee and Isadora. They'd know if he was truly dealing with some aspect of the occult, or two men doing everything they could to frighten a vulnerable young woman.

His gut knew the answer. His head needed to hear it from Delia.

"You've been a big help, Maggie." Gabe cleared his throat and buttoned his overcoat, a signal to Dodd that he was ready to leave. Randy tucked his notebook into an inside pocket. "Now I'm going to ask another favor. Let me assign two officers to go with Trula and the others. Street clothes, no uniforms. I'd feel better with my men watching over her."

Maggie hugged her satin pillow tighter, peering at him. "I'll take you up on that offer. Thank you, Gabe."

He didn't get far down the hallway before she called out.

"Gabe, I have a question too." Maggie stood in the center of the hall carpet, the red pillow dangling from her hand. She tipped her head to the side, smiling softly. "It's been almost six years. Where have you been keeping yourself?"

He fingered his wedding band, remembering the day Delia put the plain gold ring on his finger, and held up his hand. "At home with my wife. I think you'd be surprised how well the two of you would get on together. Delia's an amazing woman."

Maggie's smile wavered, but she recovered quickly and laughed. "As long as you had a good reason for staying away. Perhaps I'll test your theory of how well we'd get along and invite your Delia to lunch."

"I'll tell her." He touched the brim of his hat and smiled. "Take care of yourself, Maggie."

Gabe strode down the corridor toward the front door, giving Randy Dodd a list of people to contact and information to track down. He knew if he hurried, he'd find Delia and Isadora with Sadie. Going to the Fitzgerald house to find them would give him an excuse to check up on Jack as well.

The prospect of seeing his wife in the middle of the day, no matter what the circumstances, made him smile. Working a big case involved long days that often stretched into long nights. His job kept them apart far too much, and he'd take any stolen moments with Dee he could grab.

Gabe was in the patrol car and driving away before he remembered Maggie. He hadn't given a thought to looking back to see if she'd watched him leave.

That was for the best. He wasn't sure he wanted to know.

CHAPTER 10

Delia

Dora insisted on driving the two of us to Russian Hill for our visit with Sadie. I could have gotten there easily enough alone, either by walking or calling a cab, but Isadora was adamant about the two of us arriving together.

In all honesty, I was relieved not to be on my own. Our friendship was strong and I had faith Sadie would take the bad news in stride, but I couldn't help but worry a little. The feeling that I'd left matters until far too late made the whole thing worse.

Isadora was late as usual. I roamed up and down the walk in front of our house, unable to stand still and wait. The day was warm for late March, the sun doing its best to burn away all memories of winter. Gauzy clouds trailed across the sky, too thin and unsubstantial to build up against the East Bay hills. Daffodils and hyacinths bloomed along the front fence, their sweet scent filling each passing breeze. The plum tree in the center of the lawn was fuzzy green with new leaves, a sure sign of spring, while crocus and the first Johnny-jump-ups added splashes of color at ground level.

My cat, Mai, sat in the lower branches of the plum tree, watching me pace. Her tail swished impatiently, each side-to-side motion accompanied by loud *mrrowl*s and small chirps voicing her opinion of the two of us being outdoors. Mrs. Bauer next door peered out her front window as Mai's yowling grew louder. Most cats loved chasing butterflies or stalking beetles through the grass. Mai much preferred sleeping in sunbeams on the sitting room carpet.

"You are a disgracefully spoiled and lazy creature, Mai. I'd leave you outside to teach you a lesson, but I can't have you tormenting the neighbors." I held my arms out, catching her as she jumped down. Mai tucked her head up under my chin, purring loudly. "If you insist on wasting a glorious day, I'll put you inside. Just don't complain later."

I hurried up the front steps, well aware that Dora would be careening around the corner any moment. Mai stopped purring the instant I set foot on the porch, twisting around to stare at the front window. She growled deep in her chest, ears flat to her head and tail bushed out.

At first I thought the cat was growling at the princess ghost, something Mai hadn't done before. The princess sat in the corner of a windowpane, calm and still, her image clear and unchanging as always. A troop of faceless haunts frosted the glass around her, faint and so dim as to almost disappear against the curtains on the window. But I soon realized Mai wasn't focused on the princess or the memories that accompanied her. I shifted the way I viewed the world, searching for whatever had upset Mai.

I almost missed the phantom standing in the shadows at the end of the porch, and if not for the cat, I might not have noticed him at all. That I had seen him pulled him further out of the realm of the dead, almost as if my regard gave him permission to cross into the world of the living. His image became clearer, more solid and real looking.

He was dressed strangely, wearing loose dark trousers and a

loose long-sleeve dark shirt, but no shoes or socks. Thick, dark hair hung well below his ears, curly and untamed as his full beard. His dark brown eyes were strangest of all, changing as I watched from filmed and dim, to shining bird bright and strangely alive in a way I'd never seen in a shade before.

I understood why Mai had reacted so strongly. He wasn't just one of the restless dead wandering the world, or a simple ghost looking for rest. I wasn't sure he was a ghost at all. Letting him linger would only increase the danger.

Simple words have enormous power in the spirit realm, a power made greater by a practitioner's will. The rhythm and cadence of the words, and the number of times those words are repeated, amplifies that power even more. All the will I could summon and a great deal of what I'd learned from Dora went into my attempts to banish this ghost.

"Hear me, spirit, and believe. You weren't summoned by me nor called to cross my threshold. I won't welcome you here." I held tight to the cat, instinct or something in the spirit's eyes warning me not to let her go. Mai's tail beat against my side, but she didn't struggle to get down. She sensed the danger and meant to protect me. "Know I say this for now and forevermore. I banish you three times, spirit, and order you to go. Leave my house and never return. Leave me and mine in peace. Leave and return to where your body rests. Go now!"

The spirit's image wavered, but soon recovered and stood firm. His smug smile revealed stark white, perfect teeth, and made him appear even more menacing. Still safe in my arms, Mai snarled and lashed out with a paw. The smile faded from the phantom's face and he took a step back.

I blinked and the ghost was gone. He'd shaken off all my efforts to make him leave, but he appeared to be afraid of my tiny gray cat. Mai sniffed the air, her green eyes searching for any trace of the spirit. I knew he was truly gone when her ears came up and she started purring again.

My hand shook unlocking the front door. I kissed the top of Mai's head and let her inside. She stalked off in the direction of the sitting room, tail held high in victory.

I'd brought the cat home with me when she was a tiny kitten, an unexpected gift from the most powerful sorcerer in Chinatown. Mai was said to descend from a line of ghost-hunting cats. From the very first, she'd lived up to her heritage, chasing away spirits with ill intent and keeping Gabe and me safe. She'd outdone herself today.

The princess and her cohort of faceless memories had vanished from the front window. All my instincts told me that their disappearance had nothing to do with either Mai or the way the new spirit had left so suddenly. The princess came and went as she chose. My actions had little or no effect on her.

I locked up the house again and went back to waiting on the curb. Banishing the memory of the strange phantom's appearance and forgetting the gleam in his eyes proved impossible. Between princesses trapped in silvered glass, faceless memories, and Alina's guardian lurking in the background, I was already chin deep in spirits I couldn't explain. That they were all tied together, even this newest spirit, was undeniable. The question I couldn't answer was how.

Dora arrived a short time later, and the reason she'd been so firm about driving became clear. Her new car had arrived.

The car was a perfect fit for Isadora. Sleek, with long, low, flowing lines, the yellow 1919 Roamer was every bit as racy and sporty as Dora had claimed. With the rumble seat folded up as it was now, the car looked to be the perfect two-passenger roadster. She'd invested in the company on a lark, drawn to their slogan, "America's Smartest Car" and that the company's sales brochures quoted the poetry of the Irish playwright Oscar Wilde. The car was fresh from the factory, a tangible return on her investment.

She'd given up wearing her driving goggles and matching hat, replacing them with a plaid newsboy cap stuffed down over her blond hair. A hat like that would have looked ridiculous on me, but on Dora it was very flattering. The colors made the blue of her eyes brighter and brought out the roses in her cheeks. Randy's eyes lit up each time he saw her wearing the cap, and I suspected that was a large part of the appeal.

Dora leaned across the black leather seat and opened the door, greeting me with a bright, triumphant smile. "Hop in, Dee. Then tell me what you think of the car."

Unlike her last car, the Roamer's door latched securely on the first try. I ran a hand that trembled only a little over the smooth leather of the seat and the polished wood dashboard. Chrome trim gleamed in the sunlight. "I can see why you wanted this car so badly. It's every bit as beautiful as you said. I assume the motor is equally as impressive."

"I wouldn't have taken the trouble to have one shipped here otherwise. The man who delivered the car said it would easily do forty miles per hour on the open road. He assured me that every part of this car is top of the line." She frowned and peered at me, the triumphant smile replaced by concern. "You look absolutely ghastly, Dee. Please tell me this isn't a result of being nervous about speaking with Sadie."

"Of course not. Sadie is my oldest friend. She might be angry with me for a time, but things will work out between us." I plunged on, as certain Dora would help me find an answer as I was that Sadie would stay my friend. "But it appears that I haven't reached my full complement of bizarre spirits. Another one tried to take up residence on my porch just before you arrived. I can't even say for sure if he was a ghost or something else entirely, but he made my skin crawl. The cat came to my rescue or he'd still be lurking in the shadows. He was much more afraid of Mai than of me."

She looked away, fingers wrapped tight around the steering wheel. When Dora turned back, she was oddly calm. "Tell me about what you saw as we drive. Sadie's expecting us."

We didn't have far to go, and for once Dora drove at a reasonable speed, pausing at intersections longer than usual and not careening around corners. Even so, the time passed swiftly. I told Dora everything I remembered, from the ghost's bare feet to the wild gleam in his eyes. She remained silent until we pulled up and parked across the street from Sadie's house.

"I have a few theories about your phantom, Dee." She tapped a long red nail against the steering wheel and crinkled her nose in distaste. "You're not going to like them."

I managed a laugh, shaky and weak given the circumstances, but a laugh nonetheless. "Of course I won't like them. That's never stopped you from telling me in the past."

"You'll enjoy this even less, but I thought it only sporting to warn you in advance. What you saw most likely wasn't a ghost, at least not in the way we normally think of ghosts." Dora tugged off the driving cap and shook out her hair. "This is related to what I told Melba about raising illusions to frighten people. What I didn't tell her is that people have been known to take their own lives to escape images they thought were real. Necromancers in particular are very fond of perverting the power of death that way, or shaping ghosts for their own purposes. This one failed because you have the ability to see through the illusion to the person who created it."

"A necromancer in San Francisco? Surely you're joking." Lodging even a token protest helped ward off my own revulsion for a moment longer. I needed that time. Dora stared in that calm way that meant she expected better of me. I waved my protests away and surrendered. "All right, you're not joking. Was the crazed gleam in his eye an illusion as well?"

Dora's smile was small, quickly given and just as quickly gone. "No, Dee, whatever you saw in his eyes was undoubtedly real. The type of person who sinks to that level of the dark arts and the kinds of spells required isn't completely rational to begin with. Rumors circulated for years that the Kaiser sought the services of a necromancer at the beginning of the Great War. And though many of his followers refused to believe, Rasputin was called the Mad Monk for a reason. Necromancers are seldom sane for long."

I glanced toward the house, half expecting the front door to fly open and Stella to come barreling down the walk to greet us. That all was quiet meant she hadn't spotted us yet. "Let me take a guess at your next theory. The illusions Mr. Mullaney's men saw at the parade were sent by the same person."

"Oh yes. The chances of two different people practicing that kind of filth in our city are very slim. I've no doubt the monsters and angels the union men reported were designed to start a panic and fuel the riot." She pursed her lips, thinking. "And the entire point of the riot was to flush Alina and her family out of hiding. Someone wants her very badly. They won't stop until they find her."

"Dora . . . could the Bolsheviks be looking for Alina?" The truth of that settled in my middle as soon as I'd said the words. "Gabe told you Mr. Mullaney's story last night. The watcher, the mirror ghost, they all point to Alina being more than the daughter of a minor Russian noble. That has to be why they hunt her so relentlessly."

Grief and regret moved through Dora's eyes before she hid them away again. She dropped her hat on the seat. "I've come to the same conclusion. That someone went to such great pains to protect Alina underlines her importance. She's less likely to let her identity slip if she can't remember her past life or her true name."

I knew Isadora Bobet well. Asking straight out was the best way to get an honest answer. "You know who she is, don't you? You've known since you first met her."

"No, Dee, not at first. I had my suspicions she might be one of Sunny's daughters, but I wasn't sure. The last time I saw her girls was twelve years ago, and they were very young, not grown women. For Alina to be here in San Francisco and hunted this way means the rest of the family must be dead." Dora brushed away a tear and cleared her throat. It was a small sign of grief, no doubt the only one she'd let show. "And if the family is all dead, that makes Alina very important indeed. She may be the only surviving heir to the throne. I wasn't ready to face that possibility earlier, but avoiding the truth is always foolish."

I touched her arm. "But now you're certain of her identity."

"As confident as I can be, yes. Once Alina was inside my house and under my protection, she began remembering small things. Most of her memories are fragments and disjointed images at this point, but that will change. Sam talked with her until well after midnight and drew more out of her than I'd expected. He was back early this morning to stay with her while I'm out." Dora sifted through her handbag, checking for her cigarettes before snapping the bag shut. "The wall around her memories is crumbling. I'm not at all sure that will turn out to be a kindness for her or for Sam. He's smitten with her already, and she's less than a half step behind in adoring him."

"That's not necessarily a bad thing, is it? Both of them are very alone, Dora."

"Sam's already risked his life for her twice." She frowned and threaded her arm through mine. "And most love-struck young women aren't hunted by necromancers and revolutionaries."

Dora looked both ways down the deserted street. Not a car nor a horse-drawn wagon was in sight, but Isadora hurried us across as if trying to navigate Market Street at high noon. "I just wish there wasn't this predestined aura around the two of them. Every sign points to the fact that Alina and Sam were meant to find each other again and they've picked up their past life. Her parents had that same air of fate about them."

"That turned out well enough." I watched her reaction, trying to discover what troubled her so much. "From the little you've said, I got the impression Sunny and her husband adored each other."

"They did. Both refused to marry anyone else." She lifted a hand and let it fall, clearly annoyed. "Predestination always makes me nervous. Especially so given the dangers and complications swirling around Alina. I'm very fond of Sam. I'd rather he didn't end up badly hurt or worse."

The finality and bitterness in her voice had surprised me. I stopped on the curb and held to her arm, more than a little angry and determined to force Dora to face me. "There must be something we can do to keep that from happening. You make this sound as if the two of them were doomed characters in a fairy tale."

"Most fairy tales end quite badly, as I recall. The original tales are quite gruesome." At first she looked me in the eye, calm and unmovable, but that didn't last. She knew from experience I wouldn't back down. Dora rolled her eyes and tugged me toward the front walk. "You might be the most stubborn person I've ever met, Delia Ryan, more so than your husband. Patterns of joined lifetimes are extremely difficult to break."

"But not impossible."

Her smile was reluctantly given, but real for all of that. "No, Dee, not impossible. Just don't get your hopes raised. Once we've spoken with Sadie, we can begin tracking this necromancer to his lair. Dealing with him is our first priority."

We got as far as the top step before the front door opened. Stella slipped out and trotted across the porch to Dora, unusually quiet and subdued. Dora scooped her up and hugged her tight. "Hello, poppet. How are you?"

She buried her face in Dora's shoulder. "I'm being quiet while Papa's sleeping. Mama said to be careful not to wake him. And I am careful, Aunt Dora, honest I am."

"Of course you are. Delia and I will be quiet too." Dora smoothed a hand across Stella's curls and frowned. I couldn't sense emotion to the same degree as Isadora, but even I knew that Stella was upset. Streaks of navy and gray muddied her normally sea blue aura. "Where is your mother?"

"In the backyard with Connor. He's too young to be quiet." Stella relaxed against Dora, her aura growing clear and bright again. I'd no doubt Isadora had something to do with that, protecting Stella from emotion in much the way I'd protected Connor from ghosts. She was only three and a half, but all the fear and strain on the adults in her life were bound to have an effect.

"Dee and I need to talk with your mother. I'm afraid it's more boring grown-up talk and I need you to wait inside with Annie." Dora hugged Stella and set her down. "After we finish talking with your mama, we'll ask Annie for some cookies. Would you like that?"

"I'd like cookies, but Annie's cross with me." Stella peered at Dora. "Would you ask her?"

The truth was that Annie was often cross these days and short of patience, even with Stella. We'd almost lost her to the Spanish flu the year before, a brush with death that she hadn't fully recovered from. Her good humor had drained away with her strength.

I wasn't sure Sadie and I had recovered either. Annie's illness was a reminder that far too soon she'd be gone. Neither of us was ready for that. Annie had been a constant in our lives since we were little girls, and we were as close to her as we'd been to our mothers. Watching her grow frail, fading a bit more day by day, was difficult.

Poor Stella was too young to understand, but not too young to have her feelings hurt. I traded looks with Dora. That I felt the need to make excuses for Annie said much. "Annie isn't really angry with you, sweetheart. She's worried about your father and still very tired from when she was sick. That makes her sound angry when she's really not."

She watched me, big eyed and wanting to believe, and twisted her curls around a chubby finger. "Are you sure?"

"I'm sure. I lived in this house with Annie and your mama for a very long time." I opened the front door. "Go back inside now. Everything will be all right, promise."

Each step was reluctantly taken, but Stella went into the house. I shut the door again and followed Dora back down the front steps. We rounded the corner of the house and into the backyard. Sadie sat in a whitewashed wooden lawn chair with Connor nestled in her lap, the perfect image of motherhood and contentment. Shade dappled her face, alternating modes of light and shadow shifting with the breeze. She looked up and smiled as we entered the yard, but continued to point out animals in an open picture book, waiting after each one for Connor to repeat the name. That all the names Connor said sounded like "cat" or "bird," or even "train," didn't bother either of them.

Guilt welled up again, but I dragged two chairs close so that Dora and I sat on either side.

Dora put a hand on Sadie's arm. "We need to talk, Sadie. I wanted Jack to hear this too, but I can fill him in once he's recovered. The best way to do this is to come right out and say it."

Sadie looked between me and Dora, and her smile dimmed. We must have appeared especially grim and dour. "What's wrong? Did something happen to Sam or Gabe?"

Connor squirmed out of his mother's lap and came to me, arms outstretched. I picked him up, extending my protections around him without thinking. That I held Sadie and Jack's son close, protecting him as if he were my own child, gave me pause.

"Nothing so drastic or dire." Dora took Sadie's hand and smiled. "But it has to do with Connor, and we didn't think letting it go any longer was wise. For some time now, Dee and I have seen hints that Connor might have the ability to see ghosts much the way Esther did. He wasn't in any danger, you have my word on that, but we didn't want to say anything until we knew for sure. We're sure now, Sadie. He's a fairly strong sensitive."

Sadie sat expressionless as Dora and I took turns explaining. Once or twice, she nodded, and tears filled her eyes when I spoke about ghosts seeking Connor out during the riot, but she didn't say anything. Sadie was a rock, stronger in many ways than I'd ever be, and never shy about voicing her thoughts or questioning what she didn't understand. Silence was new. I didn't know what that meant.

We finished and Sadie left her chair, pacing a few feet away to stare into the flowerbed. Fat black and yellow striped bumblebees moved between the blossoms of white and crimson poppies, primrose and strings of bleeding hearts, their hind legs growing heavy with pollen. Sadie seemed quite taken with watching the bees, but I knew that wasn't the case.

She covered her face with her hands, just for an instant, and I went to her. Hugging her was awkward with Connor on my hip, but I managed. Sadie hugged me back, a huge relief. "Connor will be fine, I promise. Dora and I won't let anything happen to him."

"You're sure about this, Dee?" Sadie's voice was barely above a whisper. She stepped back and wiped a hand over her eyes. "No mistake?"

"I'm very sure. No mistake." I searched her face, looking for anything that said our friendship was broken beyond repair. "I know I waited too long to say something, and I'm so very sorry, but I kept hoping he'd grow out of it. And there was always the possibility that I was wrong."

"I believe you, Dee. At least now I know." She held out her arms and Connor went to her, his smile every bit the match of his mother's best. Sadie came back to her chair and perched on the edge of the seat, bouncing her son on her knees. "I survived reasonably well with you seeing ghosts all these years. I'll learn to cope with Connor seeing things I can't. And at least ghosts are something Jack and I understand. The way Connor cries when we go out . . . I'd pictured something more sinister."

Dora gave her an amused look. "For a two-year-old, ghosts are sinister enough. Things will be easier once he's a bit older and understands what's happening. Are you up to telling Jack or would you like me to explain?"

A swallowtail butterfly dipped and swooped across the yard, a slow dance of bright wings Connor couldn't resist. He slipped off his mother's lap to the ground and gave chase.

Sadie sat back in her chair, arms folded across her chest. "Telling Jack will be simple enough. He swears that when Stella was first born, he heard Mama singing to her in the nursery. That would be just like Mama, so perhaps he did." She watched her son run across the yard, giggling and rosy cheeked. "To be honest, Annie's the one I'm worried about telling, and I'm wondering if I should say anything at all. You know how she's gotten the last few months, Dee. I hate to place blame on the new pastor at her church, but that's where it lies."

Annie's new pastor had visited the house several times at the height of her illness, praying and asking God to heal her if her heart was pure. We soon discovered that Pastor Grant spent a great deal of each Sunday sermon preaching against spiritualists and mediums. The pastor saw people like me and Dora as demon cursed, working to lure innocents and the unwary into sin. As a result, Annie had grown cool toward Isadora, placing the blame for my abilities squarely on Dora's shoulders.

My attempts to convince Annie of the truth had failed, ending in a bitter argument. I'd avoided the subject ever since.

"I'd thought of that too." Connor flopped down at Dora's feet, picking dandelions and blowing seeds into the wind. I squeezed Sadie's hand, remembering Stella reciting Annie's words. "We'll talk about it later. There's no need to tell her right away."

Springs on the back screen door squealed, bringing Dora's head up. I turned, expecting to see Annie, and saw Gabe instead.

How much he'd overdone things during the course of the morning showed. Gabe walked stiff and bent as someone twice his age, one hand pressed tight to his ribs. I rushed to meet him.

Gabe smiled as I slipped an arm around his waist. "I was hoping I hadn't missed you and Dora." He looked across the yard and lowered his voice. "How did breaking the news to Sadie go?"

"I'd say all in all, Sadie handled the news better than I did. She plans to tell Jack herself, so not a word. The same goes for Annie, but for entirely different reasons." He was sweating, shaking with exertion. Crossing Sadie's backyard was a major undertaking for him, and that worried me. "What have you been doing, Gabe Ryan? You weren't in this much pain this morning."

"Leading a murder investigation." Gabe eased down into the chair I'd vacated. "I needed to talk to you and Dora before going back to the office."

"Come along, Connor. I don't think either of us wants to hear this. Time for us to see if Papa's awake." Sadie scooped her son up, nuzzling his neck and making him giggle. "You can visit with Uncle Gabe later."

She carried a laughing Connor inside, leaving the three of us to speak freely.

"A brand-new case lands in your lap, and the first thing you do is come looking for us? That's never a good sign." Dora had found her cigarettes once the screen shut behind Sadie. She took a long, slow drag and blew smoke into the tree overhead. Blue swirls caught on leaves only half unfurled, thinned and blew away. "I must confess to dying of curiosity. Are you ever assigned normal murder cases, Captain Ryan?"

"Occasionally, Miss Bobet." Gabe frowned and fiddled with the brim of his fedora, a tactic to avoid looking at Dora. He was blushing furiously, an odd enough thing in itself. Very little embarrassed my husband. "But not this time. The man who died was a wealthy Russian refugee. Mr. Rigaux was killed in a high-priced brothel, one that caters only to very rich and very powerful men. If a man has enough money, the proprietor is willing to honor—special requests."

Dora crushed her cigarette underfoot, eyeing Gabe. "I assume that's relevant."

"I know it's not a decent subject to discuss in mixed company and I don't enjoy talking about this, especially in front of my wife." Gabe cleared his throat. "But it's important for you to know and it is relevant. The young lady he'd hired for the night was one he visited frequently. He was with Trula May often enough that anyone looking for Rigaux wouldn't have a difficult time finding him. And Trula May witnessed the murder—after a fashion."

Gabe told us Trula May's story and left nothing out, his face an amazing shade of red the entire time. Dora's expression went from interested to incredulous at hearing what the dead man, Mr. Rigaux, had been doing when he died, but she let Gabe speak uninterrupted. I listened just as intently. That he was more embarrassed than either Dora or I would have been endearing if the subject matter weren't so grim.

Knowing Dora for the last four years had stripped away most of my innocence. Working on murder cases with her and my husband had taken care of the rest, but I could still be shocked at the cruelty in the world. What turned my stomach was the killer making Trula May listen to Mr. Rigaux die and then leaving her to lie next to his body until morning. How he'd died added another layer of horror.

Death magic was something I'd only read about, dark and repellent in the extreme. My one brush with a practitioner of blood rituals two years before had only reinforced my aversion. I'd learned about this horrific thing as I'd learned all Isadora wanted to teach me, so that I'd be prepared if I ever stumbled across the unimaginable. Now I had, and all the knowledge I'd gained didn't lessen how sick and angry I felt. What Gabe described was unbelievably cruel and violent.

I glanced at Dora and found her watching me, confirming we'd both come to the same conclusion. Our mysterious necromancer had killed Mr. Rigaux, but he hadn't used conjured monsters or hired gunmen on a roof. He'd strangled Mr. Rigaux with his own hands. The implications of that were the most terrifying of all.

Dora sat back once he'd finished speaking, fingers drumming rapidly on the lawn chair's arm. "Dear Lord, Gabe. You made the right call about those chants being incantations, but I'd have to know what was said to guess the purpose. Given what Trula said about it sounding like prayers sung during Mass, they may well have been speaking Latin. Old languages command a great deal of power. That would fit with what I know about European necromancers."

"I won't bother to ask if you're serious. This just gets worse." He rubbed his eyes, looking even more tired. "How likely is it that this . . . this necromancer will leave San Francisco without killing again?"

"This man isn't going anywhere, Gabe, and the chances of him not killing again are miniscule. The fact that Mr. Rigaux was

Russian only reinforces that belief. We're dealing with a fanatic who hasn't accomplished what he set out to do. What we need to focus on is finding him and doing what we can to minimize the loss of life. Unfortunately, we can't send every Russian refugee in the city into hiding." Dora lit another cigarette, but after the first puff, she let it dangle between her fingers. "Getting that poor woman, Trula May, out of the city was the right thing to do. Even that might not save her, but it should at least make finding her more difficult and buy some time. That they left her alive in the first place bothers me a great deal."

"Letting her live didn't make any sense to me either. Even if she couldn't see what happened, she heard everything and was able to give me a detailed account. But maybe that was the point." Gabe fiddled with the crown of his hat, rubbing at a worn spot and pinching the creases tighter. He was thinking, trying to fit together what he knew. "I don't believe for a second those men decided to show Trula May mercy or compassion. They left her alive for a reason."

Dora beamed at him. "Very good, Gabe. My best guess is they wanted word of what they'd done to spread in the community. Fear is a powerful weapon and can make people careless. You said this Mr. Rigaux's wife was some sort of Russian nobility with an estate on the Black Sea?"

"That's what Maggie told us." Gabe reached for my hand. "I told you about Maggie DeVere. This happened at her place."

"You did tell me." I squeezed his fingers and met Dora's curious stare. "Don't let his proper exterior fool you. Gabe has a quite colorful past and equally colorful acquaintances. Some of them pop up unexpectedly from time to time."

"I see." She smiled, quietly amused despite the topic of discussion. "We should assume Mrs. Rigaux is a target herself and may well be dead already. Regardless, we need to establish her location as soon as possible. Hopefully we can get to her ahead of the Bolshevik's hunters."

Gabe's grip on my hand tightened. "Then the rumors Mullaney heard were true, at least up to a point. The Bolsheviks are killing people with ties to the throne. I've got a hunch these people are after Alina too."

"I agree. And I think you should have another private talk with Mr. Mullaney. Quietly spreading the truth of what's happened among the Russian members of his union might be wise. Doing so before the rumors and half truths get out of hand would be best. Have him warn his people not to panic, but to be wary and on the lookout for strangers."

The kindest word I could think of for Gabe's expression was "skeptical." "Those men are waiters and kitchen workers. Do you really think they're in danger of assassination?"

The drumbeat of Dora's fingers on the chair arm grew faster. "You're making assumptions based on their jobs, Gabe. Don't underestimate how many counts and minor princes are waiting tables at the Fairmont. They're all in danger if they stay in the city. Ideally, we can flush this necromancer out of hiding soon. Once we have him in hand, the threat diminishes."

I perched on the arm of Gabe's chair, still holding his hand. "But the danger doesn't disappear."

Dora picked lint off her jacket, focusing on tiny specks I couldn't see, or that might not exist. She was stalling for time in order to think before answering. "Not for Alina. If this man fails, they'll send another. They won't stop looking for her until they believe she's dead."

Gabe looked between us, his expression closed off and careful. "Is Alina that important to the Bolsheviks?"

I watched Dora's face, knowing she struggled with how to answer, with how much to reveal and if speaking aloud would make her words unchangeable truth. Anyone who knew Alina's true identity, or sought to protect her, was at great risk. Dora and I were aware of the danger, but putting Gabe or anyone else under that same threat wasn't a step she'd take lightly. He willingly took on the dangers of his job each day, but this was different.

Until Isadora spoke, I wasn't sure what she'd say.

"She is that important." Dora sat up straighter in the chair, her face composed and regal, and looked Gabe in the eye. "If the Bolsheviks' revolution had failed, Alina would be one of the heirs to the Russian throne. Since her presence here leaves little doubt that the Bolsheviks achieved their aim of destroying the tsar—there are those who would put Alina forth as empress."

Gabe tipped his head to the side, studying Dora's face. Finally he nodded. "Then we need to convince the people after her that she's dead. Between the three of us, we should be able to think of something."

"We can't leave Sam out of this." I draped my arm around Gabe's shoulder. "He has a rather large stake in Alina's well-being."

Dora's lips twitched, but she didn't allow herself to smile. Her fingers drummed on the chair arm again, an uneven stop-and-go beat. "You're right. Sam belongs in our conspiracy, but telling him now wouldn't be wise. Alina needs to regain all her memories first. Whether she stands and fights or quietly disappears is her decision. No one can make it for her."

The springs on the back screen screeched again. Sadie stood holding the door half-open and called across the yard. "Jack wants to see Gabe before he leaves and insisted I come down and tell you. We both know he won't rest easy until you update him on the case."

I helped Gabe stand, making sure he was steady before we started off. "Gabe and I were just coming inside. You can tell Jack we'll be right up."

"You and Gabe go on, Dee." Dora opened her bag, pulling out

her cigarettes and matches. "I have a great deal to think about. Besides, I wouldn't want to antagonize Annie."

The princess ghost sat in a window as we reached the porch, her gaze serene and unruffled. I held the door open for Gabe, staring at the ghost as he went ahead of me. Faceless memories still frosted the glass around her, their number seemingly unchanged. The princess still held Alina's memories tight. I wondered if she was able to let them go.

Falling into the watcher's eyes was a gentler sensation this time and short lived, but no less overwhelming. Release was sudden and jarring, but I finally understood some of what the watcher wanted from me and why this ghost had sought me out. I stumbled into the house after Gabe, shaken and worried that I wasn't strong enough to relive Alina's memories.

Her guardian wasn't giving me a choice.

CHAPTER 11

Gabe

Gabe shifted in his desk chair, relieved that something so simple as easing the tension in his shoulders didn't hurt. A little over a week had passed since he'd cracked his ribs, a week of moving carefully and slowly, gauging how much he could do by how biting and immediate the pain was. He'd been able to work the case with Sam, Randy, and Marshall's help, even hampered and half-hunched over like an older man. Still, he wished there were a way to mend his ribs faster.

The bruises couldn't heal fast enough to satisfy him either. Delia had helped him get his shirt on each morning and undress at night, her breath catching at the sight of the darkening patches mottling his back and sides. He hated the mix of remembered fear and relief in her eyes each time she saw the marks. Dee didn't need the constant reminders of how close he'd come to dying. Neither did he.

Gabe finished the duty roster for the six officers guarding Libby's settlement house, rotating the men outside. He'd gone to the chief and called in a favor to have three of the women officers from the downtown precinct placed inside. The SFPD had hired its first women in 1913, but he'd never had any of those officers assigned to his squad room.

Adding three more women to the already busy house hadn't attracted any attention. Officer Martha Moulton was in charge, a tall, broad-shouldered woman who reminded him of his great-aunt Hazel, and was just as no nonsense. She'd been on the force since 1914, with a wide range of assignments. Everything had been quiet since Alina left to stay with Dora, but he wasn't taking any risks. He trusted Martha Moulton to get Libby and the children out of the house at the first sign of danger.

Knowing these killers were still out there made his skin itch with the need to find them. How unpredictable, how *random* the killings were made it all worse. There was no trail of evidence to follow, no pattern that would let him predict this necromancer's next move.

He didn't waste time trying to convince himself Alina was the only reason the Bolsheviks had come to his city. Once Gabe and Sam started digging, they found stories of men vanishing on their way to work, or women who never made it to the market. Landlords had reported entire families disappearing from their flats, leaving behind everything they owned. A half dozen bodies were found dumped in alleyways; bodies that were never claimed or identified.

All the disappearances happened in the two months before the riot. All the names they were able to find were Russian. Without bodies, he couldn't say if these people had run or if they were dead.

Eva Rigaux had run once they found her. She'd listened dry eyed as Gabe broke the news to her earlier that morning, asking very few questions other than how her husband was killed. Within an hour, she'd dismissed her servants, packed a valise, and left Nob Hill in the back of a squad car. Henderson had put her on a train in Oakland, bound for a small town in the Midwest. If she was as smart as Gabe thought, she'd change her name and disappear for good.

He glanced at his father's old clock hanging over the office door, automatically adding ten minutes to compensate for how slow the clock ran. Sam would be there soon and Jack with him. Today was his partner's first day back on the job since his release from the hospital. Sadie wasn't very happy about him returning to work so soon, but Jack's restlessness and his drive to solve this case finally convinced her. That Sam volunteered to chauffeur Jack to work this morning helped.

Striding down the hallway whistling or hobbling along leaning on a cane, Gabe would take Jack however he could have him. The week without his best friend and partner had stretched on too long. He still couldn't bear to think about how he'd cope if Jack never came through the door again.

Gabe had thought time and again about how to greet his partner, what to say, and how much help to offer. In the end, he decided he was worrying too much. Jack and Gabe had been best friends for going on fifteen years. A brush with death didn't change who they were or how they should act with each other. Asking Henderson to move the visitor's chair to the front of the desk was the only accommodation he'd made.

Right on time, Sam rapped on the door and swung it wide for Jack. Gabe wasn't prepared for the ache in his chest as Jack came through the door.

Jack's foot and ankle were wrapped tightly, bandages disappearing up into his trouser leg. Annie had cut down an old, worn leather shoe for him to wear over the wrappings. He shuffled slowly so the shoe wouldn't fall off and leaned heavily on a dark wood cane, fingers white with the effort of hanging on to the silver handle. A bandage hid the deep gouge in his forehead, but the bruises on his jaw and neck, the jagged scratches on his hands, were in plain view.

Gabe cleared his throat. Jack was back and he refused to think of how near they'd all come to losing him forever. "Good to see you, Lieutenant Fitzgerald. It's about time you got back to work."

"I thought so too. A life of leisure gets boring." Jack dropped into the visitor's chair, his collar soaked with sweat. He yanked off his cap and wiped his face on a sleeve. "Besides, every day I was gone was another day you got out of buying lunch, Captain Ryan. I figure you owe me at least a week's worth, maybe two."

"Don't push your luck, Jack. Sympathy goes only so far." He looked up to see Sam leaning against the file cabinet, twirling his new boater hat on two fingers and grinning at both of them. Gabe couldn't help grinning in return. "Thanks for driving him in, Sam."

"My pleasure. It gave me a chance to fill Jack in on what's been going on for the last week. He knows everything I'd already told you." Sam left his hat on the file cabinet and grabbed the second battered and dinged pine chair, dragging it over to the desk. He straddled the seat backwards, long legs stretched out and arms lying across the back. "I talked to some of the dockworkers about Nureyev last night. He's been in San Francisco since just before the war ended, but he doesn't have many friends. Other than the time he spends working on union business with Mullaney, he keeps to himself. He's not married or courting. No one can remember ever seeing him with a woman other than his housekeeper."

"He lost his wife and two daughters back in Russia. The only family he has left is a son. His boy must be about Connor's age, maybe a little younger. Mullaney told me about that." Gabe traced faint lines indented in his desk blotter with a fingertip. Something in what Sam had said bothered him, but he couldn't pin down exactly what. Or why. Sooner or later, it would come to him. "What else did they tell you?"

"Only one thing we didn't already know. About four months ago, he spent time in New York organizing a garment worker's union. He was gone only five, six weeks at the most. That all sounded pretty normal. It's what happened once he got back to town the union men thought was odd." Sam frowned, studying the toes of his shoes, thinking. He looked up at Gabe. "When Nureyev got back to San Francisco, he locked himself in his house for almost two weeks. Wouldn't see Mullaney or talk to anyone. Mullaney told all his men to leave Nureyev alone and not ask questions. Once Aleksei finally came back to the union offices, he pretended nothing had happened."

"That is strange. If I had to guess, I'd say he was hiding." Jack had a new notebook open on the desktop, scribbling notes. "I remember something in the *Examiner* about trouble over a union in New York last fall. Maybe we can find out if Nureyev was involved."

Sam shrugged. "It's worth asking. I got to know some people when I visited New York City, reporters mostly. I'll send a few telegrams and see if the name shakes loose any memories."

Aleksei Nureyev was smoke drifting on the wind, easy to see but impossible to grasp. Gabe was almost tempted to give up chasing after him or looking for anything unusual.

Almost. He couldn't shake the nagging whisper that they just hadn't found the right trail to follow. Gabe leaned back in his creaky swivel chair, rocking gently. "Send your telegrams, Sam. I'll contact the cops I know in New York and see if they've ever heard of Aleksei. Anything else?"

"I did find one other interesting piece of information. The dockworkers said I should take the time to talk to the waiters passing out handbills across the street from the Fairmont. Mullaney's trying to get a union into the hotel." Sam frowned. "I struck up a conversation with one of the men handing out leaflets. Vlad was kind of an odd duck, young and very nervous about talking to me once I mentioned Nureyev's name. But he said that if I really wanted to know about Aleksei Nureyev, I should go see the priest at Holy Trinity Cathedral. It's the Orthodox church on Green Street. He says that Aleksei and Father Pashkovsky came to America together."

Gabe rocked his chair forward and traded looks with Jack. "They sailed together from Europe?"

"From Siberia. Rumor has it that Aleksei paid off the captain of a fishing boat to take his party across the Bering Strait. The boat took them to a tiny Alaskan village called Wales." Sam rested his long hands on his knees and cocked his head to the side, watching Jack and Gabe's reaction. "This kid, Vlad, goes to church at Holy Trinity. He was sure that Father Pashkovsky and Nureyev grew up in the same city and the two of them were boyhood pals. Now, this is the really interesting part. Vlad made it sound like the priest and Nureyev were one step ahead of being shot all the way to Alaska."

"That sounds like another part of the story Mullaney told Gabe." Jack tapped his pencil on the edge of his notebook. The pencil was new, just like the notebook. "My guess is it's all true. Sadie told me about the conversation she and Dee overheard in the Palace. Mullaney said that Aleksei had spent too much time running from the Bolsheviks. It all ties together."

Sam shrugged. "Everything does tie together, but I'm not sure I trust that. The package is a little too neat."

"Whether the story is true or not, I want to make a trip over to Holy Trinity tomorrow. If Father Pashkovsky did grow up with Aleksei, I want to talk to him." He looked Jack in the eye, trusting his partner to give him an honest answer. Gabe was sure he already knew. "Is that too much for your second day back?"

Jack laughed. "Yesterday I'd have said no. That was before I walked across the squad room and down the corridor. Take Dodd or Butler with you. I'll start sending men out to question shop owners around Lotta's fountain and knock on doors. We might get lucky and someone saw those men going up to the roof. But the two of you need to promise never to tell Sadie I stayed here by choice. We argued for two days over my going back to work."

A knock on his office door cut short Gabe's reply. Sergeant Rockwell pushed the door open and stuck his head in. "Captain, there's someone here to see you." Lon glanced over his shoulder and hesitated. "He says you sent a telegram to his station commander in Chicago. He—he's come to claim his badge."

Gabe shuffled through the papers in the tray sitting on his desk, finally finding what he wanted near the bottom of the stack. He'd read the telegram from the station commander in Chicago, but he didn't remember the officer's name. "Lieutenant Lynch?"

Rockwell glanced into the hallway again and nodded. "That's the name he gave, Captain."

"Send him in, Lon." Gabe stood and buttoned his coat before coming around to the front of the desk near Jack. Sam vacated the spare chair, putting it to rights and going back to his place near the file cabinet. All of them were eager to hear the explanation of how a Chicago detective's badge ended up on a dead man in San Francisco.

Gabe understood Rockwell's hesitation as a tall, distinguished-looking Negro came through the door, ducking slightly to keep from hitting his head. Not all his men knew other police departments around the country had Negro officers on the force. Lon would have found it strange that Lynch claimed to be not only a cop, but also a lieutenant. San Francisco was still behind the times.

Lieutenant Lynch looked to be forty-five or a little more, broad shouldered and well muscled, with dark walnut skin. He stood six foot five if he was an inch. His brown suit was rumpled from travel, but Gabe guessed it was better quality than any he owned. The same could be said for the Chicago detective's fedora.

Liberal amounts of gray frosted Lynch's tightly curled black hair. He leaned heavily on a cane, favoring his left leg. Hazel eyes swept over everything in the office, lingering for a few seconds on Jack's injuries before coming to rest on Gabe's face.

Wariness sat in Lynch's eyes, his expression guarded. He wasn't sure of his welcome. That he'd traveled all the way to San Francisco anyway said a lot about him.

Gabe admired that kind of courage, and in his mind there wasn't any doubt about Lieutenant Lynch's welcome. He smiled and stepped forward, hand extended. "I'm Captain Gabe Ryan. How was the trip out from Chicago?"

"The train was comfortable enough." Lynch gripped his hand firmly, and a little anxiousness bled out of the way he held himself. "I don't usually travel this far, Captain, but I made an exception in this case. That badge belongs to me, and I wanted my shield back badly enough to come get it. My only regret is that the man who shot me in order to steal it is already dead. I was hoping to take care of that myself."

Gabe looked the older cop in the eye, weighing whether Lynch meant that or not, but let the remark pass. He finished the introductions. "This is my partner, Lieutenant Jack Fitzgerald, and Samuel Clemens Butler. Sam is a reporter for one of the local papers, but he's also a friend. He's been helping out while Jack was laid up."

Lynch shook hands with Sam and Jack in turn. "Pleased to make your acquaintance, gentlemen."

Jack tugged on the ends of his mustache, openly studying Lynch. "You seem pretty confident the man who shot you is the same man that was killed in the explosion."

"No offense, Lieutenant, but I'm damned certain. Not only did he have my badge, Amos Gary had my gun. He'd always been a petty thief, but Amos was moving up in the world. When I got too close to connecting him to a string of murders, he ambushed me. Stole my Colt and my badge, and left me to bleed to death in an alley." Lynch pointed at the spare chair with his cane. "Do you mind if I sit? I couldn't get a cab to stop and the train station is a long walk from here."

"I beg your pardon, Lieutenant. I should have offered you a seat right away. Please, be my guest." Gabe went back to his own chair. He removed a small pasteboard box holding Lynch's badge from his top drawer, staring at the bent and scratched shield before sliding it across the desktop. If Gabe had any doubts about why Lynch had come, the possessive way the lieutenant wrapped his hand around the badge settled them. "Do you have any idea why Amos Gary came to San Francisco?"

"Someone hired him. I read about what happened here in the papers and how Amos got himself killed. He wasn't smart enough to plan that riot or get those men on the roof before the parade started. Amos was hired to make sure the men on the roof didn't live long enough to get arrested. He was good at following orders." Lynch's smile was bitter, cold. "Shooting me wasn't his idea either."

Jack had begun scribbling notes early on. He glanced at Gabe. "It might help all of us if you tell the story from the beginning. Amos might be dead, but if other people are behind what happened here, we stand a chance of catching them."

"Chicago's a bigger town than San Francisco. The city's rougher too, especially since the war ended." Lynch rubbed his thumb over the surface of his badge, as if making sure it was real. He cleared his throat and tucked the badge into an inside pocket. "It's fair to say there are twice as many people living in some of the neighborhoods."

Sam moved closer to the desk. "Refugees."

"The city fathers don't call them that, but you're exactly right, Mr. Butler. When someone started murdering refugees nine or ten months ago, no one in city hall paid much attention. No one but me and my squad." Lynch rested his hands on the top of his cane. "It's harder to ignore murder when the bodies are on your doorstep.

Even with all the new faces in my precinct, it didn't take long for me to figure out all the murder victims were from the Russian neighborhood."

Gabe's heart sped up, but he'd had too much experience to let that show. "How were they killed?"

"Every way you can think of, Captain Ryan. We found people shot in their beds, and others who were strangled and stabbed. One man was thrown off the roof of a building." Lynch looked him in the eye. He was a seasoned cop, but Lieutenant Lynch didn't try to hide his anger. "The worst was when the boiler in a tenement house blew up. Killed everyone on the first two floors, seventeen people including two little babies. I might have thought that one was an accident, but the gas to the building had been turned off for a month. Someone had rigged up a dynamite charge."

Sam cleared his throat, getting Gabe's attention. He nodded for Sam to go on. "The men on the parade route used dynamite. How long ago was the explosion in the tenement house?"

"That was a damn fine question." The Chicago cop smiled, tipping his head to look up at Sam. "You sure you're not a detective, Mr. Butler?"

"Gabe's taught me a lot the last week or so. But being a reporter taught me to recognize when someone is trying to avoid answering uncomfortable questions." Sam stuck his hands into his trouser pockets and smiled. "I'd appreciate an answer to mine, Lieutenant."

The telegram Gabe had received from the Chicago commander had said Lieutenant S. Jordan Lynch was a twenty-year veteran, a man who'd risen through the ranks to command his own squad. His record wasn't spotless according to his superior officer, but Gabe's wasn't either. Lynch was a good cop, but he wasn't a suspect or a witness to any of the crimes in Gabe's files. They couldn't force him to answer Sam's question or any of the others Gabe wanted to ask.

All he could do was hope he'd read the other cop right. Gabe stopped worrying when Lynch chuckled. "You're right, Mr. Butler. Not answering is a bad habit I picked up in Chicago. The only time a Negro policeman gets asked questions about one of his cases is if the white man asking means to take credit for himself."

"I can't take credit for anything involving this case, not even a byline." Sam shrugged. "I promised Gabe I'd hold the story indefinitely. Call it a personal favor. And I'm not a cop."

Gabe stood and moved around the desk next to Sam. "Anything you say stays in this room, Lieutenant. You've my word on that. None of us are interested in credit for solving this case. All we want is to catch these men and keep any more people from dying."

"I was still in the hospital when the boiler exploded. That was close to two months ago now." Lynch looked pointedly at Jack's injured leg and back to Gabe. "My partner brought me reports twice a day. I still got back on the street sooner than the doctor or my daughter wanted."

Henderson knocked, but didn't wait for the glass in the office door to stop rattling before he shoved it open. "Captain, I just got a call. They found—" He stopped speaking at the sight of Lynch. Marshall was too well trained to go on without Gabe's okay.

He nodded toward Lynch. "Marshall, this is Lieutenant Lynch from Chicago. What did you need to tell me?"

Officer Henderson stared for a few seconds before he nodded. "Pleased to meet you, sir. Captain Ryan, Mrs. Rigaux didn't stay on the train. A cleaning woman found her body a little over an hour ago."

Gabe seldom found himself too surprised by the turn a case

took to speak, but this was one of those times. He stared at Henderson's face, noting the young officer was pale, his green eyes too bright and mildly panicked. Henderson had put Eve Rigaux on the train, thought her safely out of reach of the people who'd killed her husband.

So had Gabe. He wiped a hand over his mouth. "Where was the body found?"

"Holy Trinity Church over on Green." Henderson stared at Gabe, looking awfully young and more than a little frightened. "I put Mrs. Rigaux on the train, Captain. She was still on that train when it pulled away."

"Christ Almighty." Jack gestured at his open notebook. "That's the same church Sam just told us about."

"The killer's sending a message, Jack. I only wish I knew who it was for." Gabe clapped Henderson on the shoulder. "Have Taylor or Baker bring a car around. Then go home. I'm sure your wife would like to see you."

Lieutenant Lynch watched, but didn't say anything until Henderson left. "You coddle your men all the time, Captain Ryan?"

Gabe didn't know Lynch well enough to know if the Chicago cop was amused or not. He decided to answer honestly.

"I encourage them not to follow my bad example. Marshall's already been on duty ten hours." He unlocked his desk drawer and lifted out his shoulder holster. The weight of the gun against his side was always foreboding and ominous, never reassuring. That he found himself wearing it more and more often reinforced the feeling. He buckled the straps in place and slipped his jacket back on. "Sam, you've got the duty roster for Dora's house memorized. Who's staying with Alina right now?"

"Finlay and Maxwell. Dora should still be with Delia." Sam retrieved his hat from the top of the file cabinet. "If Jack's okay here alone, I'm going to head back over to the house. Not that anyone is likely to find Alina there or get past your men, but I'll feel better. I get antsy when neither Dora or I are with her."

Gabe wasn't sure he wanted to believe in Isadora's claim that Sam and Alina were fated to be together. He'd learned to accept most of what Dora said was true, but predestination was too close to losing control over your own life or your own decisions. The idea of being little more than a puppet made his skin crawl.

But the fact that Butler was completely smitten with Alina was obvious to everyone who knew him. And in the end, why he'd fallen for her so quickly probably didn't matter. What was important was making sure the two of them got a chance at having a life together. Finding the men after Alina was the only way to ensure that would happen.

"Don't worry about me. I've got a squad room full of cops if I need anything." Jack waved him toward the door. "Go."

Sam nodded to all of them and hurried away.

Lynch sat quietly through this exchange, lips pressed tight together, thinking. If S. Jordan Lynch was like most detectives Gabe knew, he was thinking about his own cases and wondering if there were similarities between the murders.

Gabe wondered too. He spoke before he had time for second thoughts. "Care to come with me, Lieutenant Lynch? I'd welcome the company."

Lynch looked up, startled. "You want me to go along to your murder scene?"

"Why not? You're an experienced cop." Gabe stuffed his hands into his trouser pockets and shrugged. "I could use a second set of eyes on this one."

"I can't promise to keep quiet. You should know that in advance." Lynch glanced at Jack and back to Gabe. "But I'd like to see how detectives work in San Francisco."

"Then let's go. I can fill you in on our cases on the way over."

Gabe grabbed his fedora and swung the door open. "Rockwell will bring you lunch later, Jack. My treat. Just don't get crumbs all over my desk."

Jack grinned and limped over to sit in Gabe's chair. "Make sure he brings me all the files too. I need something to do between now and lunch."

He let Lynch set the pace through the hallways and across the station lobby. The Chicago cop pretended not to notice the whispers and stares from the officers they passed, or the hostile looks from the civilians waiting their turn on oak benches, but that didn't fool Gabe. Lynch saw.

Lynch waited until the police car pulled away from the curb before he spoke. "If you don't mind my asking, I'd like to know how Lieutenant Fitzgerald got hurt. Was it during the riot I read about?"

"Jack got caught in one of the explosions. A building fell on him and some other officers." Gabe's throat threatened to close up before he got the rest of the words out. "The other men didn't make it."

"Losing men under your command is a hard thing for anyone to go through." Lynch looked out the window, his expression softer and far away. "I've lost a few over the years, and it never gets easier. I'm glad your partner made it out, Captain Ryan."

"Call me Gabe." He held his hand out, unsure if Lynch would take it this time. "We're going to work together while you're in town, and I don't see the need to be formal."

"Are you sure that's wise, Captain?" Lynch shifted his cane so it lay across his lap, gripping it tight. "Some of your men might take issue with me being too familiar and not showing proper respect. I wouldn't want to cause trouble for you."

Gabe had talked to Annie often enough about the small town where she'd grown up to understand Lynch's apprehension. San

Francisco wasn't perfect, even in 1919, but Annie could walk on the sidewalks without being spit on for refusing to walk in the gutter. "You won't cause me any trouble, Lieutenant. You've my word on that."

The hesitation was slight and Gabe might have missed it if he hadn't been watching, but Lynch shook his hand and smiled. "All right, I'll call you Gabe, but not when we're in public. Call me Jordan. Only my wife called me Scott, God rest her soul, and that happened only when she was mad enough to start yelling."

Gabe couldn't help but smile. "Was she mad at you often?"

"Often enough." Jordan's expression was more bemused than sad. "She's been gone five years, and not a day goes by that I don't miss her yelling at me. Now, tell me about your case, Gabe. Start with explaining why you've got men guarding that girl Mr. Butler rushed off to be with."

Gabe told him everything, from the start of the riot to the monsters Mullaney's men saw reaching for them to finding Rigaux's body in Trula May's bed and how the killers left her alive. Lynch was a good listener.

But most detectives were.

CHAPTER 12

Delia

The crystals inside the stone bowl sitting on my kitchen table pulsed purple, lavender, and violet. Dora dropped a folded and inscribed piece of parchment into the bowl, all the while quietly reciting charms and sketching warding glyphs on air. I'd little hope she could block the watcher's meddling with my dreams, but she insisted on making the attempt.

This was the third time we'd gone through this ritual, and the third time the parchment promptly caught fire. The words Isadora had painstakingly written charred black, and the spell packet crumbled to ash. Ginger-scented smoke rose toward the ceiling in lazy spirals.

Dora yanked her hand back from the flames, but not fast enough. "Damn it! I burned myself." She peered at the burnt fingertips and touched them gently. "Dee, would you be a dear and either fetch some cold water or some whiskey? I'd much rather have the whiskey, but dipping my fingers in water will do in a pinch. These may blister otherwise."

Some of Gabe's whiskey went into a glass, and I poured water from the icebox pitcher into a small dish. Dora plunged her fingers into the water before sipping the whiskey. She frowned at the bits of ash drifting up out of the stone bowl. "This guardian is becoming much more of a nuisance than I'd anticipated. Writing out several new spell combinations last night was a wise precaution. We'll try switching out rosemary for the ginger this time. Give me a minute to regroup and I'll try again."

"There's no need, Dora. We both know perfectly well it's not going to work." I sipped my tea, making a sour face over how cold it had grown. "The reaction is more violent each time, and I won't risk you being seriously hurt. I'm ready to admit defeat."

"Well, I'm not. I will admit this would be much easier if I'd gotten answers to my telegrams. I could come up with a solution if I knew what we were facing and wasn't reduced to taking shots in the dark." Dora slumped back in the chair, wiping water from her fingers onto a small towel. I'd always thought Sadie and Gabe stubborn and obstinate to the extreme, but Isadora made the both of them appear reasonable. "For the life of me, I don't understand why this guardian decided to pass Alina's memories on to you and not to *her*. None of it makes any sense, Dee, especially since you can't talk about these dreams in front of Alina. The mechanisms and the logic behind this elude me."

I'd tried to tell Alina about the dreams, hoping to shake loose memories of an event, a place, or the names of her family. Any attempt to speak with her—or with Gabe and Isadora, for that matter—ended with me retching and too dizzy to stand. Like Dora, I didn't understand what the watcher hoped to accomplish.

Being the unwilling vessel for Alina's past both exhausted me and made me angry. Each night brought a new dream, more pieces of a story that filled me with dread and a deepening sense of doom. I still wasn't convinced I'd be strong enough to bear the full burden of knowing how her had family died. Knowing at least a little of how the story must end, with Alina alone and hunted in a foreign land, made it all worse.

One thing was certain. Alina was the fourth sister, the young woman whose life I lived in dreams and whose face I never saw. Dora knew her true name, but refused to tell me just yet. Speaking true names can leave wakes and eddies in the spirit world—an easy trail for the necromancer to follow.

"You're assuming some kind of logic exists. Or at least one we can comprehend." I carried my teacup to the sink, rinsing away the residue of sodden black leaves, sugar and lemon, and leaving the delicate porcelain cup upended on the drain board. "You said yourself the watcher was an old-world creature, eons older than any spirit in North America. This may make perfect sense elsewhere. We just don't understand the rules."

"I wish I was as clear that there are rules here." Dora dubiously eyed the crystals in the bowl. The bright, vivid pulsing had died to a faint glimmer. "Making you suffer seems rather capricious. And if the entire point of shutting Alina's memories away in the mirror ghost was to protect her identity, that strategy appears to be a dismal failure. Her enemies are still looking for her. Nothing has changed as far as I can see."

Mai sauntered into the kitchen, ears twitching as if straining to hear some faint sound. She leapt up onto the tabletop, ignoring Dora, and giving the bowl full of crystals a wide berth as she made her way to the windowsill. I'd seen the cat crouch on the sill frequently over the last few days, her position allowing her to keep an eye on both the kitchen and the yard outside. Mai's tail thumped an angry rhythm against the wall beneath the window, her eyes narrow slits.

I couldn't say what my fierce gray cat saw or heard, but she was decidedly unhappy. Given our previous encounter with the necromancer, I took Mai's edginess seriously.

"You're thinking about this the wrong way, Dora. A great deal has changed, and Alina has far more people looking after her welfare." I sat at the table again, choosing a seat near enough to the window I could pet the cat. Mai relaxed a bit under my hand, but never lost her keen watchfulness. "Whether it's for the first time or the hundredth, Sam and Alina have found each other. He's already proved he'd do anything necessary to protect her. We both know Gabe and Randy will as well. You're acting as her guardian in place of the older couple that was killed, and I'm doing what I can to decipher the watcher's riddles. Matters are decidedly different than they were the morning of the parade."

"I wouldn't have phrased it that way, but maybe you're right. The situation and the people involved have changed considerably." She stared out the window, her eyes seeming to follow the male blue jay carrying sticks and bits of string into a cloud of peach blossoms. Within a few seconds, his mate darted away to take her turn. But Dora wasn't watching the pair of jays build a nest in the peach tree any more than Mai was. "I should have taken those changes into account without need of your prodding, but I never factored Alina's new protectors into the balance. I'm not usually so self-absorbed that anything that important would slip past. Someone, or something, didn't want me to see."

"Alina's guardian." That this creature might be powerful enough to influence Dora without her knowing was more than a little frightening. "But why?"

"For the same inscrutable reasons this creature is forcing memories on you." Dora sat back hard, arms folded. Her scowl erased my last doubt about her state of mind. "If not for my loyalty toward you and Alina, I'd be tempted to walk away and let this watcher of yours sort things itself. This creature best keep that in mind."

Prudence kept me from mentioning the watcher filling my head, or how amusement danced through its eyes. "At least the balance appears to have shifted somewhat in Alina's favor. You and I, Gabe and Sam and Randy—taken all together we're much better able to deal with her enemies than Mina and Fyodor. Maybe that was the guardian's plan all along."

"That's very likely, Dee. People who have the ability to eliminate an enemy are always useful allies. Frankly, I'm not keen on the idea of a powerful spirit viewing any of us as potential assassins." Dora sat up straighter and folded her hands on the tabletop. "I'd rather avoid violence of any kind. The sticky part comes when the other side leaves you no choice."

A small image of the princess ghost brightened into view at the top of the window. I tried to imagine Alina dressed in the same fashion as the ghost, a strand of pearls around her throat. The resemblance between them was stronger now, aided by knowing they were sisters. Or maybe I was finally able to see and more willing to believe what had been there all along.

Alina had loved her family. I didn't know which was sadder, that they were all dead, or that she didn't remember what she'd lost. But I remembered. Each dream, each moment of reliving Alina's captivity and how she's longed for her family was stark and real. That had to mean something.

The watcher's eyes swallowed me again, plunging me into depths bottomless as the night sky. I held tight to the edge of the kitchen table and fought not to panic under the dragon's regard. That I was utterly convinced the creature holding me in thrall was a dragon, the kin of Gods and myths far outside of San Francisco, was reason enough to panic in and of itself. Dragons had faded from the world centuries before I was born. Even the stories told about them had begun to disappear.

But this dragon existed, here and now. She was already ancient when the New World had been settled, her essence rooted deep in the Russian land and pulsing through every river and stream.

Stories were still told about her in far-flung villages and of castles build atop the cave where she slept. Her true name was long forgotten, but the dragon was still Russia's heart.

Tsars of old had carried images of her into battle on war flags and banners, striving to be half as fierce as the creature sworn to protect their throne. Their families.

Neither whimsy nor cruelty played a part in why I dreamed of Alina's past. I needed to remember the faces around Alina in that faraway mountain house, to memorize who was a friend and who had meant her family harm. Men could change their name, or alter their appearance, but I'd see through the illusion to the truth.

Knowing the reason didn't make me feel more equal to the task.

I came back to myself to find Mai standing on the table and rubbing her head against my cheek. Thinking the cat looked relieved when I opened my eyes was pure fancy. Still, I pulled her close and snuggled her under my chin. How loudly she purred was real enough.

There was no question of relief when it came to Isadora. She peered at me anxiously from the other side of the table and reached for my hand. "Are you all right?"

Clearing my throat several times made speaking possible. "I'm fine. The only ill effects are an unreasonable urge to cry and a slight headache. Nothing I won't survive."

"Thank heaven for that." Dora slumped back in the chair. She wiped a hand over her face. "You gave me quite a turn that time, Dee. I wasn't at all sure I could call you back. That creature has a lot to answer for."

"She didn't plan to keep me." Clouds had begun blowing in off the Bay and filling the sky. The kitchen grew colder, but I wasn't at all sure a lack of sunshine was entirely to blame. "But she needed to tell me what I'm supposed to do."

Dora grew very still, her calm expression at odds with the rapt attention and speculation in her eyes. "The guardian?"

"The . . . the watcher. She's older than we thought, Dora, one of the last of her kind. I only wish I'd been able to see what she looked like." I couldn't tell her the watcher was a dragon. Not out of compulsion or fear of what would happen if I said the word, or that I was afraid she wouldn't believe me, but because I'd been entrusted with a secret. Breaking that trust was wrong. I shut my eyes, remembering what I'd been shown, and opened them again to find Dora watching me with alarm. "I was never supposed to pass on Alina's memories."

Dora sat huddled in her chair while I explained, so still and quiet that if she'd been anyone else, I might have thought she wasn't paying attention. Some of the alarm left her expression, replaced by a frown. She was far from happy with what I had to say.

"It's times like these I regret promising Randy I'd leave the flask at home." Dora stood and began pacing my kitchen, fists clenched tight. "Dear God in heaven, old-world guardians, necromancers, Bolsheviks . . . there's no telling what else followed Alina here from Russia. I don't like this, Dee. It's too byzantine for me to be comfortable with the risk you'd be taking. Let me do this. I've had more experience."

I continued petting Mai, oddly calm for the moment. "You've no more experience with this than I do, Isadora Bobet. I've learned an enormous amount about the spirit realm over the last four years, and you've given me skills I'd never have learned from anyone else. Eventually lack of experience has to stop being an excuse for keeping me wrapped in cotton wool. You can't be my shield forever."

She leaned against the icebox, arms crossed and glaring at nothing in particular. Dora's anger was much like a summer cloudburst, intense and blustery and soon over. This time was no exception.

"Damn it, Delia. You have the most infuriating habit of being right." Dora stepped away from the icebox and busied herself filling the teakettle. "Are there any cookies?"

"In the bread box."

The wind had picked up, putting an end to the jays' nest building and scattering peach blossoms across the yard in pale pink clouds. I set Mai back on the sill to keep watch and waited for my tea.

Infuriating habit by Dora's standards or not, I was right. I had to face this on my own.

That didn't mean I wasn't frightened.

Gabe

One of the new crop of rookies had been assigned by the desk sergeant to drive Gabe to the scene. Harrison Walken drove well enough, but the young officer was new to the city and got lost twice. The delay cost only a few minutes at most, but Gabe spent the last block or two perched on the edge of the seat, peering past Walken's head and trying to catch a glimpse of the church.

Very few cars lined the street, a surprise given how much time had passed since the body was found. Most murder scenes resembled controlled chaos. New people arrived on the scene while others left, a constant ebb and flow that didn't end until his squad had gathered every scrap of information possible. Gabe had expected to see the bustle of officers gathering evidence, reporters shouting questions at anyone who looked as if he might be in charge, and neighbors gawking in hopes of seeing something gruesome or interesting.

The calm around Holy Trinity made him vaguely uneasy. Something wasn't right.

Lynch had been leaning forward too, watching intently for his first glimpse of the scene. Now he sat back, his expression openly curious. "Did all your men go home early, Gabe? Looks too quiet."

"It is too quiet." That Jordan Lynch had asked confirmed Gabe's growing opinion that the Chicago detective was a good cop. He pointed. "I expected to find beat cops, at least six or seven patrol cars, and the coroner's men waiting on us. My men know their jobs. If they're not here, someone higher up ordered them away."

"No neighbors or reporters either. They'd be even harder to run off." Jordan kneaded his wounded leg, a gesture Gabe took as a newly acquired habit. "I'm going to guess that doesn't happen often."

"Never." Gabe's smile was grim. "I'll be honest, Jordan, I don't know what's going on. I doubt I'm going to like finding out."

Jordan grinned, the first unguarded expression Gabe had seen from him. He knew then they were going to be friends.

Officer Walken guided the patrol car into a parking spot centered right in front of the church. Officer Polk and a harried-looking young priest rushed down the walk to meet the car, arriving before Gabe could gather his hat. Polk pulled the door open, but leaned in to keep Gabe or Jordan Lynch from getting out.

Gabe gestured toward Jordan. "This is Lieutenant Lynch from the Chicago PD. He's going to be helping out until Lieutenant Fitzgerald recovers. Where is everyone?"

Polk stared at Lynch for a few seconds, but nodded and touched his cap before turning to Gabe. "The body's in a changing room at the back of the church, Captain. Dr. West and most of the squad are waiting for you. Supervisor Devin ordered Dr. West to take the body to the morgue, but the coroner refused to disturb the scene before you got here."

He traded surprised looks with Lynch. Removing the body before the officer in charge signed off was against regulations. Polk knew that as well as Gabe, but the tall, dark-haired patrolman was choosing his words carefully. He resolved to adopt the same sense of caution until he knew what they were dealing with. "Thank you, Patrolman. Where can I find Dr. West?"

"That drive over to the left leads to the rectory behind the church. The coroner's van and the other squad cars are parked in the yard. Father Sakovich and Supervisor Devin ordered everyone to park out of sight." Polk looked pointedly over his shoulder. "Father Sakovich would like you to do the same, sir. He doesn't want to upset people arriving for a church supper."

Gabe wasn't angry with Polk. The man was only delivering a message. He looked past Patrolman Polk and straight at the young priest nervously fidgeting on the walkway. "Does Father Sakovich really think holding a social event right now is a good idea?"

Polk leaned farther into the car and lowered his voice. "I don't know what he thinks, Captain. He's pretty rattled after seeing the body. The supervisor and the older priest inside are giving all the orders."

He put on his public face, hiding his anger. "I'll speak with both of them. Walken, leave the car right here. You're not to move it unless I give the order."

"Yes, Captain." Walken pulled a copy of *The Argosy* weekly out of an inside pocket. It was an old issue, one he'd seen Jack reading months before. The bright cover was relatively uncreased and showed a drawing of a cowboy on horseback, reaching for his six-shooter. "Do I have permission to read, sir? Henderson said you usually didn't mind, but to ask permission first."

"Go ahead and read, but keep your eyes open." Gabe motioned Polk to step back. "Do your job and we'll be square."

He and Jordan got out of the car and started up the front walk, leaving Polk to deal with the young priest. The wind sped thin clouds across the sky, forerunners of thick evening fog that threatened to creep in from the Bay. Working murder scenes in swirling, pearl gray mist was always eerie. Gabe couldn't help but think that the ghosts of victims moved with the fog, a thought he'd never have entertained before marrying Delia.

Gabe had driven by the church more times than he could remember, and the bell tower always drew his eye. Five of the seven huge bells had been donated in 1888 by the Russian Emperor Alexander III. The story was that the emperor donated the bells as a show of gratitude to God for his family surviving an assassination attempt. By divine providence or sheer luck, the bells had been removed from their tower just before the 1906 quake and escaped being destroyed in the fire. When the church was rebuilt in 1909, the bells were installed in the new tower.

On calm, foggy days, you could hear the bells being rung in all parts of the city. Other churches in the city had bells and bell towers, but none of them sounded quite the same. That distinctive sound more than anything made him remember the church on Green Street.

A set of stairs led up to big double doors that swung open easily. He'd always been curious to know what Holy Trinity looked like on the inside. That he'd find out in the course of a murder investigation had never crossed his mind.

They entered the vestibule a step ahead of Supervisor Devin and a tall bearded priest. Gabe caught a glimpse of a chandelier and stained glass windows before the priest pulled shut the door into the sanctuary. He swallowed his disappointment and slipped his hands into his trouser pockets, working at looking relaxed and calm. The expression on Supervisor Devin's face promised this wouldn't be pleasant.

Michael Devin had been elected to the board during the Great War. His age might have kept him out of the army, but his bad leg guaranteed he wasn't called in the draft. A riding accident when he was a boy was the official story, but the leg looked withered and twisted even under his expensive suit pants. Gabe guessed he'd been born that way and for some reason didn't want to admit to that.

Devin was reed thin, his face thinner still, and might be considered tall if not for the way he hunched over his cane. The contrast between how Lynch carried himself and bore his injury was striking. The supervisor's slicked-back hair was a dull, dry-leaf brown, his eyes a nondescript hazel. Michael Devin was the type of man you wouldn't remember an instant after you saw him.

"Are you the officer in charge?" The sneer in his voice and the curl of his lip as he glanced at Jordan ensured that Gabe at least would never forget him.

"I'm Captain Gabriel Ryan." Gabe smiled but didn't offer his hand. It was a small and very real slight, the opening foray in a game he'd rather not be playing. All the rumors circulating about Devin focused on his being ruthless when opposed. He could be ruthless as well if forced to it. "You must be Supervisor Devin. I understand you're interfering with my murder investigation."

The priest put a hand on Devin's shoulder and stepped forward. "I'll handle this, Michael. I'm Father Pashkovsky, Captain Ryan. This church and the congregation are my responsibility. We have an important church function scheduled for this evening, and many of our most important parishioners are attending."

Father Pashkovsky was the name the young Russian waiter had given Sam. This man appeared to be considerably older than Aleksei Nureyev, not of an age to have been a boyhood friend. His face was a maze of fine and deep lines, and liberal amounts of gray streaked the priest's long full beard. Milky clouds filmed Pashkovsky's black eyes, a sign of both age and failing sight.

Gabe had a strong hunch this man was old enough to be Aleksei's father. The itch on the back of his neck said he was right.

Jordan cleared his throat, drawing Pashkovsky's attention. "By important parishioners, you mean donors. Money is what makes them so important, am I right?"

Gabe wiped a hand over his mouth, hiding a smile. He liked Jordan Lynch more each minute. "Father Pashkovsky, this is Lieutenant Lynch of the Chicago Police Department. Lieutenant Lynch is consulting with me about a series of murders here in San Francisco."

"I see." Pashkovsky didn't so much as glance at Devin seething behind him. That told Gabe who was in charge. "Our donors are important, but only because they benefit the whole congregation. Without their generosity, the church couldn't pay off the last of our debts or find the money to fix the rectory roof. We invite important men like Supervisor Devin to speak at dinners honoring them for the good work they do."

Gabe kept his expressions pleasant, professional. "I understand that, Father. What I don't understand is what you want from me."

"A favor. Help me find a way to hold the dinner as scheduled." Father Pashkovsky raised a hand and let it fall, a helpless gesture from a man Gabe judged to be far from helpless. "Reaching the men I've invited in time to cancel is impossible. Much of the money they donate goes toward feeding new arrivals from Russia until they find their place here. Most of them fled the Bolsheviks with little more than the clothes they wore. Without that money, many of them would starve."

Everything came back to people fleeing a revolution half a world away. The knot between Gabe's shoulders pulled tighter. "Wasn't Eve Rigaux one of those new arrivals?"

Pashkovsky and Devin both gave him blank, uncomprehending looks. Either both of them were very good actors, something Gabe found difficult to credit, or the woman lying dead at the rear of the church was a stranger to both the priest and the supervisor.

Whatever message the killer was sending wasn't meant for either man.

The message was meant for Alina. Tucked safely away in Dora's house, she'd never know—not until the killers found her.

Fear for Delia and Sam, for Isadora and Alina, snaked up his spine and smothered the last of his patience. "I can't help you, Father. Impossible or not, you'll have to cancel your dinner. I need to find the men who killed Eve Rigaux before they kill anyone else."

The clouds in Pashkovsky's eyes appeared to grow deeper as he stared. Gabe couldn't even be sure the priest really saw him.

Finally Father Pashkovsky nodded. "The dead woman is named Eve?"

"She was." Gabe ignored Devin and the cold ring tightening around his neck, trying to see beyond the milky fog in Pashkovsky's eyes. "Eve and her husband fled the Bolsheviks. Now both of them are dead."

"God sent angels to drive the first Eve from the garden. I've heard some say he sent the Bolsheviks to drive the aristocracy from Russia." Father Pashkovsky crossed himself. "Do your job, Captain. I will pray for Eve and for you."

Gabe and Jordan followed the hallway the priest pointed out and made their way toward the changing room. The corridor wound around the outside of the building, bypassing the sanctuary.

Lynch was silent until Devin and Pashkovsky were out of sight. He gave Gabe a sidelong glance. "I'm glad I came along, Captain Ryan. So far, this has been very entertaining. Mr. Devin was about what I expect out of most city officials, but I can't say I've ever met a priest like that before. I'd have thought Father Pashkovsky would be praying for Eve Rigaux's soul long before we got here. And he didn't seem at all worried about how she ended up dead in the back of the church."

"I had the same thought, but Jack maintains I have a suspicious mind." Gabe slowed his steps. He didn't want to have this conversation in front of the coroner or his men. "Do you think he killed her?"

Jordan thought for a few seconds before shaking his head. "No, but he might think he knows who did."

The corridor curved to the right and dead-ended at a set of open double doors. Baker was framed in the doorway, bent over his camera and taking photographs of the dead woman on the floor. Fingerprint powder clung in soft swirls to the brass doorknobs, darkened the white painted panels that made up the door. Taylor could be seen spreading more black powder on the other side of the room.

He and Lynch stood in the doorway, watching the bustle of activity and getting a feel for the scene. Most of the squad was inside the room, including Randy Dodd, and Jefferson West, the new deputy coroner. A few of the newer men started at Jordan Lynch a second too long, but a nudge from Baxter or Maxwell got them back to work soon enough. Randy was busy questioning an older woman sitting in a plain wooden chair, most likely the cleaning woman who'd discovered the body. West leaned against a wall, waiting for Baker to finish with his pictures.

The muscles across the top of Gabe's shoulders relaxed. Despite the attempt by the older priest and Supervisor Devin to shut things down, the investigation was progressing and well in hand. His men did know their jobs.

Eve Rigaux's body lay in the center of the room. In death she appeared older than her husband had been, but he couldn't say that was true. According to Dora, older women taking younger husbands wasn't unusual among European nobility. Her hair had been pinned up when he met her that morning, but now it fanned out in a pale brown halo, neatly arranged. The jacket to her traveling suit was missing and the diamond and ruby earrings he'd noticed.

Blood soaked the scuffed oak floor in a pool around her head and matted in her hair, leaving no doubt about how and where she'd died. Her arms were stretched out straight from the shoulders, her ankles crossed and dark blue skirt smoothed over her knees. Silver coins had been placed over her eyes, giving her face an odd, blank stare. Flower petals—roses, carnations, and pansies—were scattered over the body and in a trail that led to the outside door.

He memorized all of it, putting each detail away to think about later and describe to Jack. The coins, the flowers, the way Eve's hands were clenched into fists—all of it meant something. Leaving her this way was part of the killer's message. Gabe just couldn't read the language. Not yet.

"I'd like to hear what you think of this, Lieutenant Lynch." Gabe clapped Jordan on the back, knowing most of the squad was watching out of the corner of their eye. The men who knew him well would interpret the gesture as meaning Jordan belonged here. Those who didn't know him would learn soon enough. "Once we're done here, I want to talk to the younger man, Father Sakovich. I'll have one of my men bring him down to the station."

"His boss isn't going to like that." Lynch moved around behind Baker, positioning himself to get a good view of the body without interfering with the photographs. He gestured toward Eve Rigaux's body with his cane. "I'd say Mrs. Rigaux was still alive when the killer brought her here. There's too much evidence of bleeding for her to already have been dead when he laid her out."

"That's a good guess, but I'm not ready to make any final conclusions yet." Jefferson West appeared annoyed at first, but that didn't last in the face of Gabe's blank stare. West cleared his throat and stood up straight. "She probably was killed here, Captain. The way the blood is confined to one area near her head, I'd say he likely bashed her skull in. But I'll let you know for sure once I can move the body."

"Thank you, Dr. West. And thank you for not following Supervisor Devin's orders. I needed to see this." Gabe went back to studying the body. Jefferson West was a good coroner, but he was young and hadn't been to many murder scenes. "Go ahead, Lieutenant Lynch, I'm listening."

Jordan walked around the body again, the metal tip on his cane making dull thuds against the oak plank floor. He stopped at her feet, leaning on his cane and frowning. "Does the way she was left remind you of anything in particular, Ryan? I know what I see, but I don't want to put ideas in your head."

"I've seen pictures of angels and saints posed like this, or martyrs who were crucified. We're inside a church. My guess is that's exactly what the killer meant us to see. The question is why." Gabe moved around the body one more time, long practice allowing him to stay out of Baker's shots and not be blinded by the flash. "One thing's clear, he knew what he was doing. The coins on the eyes, the flowers—it's all staged. The killer left her this way for effect."

"That he did, Captain." Jordan looked up, eyes glittering. "And none of this was meant for the police. He wanted to frighten someone, maybe push them into making a mistake. I'd wager he wouldn't risk getting caught unless the message was important."

"I think you're right. This took time." The question of who the killer was trying to intimidate nagged at him. He could be wrong in thinking it was Alina, especially after Delia's encounter with the necromancer. A mistake on his part might get them all killed. Gabe wouldn't let that happen. "How much longer until you're finished, Baker?"

"Another minute or two, Captain." Baker moved the tripod holding his camera to a spot near Eve's left shoulder. "Before Dr. West moves her, I want to get a close-up of her hands. She's holding something."

There was room for only one of them to stand behind Baker while he took the photos. Lynch smiled and waved Gabe into place. Waiting while Baker set the aperture and the flash, focused, and snapped the first picture, then the second and third, was difficult. His mind ran through lists of what Eve Rigaux might have clenched in her fist, lists that ran the gamut of buttons from the killer's coat to beads from one of her own necklaces.

His palms itched by the time Baker finished and packed up his camera. West took the patrolman's place, putting on heavy black rubber gloves and pulling a pair of tongs out of his bag. Rigor mortis was well advanced. Eve's hands were frozen into coiled claws that refused to open—not until the deputy coroner forced them.

The sound of her fingers breaking was a sharp, meaty crack that reminded him of his mother's dog chewing open a bone to get at the marrow. He swallowed hard, refusing to be sick.

One hand held an oval locket. Diamonds around a mother-of-pearl center caught the light as West dropped the locket into a glassine envelope. Gabe slipped the envelope into an inside pocket.

Eve's other hand concealed a thin tube-shaped piece of metal as long as her palm. Gabe crouched down opposite the coroner to get a better look. Pointed on one end, the thin tube was too thick to be a sewing needle. The other end was jagged, as if snapped off against a straight, hard edge.

Rusty brown flakes clung to the shaft, crumbling to powder as soon as West prodded the metal with a gloved finger. Gabe didn't need the coroner to tell him this was Eve's blood. The evidence of what had been done to her was matted in her brown hair and soaked the white collar of her linen blouse.

This close to the body, the flowery scent of Eve Rigaux's perfume mingled with the copper aroma of blood. His stomach tried to rebel again, but he fought it back. Detective captains didn't throw up at murder scenes. Not where their men could see.

Dr. West picked up the thin tube with his tongs and held it out for Gabe to see. "What is that?"

Gabe shrugged. "I don't know. I'd guess it was broken off of something, but what that was, I couldn't say."

Lynch leaned over Jefferson West's shoulder. "Do you mind if I have a closer look, Doctor?"

West held the tongs out, slowly twisting them to different angles. Jordan nodded and straightened up again. "Sometimes my first guess at something is the best. It's a cobbler's awl, or the business end of one. Cobblers and saddle makers use them to punch stitching holes in leather. That jagged end is where the handle was. The killer couldn't hide that in her hand with a big hunk of wood attached."

Gabe stood and stepped away from the body. Even that much distance let him escape the worst of the smell. He ignored the insistent whisper in his ear that the scent of blood hadn't made him sick in years. So soon after death, the smell of rot shouldn't be this *strong*. "You sound pretty positive."

"I've seen one before. My wife's brother is a shoemaker." Lynch gestured toward the tongs. "Awls come in different sizes to make different size holes. Most of Paul's are smaller, but he's got a couple with shafts that size. If that's what killed her, I can't say it's a quick or easy way to die."

"Her husband didn't die quickly or easily either. If I didn't know better, I'd say this was personal." He looked across the room. Randy caught his eye and motioned them over. "Let's go meet the cleaning lady, Lieutenant Lynch."

He'd been told this was a changing room, likely used for weddings or for priests to don their vestments before services. But from the general clutter, the room appeared to be storage space for anything the church didn't use often. Dodd had used that to his advantage and picked the perfect spot for the cleaning lady to wait. She was tucked into a corner out of the flow of foot traffic, her view of the body blocked by an old upright piano and a low stack of pasteboard boxes.

"Patrolman Dodd, this is Detective Lieutenant Jordan Lynch from Chicago. He's working with me on this case until Jack's on his feet. Jordan, this is Randy Dodd. Randy's a friend."

Jordan gave Gabe a strange look, but offered his hand. "You do run a nice cozy little shop, Ryan. Pleased to meet you, Officer Dodd."

He gave Randy credit for smiling and shaking Lynch's hand. "Glad to meet you, Lieutenant. Captain Ryan, this is Mrs. Elise Wetzel. She cleans the rectory and cooks for Father Pashkovsky."

Elise Wetzel looked to be in her fifties or early sixties, with bright blue eyes and hair that held more gray than faded brown. She was short and slight, but Gabe didn't doubt that Mrs. Wetzel was stronger than she appeared. That she looked frightened, pale, and on the edge of panic, wasn't a surprise.

Gabe dragged over another chair, sitting so that Mrs. Wetzel didn't have to look up at him. Looming over someone smaller was intimidating, and scaring this poor woman more was the last thing he wanted to do.

Jack was better at putting people at ease and drawing out information. He'd have to do the best he could alone. Gabe braced his hands on his knees and smiled sympathetically. "I'm sorry to meet you under these circumstances, Mrs. Wetzel. I know you told Officer Dodd what happened, but I have to ask you to tell the story one more time. I need to hear it for myself. Start from the beginning and take your time."

She covered her eyes with a hand for an instant and nodded. "I came back here to find the spare table linens. We box them up after Christmas every year and there weren't enough in the rectory for tonight. The first thing I noticed were flower petals all over the floor. I thought maybe the neighbor's children had gotten in here somehow. Then—then I saw her lying on the floor and the—the blood."

"Did you see anyone else? Hear anything?"

Mrs. Wetzel shook her head. "Not a living soul. You can hear people walking the corridor or talking in the sanctuary from in here. If anyone else was around, I'd have heard."

Jordan cleared his throat. "Is the church always this empty during the week, ma'am? No quilting bees or church board meetings?"

Elise Wetzel looked at Jordan blankly, twisting her hands in her apron and struggling toward an answer. "No, not on a weekday. Most days me and the two fathers are the only ones here. Why?"

"Curiosity on my part." Lynch smiled and tipped his hat. "Police officers ask all kinds of questions. I didn't mean for mine to upset you."

More than mere curiosity prompted Lynch's question. Both he and Jordan had to assume the killer knew the normal pattern of activity in the church and that was part of the reason he'd picked this room. Even in a usually empty church, this room was set apart. Isolated.

The chance of being caught in the act of killing Eve Rigaux, or of anyone seeing this man coming or going was very slim. And if the killer knew he had time, he might set up almost anything.

Suddenly the way the body was posed, coupled with the strong smell, struck Gabe as ominous. This was more than a message being sent.

"Thank you, Mrs. Wetzel. If you remember anything else, please don't hesitate to call the station." He stood and helped her up. "Officer Dodd, have Baxter take her home. Once that's taken care of, find a telephone. There should be one in the rectory or the church office. Call my house and see if Dora is still with Delia. I need both of them to consult on this case."

Randy glanced at Lynch. "Gabe . . . are you sure?"

"I'm sure. Ask them to hurry." Gabe pulled the locket out of his inside pocket. He held the glassine envelope by one corner, cautious and wary. The expensive trinket might be harmless or a viper in disguise. "And make sure you describe the scene to Dora. I don't want her walking in unprepared."

"Neither do I. The last time that happened, she nursed a headache for two days." Randy tugged down the bottom of his uniform coat. "Let's get you home, Mrs. Wetzel. We'll go out the back door here."

Lynch leaned heavily on his cane, his expression guarded. Gabe didn't know the Chicago cop well enough to know how Jordan would react to Dora or to the idea of what she and Delia could do. He wouldn't let that stop him from doing what he thought was best. "I shouldn't surprise you either. Delia is my wife. She and Dora are experts in the occult and spiritualism. Occasionally I ask them to consult on a case. Now, go ahead and say what you're thinking, Lieutenant. It won't be anything I haven't heard before."

Jordan held a hand up and smiled. "I'm not saying anything. I said I wanted to see how San Francisco detectives worked. If you want to bring two women into this investigation, that's your business. I've seen stranger things in the last twenty years."

That made Gabe smile. He dropped the locket on the top of the piano, in plain sight but not in a place anyone would brush against it by accident. How much physical contact he'd already had made him uneasy. "You may change your mind about that before we're finished here. The coroner can move the body once Delia and Dora say it's safe."

"You're serious." Lynch tipped his hat back and looked out at the cops moving around the room. "You think the killer left some kind of booby trap in here. And your wife and her friend will be able to find it?"

"Something like that. Call it a hunch or whatever you like, but everything about this murder feels off. Delia and Dora should be able to figure out why." Gabe motioned Taylor over. "Tell Dr. West to hold off moving the body or disturbing things more than we already have. Miss Bobet is coming in to have a look, and I want everyone to wait outside until she arrives. I'll give the okay to come back in. The farther they are from this room, the better."

Taylor glanced back at the body, frowning. "Yes, sir. Will Mrs. Ryan be coming too?"

That raised Jordan Lynch's eyebrows, but Gabe was fairly sure the look on Jordan's face was curiosity. That gave him hope Lynch would keep an open mind. "Yes, Delia is coming too."

"I'm glad to hear that, Captain. This will get sorted faster with both of them here." Taylor touched the brim of his hat. "I'll talk to Dr. West and send everyone out."

He watched the room clearing, aware that the sweet smell of flowers and decay grew stronger each second. In less than a minute, he and Jordan Lynch were the only ones left in the room. "We're going out the back too, Jordan. We can talk more while we wait. I haven't told you everything about this case."

Jordan went first, squinting against the bright sunshine. Gabe paused in the doorway leading to the rectory yard and took a last look at Eve Rigaux's body. He thought he saw the air thicken and churn above her, and monstrous faces leering at him from inside the mist.

Gabe turned away and walked outside, inhaling clean air that smelled of pine and salt flats along the Bay. With the sun on his back, it was easier to believe he'd imagined the phantoms inside the church, and that this was any other murder case.

He'd settle for that.

CHAPTER 13

Delia

We parked Dora's car just across the street from Holy Trinity. Sun glinted off the church's stained glass windows, bright sparks of red, blue, and golden yellow that flew in all directions. The church was beautiful on the outside, surrounded by trees and bordered by flowers. Knowing what ugliness waited for us inside, I held tight to that image of beauty.

The princess ghost had ridden with us all the way from Dora's house, a silent passenger that never budged from the corner of the windscreen. Now she faded from view, her expression a picture of heartfelt grief. I waited for the watcher to make her presence known, but she stayed silent.

Gabe and Randy stood on the sidewalk talking, the anxious looks on their faces adding to my considerable case of nerves. Most of the squad was outside as well, standing around and watching for us. That they weren't inside gathering evidence and going about their jobs said much.

A glance at Dora earned me a raised eyebrow. "I don't know any more than you do, Dee. We'll find out soon enough. Now, be a dear and grab the basket with the candles out of the back. I'll bring the bigger one with the salt, the basil, and the sage."

Her long, stylish beaver coat swished around her ankles as we hurried across Green Street. Dora was dressed at the height of fashion as always, her skirts so short that only a few years ago, they might have been cause for arrest. She was long past being a fresh-faced young girl, but the new rookies in Gabe's squad and strangers on the street all stared, unable to look away.

Isadora attracted attention everywhere she went, most of it unasked for and at times unwelcome. This was one of those times when having all eyes watching her was especially unwelcome. Both of us would have liked to slip in with as little notice as possible.

Randy took the heavy basket from Dora and kissed her cheek. She beamed at him, but her fingers wrapped tight around his wrist and her shoulders stiffened. I was slightly uncomfortable, but the aftereffects of death, any death, washed through me and the pain didn't last more than an instant. Dora was never that fortunate.

Eve Rigaux's fear was too fresh, the echoes of how she'd suffered too strong, for Dora to avoid or face unaided. Randy was the perfect match for Dora in many ways. That he'd been born with the rare ability to bleed off Isadora's pain made me think that more than luck brought them together. With Randy's help, she could cope with a great deal of the emotion battering her.

Wrapping my arms around Gabe on a public sidewalk wasn't the proper or socially acceptable thing to do, but his smile made flouting propriety worth any amount of scandalized looks from strangers. Death always skulked at our heels in the form of Gabe's job, but over the last week, the prospect of really losing him had drawn too close. If I clung to him a bit tighter, that was to be expected.

Gabe smiled and brushed his fingers across my cheek. "I'm

sorry I had to call the two of you to come out here, but I didn't have a choice. You'll see what I mean once we go back inside."

"Don't be silly. We're in this together, Gabe Ryan." I deliberately ignored Isadora's exasperated sigh. She made a point of teasing me and Gabe about any display of affection, but that was shaky ground for her to stand on since she'd met Randy. "Neither Dora nor I would leave you to face this on your own."

He knew that was never in doubt, but I still saw relief in his eyes. That worried me more than his call for help.

Gabe gestured toward the tall Negro man leaning on a cane a few feet away. "Before we go inside, let me introduce both of you to Lieutenant Lynch from Chicago. It was his badge we found after the explosion. The lieutenant has agreed to help out until Jack can get around."

Lieutenant Lynch stepped forward and tipped his hat. "I'm pleased to meet you, Mrs. Ryan, Miss Bobet. Captain Ryan was just telling me about the both of you."

His aura was deep and strong, full of vibrant golds and the same placid greens I associated with Gabe. My guess was that Lieutenant Lynch was a lot like my husband, deeply committed to being a cop and seeing justice done. He watched me warily, giving Dora furtive glances I'm sure he'd not want noticed. Gabe had been telling him the truth about the two of us, not polite social fictions. Lieutenant Lynch wasn't sure how to take what he'd heard. I didn't blame him in the slightest.

I set my basket down and stuck out my hand, smiling all the while and trying to look harmless. Best to show him that I wouldn't bite. "I'm glad to meet you, Lieutenant, and I'm very grateful that Gabe has your help."

He smiled and shook my hand. "I get the feeling he'd do all right on his own."

Dora drooped heavily against Randy, but she found a friendly smile for Lieutenant Lynch. "Forgive me for not shaking hands, Lieutenant. I imagine that Gabe has already explained a great deal of why Delia and I are here and what he expects us to do. We should get this over with."

"I must admit I've never been acquainted with a spiritualist before. This is all new territory for me and I'm looking forward to seeing how you work." Lieutenant Lynch stepped back and waved Dora toward the sidewalk. "After you, Miss Bobet."

Gabe gave the order for his men to stay where they were and led us down the drive on one side of the church. A coroner's van and a cluster of patrol cars sat on a patch of lawn in front of the rectory. We must have looked an odd procession to the young priest watching from an upper window.

"Gabe—"

"I see him, Dee. Pretend he's not there." He took the basket from me, using the opportunity to get a good look at the window without appearing to stare. "I'm willing to wager that Father Sakovich wasn't involved in the murder, but he was with the cleaning lady who found the body. Right now he's in shock."

"Unless I miss my guess, he's under pressure from the older priest too." Lynch tugged a rumpled handkerchief from an inside pocket and mopped his face. "That smell's getting worse, Gabe. I shouldn't be able to smell anything, let alone all the way out here."

"Smell?" Dora looked between Gabe and the lieutenant. "What in the world are you talking about? I can't smell anything."

"You should be glad of that." Randy slipped an arm around her waist, prepared to keep her on her feet if need be. "We've fished bodies out of the Bay that don't smell this bad."

Dora's eyes narrowed, confirming my first instinct. The necromancer was undoubtedly involved in Eve Rigaux's death. "Really . . . how long ago did they find the body?"

"Not more than three, four hours ago." Randy looked between me and Isadora. "What are the two of you thinking?"

Gabe's squad had seen enough strange things in the last four years that they took anything Dora or I said in stride. Even those who couldn't bring themselves to fully believe in ghosts or other creatures from the spirit realm kept an open mind. And they'd seen what helping Gabe with his cases did to Dora far too often to think it anything but real. Most of the squad members were very protective of her as a result.

A stranger's reaction was always in question. I cleared my throat, keenly aware of Lieutenant Lynch watching. "The moment of death generates a kind of . . . of spiritual energy. Some texts say this energy is evidence of the soul leaving the body, or some kind of life force released back into the world. Whether it's the soul or something else, when that energy is drained away purposely, the body decays faster. Ghosts are formed out of the same energy."

"Ghosts?" Lieutenant Lynch frowned. "I haven't heard anyone talk about ghosts and spirits in a very long time, not since my grandma passed on. Grandma used to hang old bottles in all the trees around her house. She said they were ghost traps and that if she ever caught me throwing rocks at them, I'd be pulling weeds every day for the next month."

Dora's smile was arch and knowing. "Did she ever catch you, Lieutenant?"

"No, ma'am, she never caught me." He scratched the side of his neck and limped toward the open back door. "I could never hit one either. They kept moving out of the way."

The room we entered was cluttered, full of pasteboard boxes, wooden folding chairs, and an old piano that had seen better days. A door into the sanctuary stood partly open, giving me a glimpse of dark oak pews and one of the stained glass windows I'd seen from the outside. I didn't see the body until we'd come around the piano.

Randy's telephone call had warned Dora and me that the murder was recently done, the body posed in strange ways that made him and Gabe uneasy. We'd prepared as well as we could on short notice and set off for the church. I'd known that whatever we found would be bad, but warnings and preparations paled in the face of reality.

In all the cases I'd worked on with Jack and Gabe and Dora, I'd never seen a body lying cold and still on the floor. This wasn't a shadow of someone's past or a spirit remembering a day lived long ago. I held tight to Gabe's arm, staring and trying not to think of how recently Eve Rigaux's life had been ripped away.

Gabe spoke quietly in my ear, no doubt thinking only I could hear. "Are you all right?"

Dora rolled her eyes, making no attempt to hide her exasperation. "Shame on you for asking such a silly question. No, Gabe, she's not all right. You know perfectly well that a fresh corpse isn't near the same thing as a ghost. Give Dee a moment to find her feet. This is all new to her."

Lieutenant Lynch turned to her, his tone stern and almost scolding. "And this isn't new to you, Miss Bobet?"

She smiled her sweetest smile, a sure sign that Dora was annoyed. "This is far from new for me, Lieutenant. The first murder case I assisted with was more than fifteen years ago, and frankly, I find that smug tone annoying. Feeling how someone died isn't at all pleasant, it's extremely painful. And yet I'm still here, all because Gabe needs my help. Does that satisfy your curiosity?"

He looked past Dora, studying Eve Rigaux's body. Lieutenant Lynch cleared his throat and looked Isadora in the eye. "My apologies, Miss Bobet. My wife always said I turned into a pompous ass when I wasn't sure of my ground. Chances are I'm worse since she passed away. I can't say I've ever been less sure of what's going on than I am right now. That's no excuse for being rude."

"Apology accepted. You're not the only one here who's unsure." Dora let go of Randy, testing her balance before stepping away. "Dee, bring the salt. We'll contain the smell first and then we can try to discover what surprises the killer left for us."

Dora walked a circle around the body, one arm outstretched toward Eve's remains and reciting charms in a soft voice. I followed behind, pouring salt onto the floor. If I concentrated on staying precisely three steps behind Isadora and not treading on her heels, or on not letting the salt line waver or drift away from Dora's path, it was easier to forget a corpse lay inches away.

Twice we went around, leaving white crystals gleaming on the oak floor. At the end of the second circuit, Dora brought her hands together over the thick line of salt, sealing the circle.

Wind rushed past me and sped toward the open back door, rattling lids on pasteboard boxes and blowing sheet music off the piano and onto the floor. Lieutenant Lynch's hat blew away, sending Randy scrambling across the room to retrieve it for him. The gale ended quickly, leaving an eerily calm behind.

Lieutenant Lynch took his hat from Randy with a nod of thanks, his expression a mixture of surprise and speculation. Dora looked tired, but also vaguely smug. The thought was uncharitable of me, but I suspected she'd called the wind to impress on the lieutenant that she wasn't playing games.

Gabe sighed, and the green cast left his face. Dora's smile held only the tiniest bit of teasing. "Better, Gabe?"

"Much. Thank you, Dora." He moved closer, careful not to disturb the salt. "Was that what you thought?"

"Advanced decay? No." She paced next to Eve's body, hands clutched into fists and frowning. "This was the equivalent of a parlor trick, one targeted specifically at you and your men. My best guess is the killer wanted all of you sick and unable to function. Fear was a small part of it as well, but frightening a cop is extremely difficult. He misjudged that badly."

"What aren't you saying, Dora?" Randy knew her as well as I did. He stepped in front of her, forcing her to be still and face him. "Tell me what else is wrong."

She smiled affectionately and patted his cheek. "Dearest Randy, you have so much faith that all the answers are tucked up my sleeve. In this case, I have to disappoint you. *Something* is wrong; I just can't say *what*. Why he went to the trouble to set all this up is very puzzling. Any power he might have gathered from Eve's death would be wasted keeping that illusion of rot and decay going. That makes very little sense."

"But it makes perfect sense if he's not interested in accumulating power." The words were spoken before I thought. I hugged the nearly empty bag of salt, forcing myself to look, really look, at Eve Rigaux. "Making people see what he wants them to see, or making them feel a particular way, is more important. Some of your books have sketches of martyrs and saints that were crucified. When I look at Mrs. Rigaux, that's what I see, Dora. That's what he wants us all to see. The only thing that's missing is a cross."

"Or a stake for burning." She stood next to Randy, lips pressed tight together. "I can see what you're saying, Dee, but the coins don't fit. A coin placed on the eyes of the dead is an old tradition that dates from long before the Romans. The coins were meant to pay the ferryman who carried you across the river to the land of the dead. I've never seen them associated with martyrs before."

"Maybe that's not what they mean, Miss Bobet. From what Gabe said, Mrs. Rigaux was rich." Lieutenant Lynch's cane thumped hollowly on the floor as he moved to stand near Eve's head. He watched where he set his feet, just as careful as the rest of us not to break the circle of salt. "The locket we found in her hand was worth a fortune. My guess is the killer wanted us to know that money couldn't save her."

Dora groped for Randy's arm, staring at Eve Rigaux's hands and swaying on her feet. "Dear Lord, the coroner did that to her fingers, not the killer. No wonder the feel of violence is so strong."

Gabe shoved his hands deep into his trouser pockets, visibly uncomfortable. "We didn't have a choice. Rigor had set in and we couldn't get her hands open." He pointed at a pair of tongs lying next to the body. A thin metal tube coated in what must be dried blood was locked into the jaws. "That was in one hand, the locket in the other. Jordan—Lieutenant Lynch—says that's part of a cobbler's awl. I'm positive the murderer used that to kill her and broke the handle off later."

Suddenly the halo of congealed blood under her head made all too much sense. Now I wanted to be sick, but I couldn't be any less brave than Dora. "Who has the locket now? We need to see it."

"It's on top of the piano." He shrugged, sheepish and slightly embarrassed. "I had the locket in my pocket for a while, but that didn't feel safe once we all started feeling ill. I didn't want to risk anyone else handling it until you and Dora had a chance to look it over."

"You did exactly the right thing, Gabe." Dora was exceedingly pale and leaned heavily on Randy, but in this case, her prior experience with crime scenes did carry the day. She plowed through the pain and discomfort, doing what needed to be done. "Making you nauseated was a minor annoyance, but this man could have planted something truly nasty on the jewelry. Gems can hold power and spells for a very long time. Randy, be a dear and bring the locket to me."

Lieutenant Lynch was clearly puzzled as he watched Randy cross the room. "Excuse me for asking, Miss Bobet, but won't that be just as dangerous for Officer Dodd?"

"Call me Dora. All this formality is exhausting." She never took her eyes off Randy, but there was no doubt her small smile was meant for the lieutenant. "I wouldn't risk Randy for anything in this world. The same goes for Gabe and Dee, and you, Lieutenant. Randy has a special sort of immunity to this kind of thing, or I wouldn't ask. There's nothing the killer could attach to the locket that has the power to hurt him."

He studied her face, thoughtful and utterly serious. Trust was a fragile thing, constructed on a foundation that grew slowly over time. Time was one thing we didn't have, not if we were to find this killer and keep Alina safe. We were asking a great deal of Lieutenant Lynch, not the least of which was to accept that all the bizarre, outlandish things we told him were true.

"All right. I'll make the same agreement with you that I did with Gabe." Jordan Lynch pulled himself up to his full height, both hands resting on the head of his cane. "I'll call you Dora if you'll call me Jordan, but only in private. People might misunderstand if we're too familiar in public where they can hear. I'd be pleased if you do the same, Mrs. Ryan."

Dora's face fell, just for an instant, before she gave Jordan her brightest smile. She'd sensed what that admission had cost him. Having spent almost half my life with Annie, watching shopkeepers ignore her and speak to me instead, I knew the cost all too well. Jordan Lynch suffered blows to his pride and dignity every day.

Randy came back, a glassine envelope on his palm. Diamonds ringing the oval locket caught the overhead electric light, glittering with brilliant white sparks. The mother-of-pearl center shimmered with softer, multicolored rainbows. Jordan had been right; the locket was worth a large sum of money.

Dora passed her hand over the envelope on Randy's palm, careful not to touch it. She frowned and shut her eyes, concentrating while holding her hand perfectly still.

"Nothing. He didn't hide anything in the locket." She pulled her hand back, wiping it up and down on the front of her coat. I took her hand before she rubbed the skin raw. "Faint echoes of her death and the terror of knowing this man was going to kill her, but nothing else. She wasn't wearing the locket when she died, or the residue would be much stronger."

I squeezed her fingers. "Are you all right?"

How long Dora took to answer and how hard she trembled frightened me. "I will be. Give me a moment."

Gabe glanced at Dora for permission before taking the locket from Randy. He shook it out of the envelope, fumbling for a few seconds before finding the clasp and popping it open. A tiny sprig of dried flowers fell to the floor, crumbling to dust when Randy tried to pick them up. Gabe stared at the inside, his face closed off, expressionless.

"Randy, get everyone back inside. Have them finish up so Dr. West can take the body to the morgue." Gabe wrapped my hand around the open locket and kissed my cheek. "I need to call Jack and have him send a few telegrams. I'll be right back."

I opened my hand, knowing what I'd see inside the locket before I looked. On one side was a picture of Alina. She was a few years younger, her hair a bit longer, and she was dressed in the same white beaded gown and circlet as the princess ghost. If I'd any lingering doubts the ghost was made up of Alina's memories, they vanished.

The other picture brought tears to my eyes. Alina and her three sisters gazed back at me from that picture, smiling and happy. Content. I would have given much to have that be my last memory of them, to remember them full of life and hope for the future. But I had other memories of these young women, ones I couldn't dismiss. I passed the locket to Isadora and rushed out the back door, unwilling to make a spectacle of myself in front of Gabe's men by bursting into tears.

Sitting in Dora's car all alone was peaceful. Afternoon was moving toward evening, and the last warm rays of sunshine on my face burned away the urge to cry. Birds sang from the top of the bell tower, and children's laughter sounded from a yard nearby. The flowers were still beautiful, and color still gleamed in every stained glass window.

But now ghosts filled those windows, standing amongst the images of saints and angels. Among the faceless host of Alina's memories, three princesses in white beaded dresses peered at me from brightly colored panes.

All three waited, patient and serene, for me to save their sister.

Gabe arrived home hours after I did. He'd taken Jordan Lynch to stay with Katie Allen and stopped to see Jack on the way home. Filling Jack in on the case was just as important to Gabe as to Jack.

Dinner was quiet, both of us tired and lost in thought. I started to clear the table once we'd finished, but Gabe stopped me.

"Leave the dishes for now." He pulled me into his arms and held tight. "I'll take care of them in the morning."

I held him just as tight, his heartbeat fast and strong in my ear. "I'll consider that a promise, Gabe Ryan. Now, kiss me."

We fell asleep in each other's arms, warm and safe. My last thought was a prayer it would always be like this; that we'd never be torn apart the way Alina and her family were.

Each night, the dreams drew closer to the end of the story, more harrowing and vivid. Knowing who I was dreaming of made it worse.

Knowing how it had to end was worst of all.

As large as the mountain house was, I couldn't imagine just the three of us would stay there until spring. Winter would close the passes in a few weeks and snow would make even the lower roads impossible to travel. Either the rest of the family would be moved and join us, or they'd take the four of us away.

I was wrong. More soldiers arrived each week to fill the house, new faces to scowl and refuse to answer questions. These men weren't members of the Red Army. They were rough men from small villages and towns, men with few manners and no discipline. By the time winter closed the roads, the lower floor of the house and the outbuildings were full of guards. A few showed us a little respect, but only Lieutenant Dmitri was passionate in insisting my sisters and I be treated better.

The captain in charge, a man with bad teeth and bits of food in his beard, will likely send him away once the snow melts.

There was little enough for my sisters and me to fill our days with aside from cards and wandering the upstairs hallways. We weren't allowed downstairs without an escort, and the walled garden was forbidden to us. Even cold as it was, we'd have relished the wind on our face and the open sky overhead.

Once a week, we were taken downstairs to wash bed linens in a deep tin tub and hang them to dry on an enclosed porch. Wind cried and wailed under the eaves, blew through cracks around the door and rattled the murky glass in two large windows. How hard the wind blew was all that ever changed. Still, we looked forward to seeing the sky.

Guards watched us through those windows no matter the weather, smoking and making crude jokes. Others stood just inside the door leading back into the house. Our hands were red and raw from the cold and harsh soap, and we'd grown thinner from lack of food. I overhead one guard saying it was less than we deserved, making the others laugh. When he saw me staring, the smile left his face and he walked away.

After the laundry was done we hauled water upstairs and scrubbed the floors of our room. Servants worked in the house, girls and older women from the neighboring village, but they cooked and cleaned for the commandant and his officers. My sisters and I took care of ourselves, hoarding our small ration of coal to make tea and cook our meals.

I saw Lieutenant Dmitri more and more often, watching us from a distance and always frowning. He rarely spoke to us, and when he did, it was to inquire about our health and if the room was warm enough. I always answered for the four of us, pride driving me to lie about how well we were doing.

Dmitri saw through my attempts to save face. Our ration of coal grew larger, and the packets of food set aside for us in the kitchen were packed fuller. Loafs of fresh bread and wedges of cheese appeared in our room on those rare occasions when all four of us were out at the same time. I'd grown to distrust generosity, but I wasn't a fool. We found ways to hide the extra food and make it last.

Not one of the soldiers had shown kindness before now. No one smiled or said a pleasant word, but these men weren't like my father's troops. They fancied themselves as revolutionaries, guardians of a grand new world and at the forefront of a new society. I heard them brag to each other about the part they played in bringing about a prosperous new age.

But no matter how they swaggered and tried to intimidate us, I saw the truth in their eyes. My sisters and I frightened them, and our very existence called into question their glorious new society. They hated us for that.

Dmitri looked at us without fear or hate, but he was one man among many.

Winter passed slowly. Our pile of letters for Mama and Papa, the sum of our days and dreams, grew larger.

One afternoon in February, the captain with bad teeth and the unwashed beard arrived with two guards to inspect our room. Snow pelted the windows, hard, icy pellets that pinged against the thin glass and mounded on the ledge outside. We stood meekly while the guards went through our things, tossing clothing onto the beds or the floor. I watched the snow, trying not to see these men walk on our books or shake out my older sister's nightdress.

The taller of the guards found our letters in a box under the bed and handed them to the captain.

He opened one of our letters and read it, stone-faced at first, but quickly growing angry. The captain shook the letter in my older sister's face and shouted, making her cry. "What is this? Who gave you permission to write these?"

"I did." Dmitri stood in the doorway, watching my sister cry. The flash of anger in his eyes was stronger this time and not hidden as well. "I saw no harm in it, sir. No one will ever read the letters and writing kept them quiet."

The captain glared, gaping like a fish and too furious to speak. He carried the box of letters to the fire, tossing them onto the glowing coals and stirring the embers with an iron poker until the paper caught. My youngest sister buried her face in my shoulder, unable to watch our messages to Mama and Papa turn to ash.

"No more letters!" The captain threw the empty box across the room. "You do what I say, no one else. If I catch you writing again, I'll have you shot."

Dmitri shrank back out of the way as the captain stomped out of the room, the two guards trailing behind. He waited a few seconds before stepping into our room, careful not to walk on our belongings.

"I'm sorry, ladies. The captain means what he says." Dmitri

looked into my eyes, his feelings well hidden. "He won't think twice about having you shot."

All the words I wanted to say would call more trouble down on my sisters. I swallowed them, trying not to choke. "We'll remember."

He bowed before turning on his heel and striding from the room. I closed the white pine door gently, fighting the impulse to slam it shut, and slam it again and again until the door cracked into splinters.

Instead I helped my sisters gather our clothes and set the room to rights. None of us would be able to sleep until we erased all trace of the captain's visit.

Not long afterwards, the captain with bad teeth was gone. Rumors flew among the guards about his being called to Moscow, or mysterious meetings with Lenin. All my sisters and I knew from the guards' gossip was that he was gone. And with his leaving, Dmitri was in charge.

He couldn't lift all the restrictions or remove all the guards shadowing our footsteps, but he allowed us the run of the house. Food became more plentiful, and we no longer shivered in our beds. Lieutenant Dmitri did all he could to make our captivity bearable.

Twice a week, he conducted an inspection of our rooms. Dmitri came alone and stood in the center of our room, usually with a bundle of books tucked under his arm. He'd never touch our things or search through our valises, just look around and nod his approval before setting his bundle of books on our small table.

As the weeks passed, he often stayed to talk. We learned from Dmitri that there were men still loyal to my father struggling against the Red Army. He'd give us news from other parts of Russia, quoting speeches Lenin gave or telling about clashes between the Red and White Armies as they battled for control of the country. His news never mentioned my parents or the rest of the family. We were afraid to ask and hear bad news.

Dmitri spoke to me more often than to any of my sisters. My older sister insisted that he behaved more like a suitor than a jailer. I ignored her.

May brought melting snow, flowers in the yard, and a new commandant to the mountain house. He arrived in the middle of the night, rousting Dmitri out of his bed and demanding to meet my sisters and me immediately.

We were herded downstairs in our dressing gowns, barefoot and shivering, and taken to the parlor. The new commandant sat straight and rigid in a high-backed chair, gripping the knobs on the end of the arms. His hair was thinning and he wore it combed straight back, making his face appear rounder and his nose bigger. How cold his eyes were should have frightened me more than they did, but I'd grown used to fear.

Lieutenant Dmitri stood behind the new commandant, hands clasped behind his back, and studied the toes of his boots. He glanced up once, looking straight at me. Concern for my sisters and me filled his eyes, and barely contained fury. Dmitri's jaw clenched and he resumed studying his boots.

The new commandant stared and we shivered, all of us silent. Finally he leaned forward and motioned to the guards. "I've seen them now. Take them to their room."

At the door, I glanced back. Lieutenant Dmitri watched us go, his expression unreadable.

That was the last time I saw him.

CHAPTER 14

Gabe

Gabe struggled awake, sweating and tangled in the bedclothes, fleeing another nightmare about the riot at Lotta's fountain. The dream was the same every night, full of screams and confusion, and dying children that he couldn't save. He lay there panting, the taste of charred timbers on his tongue, as if he'd really been running toward the pile of brick burying Jack.

Dawn was at least an hour away, and the moon had already set, but he still saw the cat sitting on the windowsill across the room. Mai's head was thrust between the chintz curtain panels and she stared into the backyard, tail thrashing and growling deep in her throat. Gabe slipped out of bed and eased his spare pistol out of the nightstand drawer, moving quietly so as not to wake Delia.

The wooden floor was cold under his bare feet, the air seeping in around the window frame colder still. He came at the window from the side, sidling along the wall and careful not to present a target to anyone watching from outside. That Mai kept growling, never shifting her gaze from the darkened yard, was more than enough to convince him that caution was warranted.

He lifted the curtain edge enough to view the yard. Predawn

shadows filled Dee's flower beds and stretched long from the base of the trees, pools of darkness that looked deep enough to drown in. Movement caught his eye, and a long, thin inky shape detached itself from one dark pool and slithered along the fence, finally going up and over into the neighbor's yard.

A glance told him Dee was still sleeping. The faint murmur in his ear warned him to stay close. He'd learned to pay attention, and he wasn't about to abandon her to chase after a fence-climbing shadow. Gabe waited until Mai's ears came up and the thrashing of her tail quieted to occasional, annoyed flips before putting on his dressing gown and creeping into the hall.

He went from room to room, checking that all the windows were shut tight. The locks on the front and back doors were checked, and checked again to give him peace of mind.

Everything was as it should be. Gabe still couldn't relax.

He called the station and told them to send a car, issuing orders for men to watch his house round the clock. The desk sergeant reassured him no trouble had been reported from the settlement house and that Randy hadn't called anything in from Dora's. Gabe thanked him, grateful everything was quiet.

Everything but his nerves.

The big window in the parlor was covered with lace curtains that did little or nothing to block his view of the backyard. Gabe settled into the big armchair facing the window, a hand wrapped around the pistol resting in his lap. The chair was upholstered in black horsehair, allowing him to fade into the deeper darkness inside the house. No one would see him from the outside if he stayed still.

A few minutes later, Mai hopped onto the arm of the chair to face the window as well, ears up and swiveling to catch every sound. Anyone who saw them would think the small gray cat was only keeping him company, but Gabe knew better.

He stayed in the chair until the sun was well up and all the shadows under the trees and against the fence disappeared. Gabe scratched Mai under the chin and went to the kitchen to keep his promise to Delia. The weight of the pistol dragged down the pocket of his dressing gown as he stacked and washed dishes, but that was a small thing.

Breakfast was almost ready when Dee came into the kitchen, bleary eyed and with her hair hanging loose around her shoulders. He turned to watch her and smiled, taken anew with how beautiful she was and how much he loved her. "Go ahead and sit down, Dee. Eggs are almost ready."

"You're up early." She yawned and sat in her usual chair near the window, eyeing the stack of clean dishes on the drain board and the pistol on top of the icebox. "Very early. Is everything all right?"

"I'm not sure." Mai bounded into the room, leaping up onto the windowsill near Delia's shoulder. He set a heaping bowl of scrambled eggs, plates of toast and sliced ham on the table. "Let me get your tea and I'll explain."

Explaining didn't take long, and they both managed to eat before the food got too cold. Delia stared into her teacup, swirling soggy tea leaves until they stuck to the sides, then swirling the cup again.

"Mai's been watching the yard for days. Occasionally she'd growl, but nothing to the extent you described." She pushed the cup away. "I never saw anything out there and neither did Dora when she was here, but I wasn't looking very hard. This man's stock-in-trade is illusion. There's no guarantee I'm right, but the shadow you saw slither over the fence was likely what he wanted anyone looking his way to see, not what was really there. Dora thinks I'll always be able to see through those illusions, but that might not be the case if he's trying not to be seen."

Gabe took her teacup and set it in the sink, thinking hard. "Can he get past your boundaries?"

Dee studied her folded hands, forehead screwed up in thought. "No, I don't think so. He'd have crossed them by now if he could. And don't forget, he appears to be afraid of Mai. I don't completely understand why, but it works to our advantage."

"That's something, at least." Gabe raked his fingers through his hair, smiling sheepishly. He knew her answer before he asked the question. "I don't suppose there's any chance of convincing you to stay inside the house."

"Not a one, Gabe." She cleared the sugar bowl off the table and put the lid back on the jam jar. "Besides, there's no guarantee I'm the one he's after. You're the chief detective on this case. There's an equally good chance he's trying to get to you. Don't forget what happened to Jordan."

That stopped him cold. "I never thought of that."

She stood on tiptoe and kissed his cheek. "I know. You're far too busy protecting others to ever imagine you might need protection yourself. Promise me you'll be more careful."

"I promise." He hugged her and reluctantly let go. "Do you have plans with Dora today?"

"Oh yes, exciting plans." Delia looked perfectly calm, but he knew her too well to believe that. He saw through her mask just as she saw through his. "We'll be spending most of the day in her study leafing through musty grimoires and deciphering dusty scrolls. No doubt it will all be scads of fun. Dora calls it research, but I suspect it's her way of keeping me from brooding too much."

Gabe retrieved his gun from the top of the icebox, pausing to look out the window. He searched the backyard for the hundredth time since the sun rose, his eyes lingering on the spaces under trees and the back of Delia's rose garden. "The dreams are worse?"

"Rushing toward their inevitable conclusion." She folded her arms, hugging herself against a chill that didn't exist. "The end is very close, Gabe, and I still haven't seen anyone I recognize. I'm—I'm afraid the people I'm supposed to look for will appear at the very last moment. I have to live through every moment of the hell Alina and her sisters endured until I know who these people are."

"I'm sorry." He wanted to go to her, but he'd learned years ago that she didn't want to be coddled. She needed to work through things on her own. "I'd help if I could."

"I'll be fine." She smiled. "This will all be behind us soon enough. I've faith that you'll catch your killer and Alina will get to live the remainder of her life in peace. There are bright spots in the midst of all this gloom."

He weighed the pistol in his hand, unsure. "Delia . . . you know where I keep this and how to use it. If I'm not here—"

"I won't hesitate." She grabbed a dishtowel and began drying the dishes he'd washed. "You'll be late if you don't get ready for work. I'll finish up in here."

She was right. Gabe started for the bedroom, but turned back. "How are you getting to Dora's? Should I send a patrol car to take you?"

Delia finished drying one plate and picked up another. "Dora's calling round to pick me up at ten. Don't worry, I'll be fine."

Mai stared at him as he left, as if scolding him for doubting Delia could take care of herself. The truth was that he didn't doubt her or her abilities. She handled the strangeness and the risks in their life with a calmness and skill he often envied. But he could never completely forget she was in danger, or shove away the feeling he was partly to blame.

She worried about him just as much. That was the price that hung over their heads for being together.

Gabe paid it willingly.

He pushed open the door to his office to find Jack sitting behind his desk. His partner's injured foot was propped up on a wooden box shoved into the space underneath. Someone, most likely Sam, had dragged the umbrella stand from behind the door to sit just behind the desk chair. Jack's cane held pride of place in the wrought iron stand. Papers and photographs of the murder scene were scattered across the desktop.

"It's about time you got here, Captain Ryan. I've been at work for more than an hour." Jack glanced up from the magnifying glass in his hand. He gestured toward the open locket he'd been studying. "Interesting that the killer left pictures of Alina at the scene."

"'Interesting' is one word for it." Gabe swallowed away the sudden tightness in his throat. They hadn't talked about Jack's close call, not yet, but maybe letting things go back to normal was for the best. He hung up his coat and hat before dragging a visitor's chair over to the desk. "I see Baker dropped off the photographs."

"Baker must have stayed up half the night to print these. If he ever decides to take the promotion exams and do something else, we're in trouble." Jack dug out a folder from the bottom of the pile and passed it over. "A messenger brought over the coroner's report about half an hour ago. Jordon was right about the awl being the murder weapon. The biggest surprise is that the killer stuffed her mouth full of silver coins. They were all Russian coins and minted before the war. It's possible the murderer took the money from the victim."

"So the coins would all be stamped with pictures of the tsar or his father." He flipped through the report, hoping to learn something he didn't already know. "The skin on her wrists and ankles is scraped raw, but no other wounds or major bruising. Dr. West found small pieces of rope embedded in the skin around her ankles. The killer tied her up after he took her off the train, but he didn't beat or torture her. Cause of death was a severed spinal cord near the base of the skull and blood loss. I hope that means it was over quickly."

Jack gestured toward the photos. "The way she's laid out reminds me of a sideshow magic act I saw once. First the assistant was levitated above a table, and then the magician sawed her in half. That girl was younger, but it's the same pose."

Comparing the case to a sideshow wasn't far wrong. Gabe set the coroner's report in the paper tray at the top corner of his desk. "What else came in?"

"Answers to some of your telegrams." Jack eased back in the chair and shifted his foot to a more comfortable position. He hunted around until he found the paper he wanted. "This one is from a Commander Bragg. He says there aren't any records of Mr. and Mrs. Rigaux, Aleksei Nureyev, or the couple posing as Alina's aunt and uncle coming through Ellis Island. Commander Bragg said a lot of European immigrants came in under different names or entered Canada before crossing the border. I sent Marshall over to Angel Island to see what he could dig up there."

"Good work, Lieutenant. It's a long shot, but knowing when they entered the country might help us trace the killer's movements." Gabe picked up the locket, staring at the faces of Alina and her sisters. Seeing ghosts in his own way. "Did Colin send an answer yet?"

Colin Adams was a professor of antiquities, collector of rare books, and world traveler, and Gabe's former brother-in-law. He'd known Colin before meeting his first wife, Victoria, and the two of them had remained friends after she was killed in the 1906 fire. Colin was spending two years in New York and Washington, D.C. He was helping to catalog historical artifacts and books salvaged from European museums and libraries destroyed in the Great War.

"Not yet. Knowing Colin, he's holed up in some dusty storeroom and hasn't seen your telegram yet." Jack rocked back in his chair and studied Gabe's face, openly curious. "What are you hoping Colin can tell you? He's a long way from San Francisco."

"He is, but he's also an expert on the changes in jewelry styles in European courts. I had to make him promise not to bring the subject up when Dora's around. The last time we had both of them over to play bridge, they talked about tiaras and necklaces for two hours." Gabe closed up the locket and carefully set it on the desk. "We never did finish the game. I'm hoping Colin can tell me if this locket came from the tsar's court or if it's a hoax. Colin's the best judge of whether it's authentic or not."

"What does Dora think?"

He rubbed the back of his neck, tired after his early morning wake up and vigil in the chair. "Dora has an emotional stake in this. She's convinced the jewelry belonged to either the tsarina or one of the grand duchesses."

"So say Dora's right." Jack tugged the end of his mustache and frowned. "What's the point of leaving a fortune in diamonds in a dead woman's fist?"

"I wish I knew, Jack." He glanced at the clock hanging over his office door. How late it was surprised him. "Have you heard from Jordan this morning? I thought he'd be here by now."

Jack began separating the papers and photographs on the desk into piles. "He was waiting in the hall when Sam and I got here. Sam stayed long enough to get me settled and left to visit Alina. Jordan went with him. Both of them will be back after lunch." He glanced up, his smile fading as he saw Gabe's expression. "Any particular reason you're keeping track of Jordan Lynch?"

"Something Delia said after breakfast. We had an unwanted visitor before sunrise." Gabe folded his arms over his chest and told Jack everything that had happened, from the moment he woke to find Mai growling at something in the darkened yard to Delia's promise to use his gun if need be. Jack's scowl continued to grow darker. "Until Dee reminded me of what happened to Lynch, I never even considered this killer might come looking for me. And he has the perfect opportunity to finish what he started with Jordan."

"Christ Almighty, Gabe. How are we supposed to catch someone who can change what they look like?" Jack gestured toward the corridor full of cops arriving for day shift and the night shift cops going home. "He could come into the station looking like any man on the squad, and we'd never know."

"Delia and Isadora are working on that. We'll find a way." The old clock chimed nine o'clock. "I called Randy before I left the house. He should be here with Father Sakovich in less than an hour. I'd like to get through the rest of these reports before then."

"Are you finished with the photographs?" Jack held up a small stack taken in Trula May's room. Jaret Rigaux's lifeless body filled the frame. "I'll get them ready to file if you don't need them."

He thought for a few seconds. "No, leave them out. I want to see how Sakovich reacts."

The photos went to one side, still in plain view of anyone who approached the desk. "What are you up to, Gabe?" Speculation sat in Jack's eyes. "Do you think Father Sakovich is involved with Mrs. Rigaux's murder?"

"I don't think he killed her. But he knows something." Gabe dragged a stack of folders toward him, choosing one at random. "We need to think of good questions, Jack. I don't want to be too hard on the kid, not unless I'm forced. Sakovich probably doesn't realize what he heard or saw is important."

By the time Randy ushered in the young priest, Gabe had read Eve Rigaux's autopsy report in detail and compared it to her husband's, and read half the stack of reports in front of him. He set them all to the side, careful not to obscure the photos lying faceup on the desk.

He stood and held out his hand, but didn't offer Sakovich a seat. Not yet. "Thank you for coming, Father Sakovich. This is my partner, Lieutenant Fitzgerald. We have some questions we need answered. I'll try not to take up too much of your time."

Sakovich didn't look to be more than twenty-three or twenty-four, short and slightly built with brown hair and clear green eyes. His beard was sparse, adding to the impression of youth. Fair skinned, a sprinkling of freckles splashed across his nose and cheeks. The young priest looked more Irish than Russian, but his accent erased all doubt about where he'd been born.

"I'll do what I can, Captain." He shook Gabe's hand and nodded at Jack. "I don't know how much help I can be."

Gabe smiled, doing his best to appear friendly. "How long have you been at Holy Trinity, Father?"

"I arrived in America less than a year ago." Father Sakovich looked uncomfortable being the center of attention. "Like so many in our community, I left Russia to escape the Bolsheviks and their firing squads. Lenin hates the church as much as he does the monarchy."

Jack traded looks with Gabe and took the lead. "Let's start at the beginning, Father. Where were you when you heard Mrs. Wetzel call for help?"

"She never called for help." He glanced at Gabe and back to Jack, puzzled. "Not that I heard. Father Pashkovsky sent me to the storeroom to see if Mrs. Wetzel needed someone to carry boxes back to the church hall. She'd fallen just inside the back door."

"Fallen?" Gabe stuffed his hands into his trouser pockets, hiding how he'd balled them into fists. This was a different story than he'd expected. "Had she fainted?"

"I imagine that's what happened. She didn't come around for

a very long time." Father Sakovich caught sight of the photos of Jaret Rigaux on the desk. He crossed himself, his fair skin mottled with burning red patches. "I—I started to leave, to find Father Pashkovsky and get help, but that's when I saw that poor woman's body and all the blood. I knew I couldn't leave Mrs. Wetzel alone, so I tried to carry her back to the rectory. Father Pashkovsky and Supervisor Devin came out of the rectory and saw us. They helped me get her inside and went back to the church. That's when I called the police."

He wasn't at all surprised that Sakovich had called the station. Gabe stared at the ceiling, thinking hard about how the storeroom was laid out. "Father, this is important. Think hard before you answer. Did Mrs. Wetzel faint coming into the room or going out? Which way was she facing?"

Father Sakovich looked Gabe in the eye. "She'd just come in, Captain, there's no question of that. I don't think she got more than a foot or two inside the door before she collapsed."

She couldn't have seen the body.

Gabe clenched his fists tighter, picturing the way the piano and stacks of boxes hid Eve Rigaux's body until you were well inside the room. He couldn't shake the certainty that the killer had arranged that as part of the tableau he'd so carefully planned.

Mrs. Wetzel had fainted for reasons other than shock at finding someone murdered inside the church. He had to accept the possibility that she might never remember what happened or why she fainted, but he had to ask.

He came back to himself with a start, realizing Father Sakovich was still speaking to him. "Pardon me, Father. I didn't hear what you said."

"I was wondering if you would tell me the name of the woman who was killed." The young priest pulled himself up taller and clutched the cross hanging around his neck. The air of being timid and unsure fell away. Sakovich was secure in the practice of his faith. "I want to pray for her soul and ask God to forgive her sins."

"Her name was Eve Rigaux." Gabe cleared his throat and pointed to the photographs strewn across his desk. "The man in the pictures was her husband, Jaret. You should pray for him too."

"I will." Father Sakovich nodded to Jack. "Good-bye, Captain, Lieutenant."

"One last question, Father." The young priest paused in the doorway, waiting, and Gabe hesitated a second. A lot rested on Sakovich's answer. "Did Father Pashkovsky or Supervisor Devin know you were calling the police?"

Sakovich gripped his cross tight. "No, Captain. I didn't tell them until after the police were on the way. They were very angry, but my conscience is clear. I did what was right."

"Thank you, Father." He went to the door and shook Father Sakovich's hand again. "Please call the station if you think of anything else."

Gabe stood in his office doorway, watching Sakovich walk down the corridor. Once the priest disappeared into the lobby, he came back inside and dropped into his chair.

Jack was scribbling in his notebook, recording the conversation before he forgot the details. He glanced up at Gabe and went back to writing. "Explain something to me, Captain Ryan. Why would a city supervisor and a priest be angry about the police being called to the scene of a crime?"

"I can think of only two reasons, Jack." He laid a picture of Eve's body on the desk, right next to a photo of her husband. "Either the two of them killed her, or they're covering up for the person who did."

"Why would Devin get himself involved with the Bolsheviks? He made campaign speeches condemning anarchists and makes anti-union statements to the papers all the time." Jack chewed the end of his pencil, a habit Sadie couldn't break him of. "Devin has money and a good family name. I think he's got the morals of an alley cat, but people in his district are convinced he does a good job. He could be governor in ten years. Why throw that away?"

He thought for a minute, trying to find a logical way around the answer that tied his guts into a knot. "What if that wasn't Devin? If Delia's right, and I'm afraid she is, we have to take that into consideration."

Jack stared for an instant, wrestling with the implications of what Gabe had said. Finally he set his jaw and nodded. "All right, we'll consider the idea that man was an impostor. And Father Pashkovsky? Do you really think a priest would commit murder?"

Gabe stretched out his long legs, studying the scuffed toes of his shoes. "Jordan doesn't think so, and normally I wouldn't either. But you didn't meet him, Jack. I can't put my finger on it, but there's something very strange about him." He looked up to find Jack watching him. "The union man Sam talked to said Pashkovsky was a boyhood pal of Aleksei Nureyev in Russia. They were supposed to have grown up in the same village. The man Jordan and I met is old enough to be Aleksei's father."

"The girl in Maggie's house, Trula May." Jack dug through the pile on Gabe's desk until he found the paper he wanted. "She said there were two men in the room with her and Mr. Rigaux."

"Trula never saw their faces. Those two men could have been anyone." He needed to check with Maggie and make sure Trula was still safe. Gabe yawned and rubbed his face. "Assign a man to follow Devin for a few days. Tell him not to worry too much about staying out of sight. If the supervisor questions why he's being tailed, we'll make something up about threats connected to the murder. We should know one way or the other in a few days."

"Noah Baxter would be a good choice." Jack scribbled more notes in his notebook. "What about Pashkovsky?"

"Station two men across the street from the church round the clock. Send Perry and Finlay for the first shift. Have them go inside and tell Father Pashkovsky the same story we're telling Devin." Gabe stood and got his coat from the rack behind the door. "If they're on the street, he can't do anything about it, but if he pushes for them to leave, tell Perry to push back. Maybe we can make him angry enough to make a mistake."

Jack's expression was closed off, but Gabe knew him well. His partner was weighing all the facts and forming an opinion. If Jack disagreed with Gabe's decisions, he'd hear about it.

Instead, Jack nodded and closed his pencil into his notebook. "Having cops around might make Pashkovsky think twice about giving Father Sakovich trouble."

He didn't need Jack's approval, but having it always made him feel he was on the right track. "I'm hoping knowing he's being watched makes Pashkovsky think twice about a lot of things. At the very least, it will buy us some time. I want to talk to Mullaney again and see if he can arrange for me to speak with some of his men. Dora told me there are any number of Russian counts and dukes waiting tables at the Fairmont. It won't hurt to talk to them."

"Is that where you're headed now, to see Mullaney?"

Gabe didn't miss the wistful look in Jack's eye or the hint of longing in his voice. They'd worked cases together for more than fifteen years, picking up on each other's cues and taking turns asking questions. Building a case was easier with both of them assembling clues and information.

Being stuck in the office was hard on Jack. It was hard on Gabe too.

"Not until Sam brings Jordan back. I thought I'd go down the street to Allen's Cafe and bring back some sandwiches and coffee." Gabe buttoned his overcoat and took down his hat. "My treat. You can give me ideas of how to approach Mullaney over lunch."

Jack nodded solemnly and pulled another pile of report folders to his side of the desk. “Bring some strawberry pie back too. Anita Allen makes the best strawberry pie in the state. They are in season now, aren’t they?”

“If not, I’ll get apple pie.” Gabe grinned, forgetting the case hanging over their heads for a few precious seconds. As he turned to leave, Gabe caught sight of the photographs of Eve and Jaret Rigaux lying side by side on his desk. His lighthearted mood disappeared.

The only way to really forget this case was for him and Jack to solve it. That day couldn’t come soon enough.

CHAPTER 15

Delia

The distance between our house and Dora's wasn't really that far, but she'd become increasingly anxious about leaving Alina for any length of time. As a result, we made a mad dash, taking a route that encompassed shortcuts through back alleys and streets that seldom saw much traffic. I held on tight, trying not to think of the speedometer edging upward or how she navigated corners at top speed. Serious conversations were the easiest way to ignore the scenery whipping past.

"Gabe and I have been talking." The wind caught my words and snatched them away. I raised my voice. "We're considering buying a second car so I don't have to depend on others for transportation. You wouldn't have to pick me up all the time or go out of your way to bring me home. And on occasion, I could drive instead of it always falling on you."

Dora stuck her lip out, pouting prettily. Young Stella had already learned how to melt away Jack's objections to almost any request by doing the very same thing. I'd be hard-pressed to say if Stella had learned the expression from Dora or her mother. "But I have so much fun driving the two of us around, Dee. And I really don't mind picking you up, really I don't."

The three princess ghosts watched the exchange from the corner of the windshield, all of them keenly aware of what was said. I'd grown used to one ghost watching me from every shiny surface. Seeing three was still sobering and a bit startling.

"That isn't it, Dora, I assure you." Officer Bryant saw us coming and opened the big iron gate at the foot of the drive. Dora waved and gave him a bright smile as we flew past. We barreled up the drive toward the house without Isadora slowing at all. I braced myself for the jolt when she stopped. "It's really rather maudlin, if you must know. Gabe doesn't want me to have to depend on others if something were to happen to him. As a matter of fact, he held you up to me as an example."

We came to a halt in the turning circle in front of the house. Dora set the parking brake and gave me a look that fell somewhere between skeptical and aghast. "Did he, now? Your husband is full of surprises. But yes, that is rather maudlin even if it is practical. Is Gabe still having nightmares about the riot?"

"Oh yes. The two of us make a perfect pair." I gestured at the trio of ghosts on the windshield. "I dream about the terrible things that happened to them, while Gabe dreams about not being able to save the children and the two rookies who died at the fountain. Breakfast conversation is a bit on the bleak side these days. What happened this morning didn't help matters. He brought up buying me a car again after he'd dressed for work."

I'd already told her about Gabe's keeping watch in the darkened house and Mai's standing guard at his side. She'd frowned but kept silent until I'd finished.

"Gabe's had a difficult couple of weeks, but learning you're not invincible is never easy. Since he's not sure he can protect himself anymore, he's trying to protect you instead." Dora patted my hand before opening the car door. "Things will settle again soon. But Gabe does have a point about being able to cope on your own, and he was absolutely right about not hesitating to use his gun if threatened. Don't dismiss his suggestions out of hand."

"I'm not. It's just all rather sudden." I came around to her side of the car, admiring the deep green morning glory vines around the front windows and the purple wisteria framing the door. Dora's wards glimmered underneath leaves and blossoms, shining bright even in sunlight. "Were you prepared when Mikal died?"

"Not at all." She slipped an arm around my shoulders as we went up the steps. "I was very young and sure he would always be there. Mikal spoiled me outrageously, which made it all the harder once he was gone. Don't live your life dwelling on the possibility of disaster, Dee, but be ready to stand on your own, just in case."

We'd reached the top step when another car pulled up and parked behind Dora's. Sam and Jordan Lynch got out. They waited next to the car just long enough for Sam to pull a package out of the backseat before coming up the steps to meet us.

"Good morning, Delia, Dora. You're both looking lovely as always." Sam grinned and kissed Dora on the cheek. "I hope you don't mind that I brought Jordan along."

She gave him a half smile, but the skin around her eyes tightened. "Flattery so early in the morning, Sam? You must have more up your sleeve than bringing Jordan for a surprise visit."

Jordan Lynch rested both hands on the head of his cane, a position that let him take some of the weight off his injured leg. "Don't lay all the blame on Sam. I talked him into bringing me along. I saw how Gabe works yesterday, and I'd like a peek at how you and Mrs. Ryan do things. If you don't want me hanging over your shoulder, just say so. I can wait in the car until Sam's ready to leave."

I caught the look Dora gave Sam. Jordan's curiosity amused her, but she was annoyed that she hadn't had time to prepare for his visit. Dora let very few strangers into her house, and one afternoon's acquaintance didn't make Jordan any less of a stranger.

She raised an eyebrow, her tone dry. "I do hope you understand that Dee and I aren't interested in putting on a performance. Our work is every bit as serious as anything Gabe and his squad undertake. A great deal of what we plan to do today appears extremely dull, but could go a long way toward catching this killer. Watching us pore over a stack of dusty manuscripts and scrolls is far from entertaining."

Jordan pulled himself up tall and straight and looked Dora in the eye. "I'm not interested in theatrics or tricks. I got a good taste of that in the church yesterday with the salt circle and the wind blowing through. Learning more about what you do and how you manage to help Gabe is the main reason I'm here. Meeting Sam's girl would be nice too, but I'll go if you want me to."

"I never said I wanted you to go." Dora winced, her expression contrite and apologetic. "And now you're angry and extremely insulted. That wasn't my intention, Jordan, I promise. You have my word that I'll explain too, but let's get inside first." She held a hand out to him, palm up. "Scott Jordan Lynch, you are welcome in my house. Let all who ask know I call you friend."

He hesitated, head tipped to one side and studying Dora's face. I wasn't sure he'd accept the invitation, but Jordan smiled, flattered and baffled both, and took her hand. "I'm honored, Isadora. I can honestly say I've never had a friend like you."

She beamed at him and took his arm. "I'll take that as a compliment. Now, don't let go of me. I didn't have time to prepare the boundaries. Going through the door might be a little rough this first time. Dee, take his other arm. We go together."

Sam held up his package. "I told Alina I'd bring some of my family pictures today. She's waiting, so I'll go inside while the two of you put Jordan through the initiation rites. I did call, Dora, but you'd already left. Randy said he didn't think you'd mind, so we came ahead. I'll know better next time."

Dora grimaced and rubbed her temples. "I truly don't mind. And I'm not the slightest bit angry at you, Sam, just a bit out of sorts and generally annoyed for some reason. Ignore me, all of you. I'll be fine once we're inside."

"Alina and I will start some tea. Don't forget to hold your breath while crossing the threshold, Lynch." Sam hurried inside, whistling and eager to see Alina.

I slipped my arm though Jordan's, leaving him free to still hold his cane. He looked a little apprehensive. "Ignore Sam's teasing too. You don't have to do anything but walk inside. In any case, now that Dora has invited you inside, you may come and go as you please."

"My grandma fancied herself the conjurer woman for the whole parish. She had ways of keeping people she didn't know out of her house when she wasn't home. Grandma was darn near ninety when the alderman's boys broke into her house." Jordan winked at me and straightened his shoulders. "Those boys came out of her house scared within an inch of their lives. Ghost traps in the trees wasn't the only thing she knew to do. Used to embarrass the hell out of my daddy."

Jordan crossed Dora's boundaries without the slightest hesitation. Once the three of us were in the entryway, Isadora patted his arm and moved away to hang up her hat and coat. "Dee, would you please take Jordan to my workroom? I need a moment to freshen up before I join you."

"Are you all right?" She was pale and drawn, her hands visibly shaking as she took off her coat. I removed my own wrap and took Dora's away from her, hanging both coats on the hall tree. "Can I get you something?"

"Don't fuss, Delia. You know I can't abide that." She smiled to take the sting out of her words. "I'm feeling better already. I'll be down in a few minutes."

Dora took the stairs slowly, but her color was returning and she held her head up. I took Jordan down the hall to her workroom.

Alina and Sam were already seated on the settee, heads bent over an old photo album. She appeared totally entranced, leafing through the pages and pointing to pictures of a skinny young boy I assumed must be Sam and laughing. Sam spoke in her ear and she glanced our way and smiled.

"Good morning, Delia." Alina stood, clutching the photo album to her chest and smiling. I couldn't help but reflect how different the bitter, resigned young woman in my dreams was from the happy one standing before me. She held out her hand to Jordan. "You must be Lieutenant Lynch. Sam's told me about you."

Jordan didn't stare, but he looked at Alina oddly, almost as if he thought he should know her or had seen her before. Given what I knew about her identity, that wasn't out of the realm of possibility. The newspapers ran photographs of royalty more often than film stars.

"Pleased to meet you, miss." He didn't linger over shaking her hand, letting go and stepping back as soon as was polite. "Sam's told me a bit about you too. He left out how pretty you are."

Alina blushed and glanced over her shoulder at Sam. He grinned but didn't say anything.

A reflection on the side of a crystal bowl next to the settee rippled, and the three princess ghosts brightened into view. Given how deep Dora's protections ran, I was surprised, but only for a second or two. Rules didn't apply to these ghosts or their behavior. I should have expected them to follow me.

Dora breezed into the room, brighter and more chipper than when she'd gone upstairs. "I see all the introductions have been made. Alina, would you be a darling and visit with Sam in the sitting room? Delia and I have a great deal of work to do, and most of my books are here."

Sam stood and took Alina's hand. "The cook is making tea for all of us. She'll bring some in as soon as you ring."

Dora smiled and went to a small bookcase nestled in a corner. "Thank you. Be sure to say good-bye before you leave."

Jordan had followed me to a tall glass-fronted case flanking the window. Three intent faces watched me from the curved glass front, but I did my best to ignore them. The oldest of Dora's books resided in this cabinet, some with leather covers so ancient that they threatened to crumble to dust if handled too roughly.

Opening the doors brought the smell of ancient oceans, pine forests, and the salty smell of heated desert sand. Each volume carried its own scent, a marker placed by the man or woman who wrote it. Spices, long vanished meadow flowers, herbs and perfumes: each one was unique.

Not all the aromas were pleasant. That too was a reflection of the contents; dark histories from desperate times, or a survivor recounting how evil almost swept the world away. I'd avoided reading those books when I first started working with Dora, but there was no avoiding the shadowed corners for long. Best to know and be prepared.

Jordan crinkled his nose as I piled my arms full of books, but didn't comment on the smell. "Can I help you carry those, Delia?"

"That big one on the bottom shelf." I pointed with my chin. "If you bring that one, you'll save me a trip."

A large oval table filled the center of the workroom floor. I added the books I'd selected to the ones Dora had already set on the table and took my seat. Jordan hesitated, standing away from the table, eyeing the stack of books.

Dora patted the chair next to her and smiled. "Sit down, Jordan. There's no reason to be uncomfortable while we bore you."

"I'm afraid if I get too comfortable, I'll start asking questions. You won't get any work done if I start down that path." He took the chair anyway, laying his cane across the one next to it. Jordan touched the spine of one book gingerly. "Can I help in any way?"

Dora's expression softened and her smile brightened. "If you like. Many of the old books are written in such a way that makes them difficult to understand, a type of cipher or code, if you will. I'm not sure how much you'll understand, but I can give you key words to look for. If you find them, you can hand the book off to one of us."

"I'd like to try." He took a book off the stack. The smell of sun-warmed pine needles wafted up and vanished. "My grandmother was born a slave and she never got the chance to learn to read. She made sure my father learned once they moved north, and sent me off to school as soon as I was old enough. I think it broke her heart that my daddy wasn't interested in learning anything that didn't come out of his Bible."

The distant past wasn't always as far off as it seemed. That was often difficult to remember. I cleared my throat. "We're looking for anything that has to do with illusions. How they're cast, what kind of charms are used, and most important, how to break an illusion. Dora and I have more than enough evidence that this killer is a master at those spells. We're looking for ways to combat that ability."

"I'm sure Gabe told you the story of what happened at the parade." Dora fetched a pack of cigarettes and an ashtray from a side table and settled into her chair again. "A large number of the union men reported seeing monsters and angels reaching for them from the smoke. Many of the men who came from Ireland were adamant they saw banshees. The man we're looking for cast those illusions. That takes a great deal of skill."

"Damnation." Jordan sat back, mouth pulled tight and arms crossed. "What other tricks can this man pull?"

"We don't know for sure. You saw for yourself what he did at the church. Making you all think you smelled a rotting corpse was another type of illusion." I pulled my hands into my lap, keeping myself from picking at the fringe on the runner down the center of the table. "He may be able to change his face to look like someone else. I'm fairly confident he can draw shadows around himself to keep from being seen when he chooses."

Jordan had been attentive, listening closely, but now his expression changed to angry disbelief. He'd recognized something, or thought he did.

Dora watched him keenly, her cigarette forgotten. "Tell me what you're thinking, Jordan."

"I'm thinking I almost had this man in Chicago and that's how he fooled me. He changed his face." He gripped the edge of the table, anger sparking in his eyes. "Two men from my squad heard screams from one of the tenement houses. They burst in to find a woman dead and a man climbing down the fire escape. Clyde Dalton gave chase, and his partner called the station for more men. This was the third murder in a month in the Russian neighborhood. We'd already increased patrols, and it took only a few minutes until more than a dozen officers were searching that block. I was with them."

I exchanged looks with Dora. "How did he get away?"

"We'd been searching the area for hours. I had three other men with me, all of us with our guns drawn." Jordan's eyes took on a faraway look, remembering. "We saw Dalton strolling down an alley, bold as brass and in no hurry at all. One of my men called to him, but he kept on going out the other end. We found Dalton's body a few minutes later. He was already cold. The four of us spent a long time convincing ourselves we'd seen someone else in that alley."

Dora snubbed out her cigarette. "Finding a way to either see through this man's illusions or stop him from casting them in the first place may be the best means of catching him. We know that Dee can see through his illusions. I'd guess I can as well, but I haven't had occasion to test that idea just yet. Regardless, the sooner we find a solution to this, the better for all involved."

Jordan gestured toward the stack on the table. "And you really think we can find the answer in these books."

"We won't know until we try." Dora drummed her long red nails on the tabletop and frowned. "A bit of luck wouldn't hurt either. And I'm perfectly willing to manufacture my own luck if matters come down to that."

I knew Isadora Bobet better than anyone aside from Randy. She was never reckless, but she didn't flinch from taking chances when necessary. "You're thinking of setting a trap and luring him in."

She smiled, a fond parent praising a child's cleverness. "Only as a last resort, Dee. I don't think it will get to that."

Jordan nodded. "Dora's right. He'll come after one of you or Sam's girl first. The trick is to be ready when he does."

"Precisely." Dora chose a book from the pile and opened it to the first page. The scent of lavender filled the air. "And once he's inside, he won't find it easy to leave again."

Noon was fast approaching before Sam and Alina wandered into Dora's workroom. The two of them were hand in hand, and Alina carried Sam's photo album in the crook of one arm.

"It's time for me to get back to the station, Jordan." Sam squeezed Alina's hand before stepping over to the table. He picked up a book and squinted at the print along the spine. "You can stay here if you like. I can always swing by later to take you to Mrs. Allen's."

Jordan closed the book he'd been searching through, brushing his hand across the cover before setting it aside. "I promised Gabe I'd go out to the union hall with him. And these ladies are too nice to say so, but I'm just slowing them down. I'll be more useful out on the street."

Dora stuck another slip of paper in the book she was reading, marking a place she wanted to come back to. She peered at him sternly and arched an eyebrow. "I disagree, Lieutenant Lynch. You've been an enormous help."

"She's right, Jordan, and you might as well own up to that." I twisted in my chair to look up at him as he put on his jacket and found his hat. "I have some influence with Captain Ryan. Perhaps I can persuade him to share you."

"I appreciate the compliment, but I know where I'm needed most." Jordan tipped his hat. "Let's get out of here, Sam, before they charm me into staying."

Sam lingered long enough to say good-bye to Alina. Dora had convinced them that standing in the open front door, saying prolonged good-byes, was unwise. Alina stood in the workroom doorway to watch until Sam reached the front door. Each parting between them was difficult, fraught with the threat that hung over her and not knowing if they'd ever see one another again. That was a feeling I was all too familiar with, in both the past and the present.

Alina turned around, blinking too fast and flushed, Sam's photo album hugged to her chest. She was always at loose ends without Sam, but the truth was that she had little to occupy her time. "Do you need anything from me, Dora? I could fetch more tea if you like."

"Thank you, dear heart, but we have plenty of tea." Dora smiled fondly, her voice full of affection. "If you're hungry, the cook will gladly fix you something."

Isadora was always tender with Alina, gentle in a way I'd not seen from her with anyone except Stella. I often wondered if she thought of Alina as the daughter she'd never had, or if she felt responsible for easing the way for a friend's child. Either way, it was a side of Dora I'd rarely seen.

Alina stared at the pile of books on the worktable, as if noticing them for the first time. She moved closer to stand next to Dora's chair. "I've seen books like these before. They're very old, aren't they?"

Dora's smile stayed firmly in place, but all her attention shifted to Alina. She leaned forward ever so slightly, her posture wary. "Yes, very old, and very rare. There aren't many like them left in the world. Do you remember where it was you saw them?"

The three princesses popped into view, their images floating on the tea in my cup. I ignored the ghosts as best I could, but I couldn't ignore the watcher filling my head. Whether the dragon meant to help Alina remember or keep her memories locked away, I couldn't say. But I'd never understood this creature's motives.

"I remember a room full of sunlight. One entire wall was full of windows, and all the drapes were pulled back. It was wintertime, but the room wasn't cold. I wanted to play in the snow." She reached out a hand and brushed fingers across the creased blue leather of the top book, jerking her hand back abruptly. "The books were strewn across a white marble tabletop. A man was reading from one much like this. That's all I remember."

Dora and the watcher sighed at precisely the same instant. I knew Isadora was disappointed Alina's memories were still fragmented images and nothing more.

As the dragon's eyes closed, I wouldn't wager against her being relieved.

Alina drew herself up straight and squared her shoulders, attempting to hide just how unsettled these moments left her. "I'll go to my room and leave you and Delia to your work. Maybe I can finish reading the book Sam left yesterday before he comes back for supper."

Dora stood and gave Alina a quick hug before stepping back and peering at her anxiously. "I don't want you to feel that you must go away. You're welcome to stay if you like."

"I know I could stay, but I want to finish the book. Then I can talk to Sam about it." She opened the photo album, leafing through the book until she came to a picture of a barefoot Sam dressed in overalls. The photo appeared to have been taken by a traveling photographer. Sam was posed stiffly in front of a small farmhouse with a couple that must be his parents, a pair of lop-eared dogs on either side of him. He couldn't have been more than ten or eleven, but he was almost as tall as the man I assumed to be his father.

Alina pointed at the photo. "The boy in the book, Tom, must have looked just like this. Sam promised he'd explain anything about the story that I didn't understand."

Dora's eyes sparkled with amusement and she laughed. "He has you reading *Tom Sawyer*? Yes, go finish the book. Listening to him explain over supper should be quite entertaining."

Alina hurried away and Dora took her seat again, all traces of gaiety gone. She lit a cigarette, her expression pensive and brooding.

"Out with it, Dora." I leaned forward, hands folded on the table. "What's wrong?"

She made a helpless sort of gesture, something very out of character for Isadora Bobet. "I worry about her. She starts to remember, to put together pieces and odd bits, and something shuts them off. What bothers me most is that I'm not sure if this is coming from her enemies or from this so-called guardian of hers. Regardless of where it's coming from, I worry about the damage it's causing."

I sat back again, staring at my cold tea and the three princess ghosts. "I'd think not remembering her life would be more damaging."

"Normally I'd agree, but I see what this is doing to her. And I can't help but think that part of this is my fault." Dora took a long drag on her cigarette, blowing clouds of blue smoke toward the ceiling. "Before I began pushing her to remember, Alina didn't know what she'd lost. Now every instant of the past she remembers makes her hungry for more. That's taking a toll, and I can't help feeling guilty. I started her down this path."

"But what happens when she does remember? None of us can protect her from the pain once she discovers her family is dead."

"She already knows, Dee." Dora scowled, her mood grim. "Alina may not remember the details of how they died or why they were killed, but she knows her family is gone. I can see it in her face."

We left it there and went back to searching ancient texts for ways to stop this necromancer. Both of us knew we were running out of time. Neither of us could predict what would happen when the clock ran out.

Late that afternoon, we'd exhausted the resources to hand. Dora had set aside two slim volumes to study further, copies of personal narratives dating from the 1700s, and had started back through the first one. She left off staring at the crabbed handwriting filling a page and frowned. "These records cover more than five hundred years. Somehow it doesn't seem right that we can find only two small references to necromancers. I need a drink. Can I get you anything, Dee?"

"A glass of sherry would be nice." I'd put the saucer on top of my teacup and turned my back to the glass on the bookcase. Each time I'd glanced up, three young ghostly faces had greeted me, hopeful that I'd found the solution at last. I found it both distracting and very sad. "I've had quite enough tea for the time being."

Dora went to the black lacquer cabinet in the corner, pouring whiskey for herself and an inch of sherry for me. She set my glass in front of me and went back to her chair. "Let me know what you think of the sherry, it's not what I normally buy. My usual liquor merchant has closed up shop and gone into another business. He didn't want to be caught short when the temperance law takes effect in January. I had to make do with what the new man had."

"It might be a little sweeter, but it's very good." I set the glass aside, resolved to make it last. The occasional glass of sherry with Dora was a treat, one I'd miss when all the shops stopped selling liquor. "Is there anything we can use in those references?"

"As a weapon?" Dora cradled her whiskey glass in both hands. "I'm afraid not. Both of them speak of how a necromancer accumulates power and what uses they can put that power to. Most of what's recorded are things we already knew about illusion and making ghosts for his own purposes. Displays and manipulations such as the one he put on at the parade take a great deal of hoarded power. I imagine all the energy he'd accumulated from the killings in New York and Chicago were held in reserve for when he found Alina."

"So we were wrong about that. He does kill for power." I took another sip of sherry, thinking. "Changing his face to resemble someone else must tax his reserves as well. Does the book say anything about that?"

"Nothing clear cut, but what I found matches Jordan's story." She leafed through the pages, coming back to a marked page. "There was a report from Finland late in the 1600s of a necromancer who evaded capture by wearing the faces of his victims. Church authorities searched for more than a year before finding him. That echoes Jordan's experience neatly. It's implied that for this kind of illusion to work, the person being mimicked must be dead. We can't take all the details of these accounts as being absolute truth, especially when they've been handed down from the seventeenth-century Church."

"But we should be prepared for this killer to look like anyone, including Gabe and Randy. That coupled with not knowing whether he can mimic only the dead introduces a great deal of uncertainty." I drained the last of my sherry, understanding fully what drove Dora to drink. Dulling the growing panic inside, even for a moment or two, had a definite appeal. "I may or may not be able to see through his illusions, or judge a real person from a doppelgänger. What if I'm wrong?"

She reached for my hands, holding them tight. I couldn't doubt the sincerity in her eyes. "You'll know, Dee, I have absolute faith in that. That may be a purpose for these dreams we hadn't considered, to teach you how to spot the difference between real and illusion."

The dragon's eyes filled my head, radiating approval and confidence that I was up to the task. Panic faded under her regard. I wasn't the only one standing between this man and Alina, nor the only one with the ability to know true from false. The watcher, the sister ghosts, and even my tiny warrior cat all saw through illusion to the man beneath.

Time was short, the dreams meant to teach me so many things drawing to a close. I'd have to be ready.

I didn't have a choice.

CHAPTER 16

Gabe

Gabe and Jack were just finishing lunch when Sam and Jordan Lynch arrived.

"You're just in time, Butler." Jack scraped the last bits of pie off his plate and licked them off his fork. "Another few minutes, and all the pie would be gone. You know how Gabe is. He has no control when apple pie is around."

"Keep slandering my name, Jack, and you'll be buying your own lunch." He took two wrapped plates, each holding a big piece of pie, off the top of the file cabinet and offered them to Sam and Jordan. "Everything quiet at Dora's?"

Sam spoke around a mouthful of apple pie. "I caused a bit of a stir bringing Jordan unannounced, but we sorted things out. Not a hint of trouble otherwise."

"Good. Let's hope it stays that way." Gabe gathered up discarded sandwich wrappings and tossed them in the wastebasket. He glanced at Jordan while stacking dirty plates and forks in the box lunch had come in. Dropping the dishes off at the café on his way out would take only a minute. "How did you and Dora get along?"

"We got on fine. I spent the morning working with Dora and your missus. They helped me figure out how this killer got away from me in Chicago. I'd never have understood without them." Jordan set his pie aside and offered Gabe his hand. "I owe you an apology, Gabe, and I hope you'll accept it. Turns out, I'm not near so smart as I should be. This is your case. I never should have questioned how you were working it."

"No harm done." He smiled and shook Jordan's hand, knowing full well that the older cop would take offense if he didn't. The last thing he wanted to do was offend Jordan Lynch. "What Delia and Dora do takes some getting used to. You're not the first to question them working with me and Jack."

Lon Rockwell knocked and pushed open the office door at almost the same instant. At times Gabe was tempted to think that some of the younger cops had adopted the worst of Jack's bad habits, but he'd never make that statement about Sergeant Rockwell. Something had happened.

The expression on Lon's face was all the confirmation he needed. Gabe stepped away from his desk and into the middle of the room. "What is it, Sergeant?"

Lon saw Jordan and hesitated, looking for Gabe's slight nod before continuing. "I'm sorry to interrupt your lunch, Captain. A report just came in that a body was found by a street sweeper in the Dogpatch neighborhood. The patrolman on the scene identified the man as Supervisor Devin."

His heart caught between beats and moved on. Gabe didn't dare look at Jack; his calm façade would shatter if he did. "Has the coroner arrived on the scene yet?"

"No, sir. Not when I talked with Officer Dodson."

Gabe did glance at Jack now, seeing the same speculation on his partner's face that ran through his own head. This soon after Eve Rigaux's murder, finding Devin dead wasn't a coincidence.

His gun was locked in the top drawer, but he'd gotten in the habit of wearing his holster in the office. What that said about the changes in his job didn't bear thinking about. Gabe unlocked the drawer and slipped the gun into the holster, settling the weight against his side. "Send three cars to back up Officer Dodson, Lon. If any of the men on patrol are armed, they have priority for going to the scene. Make sure Baker and his camera go out there too. Have a car pull up out front and wait for me. I won't be long."

"Yes, sir." Lon hesitated with his hand on the doorknob. "Should I issue a sidearm to your driver? I don't think Walken carries one of his own."

A part of him flinched, haunted by visions of the dead rookies at the Saint Patrick's Day parade. Gabe gave the order anyway. "Make sure he knows how to use a gun first. I'll be out in a few minutes."

Jordan added his plate and fork to the pasteboard box of dirty dishes. "Dogpatch is a strange name for a neighborhood. What is this place?"

"A long time ago, there were slaughterhouses on the nearby creek. Story was that packs of dogs used to live there and scavenge scraps from the refuse piles. People started calling it Dogpatch, and the name stuck." Gabe rummaged through the piles on his desk, looking for the key to his desk drawer. He found it dangling from the bottom drawer lock. "There's a mix of factories and boardinghouses there now. More than half the people living there are Irish immigrants, but the rest are Russians, Slavs, and Italians. It's a lot like the neighborhood most of your Chicago murders happened in."

"Do tell." Jordan rubbed the back of his neck, his expression closed off and careful. "I don't suppose you'd like some company out there? Assuming Jack doesn't object."

He blessed Jordan for thinking to ask. Jack shrugged, appearing unconcerned, and tried to make light of being left behind again. "Why would I object? Gabe needs someone to look out for him."

"I can take care of that." Lynch pulled his coat open, revealing his long-barreled Colt holstered at his side. "I didn't think walking around without this was a good idea. Turns out I was right."

"You were right. And you saved me from answering the desk sergeant's questions about why I'm issuing you a sidearm." Gabe tossed the desk keys to Jack. "Lock up when you're finished with the files. I'll get the keys from you later. Sam, I need a favor."

"Sure. What do you need, Gabe?"

"Drop by the union hall. Find out if Mullaney will meet with me at Saint Mary Magdalene this evening." He stuffed his old fedora on his head and put on his overcoat. "I don't want Aleksei to know I'm talking with Dominic. And make sure Dominic knows that Father Colm is welcome to join us. That might make him feel better about talking to me."

Sam checked his pocket watch. "I need to be back at the paper a little over two hours from now. Should be plenty of time to visit Mullaney first."

"Thanks." Gabe held the door for Jordan. "Do me another favor, Sam. Be careful."

Butler nodded gravely. "You and Jordan do the same."

Gabe and Jordan Lynch hurried down the hallway. They all needed to be careful, to watch each other's backs, and look out for the people they cared about. He was rarely afraid, but something—no, everything—about this case scared him. The overwhelming feeling that he couldn't trust his own eyes was at the heart of that.

The only cure was to catch the killer. Maybe then the nightmares would stop and he could sleep at night.

Fog had begun to move in by the time Gabe and Jordan drove out to Dogpatch. Swirling mist caressed the car windows, leaving smeared fingerprints of moisture behind. That the sun was out, hidden by the lowering clouds, made the fog all the more ominous to Gabe. Working in the shifting half light meant taking extra care not to miss things. And the concealing nature of fog made it all too easy for someone to come up on them unawares.

Jordan had never seen San Francisco fog. He got out of the car and stood on the curb, watching gray tendrils creep down the side of dirty brick buildings and slither along the sidewalk. Lynch watched silently for a moment, fascinated. "I've read about San Francisco fog, but I had to see for myself to believe. Easy to understand why people describe it as something alive. Lake fog in Chicago is nothing like this."

"Work a few murder scenes on foggy nights, and you'll be convinced all the stories are true." Gabe buttoned his overcoat and flipped up the collar. Damp chill still clung to his skin, trying to work its way to the bone. "Funny how many times thick fog comes in around a murder scene too."

Lynch's eyes were full of mirth, but his expression remained serious. "Are you saying the fog's full of ghosts, Captain Ryan?"

Gabe smiled and moved toward where Maxwell waited, Jordan matching his pace. The mouth of an alley gaped behind the patrolman, an open maw full of mist. "That's for you to decide, Lieutenant Lynch. You might want to have a talk with Delia before you make up your mind. For now, let's go see what my men have to say."

Maxwell was huddled into his uniform coat, hands in his pockets. He nodded to Jordan, his brief smile friendly. "Afternoon, Lieutenant. The body's at the end of the alley, Captain. Dr. West hasn't said yet, but from the looks of things, he's been there for days. Maybe as long as a week."

Jordan touched the brim of his hat and returned Maxwell's smile. "Afternoon, Officer. Are you sure the dead man is Supervisor Devin?"

"Three of us were assigned guard duty during his last campaign. I spent a month following him around the city, listening to him give speeches, and watching him shake hands. Even after what the rats did to the body—there's no doubt it's Devin." Maxwell frowned. "None of it makes any sense, Captain. How could his body have been lying there for a week? I saw him at the church when that woman was murdered. That was only a few days ago."

"We all saw him, Maxwell." Gabe clamped down hard on the shivers threatening to well up and rattle his teeth. *He'd looked the man in the eye, stood not three feet away from the killer, and not known.* Clearing his throat let him speak. "How did a street sweeper get to the end of that alley?"

"Mr. Jansky needed to relieve himself, and he didn't want to do so in sight of the street." Maxwell pointed at the blank walls overlooking the alley on either side. "There aren't any windows for people to look down and see him. Lots of tradesmen use alleys in neighborhoods like this. He knew something was wrong when he heard the rats and went looking for what they were after. Mr. Jansky found a beat cop, who called it in."

"Thank you, Maxwell. Pull Walken out of the car. I want the two of you to keep anyone who doesn't belong from wandering down the alley. Coroner's men and squad members only." Gabe clapped him on the shoulder on the way past. "Anyone else comes nosing around, find me."

"Yes, Captain."

The alley trapped the fog, making it thicker, darker. Not only weren't there any windows looking down from above, but the two doors Gabe saw were boarded over and padlocked as well. Broken glass crunched underfoot, bigger pieces spinning away when he or

Jordan kicked one by accident. No ash cans lined the alley, but the ground was strewn with all kinds of trash nonetheless.

He saw food scraps in the mix, discarded remnants of a half-eaten lunch left behind, or food stolen from the grocer a block over. That helped explain the large number of rats. Dark forms scuttled into holes chewed into the bottom of walls as Gabe and Jordan approached, glittering black eyes angry at being chased away from their feast.

They came upon the street sweeper, Mr. Jansky, being questioned by Officer Warren. The street sweeper was well over seventy, slight and stoop shouldered, his clothes patched and threadbare. Jansky's coat was too thin for the weather, but he'd expected to be working, not standing still in clammy fog, answering questions.

Gabe considered having Warren send the old man home and quickly changed his mind. The chances of Mr. Jansky having seen anything useful were slim, but they wouldn't know that until Warren got all his answers.

The flash from Baker's camera was muted by the fog, light diffused into an indistinct glow. Long experience said Baker would get his shots anyway.

Devin's body lay facedown, the top of his head hard up against a brick wall. One arm was thrown up over his head as if to ward off a blow. Water dripped off the eaves, each drop landing square in the middle of Devin's back and soaking his suit coat. The puddle around him was stained with blood, part from where the rats had chewed exposed flesh, a larger part from the knife shoved into the base of his skull.

"Gabe." Jordan's voice was a low rumble that carried in the fog. "The knife. Do you see it?"

"I see." He stepped back, getting out of Baker's way as he moved the camera. "The blade's bigger, but it's the same spot he used to kill Eve Rigaux. Wish I knew what the hell that means."

"Does it have to mean something?" Jordan edged around the body, bending down to take a closer look at Devin's hands. "I'm not disagreeing with you, Captain, just trying to see where you're headed with this."

Dr. West stood a few feet away, still wearing his black rubber gloves and scribbling notes in a large notebook. He looked up, openly amused. "Lieutenant Lynch is right. The placement of the knife is almost identical to Mrs. Rigaux. I didn't find anything hidden in Devin's hands or in his pockets. My instincts say that he died where he fell, but that's only a guess. Given the way evidence has been washed away and the animal damage to the body, an educated guess is probably the best I can do."

Gabe nodded, still studying the way Devin's body was placed. West was right; there was no hidden message here. "I can't ask for more. How long do you think the body's been here?"

"A week to ten days, maybe a little longer. Rigor's been gone for a long time." He squatted next to the body, pointing with his pencil. "These bite marks on the back of his hand, and over here on his neck, are fresh. You can't see any evidence of bleeding or blood weeping from either one. That's a good indicator that the body's been here for some time. Any blood left in the body is pooled in the lowest parts."

"If Mr. Jansky hadn't picked this alley as a privy, he might never have been found." Some tiny and unrelenting detail still bothered him, dancing out of reach each time Gabe reached for it. "Can we turn him over?"

Jefferson West gave two of his men instructions to do as Gabe asked. They rolled Devin faceup, an awkward job at best. Still, the two men were careful not to splash blood-tainted water on Baker's camera or on any of the cops watching.

A pearl-headed hatpin secured a folded piece of paper to the front of Devin's jacket. The paper was soaking wet, the ink smeared and running together. West slipped the hatpin out and looked up at Gabe with an apologetic smile. "Maybe I was wrong about hidden messages."

Jordan braced himself with a hand on Gabe's shoulder and leaned in for a closer look. "Maybe not, Doctor. That may not be meant for the captain and his men at all, especially if the killer never expected the body to be found."

"What do you think it is, then?" Gabe held open a large glassine envelope while West gingerly placed the paper inside. As wet as the paper was, the real danger was that the folded square would either fall apart or fuse into one solid mass before they had a chance to dry it out.

"I think the best people to ask are Miss Bobet and Mrs. Ryan." Jordan looked him in the eye, clearly reluctant to say too much in front of the deputy coroner. "I think they'd be interested in taking a look. Chances are, Miss Bobet will know a way to open it up without the whole thing falling apart."

"That's a good place to start." Gabe held the envelope flat on his palm, trying to puzzle out smeared ink lines in the dying light. The fog was growing thicker, deeper. He tried to convince himself that the murk wasn't gathering around Devin's body, a shifting pearly gray shroud that sought to hide the supervisor's ravished face. Gabe slipped the envelope into an inside pocket. "Thank you, Dr. West. Please send your report over to my office as soon as you're finished."

"You'll have it by morning." West tugged off his black gloves, letting them dangle from his hand. The young deputy coroner looked uncomfortable and embarrassed. "Gabe—do me a favor, if you would. Tell me what Dora says. I'd really like to know."

He hesitated but finally nodded. "I'll get word to you."

The walk back to the car was silent. Gabe hunched into his overcoat once he'd given Walken the directions to Dora's house, trying to get warm. Jordan stared out the window, making a point of studying the fog and the veiled landscape. He had faith that if Lynch wanted conversation, he'd speak up.

Gabe took the envelope from his pocket, laying it flat on the seat between them. Dora would know what it was.

Dora would know.

Dora passed her hand over the glassine envelope for the third time, eyes shut. Each time, her frown deepened and she winced slightly.

Each wince added to Gabe's guilt. Delia slipped an arm around his waist, leaning against him. That she wasn't angry with him too was a blessing.

Isadora was furious. She slumped back in her chair and opened her eyes, giving him a baleful look. "I thought you understood not to bring things into my house without calling first. You of all people should know better, Gabe Ryan."

"Gabe's already apologized, Dora." Dee gave him a quick hug and went to stand next to Dora's chair. She planted her feet, watching Isadora sternly. "He's apologized five times by my count, and that should be enough. Why don't you tell us the real reason you're upset?"

The two of them glared at each other, both equally stubborn. Dora gave in first, rolling her eyes and tossing a hand up in exasperation. "All right, you win. I'm not as angry with Gabe as I am shaken by how narrowly we avoided disaster. It's a finding spell, Dee, and it was designed specifically to find Alina."

"Mother of God . . ." Gabe extended a hand in apology and let it fall again. "Dora—I'm sorry. I should have called first or asked you to come to the station."

She peered at him and raised an eyebrow. "I'd appreciate you remembering that beforehand in the future. We got lucky this time.

The spell is badly degraded from the paper spending so much time in the water. All the lines have run and the ink is smeared, but the energy mined from Supervisor Devin's death still lingers. I've done what I can to shut it away. Once Randy comes home, I can finish the job."

Jordan sat in a chair near the window, brooding and pensive. "Devin was already dead the day we were all at the church. This is twice I've looked this man in the face and thought he was someone else. That's an uncomfortable feeling."

Images, pieces of what they knew and what he'd seen, ran through Gabe's head. He couldn't find a pattern.

Maybe there wasn't one. Maybe he'd been looking at this the wrong way.

Gabe retrieved his jacket from the back of an armchair and slipped it on. "I arranged a meeting with Dominic Mullaney at Saint Mary Magdalene. If I don't leave now, I might miss him, Dee. I'll call the station before I go and have them send a car to take you home. Have one of the men watching the house wait inside with you until I get home."

"I can wait with her." Jordan pushed himself up out of the chair and leaned heavily on his cane. Another pang of guilt hit Gabe. He hadn't given Jordan's leg or that the older cop might be in pain a thought. "That is, if Delia doesn't mind having me underfoot. Mullaney doesn't know me, and he might think twice about talking with me around."

Delia smiled. "Of course I don't mind. Perhaps you could tell me more stories about your grandmother."

Relief made Gabe smile in turn. They'd take care of each other, and neither would feel smothered or slighted. He kissed Delia's cheek. "Then it's settled. Don't wait supper for me."

Dora stood and gave him a hug. "Be careful who you trust, Gabe Ryan. Be very careful."

She wasn't talking about Jordan, he was certain of that, nor Sam and Jack, or Randy. That left most of San Francisco to watch with a wary eye. He couldn't think about that right now.

He thought of patterns instead.

Four nights a week, Father Colm stood in the front of the church and handed out baskets of groceries to the wives of men who'd lost their jobs over wanting to join the union. He believed in the phrase "bread or revolution" as deeply as Mullaney or any of the union men, but his belief ran toward handing out bread to stave off the need for violent revolution. Even so, he wasn't above strong-arming rich parishioners and business owners for donations. No one in his flock went hungry for long if Father Colm could help it.

Twice a month, the priest hosted parish dinners for anyone who wanted to come eat, sitting entire families down at big tables in the church hall and serving them stew and fresh bread. Husbands and grandfathers came to eat with their families on those nights. The social air of the evening and the open invitation for the whole congregation soothed their pride.

He'd forgotten that a dinner was being held this evening. The hall was filling with people when Gabe arrived, making it less likely his arrival would attract notice. Women and men stood in knots exchanging news and gossip, while excited children dashed around and somehow avoided being underfoot at the wrong moment. Father Colm spotted Gabe right away, nodding toward the back.

Gabe found Dominic in the church kitchen, ladling boiling hot stew into bowls. The union leader glanced up but kept working. "There's an apron on a hook over by the stove, Ryan. Lend a hand, and no one will think twice about the two of us talking."

He traded his overcoat and jacket for the apron, adjusting the patched white canvas around his waist until most of his pistol and holster were covered. Even inside the church, Gabe didn't feel easy about going unarmed.

Mullaney eyed the gun. "Things must be bad for you to wear that where Father Colm can see. Tell me what's so important, we need to meet in secret."

Gabe arranged more bowls on empty metal trays, getting them ready for Dominic to fill. "I need information about your friend Aleksei and his trip to New York a few months ago. And I thought it best to make sure he wasn't hanging over your shoulder while we talked. This is important or I wouldn't involve you."

"Alek has his own life, Captain." A wheeled serving cart with three shelves sat next to Mullaney. He put the full tray on the bottom shelf and began filling another tray's worth of bowls. "He keeps lots of secrets, but that's his right. There's no guarantee I know the answers to what you're asking."

He shrugged. "Maybe not. But hear me out first."

Telling Mullaney everything was risky, but Gabe didn't see another way to convince the young union leader to trust him. He started with the murders and disappearances in Chicago's Russian neighborhoods, how the rumors and whispers among immigrants of the Bolsheviks hunting down anyone with royal blood were true, and how the pattern was being repeated in San Francisco. Gabe didn't hold anything back when it came to detailing how Eve and Jaret Rigaux were killed.

He didn't come right out and say Aleksei was at risk, but he didn't have to. Dominic understood.

Mullaney leaned heavily against the worktable, shaking his head and swearing softly. "Damn it, damn it! I told Alek to go to the police. I warned him not to try and handle this alone."

Gabe kept stacking chipped pottery and dented metal bowls

on trays, holding tight to the anger trying to surface. "Nureyev knew about the killings?"

"Not at first." Dominic gave Gabe a considering look and went back to ladling stew. "He heard the same rumors as the rest of the men, but no one could say if they were true or just talk. I don't think Alek wanted to believe any of the stories, not at first. His son was here, and that boy is all he has left. If someone came looking for Alek and meant to kill him, they'd kill the boy too. He couldn't stand thinking about that."

He understood Aleksei's need to protect his son, but that's where his sympathy ended. People had died because Alek hadn't come forward or told what he knew. "When did Nureyev find out the stories were true?"

"Just before his trip to New York."

Father Colm picked that moment to push open the swinging door and step inside. The priest eyed Gabe's gun and frowned, but didn't comment on his being armed. "I'm glad to see the two of you can talk and work at the same time. The children are hungry, and there's no keeping them still about it. I'll take the full trays out on the cart. The two of you finish up, if you would. You're welcome to stay and eat too, Gabe."

He smiled. "Thank you, Father, but Delia's waiting for me. Another time."

"I'll hold you to that, Gabriel." Father Colm backed out the door, pulling the serving cart with him. "Bring your wife when you come."

Dominic glanced at Gabe, his sheepish smile making him look younger. "He came to check up on us, you know. I think he was afraid we'd come to blows if left on our own too long."

"I'm not surprised." Gabe found the last of the trays and laid them out on the worktable. "If Aleksei discovered the stories of people dying were true, why did he go to New York?"

"Alek was already set to help start up a union out there. He took his son and the girl who looks after the boy with him. Alek sent them into hiding, but he won't say where." Dominic scraped the last of the stew out of the kettle, filling the last bowl. "A day or two before Aleksei came back from New York, an old man came looking for him at the union hall. The old man said to tell Aleksei that Josef had tracked them to San Francisco."

Gabe wiped his hands on the apron, his mind racing. He knew, *he knew,* the old man was Alina's uncle Fyodor. And now he knew the killer's name. "Did he say anything else, or leave any other message for Alek?"

Dominic frowned. "No, nothing. He wouldn't leave his name or tell me where Alek could find him. The old man said Aleksei would know. I told Alek as soon as he came back, but he didn't act as if the message meant much to him."

"You've been a big help, Dominic." Gabe hung the apron back on the hook and put on his jacket. What Mullaney knew put him in danger, and he felt honor bound to warn him. "I don't want you telling anyone else about this or talking to Aleksei. Let me talk to Nureyev first. Do you know where I can find him tonight?"

Mullaney hefted the empty kettle into the sink. "He might have locked himself in the house again, but that's only a guess. I haven't seen Alek in two days, Captain."

Gabe wouldn't let himself think the killer was a step ahead again, that the chance to find out who this man named Josef was, what he looked like, and where he might hide, had slipped away. He couldn't.

"Get a message to me when Nureyev shows up again." Gabe started to leave and turned back. "Be careful, Dominic. If this killer decides you're in the way, it won't matter that you're Irish and not Russian."

"You do the same, Captain Ryan." Dominic scrubbed at

burned-on stew and didn't look up. "I don't want the banshees wailing your death any more than I want them keening for mine."

That made him smile. Gabe hurried away, knowing he'd have to go back to the station before going home. The list of things to check on reeled through his head, one remembered detail sparking ten more. Calling Delia and letting her know he'd be late, and then calling Dora, were at the top of that list.

He stopped at the donations box just inside the front door, looking back across the hall. All around the room, people chatted over their dinners, eating their fill. Children smiled and laughed as Father Colm went from table to table, handing out cookies.

Gabe counted the bills in his wallet, pulling out half and stuffing the money into the box. He left, more convinced than ever that Father Colm had the right idea.

CHAPTER 17

Delia

Gabe and I talked until well after midnight once he got home, going over everything Dominic Mullaney had told him about Aleksei Nureyev. I'd agreed that the man Alina knew as her uncle Fyodor had to be the older man who'd gone to the union hall. Why he and his wife hadn't taken Alina and run was a question neither of us could answer.

The three princess ghosts watched from the kitchen window while we talked, their images distinct against the night-dark sky. Faceless ghosts still filled the glass around them, but they were harder to see. I tried not to look at the princesses too often, unable to bear the pleading look in their eyes. I wanted to save their sister as much as they did.

Falling asleep was difficult, but the combination of Mai's soft purring and Gabe's warmth next to me finally allowed me to drift off. If I dreamed of Alina's life, I didn't remember.

I woke the next morning as the parlor clock chimed half past nine. Mai crouched on my pillow, but she was relaxed and sleeping. How hushed and still the house felt was a sure sign Gabe had already gone to work. He'd warned me about leaving early the night before, but I still wished I'd been able to say good-bye.

All houses groan and settle, timbers creaking as they warmed in the sunlight or cooled again at nightfall. I almost never noticed the noises our house made, but today every tiny sound made me jump. Mai stayed close as I dressed, and I watched her for any sign that things weren't as they should be. By the time I'd finished my second cup of tea, I'd come to the conclusion that the constant need to look over my shoulder was edging toward irrational.

As long as the cat was relaxed, I should be as well. Knowing that to be true was easier than putting it into practice, but I was determined to try. I fetched more tea and settled down in the sitting room with a book Sadie had lent me. Written by a young novelist named Sinclair Lewis, *The Job* was about a young woman holding down a position normally reserved for men, and doing that job very well indeed. I found the story of Una Golden's life fascinating, and I could well see Sadie or myself in her place. It didn't take long before I forgot my case of nerves.

The front doorbell chimed. Mai's ear twitched, but she didn't so much as open an eye or move from her spot on the sofa cushion. Gabe's men knew not to walk in unannounced, and I fully expected to see one of his men when I opened the door.

Dora's bright smile greeted me instead. Her hair was a bit mussed from wearing her plaid driving cap, but otherwise her green silk suit and white batiste blouse looked impeccable and stylish as always. That the cap was totally out of place with her outfit didn't matter in the slightest to Isadora.

Her smile grew wider at seeing me. She viewed my clothing with a critical eye. "I'm glad to see you're already dressed to go out. That will save time. Get your coat and your bag, Dee."

"Good morning, Dora. How are you today? Sleep well? Perhaps you'd like to come in." I waved her inside, succumbing to the urge to shut the door and close out the outside world. The thought of hiding in my book all day possessed a great deal of appeal. "Most people indulge in at least minor social niceties before announcing they're whisking you away for impromptu journeys. Not that I ever mind going places with you, but perhaps you could tell me where we're going. Knowing why would be appreciated as well."

She raised an eyebrow, her expression making it clear she was torn between laughing and being annoyed. "My, my, you are touchy today. We're going to see Sadie. Any particular reason for the foul mood?"

"I can't point to any one thing as the cause. Too many terrible dreams, too many unanswered questions." I waved it all away and took my coat off the hall tree. "I woke up on edge, but I'm sure it will pass. So tell me, why are we going to Sadie's?"

Dora beamed at me, well pleased with herself. "I found a more effective protection charm for Connor. This one should last longer and work reasonably well even when he's away from home. I thought you'd like to be there when I give the charm to Sadie. We can attune it to Connor together if you like."

"Oh yes, I'd like that a great deal. Let me get my bag." Tears filled my eyes. Having stronger protections in place for Connor would be a huge relief. "I thought we'd found everything there was to find."

"So did I, Dee." She waited patiently as I locked up the house. Dora slipped an arm through mine for the walk to the car. "But there was a note in one of the chapters I'd marked for references to necromancy. I'd never have looked in that volume otherwise. The rest of the incidents recorded in that chapter were totally unrelated to Connor's problem."

Luck wasn't anything I wanted to rely on at any time, but I'd take whatever bits of fortune that wandered by. I held tight to the door handle as Dora shot away from the curb and waved gaily to

Gabe's men. They looked amused, but then again, they weren't riding with her.

Isadora picked up speed at a rate that was alarming even for her. I cleared my throat, hoping that conversation would distract me from the threat of disaster. "Is Sam staying with Alina?"

"No, Libby came by to visit early this morning. Sam is supposed to collect Jordan at Katie's and then swing by for Jack." Dora barely paused at the corner before turning. "Libby volunteered to stay and play cards with Alina until I come home. Inside my protections and with Gabe's men standing watch outside, I felt it was safe enough, so I agreed. Sam and Randy are both working, and I hate leaving Alina alone. Libby's visit turned out to be the perfect solution."

Neither of us said it aloud, but we both knew that Libby's visits were made in hopes of seeing Sam. She'd stayed away at first, and I'd wondered if we'd ever see Libby Mills again. That had changed over the last week or so. She was unfailingly friendly and kind, and spent long hours with Alina, but I knew what that cost her. Libby couldn't quite keep the heartache out of her eyes when Sam was around.

Dora came near to stopping my heart another time or two, but we arrived at Sadie's in one piece. Stella sat at one end of the front porch as we started up the walk, all her china dolls and stuffed toys arranged in a circle. She loved throwing elaborate tea parties for her dolls and making up stories about the other guests.

Sadie had insisted that Jack's stepmother, Katherine, allow Stella to accompany her to small garden parties. Given Katherine's dislike of being a grandmother, that Sadie had won the concession was a victory for her. I suspected Stella's skill at mimicking gossip meant she'd spent a great deal of time listening in to adult conversations at Katherine Fitzgerald's parties.

She saw us coming up the walk. Stella abandoned her dolls and came running. "Aunt Dora! Aunt Delia!"

Isadora opened her arms wide and caught the little girl as she reached us, sweeping Stella off her feet and hugging her tight. "Good morning, poppet. How are you?"

"I didn't know you were coming today. Do you have time for a tea party with me and Annabelle?" Stella wrapped her arms around Dora's neck. Annabelle was her favorite, and the curly-haired china doll went almost everywhere with her. "I know you don't like sitting on the ground. But I can move everything inside."

Dora glanced at me, checking to see that I agreed. "Dee and I need to talk to your mama first, but afterwards we can have a tea party. Do you know where your mother and father are right now?"

"Papa's getting ready for work. Mama's upstairs in Connor's room." Stella wiggled out of Dora's arms. She tromped up the front steps and across the porch, gathering Annabelle into her arms. "Mama said he's too big for his clothes. She's packing the little ones in boxes."

Saving them for another child. I fought back the unexpected pang of envy. Sadie would likely have more children in time, brothers or sisters to join Connor and Stella. I'd made my peace with knowing that I'd never have children of my own, telling myself over and over that loving Sadie's children was enough. The pain still rose up at times, knife edged and unwanted.

We joined Stella on the porch. Tiny china cups sat in front of each doll and stuffed toy. A small teapot and a plate from the kitchen, heaped with sugar cookies, sat in the center of the circle.

"Coming outside to have a party was a wise decision. It's a beautiful day." Dora crinkled her nose, making Stella giggle. "And packing away clothes sounds boring. Is Connor helping your mother?"

"Annie took him to the backyard. He was in the way." She fussed with the doll's hair, twisting curls around her fingers, and smoothed the front of Annabelle's dress. "I wanted to have my party in back, but Connor runs off with my dolls."

Dora put a hand on my shoulder and leaned close, speaking quietly. No doubt she thought to keep Stella from overhearing, but the sidelong glances Stella gave us told a different story. "I'd like a moment to talk to Sadie alone, but we'll need Connor to bind the charm properly. Be a pet and take Stella with you to collect him. Give me just a minute before all of you come up."

The three of us went in the front door. Jack's voice came from upstairs and Sadie's laugh soon followed. Dora blew Stella a kiss and hurried up the stairs to find them, calling to Sadie as she went.

I strolled through the entry hall and toward the dining room, holding tight to Stella's hand and listening to her talk to her doll. All the years I'd lived in this house with Esther and Sadie didn't stop me from feeling like an intruder, a stranger that no longer had a place here.

Small changes contributed to that: furniture that had been moved, new pictures that had been hung, vases and small mementos of Jack and Sadie's life together in curio cabinets. My home was with Gabe now, I knew that, but the realization that this would never be home again struck me hard. That was new.

The restless unease that had plagued me all morning increased tenfold, growing stronger still as Stella and I entered the kitchen. Eyes opened in my head as the watcher woke. The dragon growled a warning, a low rumble that filled my chest and made me dizzy. I couldn't ignore how I felt or keep pretending the overwhelming need to be cautious was merely a product of too little sleep and nerves stretched thin.

Both doors to the utility porch stood open to let in air, the screen door into the backyard a thin barrier to keep the bugs outside where they belonged. I heard voices from the yard, Annie and a man's voice I didn't recognize, and the muted sound of Connor crying.

"Stella, stay right here." I lifted her into one of the kitchen chairs, far back from the screen door and any chance of being seen. "Be very quiet, sweetheart. Don't move unless I say it's all right."

Her eyes grew round, and she hugged her doll tight, but Stella nodded and did as I asked without questioning. I crept onto the porch, being careful to stay well back from the screen and the windows facing the yard. The relative darkness inside would let me see out without being seen myself.

Or so I hoped.

Annie stood under the big shade tree holding Connor. The lines in her face were deeper, harsher looking than I'd seen just a few days before. I lied to myself that it was a trick of the light, wanting to believe the bright sunshine was to blame for how she appeared, not that she'd edged closer to death.

Connor's face was buried in Annie's shoulder, muffling his sobs. Ghosts crowded around them, both the freshly dead who looked almost alive, and those faded haunts who were long buried. My throat grew tight, knowing how terrified he must be. Many of the phantoms crowded close to reach for Connor, but stopped short of touching him or stroking his hair.

All the charms that Dora and I had laid around the yard, layered on the house and anything belonging to Connor, were meant to shut out ghosts completely. Something had caused all of them to fail. I thanked God they still functioned well enough to protect him from a spirit's touch.

Reverend Grant, the new pastor of Annie's church, stood in the shade with them. He reached toward Connor as well, but stopped short before his hand touched the little boy's head. His movements were the mirror image of the entire host of spirits filling the backyard, a puppet master pulling a web of strings. Pastor Grant frowned and tried again, straining to reach the little boy in Annie's arms. His face blurred for an instant, features slipping to resemble another man.

"Oh dear, God . . . no." I whispered charms as fast as I could, strengthening everything Dora and I had labored to put in place, and adding more layers where I could. Stalling for time was all it amounted to, but I needed time to summon Dora. I knew better than to face this necromancer alone.

Pastor Grant looked toward the house, scowling. I slid along the back wall of the porch and back into the kitchen. Stella still sat in the chair, quiet and frightened. Memories of the parade and the aftermath sat in her eyes, as well as the trust that I'd keep her safe again this time. I scooped her up and carried her into the dining room. That was as far as I dared go. I put Stella down and knelt in front of her, putting myself eye to eye with the little girl.

"I need you to do something for me, Stella. Listen carefully, sweetheart." I brushed curls back off her face with a shaking hand. "Run upstairs just as fast as you can and tell Aunt Dora I need her. Tell her it's very, very important she come right away. Can you do that for me?"

"I can do that." Stella frowned and patted my cheek. "Should I tell Aunt Dora you're scared?"

"Yes, tell her I'm very scared." I hugged her tight and turned her toward the stairs. "Now, go quick as you can. Make sure you and your mama stay upstairs. No matter what, stay in the house."

I watched Stella climb the first few steps and rushed back into the kitchen. The dragon's low growl rang in my ears, urging me to hurry. This time I didn't try to hide my arrival or conceal that I could see out in the yard from inside the porch. I called Annie's name loudly and shoved open the screen door, careful not to step over the threshold. The wards around the house were older, stronger. I didn't think he could cross those.

If he could, this man would already be inside.

"Annie! Oh, there you are." I smiled and nodded to the man wearing Pastor Grant's face. Keeping up a pretense of normality would win me time as well. "Sadie wants you to bring Connor inside to get changed. Dora and I are taking them to lunch."

Pastor Grant stepped forward, his kind, puzzled expression a startling contrast to the gleam in his eyes. Ghosts trailed behind him, row upon row of spirits that stretched beyond the back fence. That he made no attempt to hide them meant he didn't know I could see. "Have we met, sister?"

But that was another pretense on his part, another attempt to fool me into thinking him less dangerous. The day he'd hidden on my porch, I'd seen through his illusions. This same man had crept around my house in the dark and failed to cross my boundaries. He had to know who and what I was.

"Several times." Best to leave no doubt or room for misunderstanding. I sketched a warding glyph on the screen, and the watcher rumbled approval. Now wasn't the time to be coy or subtle, not if I wanted to get Connor and Annie safely away. I prayed for Dora to hurry. "I'm surprised you don't remember."

"You'll have to forgive me, sister, my eyes are failing." He took another step away from Annie and toward me. I wanted him closer still. My chances of getting Connor and Annie safely away were better with distance between them. "Come here so I can see your face."

"Delia Ann Ryan, mind your manners and stop embarrassing me. I taught you better than that." Annie shifted Connor to her other shoulder. He was crying inconsolably, red faced and sobbing with his eyes tight shut. Annie patted his back in a distracted way, more concerned with scolding me than with Connor's distress. That wasn't at all like her. She moved to within a handbreadth of Pastor Grant. "Step over here and introduce yourself to Pastor Grant properly."

All the protective and prohibitive charms were keyed to Connor. Nothing we'd put in place stopped the necromancer from putting his hand on Annie's arm, or patting her shoulder, or slipping an arm around her waist as her knees gave way. Ghosts crowded closer, phantom hands that couldn't grasp Connor reaching for Annie instead.

Stepping out the back door was one of the hardest things I'd ever done. Losing the woman who'd helped raise me, a woman I loved dearly, would be harder.

The watcher filled my head again, showing me things I'd not see on my own. Ghosts were part of this man's strength, his to summon and command, and a source of power to draw on. Why the necromancer had been so frightened of my ghost-eating gray cat became clear.

I banished ghosts as I crossed the yard, using charms I knew well and words whispered by the dragon. Spirits vanished rapidly, thinning the crowd around Annie and Connor, but there were still far too many. I prayed for enough time to turn the odds in my favor.

What the dragon couldn't show me was how to get Annie away from this man, and with her, Connor. Dragging her away was out of the question, as was letting this man get close enough to touch me. He'd turn my connection to ghosts and the spirit realm against me. I kept telling myself there had to be a way. I couldn't let myself believe otherwise.

I circled around him, staying just out of reach, and forcing him to turn in order to keep me in sight. Seeing Annie drooping in his arms was difficult, as was watching his face shift faster and faster. His control was slipping as he turned all his power toward keeping a wall of spirits between us, his features never settling into the face of one man for more than an instant. I whispered banishing charms faster, counting each ghost that vanished a step toward victory. Just as quickly, he summoned more into existence.

He never said a word in return, nor uttered a spell to counter mine. It was an odd, silent struggle, one I'd never imagined being involved in, but no less serious or deadly for the lack of battle cries.

Connor was mindless with panic. He kicked and shoved against Annie's hold, fighting with all his strength to break free and slip to the ground. Each ghost the necromancer called added to his terror. I couldn't believe Annie was able to keep hold of the squirming, flailing little boy, but that too was a result of the necromancer's power.

The screen door slammed. Dora ran across the lawn to my aid, weaving charms of her own as she came and strengthening my efforts. What I hadn't expected to see was Jordan Lynch at her side, his long-barreled Colt in hand. How he managed to run on his bad leg, I couldn't say, but he kept pace with Isadora.

Annie's eyes rolled back and she crumpled to the ground, limp and unmoving. Connor fell on top of her, oddly quiet and clinging to Annie with all his strength. The necromancer reached for him and Dora yelled in a language I couldn't understand, words whose power made the dragon roar and caused the world to spin around me.

Words whose power brought the necromancer up short. The wall of ghosts between us vanished.

I swept Connor into my arms and found myself staring into the clouded eyes of the man I'd seen in the shadows of my porch. This was his true face, I was sure of that, not an illusion or the doppelgänger of a man he'd killed. This was the face I needed to remember, the face I needed to search for in my dreams.

He backed away from Annie and from me, calling new ghosts to himself and bleeding them for the power to wrap himself in illusion. Spirits vanished as quickly as they appeared, all their substance gone. The startled expression on Jordan's face and the bitter frustration on Dora's told me they couldn't see him now. As far as they saw, the necromancer had vanished into the air.

That I was the only one to see him run from the yard out to the street was equally frustrating. Even if I gave chase, I'd no hope of catching him and no way to keep hold of him if I did.

And I didn't dare leave Connor alone. Going after the necromancer meant leaving him behind, at the mercy of phantoms and haunts, and in very real danger of losing his sanity. Wrapping my protections around the little boy was second nature now, taking no more than a thought. Connor huddled against me, shivering and hiccuping, face buried in my shoulder as he cried. I fought not to cry myself. He was so small.

Dora dropped to her knees next to Annie, rapidly whispering incantations and sketching glyphs on Annie's skin. Each glyph glowed briefly before vanishing. Isadora placed her hands over Annie's heart, on her forehead and throat, and back over her heart. The dragon watched through my eyes but didn't interfere.

That the dragon remained quiet filled me with both hope and despair. Hope that Dora's attempt to break the necromancer's hold was going to work, despair that the watcher's silence meant there was no saving Annie. I hugged Connor tight and rocked him side to side, feverishly praying I hadn't sacrificed one person precious to me to save another.

Jordan hovered around all of us, his expression mirroring my own helplessness and anger, and the battle he fought with his cop instincts to give chase. He kept his Colt to hand, watching the corners of the yard and the shadows. I didn't blame him for being wary. If this man returned, Jordan might not see him until it was too late.

Annie groaned, flailing her arms and attempting to bat away Dora's hands. The chants Isadora muttered changed and all the fight went out of Annie, leaving her limp and resting easy. I did cry then.

"Jordan, would you hold Connor for a minute?" He looked doubtful, but I wiped my eyes on a sleeve and held Connor out to him. "I need to help Dora. It will be all right, I promise. That man is gone."

"I'll take your word on him being gone, Delia. The way he disappears—I couldn't say one way or another." Jordan holstered his gun and held his arms out. "It's been a lot of years since my boy was this small, but I remember he only wanted his mama when he got scared. Connor looks like he's had a rough time of it already, and I don't want to frighten him more."

"It's only for a minute or two." I kissed Connor's cheek and handed him over. "And I wouldn't ask if I had a choice."

Jordan wasn't wrong about all Connor had been through, but the little boy relaxed from the start and rested his head on the big man's shoulder. He patted Connor's back. "You're safe now, son. Rest easy and we'll go find your mama real soon."

Between the two of us, Dora and I got Annie on her feet. She looked dazed, confused about where she was and what had happened. We slowly made our way across the yard with her, Jordan following a step behind and holding tight to Connor.

Sadie waited on the other side of the screen door, wringing her hands but obeying my orders to stay indoors. Sam and Jack stood just behind her. I could well imagine that Dora had issued her own orders not to cross the boundaries around the house.

Annie was even more confused by the fuss everyone made about getting her inside and seated in a kitchen chair. Sam and Jordan stood back, staying out of the way as Sadie bustled to get Annie's shawl and make her a cup of tea. Jack stood with them holding Connor close, as if he'd never let his son go again. Grim expressions mixed with relief on everyone's faces.

Stella stood with her back against the swinging door into the dining room, clutching Annabelle, looking small and alone, ashen with fright. I picked her up, angry beyond words at how hard she trembled and that this man—this killer—had terrified her so deeply for a second time.

I looked up to see Dora watching us. The same anger sat in her eyes and the same silent promise.

There wouldn't be a third time.

Gabe

Gabe paced Jack's sitting room, waiting for Dee and Isadora to come downstairs. They'd sealed all the windows and doors downstairs, layering protections on top of the ones already in place, and moved on to the second floor. The house would be a spiritual fortress when they finished, on a par with Dora's house and his own.

A fortress would keep this man out. The drawback was that shutting him out meant Sadie and the children were trapped inside. Even the backyard was off-limits, at least until they caught this man. Gabe clenched his fists and swallowed the anger threatening to choke him. Punching a hole in the wall wouldn't accomplish anything.

Sam and Jordan had gone to stay with Alina and make sure an officer saw Libby home. As skeptical as Libby Mills still was about spirits, telling her why she needed protection wouldn't be an easy job. Gabe didn't envy Sam the task.

He had most of the squad out on the street, working in groups of two or three, and under strict orders to stay together. Dora had agreed that was a wise precaution, one that would keep the necromancer from replacing an officer and walking away in plain sight. The man they were after was capable of some strange and incredible things, things that Gabe had a hard time believing. That made catching him even more difficult.

Dora didn't hold out much hope of his men being able to find this man. The only one who knew what the necromancer's real face looked like was Delia, and the thought of sending her out to hunt for a killer made his skin crawl. He ran his fingers through his hair, counting how many men he could pull from the next shift. The entire squad was spread thin with rotating guard shifts at Libby's settlement house, keeping an eye on Dora's place, and handling the day-to-day cases that came their way.

"Sit down, Gabe." Jack lounged on the settee, his bandaged foot propped up on a cushion. He gestured toward an overstuffed chair, whiskey from his glass sloshing onto his hand. "Wearing a hole in my carpet won't hurry things along."

He dropped into the chair, slouching and stretching his long legs out. "You might as well admit it, Jack. You'd be pacing with me if not for your leg."

"I never denied that, Captain Ryan. And if you weren't on duty, you'd be drinking with me." Jack lifted his glass in a toast before taking another sip. "I trust Dora and Delia completely, but I'm not sure I'll be able to sleep at night until we find this man. I know Sadie won't."

Once they'd gotten Annie to bed and Dora had reassured them Connor was unharmed, Sadie broke down completely. How distraught and shattered she was frightened Jack and Delia as much as or more than Annie's near miss. Sadie was stronger than any of them, and they all depended on her being calm and unwavering. Seeing her undone was sobering.

He shifted in his chair, still restless and unable to keep still. The sound of crackling paper reminded him of the telegram in his pocket. Gabe took the folded yellow paper out and passed it to Jack. "I heard from Colin. He's positive the locket was part of the Russian crown jewels. Colin's just as sure that it belonged to the dowager empress. He doesn't remember the occasion, but the locket was a gift from her son."

Jack read the telegram quickly. "Damn, Dora was right."

Dora's voice right behind him made Gabe jump.

"Of course I was right. I usually am." She sat in the overstuffed chair at the other end of the settee and rubbed her eyes. "Remind me what we're talking about. I seem to have forgotten."

"A telegram from Colin. He identified the locket in Eve Rigaux's hand as belonging to the Russian royal family." Gabe glanced over his shoulder, looking for his wife. "Is Dee coming down?"

"Not just yet. She's helping Sadie lie to Annie. The three of us decided telling her the whole truth wasn't a good idea. Thanks to Pastor Grant's influence, Annie's convinced I'm in league with demons." Dora was tired or she'd never have allowed an edge to creep into her voice. That she did was a measure of how much Annie's poor opinion bothered her. "Telling her that Connor was attacked by a foreign necromancer would add fuel to that fire and upset her more. She doesn't remember a thing before I brought her around. Concocting a story about fainting was much kinder."

Jack drained the last of his whiskey and set the glass aside. His cheeks were flushed, but his eyes were clear and focused. "I keep asking myself why this killer went after Connor and Annie. If you've got an answer to that, Dora, I'd like to hear it."

"I don't think he came looking specifically for Annie and Connor, but once here, he took advantage of the opportunity. I've no doubt he was hoping to find Alina." Dora frowned, her long nails tapping silently on the padded arm of the chair. "The type of protections on the house may have had a great deal to do with drawing him here. What Dee and I put in place to protect Connor are precisely the kind of barriers that keep him from finding Alina. That made him curious about what you were hiding. It's a double-edged sword. For the life of me, I can't see another way."

"They were easy targets, Jack." Gabe cleared his throat. So many people they knew and cared about were easy targets. "We need to remember that this man isn't entirely sane. Delia's convinced he'll use anyone to find Alina."

Jack looked between Dora and Gabe, his voice flat, unemotional. "Even a two-year-old."

"Even a two-year-old." Dora leaned forward, fingers gripping the arm of the chair tight. "He didn't flinch from killing innocents at the parade or from harvesting power from their deaths. Dee's right in believing a necromancer will use anyone who comes to hand. She's just as right to believe him more than a little mad."

"All right." Jack toyed with the rim of his glass, running a finger around the edge and staring at melting ice. He looked up, all his carefully hidden anger sitting stark in his eyes. "Fair warning, Gabe. I won't flinch either. I'll shoot him if this man comes near my family again."

He didn't argue. Gabe stood, pulling out his pocket watch to check the time. "I have to get back to the station. Will my going upstairs to tell Delia good-bye complicate things for her?"

Dora's dismissive wave was another measure of how tired she must be. She rarely passed up the opportunity to tease him. "Go kiss your wife, Captain Ryan. I'll get Dee home safely."

Gabe went to her chair, leaning down to kiss her cheek. "Thank you, Dora. Be careful."

She smiled. "I'm probably in the least danger from this killer, and I'm always cautious. You and Randy are the ones I worry about. Promise me you won't forget that this man can look like anyone."

"I promise. Don't fret about me." He glanced at Jack, noting the harsh new lines in his partner's face and the hollow, haunted look in his eyes. Gabe wasn't about to forget, and neither would Jack.

Not a chance. They had too much at stake.

CHAPTER 18

Gabe

A phone call from Randy Dodd granted Gabe's wish to see inside the sanctuary at Holy Trinity Cathedral.

His driver double-parked in the middle of the street, sparing Gabe a long walk through the crowd of neighbors straining to see what was happening. He stood next to the car, buttoning his coat and looking around before going inside. The scene was much different from his first visit, more like an active murder investigation and less like a sleepy church supper.

Six patrol cars crowded the curb in front of the church. The coroner's van and two more police cars filled the drive leading to the rectory in back. A line of officers on horseback held the press and a throng of curiosity seekers at bay across the street. Reporters who recognized Gabe shouted his name, their raucous voices accompanied by the pop and snap of photographers' flash being set off. He turned his back to them and started up the walk.

The bell tower cast long, jagged shadows in the late afternoon light, rippling over the lawn and creeping onto the sidewalk. Deeper shadows darkened the covered entry into the church. Mindful of

Dora's warning, Gabe slowed his steps as he approached and made sure that the man waiting for him near the door was Randy Dodd.

But even after Gabe reached the front doors, he found himself watching Randy for an extra few seconds, his heart beating just a little faster. Not being able to trust what he saw was unsettling.

Gabe shoved the feeling down deep. He couldn't work that way, and if he was going to catch this man, he needed to think. "Your phone call spoiled a perfectly good afternoon of paperwork, Officer Dodd."

Randy looked up from his notebook, his smile grim. "I'm about to finish ruining your day, Gabe. Father Pashkovsky is dead. Based on how it looks right now, Aleksei Nureyev may have killed him."

Gabe tipped his hat back to get a better look at Randy's face. "But you don't think he did it."

He went back to studying his notebook, avoiding Gabe's eyes. "No, I don't. I think someone did a damn good job of setting him up to look guilty. Aleksei was the one who called us." Randy stuffed his notebook in a pocket and pulled open one of the double doors. "He's waiting inside. He was sitting in the same spot when the beat cops arrived."

The doors into the sanctuary were propped open. Bursts of bright light flared and faded again as they stepped inside. Baker's flash. An oversized chandelier filled the center of the ceiling, wired with dozens of electric bulbs. Opaque, amber-colored mica shades covered each bulb, softening the light.

Stained glass windows ranged around the room, all set into the top of the walls to shine colored light down on the pews. This late in the afternoon, the sun had sunk too low to light more than a few windows. Gabe didn't know the names of the Russian saints pictured, or the stories told, but he couldn't deny they were beautiful.

Aleksei sat in the front row of pews, staring at the large wooden crucifix hanging behind the altar. He muttered in Russian, but the singsong rhythm of his voice and the way he crossed himself every few seconds painted a picture of a man in prayer.

Gabe didn't need to ask why he prayed or who Aleksei's prayers were for. Father Pashkovsky's body was nailed up behind the altar, the light gone from his milky eyes. In death, the priest looked younger, a man closer to Nureyev's age and who might have been a boyhood friend. Another piece of the puzzle clicked into place.

Blood splattered the wall beneath the crucifix. More blood stained the altar, splashed the carpeted steps and the runner down the center of the aisle. Square-headed spikes, the kind used for railroad ties, were driven through Pashkovsky's palms. More spikes were used to secure his wrists and shoulders, and through his crossed ankles. That explained much of the blood, but the knife driven into the center of his chest was what killed him.

The way Eve Rigaux's body had been laid out was only the start of the killer's message; this was the ending flourish. She'd been killed quickly, even gently, in comparison. Only a blind man would miss the symbolism in this, or a stupid man miss the hate.

Aleksei Nureyev was neither blind nor stupid. One look at his face told Gabe he understood.

Baker moved his camera a few feet to the left, taking more photographs. The flash reflected off gilt carvings of saints and statues of the Virgin Mary set into niches along the back wall. A carving of Jesus, torn from the crucifix before Pashkovsky was nailed up in its place, lay in pieces.

Gabe took it all in and came to the same conclusion Randy had. Aleksei wasn't the killer. The man who'd attacked Annie and Connor was responsible, just as he'd been responsible for the riot at the Saint Patrick's Day parade and killing Alina's guardians. Proving that, and catching the killer, was an entirely different matter.

He skirted around the blood on the floor and slid into the pew next to Aleksei. Gabe glanced toward the altar and tried not to flinch. Details revealed themselves in the light of Baker's flash. A gag had cut into the corners of Father Pashkovsky's mouth and dribbled blood into the priest's beard. From the front row, Gabe could see echoes of pain in Father Pashkovsky's eyes; the suffering set into his face. The priest had hung there for a long time before the killer stabbed him and ended his agony.

Gabe leaned back, resting an arm along the back of the wooden bench. "Who did this, Alek? I know you didn't kill him. Help me find the man who killed your friend."

"I have no friends, Captain Ryan. Sasha Pashkovsky was the last." He shut his eyes and crossed himself again. "Josef has turned all of them into ghosts."

"Josef?" The killer's name sent cold trailing down his neck and set off a flurry of whispers in his ear. Gabe couldn't help hearing. What he heard made him ill. "Who is he?"

"A man I shot and left for dead in the Ural Mountains. God have mercy on my soul, I shot him and drove off. I discovered later he'd already betrayed us." He crossed himself again, but didn't turn away from the blank, accusing stare of Father Pashkovsky's eyes. "Josef works for Lenin and the Bolsheviks. Killing him was the only way to keep him from following us, but I failed even at that. I've failed at so many things."

"Start from the beginning." Gabe twisted in his seat to face Nureyev. "You weren't alone on that road. Who else was with you?"

Aleksei shuddered, forcing his eyes away from the corpse on the cross. "A young officer in the Red Army came to me with news of where the tsar and his family were being held by the Bolsheviks. He'd put together a desperate plan to save the grand duchesses, but he needed my help to pay a hired assassin known as Josef the Undertaker. I'd heard rumors about what this man was capable of, but this young lieutenant had already agreed to his price. Backing out meant losing any chance of freeing the family, so I went along."

The distant, detached cop inside him needed to collect details, to know what freeing a tsar's daughter cost. Another part, the man who'd sat up in a darkened sitting room, gun in hand while his wife slept, flinched from knowing. That man didn't want to know, but he asked anyway. "What did it cost the young lieutenant to free Alina?"

Nureyev glanced at him, but didn't seem surprised that Gabe knew. "Josef's currency is death, Captain, and he demanded payment in people's lives. I didn't find out what Dmitri had agreed to until it was too late. Alina was the only one of the family to leave with us."

Baker was finished with his photographs. Randy Dodd and Marshall Henderson stood with the deputy coroner, arguing about the best way to remove the body. Getting Nureyev away from here before they started was for the best. He considered himself a somewhat hardened detective, but the thought of watching the coroner pry the spikes out of Pashkovsky made Gabe's stomach flip. The idea of forcing Aleksei to watch hit him even harder.

He stood and got a hand under Nureyev's elbow. "You can tell me the rest of the story in my office."

"Are you arresting me, Captain Ryan?" Aleksei paused before stepping into the aisle, looking back toward the altar and crossing himself again. He didn't resist as Gabe led him away. "Josef will find me in a cell as easily as on the street or in the union office. I'll be dead by morning."

The hair on the back of Gabe's neck rose. He believed him. "You're not under arrest. And I've no intention of letting you die in my jail. I have the means to protect you if necessary."

"You mean Mikal's widow, Isadora." Alek pulled himself up straighter. "Thank you, Captain, but no. She has too many people to protect as it stands. You and I will talk, and once we're finished, I will do my best to disappear. Maybe I can lead Josef away from San Francisco and buy you some time. I don't hold much hope he'll follow, but he's fooled me before."

They stopped just inside the front doors, giving Aleksei time to button his overcoat and flip up his collar. Gabe thought about the crowd outside, the press of bodies and the reporters shouting questions. Every instinct he had told him not to parade Nureyev past the photographers.

Gabe put a hand on Aleksei's arm to keep him from stepping outside. "I've changed my mind. You're not going back to the office with me, you're leaving now. I know from experience the coroner carries extra coats and caps in his van. No one should look twice if you go out the back dressed like one of his men and drive away with them. I'll square things with Dr. West. Call it a head start if you like."

Nureyev smiled, the first real smile Gabe had seen from him. "Thank you, Captain Ryan. For a police officer, you have a very devious mind."

"My partner says the same thing." Gabe stuffed his hands deep into his pockets, thinking. "I need to ask something before you go. I can understand Josef wanting revenge against you for shooting him. But why kill Eve Rigaux, or Father Pashkovsky?"

He stopped short of asking why this man had Jordan Lynch shot, or killed entire families, or why all the children that haunted Gabe's dreams had to die. Once he started asking why, stopping might be impossible.

"Do you know much about Russian history, Captain?"

Gabe shrugged. "No, not a thing."

Nureyev pursed his lips and nodded, as if he'd known the answer all along. "Russia has been ruled by an emperor or an empress for centuries. Rightly or wrongly, all the ills that befall Russia are blamed on our rulers. That has always been true, but Lenin and his thugs won their revolution by making Nicholas appear to be an unfeeling monster. From there, it was but a small step to seeing the entire aristocracy as vermin, needing to be trapped and killed. Lenin loosed Josef on the world. I don't know if he can be called back."

Gabe chewed his lip for a few seconds, thinking. "Then we need to find a way to stop him once and for all."

"I wish you luck with that, Captain. Be very very sure when you shoot him that Josef dies. Don't make the mistake of showing any mercy. Alina's life, and the life of my son, depend on you."

Gabe stared, ready to argue that there were other ways to stop Josef and that he was sworn to uphold the law, to see justice done, not gun down criminals in the street. He couldn't get the words out. In his gut, he knew Aleksei was right. Isadora would likely agree, however reluctantly.

He gripped Nureyev's shoulder. "I'll do my best, you've my word on that. Now, let's get you on your way."

By the time Gabe went out the front door, Aleksei Nureyev was blocks away, riding in the back of the coroner's van. If anything, the crowd outside was thicker, the shouts from the throng of reporters more insistent. He ignored them all, striding to his waiting car and climbing inside.

He watched people from the safety of the backseat, scanning each face, looking for a sign he hoped he'd recognize.

Josef could be any one of them. That he'd never know until it was too late made Gabe's skin crawl.

Delia

Gabe got home long after supper, exhausted and discouraged. He told me about Father Pashkovsky's murder and his conversation with Aleksei Nureyev. I assured him that having a name for this man, whether Josef was his true name or not, was a good thing. Names opened new ways for Dora and me to search for him. Our chances of finding him had increased enormously.

The one truly bright spot in his afternoon was finding Pastor Grant alive and well, and confused about why the police came looking for him.

He used the parlor phone to speak with Dora while I dished out the food I'd kept warm for him. We went to bed as soon as he'd finished eating.

I'd covered the dressing table mirror earlier. Gabe offered to turn the mirror to the wall, but draping it with an old sheet was just as effective. I couldn't fall asleep with all three princesses watching me, especially knowing where my dreams led and what I might see.

Being accustomed to seeing ghosts, to knowing that the restless dead were always a part of my world, was far, far different from watching someone die. In all my years of dealing with spirits, I'd never before been forced to witness a death or the events that led to a last moment. A last good-bye.

The watcher had changed that for me. I understood the necessity, but I didn't thank her for the experience.

I struggled with sleep, fought hard against drifting away from the comforting warmth of our bedroom into the forbidding chill of that far distant mountain house. All the dreams were vivid, stark in their harshness and the terror that made my heart pound before waking. But I always knew before dreaming what I'd remember and what would pass away.

This dream I'd remember.

After that first night, the commandant ignored us. He slept in the village each night, coming to the house only to make sure we were being fed and that the guards hadn't abandoned their posts. I heard one of the guards call him Yuri or I might never have learned his name. When he did speak to us, it was to deliver lectures, reminding us again and again we were citizens of the state now, with no more status than the village girls scrubbing pots in the kitchen.

As spring ended, a few of the younger guards gossiped where I could hear, raising my hopes that I'd see my parents soon and that the whole family would board ship for England. Exile might be a different kind of captivity, but one I'd welcome.

Commandant Yuri's next visit crushed even that hope. In the midst of his lecture, he made a point of telling us the English king, my father's cousin, had refused us asylum. Lenin could have washed his hands of us if we'd gone as penitents to England. The flatness in Yuri's eyes and the finality in his voice stole my last bit of hope.

By the time my parents and my brother arrived at the end of June, I'd given up all thoughts of leaving the mountain house alive. My father was thinner, my mother barely able to walk or stand for more than a minute, but the family was together. I was grateful, no matter how short the time we had left.

Papa refused to believe the Bolsheviks would go so far as assassination, but I'd overheard the guards talking and I saw the way they watched him. He couldn't see the hate while I saw little else. My thoughts were full of nothing but ways to escape, elaborate plans to save my family that had no chance of success.

More soldiers, more strangers, arrived. We hugged our parents and laughed with our brother and I tried to be happy. All seven of us were together in the same house for the first time in more than a year. Dinner was in the downstairs dining room that night. There was fresh milk and cake, and Papa told stories of when he was a boy.

Twice I thought I saw Dmitri standing with the guards in the hallway, and again as we went upstairs to bed. Each time I looked again and the face belonged to an older man, a stranger with a scarred face and a crooked nose.

I lay awake thinking about that. He'd been my only friend here, the only one to show kindness. Dmitri had gone so far as to smuggle in a cake for my birthday, something I'd not forgotten. I decided that seeing his face among a crowd of strangers wasn't so odd.

Midnight was long past when insistent pounding on our door woke my sisters and me. Yuri and three guards stood in the hallway when I pulled the door open. "Get dressed and pack your belongings. I've had word that fighting with the White Army is moving this way. You're to be moved tonight."

"Tonight?" My throat tightened and for an instant I couldn't speak. "Where are you sending us? We've barely had time to see each other."

He smiled and touched his cap. "The family will stay together. Now, hurry. The trucks will be here before dawn."

Yuri's smile frightened me more than leaving in the middle of the night, but we did as he said. Guards came and gathered our bags, carrying everything downstairs. The family, my brother's doctor, and the few servants that had followed my parents into captivity gathered in the hallway to wait. My younger brother was ill and couldn't walk, so Papa carried him. I picked up my sister's little dog to keep her from racing around our feet.

A minute or two later, Yuri returned with five or six guards, all of them new men I'd not seen before now. One was the stranger with the scarred face and crooked nose. I avoided looking at him for fear my mind would play tricks on me again.

"I've had word that the fighting is getting closer." Yuri stepped back and gestured toward the stairs. "You will wait for the trucks in the basement. No one from the village will see lights on or wonder why so many people are up and about at this hour."

Yuri led the way downstairs, guards flanking my family when

the corridor was spacious enough, and following when it narrowed. I went last and trailed a few yards behind my sisters, not from any reluctance to leave the mountain house, but to keep my sister's dog from growling and snapping at the guards. Two of the guards stayed close to me, as if I might attempt to stay behind.

I paid them little attention. My heart was pounding too hard, my stomach churning with fear. We'd moved at night before, but this felt different. And I couldn't forget Yuri's smile.

My parents had already started down the steep steps into the basement when the dog wiggled free of my arms and ran back the way we'd come, disappearing around a corner almost immediately. I raced after her, not stopping to think or ask permission. My sister's heart would break if her dog didn't go with us. And there was the chance that Yuri would give the order to kill the dog rather than try to catch her.

Yuri shouted for the guards to stop me, and the one closest gave chase.

A door along the corridor stood open, a large temptation for a small dog with the urge to run. She sped inside and I sent up a prayer that other doors in the room were closed. I ran after her, thinking of nothing other than catching her quickly and rejoining the family.

The guard with the crooked nose caught me, yanking hard on my arm and pulling me off balance. He clamped a hand over my mouth and instead of hauling me back toward the stairs, dragged me into the room. The door closed behind us, shutting out the lights in the hall. Another man partly raised the shade on a small tin lantern. Not much light escaped, but enough to show me a girl holding my sister's dog and a tall bearded man standing in the corner. We were in an unused parlor or office, the furnishings all covered in dusty canvas.

I twisted and fought, trying to break free, but the man holding me tightened his grip. He spoke next to my ear, each word rushed and quavering and spoken in Dmitri's voice. "Be still, Maria! I've come to take you out of here. You're safe, I promise."

"Listen to him, Your Grace. We don't have much time before they come looking for you." The man holding the lantern set it down. Light fell across his face, showing me a man I'd known all my life. Count Aleksei Nureyev was a distant cousin and had visited my father's court often. Now he was dressed in a scruffy uniform that could have passed for one of Yuri's men or an officer in any of the local militia. "Trust us and we'll get you away from here."

Rescue was something I'd often dreamed of, but never dared hope would really happen. I did trust Aleksei and believed he'd keep his word. So many thoughts, so many questions about how he'd get my family away from Yuri's men crowded my mind. I wanted to ask each and every one, but Dmitri kept his hand clamped tight over my mouth.

Aleksei motioned the girl with my sister's dog forward and pulled a small pouch out of his shirt. She stood toe to toe with him in the small room, trembling with fear. The sound of coins clinking came to me as he stuffed the pouch down the front of her dress. "That's all I promised and a bit more for getting word to me in time. Now, stand still, Alina. Are you ready, Josef?"

The tall stranger, Josef, stepped forward and touched Alina's face. She flinched and tried to pull away, but Aleksei shoved a pistol into her back. "You've no choice but to keep your part of the bargain. Hold still and this will all be over."

Dmitri's arm tightened around me to the point I could barely breathe. Josef whispered in a strange language, each harsh word I couldn't understand making my heart stutter. I wanted to scream, to run from the sound of that voice.

Alina's eyes clouded over and her features went slack. She didn't see Josef cup her face in both hands, or Aleksei loop an arm around her chest to keep her from dropping the dog as her back arched and her body convulsed.

Pain burned through me and tears flooded down my face, the sensation of bones shifting under my skin more than I could bear. Dmitri murmured in my ear, a string of nonsense words a parent might use to comfort a child waking from a nightmare. I couldn't move or see, helpless to escape or understand the torture visited on me.

Josef's whispers stopped and so did the pain. I sagged in Dmitri's arms, fighting the urge to weep uncontrollably and holding on to hope, cracked and fragile. Aleksei would explain. He would save us all.

Dmitri rested his cheek on the top of my head and spoke next to my ear. "The worst is over. We're leaving soon, I promise."

My vision cleared and I saw that Dmitri had lied. The worst was far from over.

I stared at the woman standing with Aleksei, the woman who had been Alina just a moment before. A doppelgänger wearing my face—my eyes, my hair, *my skin*—stood in Alina's place, hugging my sister's dog close. I screamed, the sound muffled against Dmitri's hand.

Aleksei reached down the front of my double's dress, retrieving his bag of coin and tucking the money back inside his shirt. She didn't react, staring toward the closed door with a blank expression. He tipped her chin up so that she looked into his eyes. "Remember this. Your name is Maria. You went looking for the dog and came back to join your parents as soon as you found her. You never meant to cause trouble. Hurry to the basement now before the guards come looking for you."

My double turned on her heel and rushed from the room, the sound of footsteps running toward the stairs echoing in the empty hallway. Not long after, my sister's dog barked and a guard shouted. "I found her!"

Muffled, angry voices came from the hallway. Aleksei stood with his ear pressed to the door, pistol drawn. Yuri's shout carried over all the rest. "Get her downstairs! We're running out of time."

Silence filled the small room, tense and expectant. I heard a door slam on the ground floor, heavy footfalls, and the voices of a large troop of guards. One of them laughed loudly, but the voices moved away before I heard more than a word or two. Aleksei and Dmitri traded grim looks, but Josef smiled.

Aleksei flinched when the gunshots began and crossed himself. My sisters screamed and screamed, the terror in their cries filling the whole house. I surged against Dmitri's hold, desperate to fight my way free and go to my family. Yuri shouted orders for his men to keep shooting, to use their rifle butts and bayonets.

I couldn't let Yuri murder my parents, my sisters and brother. I stomped on Dmitri's foot and bit his hand.

Dmitri shoved me against a wall, trapping me between faded wallpaper and his body. He whispered in my ear, his voice breaking. "I'm sorry, Maria, I'm so sorry. I couldn't save them all, only you. Don't cry, it will all be over soon and they will rest with God. Soon you won't remember."

Aleksei swore violently, and hit the wall with a fist. My sisters' screams and the sound of gunfire went on forever, my heart breaking a little more each second. I prayed for their souls and that I'd remember more of them than agony and fear.

I added Alina to my prayers. She was dying in my place.

Silence, paired with the gloating tone in Yuri's voice as he issued orders, told me when my sisters died. My knees gave way and I slid down the wall. Dmitri pulled me into his lap and held me, his hand over my mouth to muffle my sobs.

Josef and Aleksei argued violently in hushed voices, but I didn't pay attention to why or what they said. Trucks pulled into the yard below, men swore and made jokes at my father's expense, and the trucks drove away again. I huddled against Dmitri, numb and wondering if hiding in airless rooms was the only future ahead of me.

"Get her on her feet." Josef's voice was sandpaper on my skin, awaking pain. Dmitri did as he was told, pulling me up to stand next to him. Josef touched my face and I whimpered, all the fight in me draining away. The feel of my body changing, shifting, was less painful but still unpleasant. "Take her out the front door. The guards will see one of the kitchen girls, not the grand duchess. You know what to say if the guards question where you're going. Alek and I will meet you at the truck."

"I know what to do." Dmitri dried my face on the hem of my dress and pulled pins from my hair. He took my hand. "Yuri took all but three or four men with him. The men left behind are well on their way to being drunk by now."

Aleksei opened the door a crack, peering down the hallway before stepping out. "Even more reason to be cautious, Lieutenant. Drunk men don't hesitate to cause trouble."

Dmitri led me down the steps to the front door. He paused before going out, checking his pistol. I caught a glimpse of myself in the entryway mirror and stared. Panic at what Josef had done penetrated the fog I moved through.

The woman I saw was older, thicker through the middle, and not as tall. Her dress was low cut, her breasts threatening to spill out the laced top. Dmitri caught me staring and turned me away from the mirror. "Forgive me for anything I say or do out there. Yuri's men need to see what they expect."

I couldn't speak. Dmitri wrapped his arm around me and pulled me close before we stepped into the courtyard.

Dmitri was right; the guards were already drunk. Men in

sloppy uniforms lounged against a parked truck and passed a jug of wine between them. They eyed Dmitri as we drew even and leered at me. One of them said something, his voice too low for me to hear, and the three of them burst out laughing.

"Wait a moment." A short round guard pushed away from the truck, moving toward us on unsteady legs. The guard's black eyes glittered in the moonlight. "What have you got there?"

Dmitri's arm tightened around me, his other hand resting lightly on his pistol. "Have you been away from your wife so long you don't recognize a woman when you see one?"

The two guards still leaning on the truck laughed and passed the jug of wine again. Dmitri tugged me forward a few feet, and the round guard stepped in front of us again. "You haven't answered my question. I want to know who this woman is and where you're going with her."

"All you need to know is she belongs to me." Dmitri nuzzled my neck, his breath hot on my skin, and stepped between me and the guard. He loomed over the shorter man, his voice a low growl. "As for where I'm going with her, I'm taking her home and to bed. Is that a problem?"

They stared at each other, each scowling fiercely. Finally the round-faced guard stumbled back a few feet and waved in the direction of the front gate. "Go on, then."

All three guards made jests at Dmitri's expense, calling after him and making drunken suggestions about how to spend his time with a woman. His jaw tightened and he gripped my arm harder, but he called back crude comments of his own. Once we'd passed out of sight, he hurried me along faster.

The streets of the village were deserted, windows on the houses blank and dark. July nights were warm even in the mountains, but bone-deep tremors threatened to rattle my teeth. I wanted to lie in the road and wail at the full moon, to give voice to all the pain and fear trapped inside. Dmitri kept me moving, not allowing me time to grieve.

A small lane led off the main road. Aleksei and Josef waited for us next to a truck much like the one that had brought me to the mountain house. Dmitri helped me into the back and pulled the flap closed. He held me as the truck lurched around corners and labored up inclines, moving higher into the mountains. Sleep was impossible. I couldn't get the sound of my sisters' screams out of my ears.

Dawn was brightening the sky when the truck stopped. Aleksei opened the back flap and Dmitri handed me down. A smaller truck was parked just ahead. Wooden slats held a load of turnips and cabbages in the back, a weathered piece of canvas thrown over the top to keep off rain.

Josef paced the road, his fists opening and closing with each step. He came to meet us, his smile making me shiver harder as he reached for me. I struggled against the hold Aleksei and Dmitri had on my arms, frantic to keep Josef from touching me again.

"Don't fight us, Highness." Aleksei nodded at Dmitri to let go and wrapped his arms around me, hugging me to his chest. "This will be the last time. You'll forget all that's happened until it's safe for you to remember."

They didn't keep me from screaming this time, but there was no one to hear. The shift of bones and flesh took longer, but when Josef stepped back, the faint reflection in the truck window belonged to me, not a stranger. Numbness stole over me, pushing grief and memory into the background.

Dmitri helped me into the truck and shut the door. He turned to find Aleksei pointing a pistol at him. Aleksei motioned him away from the truck, but I missed him stepping away. What I saw lurched, skipped ahead like a cinema film that had slipped the projector sprockets. I watched from a distance as Dmitri knelt at the side of the road and Aleksei put the gun to the back of his head. His body was facedown in a water-filled ditch the next I knew. Tears welled up in my eyes, but I couldn't remember why.

Raised voices made me turn my head. Aleksei had his back to my side of the truck, his shoulders stiff with anger. "I let my emperor—*my friend*—and his family die because that's the price you demanded for saving one of his daughters. Dmitri is the last life I owe you for your services, Josef. Even a necromancer must get his fill of death. Kill the others yourself, I won't do it for you."

Josef smiled, his clouded eyes empty and cold. "You don't understand, Count Nureyev. You've no choice but to pay my price."

"I have a choice." He pointed the gun at Josef. "I should have made it sooner."

The shot echoed, scattering a flock of rooks roosting in the pine trees. Aleksei fired again before coming around and climbing into the truck.

We were far down the road when I remembered to ask. "I—I can't remember. Who are you?"

"Call me Alek." Tears filled his eyes. "I was a friend of your father, Alina. He'd have wanted me to take care of you."

"Alina." I touched my face, uncertain what I was searching for or why the gesture made my hand shake. "Is that my name?"

"Yes." He jammed the truck into a lower gear, the engine laboring to climb the steep grade. Alek glanced at me, his face tight and closed off. "Alina is your name. Remember it."

I woke screaming, fighting to leap up and run. Gabe reached for me, but I shoved him away and half slipped, half fell off the bed. The sound of gunshots and the smell of pines faded slowly, becoming more distant. I curled on my side and dug my fingers into the rough wool carpet, weeping inconsolably for people I'd known only in dreams.

Gabe lay on the floor with me, pulling me close. "It's all right, Dee, it's all right. You're home and safe with me, not trapped in that house. Nothing's going to hurt you."

The watcher's eyes filled my head, softening images of Josef's face and the hardness in Aleksei's eyes, muting the sounds of screaming and terrified young women crying out. I wanted to be angry, to rage that a powerful guardian who couldn't save her charges was less than useless. But the dragon's sorrow dampened my rage. She didn't have the mercy of forgetting either.

I pulled away from Gabe, crawling to the dressing table on hands and knees. One sharp tug, and the sheet covering the mirror cascaded around me. I sat on my heels and hugged the mound of cool white cloth to my chest, knowing what I'd see.

Three princess ghosts gazed out at me. Roses still bloomed in their cheeks, their eyes bright and lively as they'd been while alive. I knew their names now, which one was the trickster, which spent hours by her brother's sickbed, which one had dreamed of children of her own.

Hope sat in their eyes, and trust that I'd understand and always remember who they'd been.

I knew their secret now. That secret tore pieces from my heart.

CHAPTER 19

Gabe

Gabe jumped each time someone knocked on his office door, rattling the glass in the frame. Far too often over the last week bad news had followed that knock, more bodies found and more people missing. Twice Mullaney had been at his door with reports of Russian waiters vanishing on the journey between work and home.

He'd come to associate knocks on his door with death. This morning he'd left the damn thing open.

About the only bright spot he could point to was that none of the bodies found belonged to Aleksei Nureyev. He clung to the hope that Alek had gotten away.

Jack arrived a little after nine, his cane slung up over his shoulder. He was still limping, but each day brought more improvement and he'd driven himself to work for the last several days. That he brought the cane with him at all was to keep Sadie happy.

Gabe didn't blame Sadie for fussing over Jack. The last few weeks had been rough on her. They'd been hard on all of them.

"Good morning, Captain Ryan." Jack hung his cap on the coatrack and dragged the extra chair closer to the desk. "Lovely day out. Sadie says I'm to drag you outside at lunch and force you to get some fresh air. She may have said something about your office being an airless cave as well, but I didn't catch it all. Stella was telling me something at the same time."

"My goddaughter might be the only person alive who can outtalk her mother." Gabe tossed the coroner's report he'd been reading onto the stack of files he'd read a half dozen times. He was starting to see a pattern in the way some of Josef's victims died. "Sadie's never shown this much interest in my health before now. Being cooped up inside the house all day must be boring for her."

"She's holding up pretty well for now. Knowing the children are safe has a lot to do with that. Ask me again if she's forced to stay in another week." Jack picked up a file and began leafing through. "Find anything new I should know about?"

"Maybe. I need to ask Dora what this means." He thumbed through the files, picking out the ones he wanted. Gabe passed six folders to Jack. "I've been hoping to find a pattern of some kind in Josef's murders. The bodies we've found are scattered all over town and the way people died is just as random. That makes it damn near impossible to know for sure if he's the one who killed these people. But take a look at the cause of death in these reports."

Jack read through the files quickly. "I'll be damned. The way they were killed matches the way Devin and Mrs. Rigaux died."

"It's a perfect match. We know for certain that Josef killed the two of them." Six people with a spike, an ice pick, or a knife shoved into the base of their skull. Supervisor Devin and Eve Rigaux made eight, all killed the same way. Gabe had wanted a pattern. Now he'd found one that made him ill. "What I want to know is why. What made them different?"

"Good question. I'd like to know that myself." Gabe and Jack looked up, startled, to see Sam Butler leaning against the doorframe, arms crossed over his chest. Sam's posture was relaxed, but a muscle jumped along his jaw. "I've been trying to figure out how this bastard stays one step ahead of us and Dora. Last night I started to wonder if we're thinking about this the wrong way."

Jack tugged his notebook out of a pocket and opened the book to a fresh page. He glanced at Sam, pencil poised. "What do you mean?"

"Instead of asking what's different about those people or thinking so hard about how they died, maybe we should ask what Josef stands to gain killing that way. There has to be something." Sam pulled off his straw boater, tapping the hat against his hand and frowning. "What do we know happened after he killed Devin?"

The answer crept up on Gabe slowly. "Mother of God. He changed the way he looks."

Jack frowned. "There has to be a limit on how often he can do that."

"From what Dora's told me, the only limit is how many people he kills." Sam wandered over to the map of San Francisco on Gabe's wall. Round pins marked all the places bodies had been found. Butler counted them all, a daily ritual. The longer this went on, the more afraid he was that one of those pins would come to represent Alina. "Dr. West can likely tell us how much time passed between the murders of these poor souls. That might give us some idea of how long a change lasts."

"That still won't tell us what Josef looks like." Jack tugged at the ends of his mustache. "After what happened with Pastor Grant—"

He didn't need to finish the sentence. They'd all assumed that Josef always took the faces of his victims. Discovering that wasn't true had been another blow.

"One step at a time, Lieutenant. It's more than we knew before." Gabe tapped a pencil on his desk, thinking hard. "Have you spoken with Jordan this morning, Sam?"

"He was still having breakfast with Katie Allen when I went

by to pick him up." Sam turned away from the map and pushed his hands into his trouser pockets. "Katie was telling him all about growing up in Harrogate. Jordan was having a good time, so I let him be. I'm supposed to catch up with him at Dora's house around noon. I have to go into the paper for a couple of hours first."

That made him smile. "As much time as you spend at Dora's, I'm surprised you still have a job."

Sam shrugged, pretending nonchalance. "Being a reporter is the best job in the world, Gabe. No punching a time clock and I get to make my own hours. As long as I turn in stories, my boss is happy."

Gabe rocked back in his creaky desk chair, considering. "What would your boss think about running a series of small stories linking the Bolsheviks to people disappearing in San Francisco? The more wild and sensational, the better."

"My boss will print anything that sells papers. What made you think of this?"

"I want people looking over their shoulders and suspicious of anyone they don't know. They'll be twice as suspicious of seeing people walking around who are supposed to be dead or missing." He traded looks with Jack. "Maybe we can take away his ability to hide in plain sight. I'll settle for making Josef's life more complicated if nothing else."

Sam glanced at the clock. "I might make the early afternoon edition if I hurry. That will give me plenty of time to write one for the evening run too."

He grabbed another folder off the stack he hadn't read. "Keep your name off these pieces, Sam. We want Josef paying attention to the stories, not to you."

Butler waved him away as he went out the office door. "No need to teach granny how to suck eggs, Captain. I know what I'm doing."

Gabe gave Jack a sidelong glance. "I forget how young he is at times."

"We were young and cocky once, Gabe. We survived." He went back to leafing through reports and photographs, jotting down names from the files Gabe had given him. "Sam does know what he's doing. Don't worry, he'll be all right."

Delia

Shutters were pulled tight across the windows in Dora's kitchen, preventing anyone outside from looking in. Sunlight still managed to sneak between the slats. Glass doors on the cupboards reflected sunbeams onto the ceiling, painting rainbow streaks that rippled as clouds moved across the sky. I'd forgotten how bright and cheery her kitchen could be. We rarely sat in this part of the house.

Three princesses looked down from the cupboard fronts with grave expressions. They were my constant companions, defying even Dora's strong boundaries in order to watch everything I did and listen to all I said. I paid as little attention to them as I could. Looking at them reminded me of how they'd died, awoke the memory of screams that never seemed to end, and of how Isadora had sobbed in my arms after I told her how Sunny's family died.

Those memories would never leave me, but the less I thought of them, the better.

Dora's latest cook was gone, sent away for her own safety. As things stood, we were forced to make our own tea and sandwiches. That was far from a hardship, but Dora had insisted she needed my help, a transparent ploy to speak to me alone that roused Libby's curiosity. We'd left her losing another game of gin to Alina and retired to the kitchen.

I shuffled the deck of tarot cards I'd brought from the sitting room and cut them into three stacks, flipping the top card on each faceup and starting again. The cards took very little of my attention, watching the teakettle even less. Both were idle distractions, something to do while I waited for Dora to tell me what was wrong.

She was decidedly unhappy. Dora paced from one end of the long, narrow room to the other, fists clenched at her sides and heels clicking on black and white linoleum. She scowled fiercely, talking to herself in Russian. That she didn't so much as glance in my direction was a measure of how upset she was.

My getting up to fix tea and sandwiches, and arrange plates, cups, and napkins on a tray didn't slow her. Once I'd finished, I leaned against the kitchen worktable with my arms folded and watched her. "Finding a solution would be easier if I knew what was wrong, Dora. Talk to me."

She glanced my way, her scowl lightening. "The last finding charm I sent out just failed. If I were a novice or extremely foolish, I might be tempted to believe that murdering scum had moved out of range. I know that's not the case. Josef destroyed this charm, just as he destroyed the rest. Only this time, he flung the shards back at me."

"What? How could he?" I shivered and stepped away from the table, hoping I'd heard wrong. "Oh, God, Dora. Please tell me he can't use your charm to find his way here. Please."

Her smile was tight and brittle and resigned. "I promised years ago I'd never lie to you, Dee. I won't start now. If I were sure you wouldn't walk straight into his arms, I'd send you and Libby out of here this instant and face him alone. Since I can't guarantee he's not lying in wait, you're both staying here. We're all safer inside for the moment, even if we are trapped. He can't cross my boundaries without permission."

The watcher's eyes opened in my head, but she held herself

apart, distant, and allowed me to think. That she was there and paying attention was an odd sort of comfort. At the same time, she made me nervous.

"All right. At least we have a small advantage." I sat in my chair again and folded my hands on the table. That my hands remained steady was a bit of a surprise, and no doubt a sign of how much faith I placed in Dora. "Explain to me how a—a necromancer could turn your own spell back on you. Everything I've read says they don't have that kind of strength or knowledge. All their skill lies in manipulating the dead."

Dora winced. "Josef killed someone. It's that simple, Delia. He used the ghost created when this poor soul died to trace the threads binding the charm back to its maker. Back to me. The impact when the spirit slammed into my wards was enough to give me a headache."

"And more than enough to tell him where you are." Now that I knew what we faced, shock wore away rapidly. "There has to be a way to locate him without the charm."

She sat in the chair opposite mine, a hint of amusement showing in her eyes. Dora gestured in the general direction of the sitting room. "Locating Josef won't be a problem. He'll come looking for me. I have what he wants."

Alina.

"Should we call Gabe and Randy?" I frowned, undecided. "And do we warn them to stay away or issue a call for help?"

That amused her even more. "I'd already called Randy before I brought you in here. He's passing the message on to Gabe. A call for help is definitely in order. If matters come to a head . . ."

Dora's voice trailed off, her eyes unfocused and far away. She stood suddenly and stalked over to the pantry at the end of the kitchen, disappearing inside. When she reappeared, Isadora carried a rather large wooden box. She set the box in the middle of the table. "You do have a pocket in that skirt, don't you?"

"Of course. Why?"

Dora lifted out jars of dried herbs and spices, setting them to the side. Removing the box's false bottom took only a few seconds more. She gingerly lifted out a small pistol and laid it on the table. "I have another small revolver in my workroom that I'll get for me. Keep this one in your pocket, Dee. It's smaller than the gun Gabe keeps at home, and you should be able to use it easily. I need you to make the same promise to me that you made to Gabe. Don't hesitate to shoot."

The gun was much lighter than Gabe's and fit my hand perfectly. Promising to shoot, to kill Josef if necessary, made me ill. I promised anyway. "If there's no other way, I won't hesitate. But please tell me we'll find another way."

She touched my cheek. "I will do my very best not to put you in that position. Now, let's take the tea and sandwiches out. I'm surprised Libby hasn't come looking for us already."

Dora balanced the tray holding the teapot and cups. I took the larger platter of sandwiches and cookies. "Should we warn Libby?"

"No, not yet. No need to alarm her until we have cause. I might be jumping at shadows."

I shoved the swinging door open and held it for Dora. "You've never jumped at a shadow in your life, Isadora Bobet."

"There's always a first time." She smiled and squeezed past me. "Pray that this is it."

Gabe

Gabe's meetings with the chief of police were never brief. This one had dragged on longer than usual. He understood the pressure on the chief to find the people behind the riot at Lotta's fountain and the string of murders that followed. Demanding that Gabe detail every step he and Jack had taken in the investigation didn't provide any new answers.

That there were things he couldn't say, things Gabe knew to be true that the chief would never believe, made it all worse. Telling the chief that a necromancer working for the Bolsheviks was responsible for the riot was a sure way to lose his badge. His response to any question the chief asked was to slide around and evade the truth. He left the two-hour meeting feeling bitter about the waste of time.

Gabe headed back to his office, his mind on details of what he needed to tackle next. He rounded a hallway corner and almost ran headlong into Randy and Jack.

"Christ Almighty, Gabe." Jack wore an overcoat and his plaid cap. He thrust Gabe's coat and hat toward him. "I didn't think the chief was ever going to stop talking. Dora called. We need to get over there."

His heart sped up, but he kept his voice calm and even. Ignoring the icy whisper telling him to run was harder. "How long ago?"

Randy didn't have as much practice keeping panic from showing. He wiped sweat from his forehead on a sleeve and set a brisk pace down the corridor. "More than an hour. Josef found a way to trace the finding charms back to her. Dee's with her, but she needs reinforcements. He knows where they are, Gabe. He knows."

"He can't get past her boundaries, not without an invitation. Dora's sure of that." Jack limped a little more, but he gamely kept up with the two taller men. "I sent more men to surround the house and patrol the street. They all know not to separate and to check in frequently."

"Good. I'd have done the same." They wove through the always crowded lobby and hurried toward the front doors, avoiding eye contact with anyone who looked their way. Gabe didn't trust himself not to snarl at anyone trying to delay them. "What about Sam and Jordan? Did you warn them away?"

"Sam's still at the paper. I sent Finlay and Perry over to his office to make sure he stays there. They're under orders to arrest him if that's what it takes." Jack frowned. "Jordan called from Dora's not long after she phoned me. Lynch knows everything and insists on staying put. He made a point of telling me he's got his gun."

They shoved through the front doors and outside. The sun was shining in a fresh blue sky, giving an impression of warmth that wasn't there. Chill, sea-damp air seeped under his coat, raising gooseflesh. Gabe flipped up his collar. "Lynch is a good cop. I can't see him walking away when Dora and Dee need him."

Randy Dodd yanked open the car door, stepping back to let Gabe and Jack climb into the backseat. "Libby's there again too. Jordan can keep her from charging out the front door if nothing else."

Gabe wiped a hand over his mouth, counting. "We have five people inside. Anyone else we have to worry about?"

Randy's smile was grim. "Five is enough."

"Five is more than enough." He climbed into the back next to Jack and slammed the door. The hollow echo reminded him of gunfire. He saw the same thought sitting in Jack's eyes.

Dodd slid into the driver's seat and started the engine. The car lurched away from the curb, picking up speed rapidly. Gabe hunched into his coat, silently watching people on the sidewalk and buildings hurtle past.

They didn't have far to go, but the drive would seem endless. Not knowing what they'd find tied his stomach in knots.

CHAPTER 20

Delia

Laughter from the sitting room signaled that Alina had won another game of cards. Jordan Lynch's deep, rumbling voice followed, consoling Libby. She took it well, as she always did, but the edge in her voice betrayed the strain.

Libby might not believe in spirits and ghosts, in Dora's abilities or mine, but she'd seen the riot and the aftermath. When Jordan took her aside and flatly told her it was too dangerous to leave, and why, she hadn't argued for long. I was enormously grateful she hadn't made a bigger scene.

Plum-colored shadows bruised the skin under Dora's eyes. She sat upright in the straight-backed chair at the head of table, but that didn't erase the image of her wilting as I watched. We'd spent most of the last two hours reinforcing the barriers around her house, adding layers to protections that had grown thicker with each passing year. I'd done all I could to help, but by necessity, the majority of the effort came from Dora. I'd rarely seen her so exhausted. That she was still on her feet was nothing short of remarkable.

She pinched the bridge of her nose, eyes closed. "Chief Michael's meeting with Gabe couldn't have come at a worse time. The temptation to send a silence hex his way is almost overwhelming. Randy and Gabe should have been here more than an hour ago. I'm beginning to worry that something's happened."

"Something more you mean. I don't believe that's possible." Heavy damask drapes covered her workroom windows. The dim yellow light of two small electric lamps provided enough light to see, but shadows filled the corners and veiled the ceiling. Dora found the near darkness restful, soothing. Normally I'd agree, but today the lack of light grated on my nerves. "Gabe and Randy will be here soon. I'm confident Jack will come as well. He won't want to miss the fun."

That made her smile. "Sadie would be horrified to hear you say that, even if it is true."

"Then we shan't tell her." The watcher's eyes still filled my head. She kept a constant vigil, ever alert, and added to the restless anticipation I couldn't shake. "Do you have any of that sherry left?"

Dora stared. "Delia Ann Ryan, I don't think you've ever asked me for a drink before. I'm starting to think I'm a bad influence."

"You've always been a bad influence. I adore you anyway." I stood and went to the doorway, peering down the hallway in hopes of seeing Gabe. He wasn't there, but I'd known that. The gun in my pocket bumped my leg as I turned around, a sober reminder of my promise. "But perhaps I should skip the sherry for now. I'll reconsider once Gabe arrives."

"More tea, then." Dora braced against the edge of the table and stood. "Tea and a bite to eat will do us both a great deal of good."

She slipped her arm through mine for the walk to the kitchen at the other end of the house. We found Jordan at the bottom of the staircase, frowning up at the second-floor landing.

Isadora's fingers tightened on my arm. "Is something wrong?"

"Not a thing." He looked slightly embarrassed. "I know this man can't get inside on his own, but do you mind if I take a look around upstairs? I'd feel more sure of my ground and a little less jumpy. Old cop habits die hard."

Her smile was warm and bright, if a bit frayed around the edges. "I don't mind at all. Tea will be ready when you come back down."

We waited until Jordan reached the second floor before going into the kitchen. Dora hunted in the icebox for lemon wedges and rounds of cheese while I filled the kettle. Slices of bread, the last few apples, and a plate of cookies went on the big tray as well.

The fuzzy images of three princesses gazed back at me from inside empty teacups and the back of a silver teaspoon. I turned to find their anxious faces watching from each glass cupboard door, the sides of water tumblers, and serving dishes. Everywhere I looked, Alina's sisters gazed back, voiceless and desperate to speak.

They were frightened. The front door chimes rang and the dragon growled. "Dora—"

Libby's cheery voice carried from the entryway as she greeted Sam and told him to come in. Isadora's head came up abruptly and she dropped the cheese knife, grimacing in pain and grabbing the table edge to keep from falling. "Oh dear God, she invited him in . . . no."

I didn't wait. I pulled the gun from my pocket and ran.

Hurtling headlong into Libby outside the kitchen knocked the wind out of me and sent the gun tumbling out of my hand. She retrieved the pistol, staring openmouthed. "Dee, what are you doing?"

"That man—that's not Sam. Give me the gun!" I couldn't think, couldn't see round the dragon's angry red eyes. She roared in rage and terror, and I fought not to go to my knees. "Please, Libby. It's not him. That's not Sam!"

"You've lost your mind." She backed away as I lunged for the gun, her expression growing more horrified. "No, I'm not letting you go in there with this. Jordan! Jordan!"

"Yes, call Jordan." I steadied myself against the wall and took a step. "Tell him to hurry."

Libby shrank back, shaking and obviously terrified, and didn't try to stop me from continuing down the hallway. This wasn't at all like the fearless woman I'd come to know. I wondered what Josef had done to her, or if he'd given her a vision of how death would find her.

The man on the settee was a perfect double for Sam, and to anyone watching, the way he cupped Alina's face appeared tender and loving. Libby wouldn't have questioned allowing him inside, but I saw through his illusions. Sam's face stuttered in and out of view, replaced by a bearded older man with dark hair and clouded eyes.

Remembering my dreams, how Josef had held her face just that way and the feel of bones shifting, made my skin crawl. Alina whimpered the same way now, wide eyed with horror, and terrified tears slid down her face. She couldn't escape, couldn't move as long as he held her.

An army of ghosts filled the sitting room, arrayed in rows that stretched from the door and beyond the far wall. Most were Josef's victims, angry-eyed phantoms he refused to release. He'd bound these men and women as they died, forcing them into his service. They glared at him and didn't try to hide their hatred.

A shrinking circle of spirits surrounded Alina, faceless memories trying to shield her and hold back the tide of haunts Josef called. They faded as I watched, growing distant. Soon they'd vanish completely and leave Alina unprotected.

Josef didn't so much as glance my way. The wall of ghosts between us was meant to keep me out, to shut Dora off from Alina. I pushed into the room anyway, whispering banishing charms and commands for restless spirits to go, to move on and seek their rest.

A few gave way, but most reached out to brush cold fingers across my face, to grasp an arm or touch my shoulder. I relived each tortured soul's last moment and each painful death delivered by Josef's hands. The dragon growled with each ghostly touch that drove the chill deeper, but she couldn't stop the dead or send them away. I clenched my chattering teeth and held on.

One faded spirit, an old man dressed as a monk, stepped in front of me, blocking my path. I plowed through him, shivering with cold and the agony of his last moments. When I could see again, I was within arm's reach of Josef.

A slender pewter vase sat on a half table at the end of the settee. I grabbed the vase round the top and swung at Josef, landing a solid blow on the back of his head. He snarled and caught the vase with one hand, twisting it away from me, and wrapped his other hand around my throat. Alina slumped in the corner of the settee, limp and unable to move.

"Are you that eager to die, little witch?" He chanted in a mix of Russian and Latin, a singsong rhythm that drew his ghosts in closer. Josef's voice rasped over my skin, tiny thorns of pain hidden in each word. The mask of Sam's face fell away completely and his grip on my throat tightened. Darkness reached for me, clouding my vision until all I saw was Josef's face. I clawed at his hands and face, desperate to get air, frantically trying to break free.

Death didn't frighten me. Having my spirit bound to him to use as he wished utterly terrified me. I raked my nails across his face, drawing blood. He smiled.

The dragon roared, deafening me. Josef stopped chanting, eyes full of shock and face slack with surprise. I didn't hear the second shot, but blood splattered the front of my dress and Josef staggered back, going to his knees. He touched his side and lifted his hand, staring at the blood on his fingers before pitching onto his face.

Dora moved farther into the room, a pistol gripped in both

hands and her full attention on Josef. She glanced at me. "Are you all right?"

Josef groaned, his hand reaching for my ankle. His phantoms crowded closer and I edged away, fighting the need to cry, to scrub his blood from my clothes, my hands and face. I cleared my throat several times, trying to speak, but managed only a hoarse croak and a nod.

"Dee, take Alina out of here." Dora spoke firmly, but her hands shook. "Jordan's in the hallway near the kitchen. Leave Alina with him and come back. I need your help."

We stumbled from the room, Alina and I holding each other up in equal measure. I don't know what Dora told him, but Jordan didn't budge from his post in front of the kitchen door until the last second. He took Alina from me, wrapping an arm around her shoulders protectively.

"Sweet Jesus, Delia." He took out his handkerchief and wiped my cheek. It came away splotched with crimson. "Say something. Tell me you're all right."

I cleared my throat again and swallowed, wincing. "No, I'm not. Where's Libby?"

"She's in the kitchen." Jordan frowned. "Dora made me promise to keep her there and to keep Libby away from Alina."

I'd been right about Josef doing something to her. Dora had sensed it too. "Do what she said, Jordan. There's a reason to keep Libby confined for the time being. I have to go back. Dora needs me."

Dora stood where I'd left her, the gun pointed at Josef. He lay quiet and didn't move, but phantoms still packed the room. The ghosts moved aimlessly, restlessly. They wouldn't leave until he was truly dead. I wasn't sure they could leave. Not unless Josef sent them away.

"Tell me what to do, Dora." I screwed up my courage and

squared my shoulders. "I know we can't let him walk out of here."

Her grim smile made it easy to see how very tired she was. "We don't need to go quite so far as murder, Delia. Josef is already dead, and I suspect he has been for some time. Necromancers really are foul creatures. The worst of them siphon off the death energy of their victims to prolong and restore their own lives. They become like morphine addicts, craving more and more death."

Josef moaned and his fingers twitched. I stared. "He's dead?"

"Very. He was already dead when Aleksei Nureyev shot him." She gestured toward the ghosts crowded around Josef. "Look closely, Dee. If I can see the bond that holds these ghosts in thrall, it should be very clear to you. That bond is what enables Josef to maintain the illusion of life."

The bonds were clear, now that I knew to look. Braided strands of yellow, silver, red, and green—captured pieces of aura—tied each phantom to Josef. They all pulsed in the same rhythm, beating in time with his heart. "Can we sever those bonds?"

"Setting the ghost free is supposed to break the connection." She shrugged and gave me a rueful glance. "It's a lot like sending on someone who doesn't know they're dead yet. I've read about this, but I lack practical experience."

I'd sent on thousands of confused haunts, and banished twice that many stubborn spirits who refused to leave the world of the living. And from the baleful looks these phantoms gave Josef, they'd be grateful to leave. He held them here, nothing else.

I shut my eyes and looked inward, searching for the best way to start. The dragon's night-dark eyes greeted me, and I knew what to do. Fear set my heart to racing, but being afraid didn't mean I wouldn't try. That the watcher made it appear so simple, so easy, scared me most of all. Dealing with the spirit realm was seldom simple.

"Hear me, spirits, and know I speak truth. Your tie to life is broken. No man can bind your spirit to his will, no man use the essence of who you were to cheat death." I couldn't raise my voice above a whisper, but whispers worked just as well. The phantoms turned as one, watching me and listening. "I free you to seek rest and peace, I free you to find a place beyond this living world, I free you from the bonds that keep you here. No man can force you to his bidding or bend you to his will. Three times I've said the words, three times I've cut the bond, three times I've granted peace and rest. You have your freedom. Go."

For a moment, I thought I'd failed. But slowly, one by one, the pulsing of the bonds slowed and stopped, the colors fading. Phantoms crumbled to dust and blew away on a wind I couldn't feel, or rose in misty tendrils to vanish through the ceiling. They followed each other faster and faster, until the room was empty of ghosts.

Blood still stained Dora's carpet, but all that remained of Josef was a pile of yellowed bone wrapped in rotting fabric.

Dora carefully set the pistol on a side table and put her arm around me. "Well done, Dee. We'll need to burn the bones and salt the earth where we bury the ashes. Far from the city would be best, but we'll find a spot nearby if forced to it."

The front door slammed open, followed by Randy's frantic shouts. "Dora! Dora, where are you?"

"We're in here! Everything's all right!" Tears slid down Dora's face. She squeezed my shoulders and went to meet him. "Everything's all right."

The bruises on my throat healed slowly, and my ability to speak in a normal voice took nearly as long to recover. I saw Gabe watching me when he thought I didn't know, that horrible knowledge of how close he'd come to losing me sitting stark and raw in his eyes. That

I'd looked at him the same way after the riot didn't make it easier to bear for either of us. If we held each other a little tighter, that was to be expected.

Dora sent a series of letters to Europe and telegrams to New York with the truth about the murders of the tsar and his family. People she trusted were asked to spread tales of what had happened. Rumors followed quickly, stories of sightings of his daughters alive and well, and reports of the tsar living quietly in exile.

None of the stories were true and grew wilder with time, but they got people talking about Lenin and his revolution, and chasing after false trails. That was exactly what Isadora wanted.

Sam was alive and well, and he did his part to throw the hounds off the scent. I didn't ask how he managed, but a photograph and a story about the tsar's daughter Maria being killed in the San Francisco riot spread across the country. The story appeared in all the biggest papers, from Los Angeles to New York and points between. It was quite the sensation and lasted for several weeks. That story spread to Europe as well and brought more scrutiny to the Bolsheviks.

Alina—Maria—was as safe as we could make her. With Josef's death, all her memories had returned, as well as all the sorrow. She had no interest in being a rallying point for the royalists. With most of the world believing she was dead, she had a chance for a quiet life with Sam.

We'd done our best for Connor over the last few weeks. There was no cure, no guarantee that spirits wouldn't continue to frighten him, but a protection spell Dora obtained from an old friend kept the ghosts away when he left the house. He was a happier, brighter little boy as a result. That made Sadie and Jack happier as well.

Dora and I worried about him less, and my fears of madness and possession receded into the background. Once he learned to talk and could understand, we'd start teaching Connor ways to protect himself. He wouldn't be left to fend for himself.

Jordan Lynch put off his trip back to Chicago until everything had settled. He filled his time by making small repairs around Katie Allen's boardinghouse and listening to her stories. I couldn't say which of them got the most enjoyment out of their time together. Jordan might not have gone back at all, but Gabe couldn't get the chief of police to hire a Negro. As it was, Jordan wanted to stay long enough to see Sam and Maria married. He got his wish.

Gabe and I filled our parlor with flowers on a late June night, roses and lilies, carnations and the first sweet peas from my garden. Candlelight lit the room, adding soft shadows. Food and a wedding cake waited in the dining room, all paid for by Dora.

Libby had been invited, but she sent a note saying she had other obligations and couldn't come. It was all very polite and proper, and a lie from beginning to end. She was still deeply smitten with Sam. Watching Maria marry him was more than Libby Mills could bear.

Annie came with Jack and Sadie and the children, leaning heavily on Jack's arm and looking more frail than even the day before. How confused she'd grown since her encounter with Josef reminded me of Esther Larkin's last days, a slow fading away that ended in death. I visited daily and spent as much time with Annie as I could. Sadie and I both knew we wouldn't have her for long.

Dora had bought Maria a proper dress and a going-away suit, and fussed with arranging flowers in Maria's hair as much as any mother of the bride. Maria looked radiant and the picture of happiness as she came into the parlor on Gabe's arm. Sam's eyes lit up as soon as he saw her. I knew in that strange way I could never describe that they'd have a long, happy life together.

Sadie and I stood on either side of Annie's chair, holding her hands, and watched the happy couple take their vows. A cheer went up and we all clapped when Sam and Maria shared a kiss. If a few tears were shed by Isadora Bobet, we all pretended not to see.

Three princess ghosts watched their sister marry as well, roses that would never wither in their cheeks and bright eyes brimming with happiness. I'd thought the memory ghosts would fade away, but they still followed Maria everywhere. That was just as well. Knowing someone who loved her still watched over Maria gave me comfort.

The dragon's eyes opened, plunging me into night-dark depths and wrapping me in amusement. Maria's guardian would always be there for her, for her children and grandchildren. She released me slowly this time, affectionately, and left behind a promise. Maria and Sam would never truly be alone.

Dora and I drove Sam and Maria to the train station at dawn. The buildings downtown were dark outlines against a brightening sky, shadows retreating moment by moment with the approach of daylight.

Sam and I hung back as Dora said good-bye to Maria. There were tears in both their eyes and I wasn't sure Dora would let go. Of course in the end, she did.

Isadora and I stood with arms around each other, waving and watching the train pull away. She was still waving long after the train was out of sight.

We linked arms for the walk back to the car. The sun rose over the rooftops as we left the station, sending rainbow sparks out from windows to dance on the sides of buildings. I took that as a sign.

My life held more light than darkness, more love than sorrow. I needed to remember, and keep pushing back the shadows.